"A spirited woman ahead of her time makes this well-paced novel in an extraordinary setting shine. Rife with suspense and romance, *The Secrets of Emberwild* is as much history as mystery—and a horse lover's dream!"

Laura Frantz, Christy Award–winning author of *A Heart Adrift*

"Saddle up for a ride you won't want to end. This story of secrets and second chances is full of everything I love: fully developed characters, a well-drawn plot, and a pace that's just right, whether it's trotting through unfolding revelations or galloping through the climax to the end. Stephenia H. McGee writes with both authority and heart. She's an author I trust for historical integrity and a captivating tale every time."

Jocelyn Green, Christy Award–winning author of *Drawn by the Current*

"Stephenia H. McGee is a master at writing Southern charm and historic detail, and she's outdone herself with *The Secrets of Emberwild*. This fascinating story draws you in with characters who come alive from their first step onto the page. McGee's clear knowledge of horsemanship shines throughout. This is one for the keeper shelf!"

Misty M. Beller, *USA Today* bestselling author of the Brides of Laurent series

"In her book *The Secrets of Emberwild*, Stephenia H. McGee will enchant readers as they discover a bygone era filled with mystery, romance, and realistic characters. Her masterful ability at creating stories will have readers searching out her books for years to come."

Dawn Crandall, award-winning author of *The Hesitant Heiress* and The Everstone Chronicles series

the
SECRETS
of
EMBERWILD

the

SECRETS

of

EMBERWILD

STEPHENIA H. McGEE

Revell

a division of Baker Publishing Group
Grand Rapids, Michigan

© 2022 by Stephenia H. McGee

Published by Revell
a division of Baker Publishing Group
PO Box 6287, Grand Rapids, MI 49516-6287
www.revellbooks.com

Printed in the United States of America

Library of Congress Cataloging-in-Publication Data
Names: McGee, Stephenia H., 1983– author.
Title: The secrets of Emberwild / Stephenia H. McGee.
Description: Grand Rapids, MI : Revell, a division of Baker Publishing Group, [2022]
Identifiers: LCCN 2022014416 | ISBN 9780800740238 (paperback) | ISBN 9780800742270 (casebound) | ISBN 9781493438884 (ebook)
Subjects: LCGFT: Novels.
Classification: LCC PS3613.C4576 S43 2022 | DDC 813/.6—dc23/eng/20220328
LC record available at https://lccn.loc.gov/2022014416

Published in association with the Hartline Literary Agency, LLC.

Baker Publishing Group publications use paper produced from sustainable forestry practices and post-consumer waste whenever possible.

22   23   24   25   26   27   28   7   6   5   4   3   2   1

For Jason.
You are the hero of my favorite romance.
No story could ever compare to the beauty
of every day spent with you.

Not to us, LORD, not to us but to your name be the glory, because of your love and faithfulness.

Psalm 115:1

chapter
ONE

Emberwild Horse Farm
Neshoba County, Mississippi
March 3, 1905

Freedom rushed through Nora Fenton's veins, erupting with each breath. Invisible shackles didn't bind out here.

Her independence always came at a price.

Nora leaned forward in the saddle. The wind slipped through her hair and snatched it from its pins, letting the honey-brown tresses fly out behind her. Hoofbeats pounded in rhythm with her heart.

The colt's exuberance for the open terrain would soon have to be contained once more and their ride brought to an end. Wild abandon never lasted long, and Arrow's reckless gallop could snatch life away from the both of them without warning. Caution demanded she draw back on the reins.

Not yet.

Freedom tasted far too sweet. It broke through the cloud of oppression and the pall of death that had made the delicate balance of her household all the more unstable these past months. She would pay for the reprieve.

And it would be worth it.

Nora took in one last look at the morning sky painted brilliant pink, then laid her left rein across Arrow's neck, asking him to make the turn toward home. He pinned his ears in displeasure and lowered his head, resisting her attempt at control. He lengthened his stride until they nearly soared above the ground.

Apparently the neck-reining lesson hadn't lasted past the corral. So be it. Gripping the rein in her leather glove, Nora pulled back and applied pressure to the side of the bit. Arrow shook off the command.

Stubborn colt. He would learn. He might be a stallion, but she was alpha of this herd. Nora planted her foot in the left stirrup and snatched the rein down to her hip, holding firm until his stride jerked to a halt. She dropped from the saddle.

"Got the better of you, didn't it?" Nora laughed, ruffling the shock of mane between his red ears already flecked with gray.

Arrow pinned his ears again and tossed his head. Nora squared her shoulders and pushed into his space. He snorted, then flicked his ears forward and lowered his head in submission.

She patted his neck. "See, now. No reason to get ornery. Keep acting like that and you'll spend your sunrises in the stable."

Arrow tilted his head and gave a good shake. As he did, her saddle slipped to the side.

Nora reached for the girth only to find the leather on the right side splitting. It probably wouldn't safely survive another battle of wills with Arrow, and she couldn't risk falling under his hooves if it broke. Roger would likely use this as a mark against her competence. The surly stable master took any excuse he could find.

Sighing, she gathered the reins and turned back toward the stables. They had a long walk ahead of them, and now she wouldn't have time to change. The best she could hope for was to deliver Father's tray before he woke.

Nora strode through the new stalks of bermudagrass, bright green from the spring sun. If the weather held this year, they'd have plenty to sell after they stocked their herd for the winter.

Arrow snorted and pranced. The stallion, two years old last month, was as high-strung as he was beautiful and brimmed with potential. A few more weeks of training and he'd be ready for his first qualifying race—just in time for the fair.

She hoped.

If only she could work with him longer each day. Father's insistence that a woman had no place training horses hadn't waned as his illness worsened, and the stable hands still thought they were doing her a favor by thwarting her efforts. Mother, for her part, seemed to think it her duty to carry on Father's archaic ideals with a fervor. As though doing so would smother Nora's modernized way of thinking and suddenly turn her into the pristine lady they'd both somehow failed to produce.

Nora swatted a thick seed head. She'd show them. Her methods worked faster and better than any of the stable hands', but none of them would admit it.

She smirked. They wouldn't have a choice if she got Arrow ready on her own.

If she could prove to Mother that women were capable of more than just tending home and hearth, then perhaps she could convince Mother to entertain her other ideas for the farm. Father wouldn't get better, and they needed to prepare. Arrow was the key to her independence.

The horse suddenly tossed his head, nearly snatching the reins from her hand as though in direct defiance to her thoughts. As they neared the stables, he let out a shrill call for the other horses, awakening the rest of the barn and earning a chorus of nickers and whinnies in reply.

So much for going unnoticed. Nora glanced up at the sky, its masterpiece of purple and orange light now a swath of blue.

Late. Again.

For the briefest instant she considered leaving Arrow in his stall while she tended Father and then brushing him down later, but she dismissed the notion as swiftly as it came. She wouldn't neglect

Arrow just because she'd let herself enjoy his first real ride too long or because they had to walk all the way home.

The massive stone barn of Emberwild fluttered with morning activity. Nora inhaled deeply, breathing in the earthy scents of hay and oats. She felt more at home surrounded by horseflesh than humanity, something her parents never understood. Horses were creatures with pure motives and unveiled intentions.

She led Arrow into his wide stall, pleased it had already been raked clean and the straw replaced in their absence. Her colt thrust his muzzle into the hay bag and snatched out a mouthful with a snort of contentment.

Making quick work with the brush, Nora combed over Arrow's frothy coat and checked his forelocks. After inspecting his hooves for rocks, she tossed him his morning oats and secured the latch to his stall. She replaced her saddle on the stand in the immaculate tack room. She'd have to find a new girth soon.

The heels of her boots clicked down the stone center aisle as the two stable boys, Pete and Andrew, scurried out of her way. She'd long since stopped trying to befriend them. Nora exited through the barn door and quickly surveyed the yard between the house and the stable. Other than the boys tending the horses in the barn, Emberwild roused slowly. Even the hounds didn't seem interested in greeting this humid day.

She passed the exercise track and skirted the pristine, overflowing flower bed on her way into the house. Mother cared about her flowers and the state of the house more than anything—or anyone—else.

The day Father had presented the finished house to Mother, she'd said it looked like a doll's house, with all that gingerbread molding in the eaves and the porch that wrapped around both sides.

For Nora, home became a gilded cage woven with conditional affection and cold conversations.

She entered the still-silent house, praying she didn't leave a trail of dirt behind on the wood floor to condemn her. She rushed through gathering the honeyed milk, the teapot, and the two eggs she'd boiled the night before and assembled them on a silver tray, making sure to leave Mother's sunny yellow domain as spotless as she'd found it.

She lifted the tray and pushed open the door between the kitchen and dining room with her hip, turning toward the wide staircase to the upper floor. All she had to do was slip into Father's room, drop the tray, and then get herself cleaned up before either parent saw her.

She took the steps carefully, avoiding the fourth one, which squeaked. How long had she dallied? She hadn't paused to look at the grandfather clock in the foyer. The chandelier overhead caught morning sunrays, sending diamonds of color over the green papered walls.

She hurried across the thick carpeted hall, coming to a stop next to Father's room, a room he'd once shared with Mother but now called his prison. Maybe that gave him a taste of what life had been like for her all these years. She pushed the bitter thought down and balanced the tray with trembling hands before carefully turning the knob. With any luck, she wouldn't wake him.

The door swung inward on silent hinges, the sunlight barely piercing the shadows. Nora held her breath and listened for her father's ragged breathing. She moved closer to the bed and set the tray on the bedside table, cringing as the rattle of porcelain gave her away. She paused, waiting.

Silence.

There. She'd left his breakfast for him to partake when he woke, just as he liked. She should hurry to her room to don a gown before anyone saw her in men's pants.

But still she lingered.

The silence in the room unnerved her. She needed to get close enough to make certain only sleep claimed him.

Nora inched toward the carved canopy bed draped in summer mosquito netting. With the scant light filtering through the curtains covering the double window opposite, she could make out the shape of his form under the blankets.

She peered closer. Did his body move with breath?

His form suddenly lurched. Nora yelped and stumbled back, her pulse thudding in her ears.

"Nora?" Her father's voice, raspy yet edged in steel, found her in the gloom.

Maybe he hadn't seen her, and she could still slip out. She took another step back.

"I know it's you. I can smell the horse sweat."

Nora set her teeth. "Good morning, Father. I've brought your tray. I didn't mean to wake you."

"But you did."

She turned and headed toward the safe harbor of light beckoning from the hallway.

"Please . . . stay."

Nora froze. Sweat beaded on her brow, and she swiped the moisture away. She turned reluctantly, despising the long-buried need within that still sought his approval.

"Yes?"

"Come closer."

"I've already brought your tray. Do you need me to pour the tea?"

"I . . ." His words dissolved into a racking cough more strangled than yesterday's.

By the time she took hold of the heavy velvet curtain, his fit had subsided. Nora thrust the fabric aside, allowing the daylight to breach the room and fully reveal her disgrace.

"Come. Sit."

Surprised he said nothing about her attire, Nora grabbed a ladder-back chair and positioned it by the bedside. She sat and clasped her hands in her lap, eyes downcast.

She waited, listening to his breathing. Each inhale came with a faint whistle, as though his lungs struggled to fill with air.

"Need to tell you . . . something."

"I know. I shouldn't have been out at the stables this morning—"

"Enough." He barked the single word, cutting off her explanation.

Hiram Douglass Fenton thought women should listen to orders without comment, and children, daughters especially, should be seen more than heard. Nora clenched her teeth to keep her tongue tamed.

Father settled against the multitude of feather pillows behind his back. He'd become a skeleton draped in papery skin. He hardly resembled the thickly muscled man of her youth, and his eyes held none of the laughter that, if she thought hard enough, she could remember from her childhood.

Somewhere deep in her heart, she recalled calloused hands that would hold hers and lips that were quick to form a smile or story in the evening's firelight. Somewhere around her twelfth year, Father had suddenly ceased to be the cheery man she'd loved. As she'd grown into womanhood, she'd seemed to displease him more with each passing year until the man before her was little more than a demanding stranger.

She could feel his eyes upon her but would not lift her head until he spoke again. He kept her in suspense. Another lesson on humility.

"I have something I need to tell you." Father cleared his throat, but his words remained thick. "Something I need to confess before I die."

Her gaze shot up to his face, and she noted the trickle of blood from the side of his lip. Without comment, she handed him a handkerchief. He wiped the blood away, his eyes never leaving her face. Did he expect her to argue? Say he shouldn't talk about death or assure him he would recover?

Such claims were lies they'd both recognize.

He wadded the linen in his gnarled hand. "Everything we have is built on a lie."

Her pulse skittered. "What?"

Father leaned his head back and closed his eyes. "For once, girl, stop talking and listen. I don't have much time, and I need to get this stain off my soul. I've carried it far too long as it is, and if God will have mercy on me, I don't wish to carry it to my grave."

Nora sat back in her chair.

"Fifteen years ago, this place had nothing but four half-starved mares and a floundering stallion that wasn't worth his weight in manure."

While she waited for another fit of coughing to subside, Nora averted her gaze. An uneasy feeling settled in her stomach. She remembered those days. Times when the long winter nights with wind beating at their rickety door left them yearning for thicker blankets and fuller stomachs as they huddled together around the fireplace. Hard times, but happier ones.

"I was desperate to make things better for her, so I didn't question him. That horse was just . . . something."

Nora frowned. What was he talking about?

"But . . . should have known better. Then, all these years, I didn't say anything. Just . . . kept building on the lie."

He clutched at his chest, the coughs racking his thin frame.

"I'm going to get Mother."

"No!" He gasped for air. "I don't like her . . . seeing me . . . this way."

Nora paused, indecision biting at her. He didn't look well. Much worse than yesterday, when she'd honestly thought he wouldn't see another sunrise. Mother needed to know.

"Let her remember me like I was."

His eyes held such pleading and vulnerability that Nora couldn't get herself to move. He clutched his chest again, breaths seeming harder for him to find. His features deepened to a bluish tinge.

"Don't tell her. Don't you d-dare tell her what I told you. Not a . . . burden for her . . . to bear."

Palms sweating, Nora ran them down her hips, only gathering dust in the process. With her hands too dirty to reach for him, she merely watched him instead.

"Promise."

Promise what? What did he want her to do? Promise she would never tell her mother something she didn't even understand? She had no idea what he was talking about.

"Promise!"

Nora nodded, tears clouding her vision. Then he shot forward, his mouth agape, as though he could not catch the breath he desperately needed.

"Mother!" Nora dropped down beside his bed. "Mother!"

Father grabbed her hand, his eyes wild. Not knowing what else to do, she held on, praying that God in his mercy would remember the faith of a younger man and forget the bitterness of the older one. Helpless, Nora watched until her father's body stopped flailing and he slumped back against the pillows. His fingers slacked, then his eyes stared up at nothing.

Biting her fist, Nora fought back the sobs.

Footsteps pounded down the hall, and then Mother's shrill cry splintered the silence.

chapter
TWO

Pecos County, Texas
May 11, 1905

A man could never fully be prepared for death, but Silas Cavallero tried to withstand its sting. His chest constricted with pain as damp earth clung to his spade. He wiped the beads of sweat from his brow and paused to survey his work. It had been a quiet ceremony, just him, the preacher, and a handful of ladies from church. With little fanfare and short goodbyes, he'd lain to rest the person most dear to him.

He rested a hand on the cross that marked his mother's final resting place, its rugged construction similar to the others dotting this tiny cemetery. Hot Texas wind stirred damp hair hanging down the back of his neck.

"What will you do now?"

The preacher's voice startled Silas and made him drop his spade. Will Haby looked better fit for the saddle than the pulpit, with his weathered complexion and stringy pale hair stuffed under his wide-brimmed hat. He stared at Silas with compassionate eyes, never one to skirt or soften a hard subject. Or push a man into answering before he'd considered his words.

"Reckon I'll head back home." An obvious answer, though not what the preacher wanted. Silas had nothing else. He could hardly think beyond this moment.

Will waited a few more painful heartbeats. "And then what?"

"What do you mean?" Silas handed him the shovel. Waning daylight snagged on the dull metal. Had he truly spent all afternoon out here by himself covering Mama's coffin?

"It's all right to grieve, you know."

Silas pushed open the small fence surrounding the land of the dead with his scuffed boot and brushed off his hands. "I know."

Truth be told, he'd been grieving for months. That's the way it went with a long death like the wasting disease. Prolonged suffering gave a man plenty of time to mourn long before its victim's last breath.

Will stepped into his path. "I hate for this to be the day you find out, but we figured it would be better for me to tell you than Eakman."

The name brought Silas to a halt. "What does Eakman want now? I made last month's payment, and he'll get this month's after the sale." And after that, there'd be nothing left. A worry for later.

"Well, seems that's the thing. With your mother's death . . ." At Silas's look, the man hesitated a heartbeat, then continued in the forthright manner Silas had always appreciated. "Since the property went to Mrs. Cavallero when your father died"—Will turned out his calloused palms—"the bank is calling the loan."

"I don't have the money. You know how bad these past few years have been."

Will clasped him on the shoulder. "I know, son. I tried to talk to him, but he says the bank is insistent."

"So, I'll get a new loan in my own name." Even as he said it, the thought soured his stomach.

The day's dwindling light cast pink shadows over the face of the man who'd been almost like a second father. Despising his own boorish behavior but too exhausted to apologize, Silas bid the preacher a good evening and mounted his mother's beloved Starlight. Only the tired old mare remained of what had once been a prominent herd. Now, she served as just another reminder of everything he'd lost.

"Get some good rest," Will said. "You've had a hard day."

Silas dipped his hat, his throat too thick for words. He turned Starlight and gave her sides a good squeeze. In a few pounds of her hooves, they left the peeling paint of the little church behind.

They passed through the settlement comprised of little more than a few pitiful buildings and a swath of dry ground pierced with sharp plants too stubborn to realize no one wanted them.

He slowed Starlight to an easy walk, in no hurry now to get home. Her hooves stirred up the relentless dust, its particles hanging in the still air like dirty fog. The constriction in his chest squeezed tighter the closer he got to the crumbling house, and, as Silas tried to draw in a deep breath to ease its ache, he found himself coughing instead.

He'd been prepared, he reminded himself once more. He'd known for weeks that death lurked in the shadows. He and Mama had said their goodbyes, they'd shared laughter and tears, and, in the end, they'd both been ready for the peaceful release of her joining Papa at the Creator's side. So why had he been unprepared for how much covering her grave would take out of him?

He drew Starlight to a halt in front of the barn and gave her ebony neck a pat before sliding from the saddle. It took three tries to get the barn door to move on its rusty hinges, and, at his final yank, one of the boards splintered.

As he held the crumbling door, an unusual temptation to curse overtook him. But doing so would dishonor his father's memory, and no release of emotion could justify that.

He kicked the door aside and led Starlight into the dark space. She nickered as though still hoping for some equine companionship. But they'd sold off the last of the horses in January in order to make the payments and have at least something to give the kindly doctor. By the end of the week, the last of his scrawny cattle would be gone.

By the time he'd tended Starlight and mounted the steps to the cabin, the day had faded into the relative cool of evening. Silas took his time lighting the lamp and setting it on the hewn table. Then he settled into the chair and picked up the letter he'd left there this morning.

He'd stared at the envelope for a week now, ever since Mama had handed it to him and made him promise not to read the letter until after she'd stepped into the next life. He ran his finger over her sweeping script, one of the few remnants of the life she'd lived as a lady back East. He opened the seal, an ache smoldering in his chest.

Silas, my dear son,

I'm sorry I wasn't able to give you more. I know how hard you worked trying to sustain us. But this is not the life your father intended. This isn't the dream he held in his heart when he first came to this country as a bright-eyed youth, so full of life and adventure.

I know you did your best, and I know my broken heart was a burden you shouldn't have had to bear. You grew up too fast, and I wasn't the mother I should have been. Your forgiveness makes it easier to leave this life, and I'm grateful for it.

I'm writing this for you to read after I'm gone so that I don't have to argue its contents with you. This is my request, and I pray you will honor it after my death. My son, I want you to leave this place. Sell it, or let the bank have it, and do something more. Live the dream your father wanted or find one of your own. Don't let this land siphon the life out of you any more than it already has. Go, and know that you will not be betraying me or your papa by doing so.

Find a better life. Love a good woman. Rest once in a while.

I love you and ever shall.

Mama

Silas folded the letter and placed it back on the table. He stared at it, then opened the single page and read it again. By the third time, the words started to sink in. He shoved the letter into his breast pocket, crinkling the edges. Mama was gone. The bank wanted the land.

And he needed to find his father's killer.

The memory of his father's crumpled body rose like bile. He ground his teeth and pushed the gruesome image aside. Nothing remained for him here.

Come morning, he'd leave it all. He was going back to Mississippi.

chapter
THREE

Emberwild
May 14, 1905

Two months were enough to uproot one's life entirely.

Nora watched Arrow trot in the corral, but her mind wouldn't focus. Her thoughts kept stubbornly returning to Father's death and Mother's cold distance that handed out a daily sentence of blame. As though Mother thought Nora's delivering his breakfast that morning and listening to his cryptic confession had somehow been his demise rather than the consumption, the disease that had withered his body and devastated his lungs. Not that Mother would really know how terrible he'd looked in his final days, seeing as how Father had refused to let her enter.

Arrow made another smooth round. She hardly remembered the service, other than the pervading guilt for not feeling something more sorrowful than relief. Tears pooled in the corners of her eyes, and this time Nora let them find release upon her cheeks. If anyone were to see her, they might not blame her for such a display of emotion.

She was technically supposed to still be in deep mourning, after all. Even if she had shunned her mourning blacks for trousers when the itch to leave her room and return to Arrow proved too great. Besides, Mother wouldn't notice.

Nora held out her riding crop, signaling for Arrow to change directions. He pivoted on his hindquarters and pranced for a moment before resuming his trot in an opposite circle around where she stood in the center. He tossed his crimson mane in the air, all flash and fire. By the time the sun found its way over the pines, he'd worked up a good sweat. She stepped forward and put her crop out toward the fence. As Arrow neared, he slowed and then came to a stop. Sweat foamed on his broad chest, and the muscles in his neck quivered when she caressed his damp coat.

"There, now. Did we release enough energy to try you at the harness?"

As though answering her question, Arrow shook his big head and gave a snort.

Nora lifted her eyebrows. "We'll just see about that, won't we?"

Arrow's head jerked up, and he looked over the top of Nora's uncovered hair to something behind her. Reminding herself her father could no longer berate her appearance or banish her to her chamber, she kept her chin lifted as she turned.

She let out a breath, shoulders relaxing. Uncle Amos. She smiled, walking across the corral to stand at the fence next to him. Amos was opposite of Father in every way. Where Father had shared Nora's fine honey-brown locks and blue eyes, Amos had thick ebony hair and cocoa-brown eyes. He wore his medium length curls meticulously combed back into glossy waves. Today his customary smile was absent from his generous lips. Dark rings smudged beneath his eyes. Father's death must have taken its toll.

Amos had shown up several times over the past weeks, checking on the women and speaking at length with Roger. While she appreciated his concern and understood his feelings of duty toward his brother's widow and daughter, she looked forward to the solicitor finalizing her father's will, officially leaving the property in Mother's control.

Amos glanced back at Arrow and then to Nora as though not quite comprehending what sort of training she used.

"What are you doing out here?" His voice rasped, an effect she assumed stemmed from the private expressions of grief he had not shared graveside. Of all those who'd attended the service, only Mother had succumbed to tears.

"Just exercising him a bit before we start with the harness." Nora clasped her hands behind her. "It helps keep him a little calmer."

Creases formed between his eyes. "You're in trousers."

She didn't expect the bite in his words but wouldn't begrudge him. Nora forced levity into her tone. "Arrow is ready for his harness training, and I'll not go about it in a dress. Trousers keep me from getting tangled up in skirts. Men don't know the inconvenience of training with a big swath of cloth wrapped around one's legs."

"Perhaps that's because as a man shouldn't be in a woman's dress, a woman should not be in the indecency of men's trousers. You should be helping your mother, not playing stable boy."

Nora drew back at the snap in his words. Now he would take up the mantle of her father's wishes? Nora had always thought him a bit more progressive. She lowered her eyes.

A sigh lifted his shoulders, the ire sliding off him and his usual friendly smile returning. "Forgive me, my dear. I didn't mean offense."

They stood in silence for several moments, watching Arrow prance as though he'd not just had a thorough exercise. Finally, Nora gathered the courage to ask about what had been needling her for weeks. She trusted no one else with such a revelation. "Before my father died, he said some strange things."

Amos grunted. "Probably had fever again."

"No, it wasn't that. He said something about a lie."

A spark flashed in his eyes, but he looked away before she could identify the cause. When he met her gaze again, he seemed to age a score of years. "What exactly did he say?"

"Not much." She swatted a fly. "He mentioned something about a horse that was, as he said, 'just something.'"

"Ember?"

Arrow came up behind her, nosing her in the back. He rubbed his big head over her shoulder blades, nearly lifting her from her feet. "I don't know." Their foundation stallion would make sense in context, she supposed, but he could have been talking about any horse. "He said he continued to build on a lie." She gripped the railing as Arrow rubbed harder, the sweat apparently making him itchy. "Do you know what he meant?"

Amos chuckled. "Looks like you've made yourself into a scratch post."

Heat rose up her neck. She sidestepped Arrow, gave him a good rub between the eyes, and then scrambled over the rail to join her uncle.

"Come on," he said. "We better get you back inside before your mother has a conniption."

"She won't notice." At his questioning gaze, she lifted her shoulders. "She hasn't left her room."

"She's taking it hard."

The statement required no response, so Nora turned toward the stable to gather her equipment. "Do you know what Father was talking about? I'm too afraid to ask Mother." Not to mention that Father had made her promise not to.

Amos fell into step beside her and remained quiet for so long that she didn't think he would answer. Then, he took her arm and guided her to the big oak shading the north end of the barn. After glancing around to make sure no one loitered nearby, he put a hand on her shoulder.

"I'd hoped to keep this from you, but since you are a lady of a certain age"—he gave her a gentle squeeze—"and an insatiably curious one at that, I suppose it would be better for me to tell you."

The words held a hint of mystery, and her pulse quickened.

"But then we will not speak of it again, agreed?" The concern in his eyes made her all the more uncomfortable. "And you must promise to keep this information close. No sense causing your mother heartache over wagging tongues."

At Nora's hesitant nod, he continued.

"Your father was desperate in those early days. The farm was struggling, and he was having trouble keeping enough food on the table for you and your mother. One foal after another had died, and those that survived brought less than half of what he'd hoped."

"Four half-starved mares and a floundering stallion?"

A sad turn lifted his lips. "Your mother kept praying, and I told Hiram we needed a racer. Something more exciting than plow horses and cutters. He called the idea foolhardy, since this wasn't Virginia or Kentucky and no one around here cared for such nonsense. He was right, of course, and harness racing hadn't come into vogue back then. But I had a hunch, you see."

He released her shoulder and stepped back, tilting his head to gaze into the umbrella of branches overhead. Nora waited, wanting to prompt him to continue but knowing she might not get the information she desired if she did.

Finally, he cleared his throat and looked back at her. "I thought that was the end of it. But then one night, he came home with a magnificent colt. Fire-red and as fine a piece of horseflesh as I had ever laid eyes on."

Nora smiled. "Ember."

"A fitting name too. I've never seen another stallion throw red colts that turn white by their fourth year. The whiter he got, the more Hiram would say he'd picked the perfect name. Red as a coal and then white as ash when his fire burned out." Amos's smile turned melancholy. "But old Ember, he never has quite lost that fire."

Nora watched Arrow, the colt she had helped usher from his mare into the world. "Arrow is a lot like him."

"I asked him where he'd bought the horse, but he never would say. Told me to mind my own affairs." He sucked his teeth. "After that, he started changing. Slowly at first, but more over the years. I've always wondered if something happened with Ember that withered part of my brother's soul."

The words sent a sudden chill down her spine. "You don't think . . ." She drew a breath, unable to form the words.

Amos looked away with a small shake of his head. "Whatever lie Hiram meant, Ember has official registry papers."

Nora pressed her lips together. What had Father meant? Would the truth now come out after his death, somehow costing Emberwild their future? Why leave the half-told secret to her instead of Mother?

"Did you hear me?"

She snatched her wayward attention back to her uncle's concerned face. "I'm afraid not."

"I said, how about we get you back to the house and dressed properly? I've an important reason for today's visit." Before she could ask, he gestured toward the house. "To save a repeat telling, how about we wait until your mother can join us? Perhaps over the midday meal?"

Nora withheld her groan. Of course he would expect her to prepare food. She cast another look at Arrow and opened her mouth, but before she could speak, Amos let out a shrill whistle.

The stable door flew wide, and Roger hurried out, his thin frame ever resisting the bulk his labors should have heaped upon him. He came over smelling of horseflesh and hay and wiped his hand across his brow. He gave a polite nod to Nora, though clearly uncomfortable, and turned his attention to Amos.

"Yessir?"

"Would you see to Arrow? The lady has indicated he needs harness training today."

The stable master cocked his head. "But, sir, that colt ain't ready for—"

"As Miss Fenton wants him trained, and you are under the employ of this farm, I say it's best to see to her wishes."

Roger gave a brisk nod. "Yessir. I'll see to it myself."

"Good man."

At a loss for words, Nora watched Roger trot off. No one had ever made Roger do anything for her. In fact, she often had to skirt around the pernicious man to accomplish anything at all. Well, perhaps *pernicious* was unfair. Bullheaded, certainly. At least insofar as his attitude applied to women and horsemanship. A glimmer of satisfaction burned as she watched him hurry off to fulfill her wishes.

Amos took her hand and placed it on his arm. "Now, how about we head inside?"

He led her away, leaving behind the sound of Arrow's shrill whinnies and Roger's answering curses.

chapter
FOUR

Avoiding the squeaky fourth stair out of habit, Nora climbed to the second floor and slipped into her room. If Mother by chance opened her door and saw Nora dressed in trousers, she'd risk another bout of hysteria. Amos would simply have to wait.

Crossing carpeting that had begun to show signs of wear, Nora hurried to her walnut wardrobe. She hadn't made her bed this morning, and the jumble of blankets lay in a heap on the floor where she'd tossed them aside. Had Amos noticed their state of disarray downstairs as well? How long had it been since anyone had scrubbed the floors? She couldn't remember.

Mother had dismissed the housekeeper when Father had fallen ill, and Father gave the domestic chores over to Nora. A fair compensation, he had said, since Nora refused to marry during her most fetching years and now insisted on living on her parents' generosity.

Nora huffed out a breath. If the men paraded before her hadn't all been so weak, maybe she would have chosen marriage. But she simply wouldn't follow a man she couldn't respect.

She selected a black cotton day dress from the wardrobe and changed out of her barn clothes as swiftly as she could, shimmying into all the absurd layers required of a woman. She wouldn't dare show herself to Mother without proper mourning attire. She eyed the white porcelain basin.

No time for washing.

She ran a hand over her mussed hair, straightened her shoulders, and strode back into the hallway. She glanced at the end of the hall. The door to Father's room stood open, a dark cave she'd not set foot in since the morning he died.

A chill washed over her, but she shook away the feeling and turned with purpose toward her mother's room. She rapped firmly on the door. "Mother, Uncle Amos is here to call on you."

"Tell him I am indisposed." Mother's reedy voice barely penetrated the door. She wouldn't soon suffer from sickness as well, would she?

"I did. He insists he must speak to you. Says it is a matter of great importance."

Nora waited for several moments, but when no reply came, she heaved a sigh and returned downstairs.

Amos stood stoically in the entry hall, his hat tucked under his arm, an expectant lift to his chin. The hush of the house amplified with his presence, as though the residence held its breath.

"Mother will not leave her room."

"She must." Amos spoke with the tone men used when they expected no arguments. "My news is of the utmost importance. Both to her and you. It cannot wait."

What could he possibly have to say that required Mother's presence? She started to ask, but the look in his eyes stilled her.

Pleading, nearly.

Amos shifted his stance in a subtle gesture she recognized. One that meant stubbornness would soon follow. "I would like to see her."

Perhaps that look was determination. Men never understood a woman's capacity to sink to depths of darkness so thick that neither sunlight nor good intentions could pierce.

Nora tried again, speaking with as much calm deference as she could muster. "Perhaps if I let her know you came calling, then maybe tomorrow . . ."

He forced a smile. "Very well. I suppose you and I will discuss the necessities, and you can relay them to Mrs. Fenton at another time."

What a grand idea. It was almost as if he'd been advised of that already.

Pushing down a retort, Nora offered a small smile instead. "A pertinent suggestion, Uncle."

The side of his mouth twitched. "I'll wait in the parlor. Please inform me when the meal is prepared."

He still expected her to make dinner for him? Struggling to keep her resentment from showing, Nora obediently inclined her head. Clearly satisfied by his victory, Amos strode to the parlor.

Did she have anything he'd find acceptable? She'd been taking Mother broth—which she usually refused—while Nora had existed on salted meats and canned vegetables from the cellar. One would think after a year of attempting to learn to prepare their meals she'd be more accomplished in her cooking skills, but despite Mother's instructions, she fell short of adequate.

She lifted the top on the wooden icebox and chopped off two large chunks with the ice pick. Perhaps Amos would be more agreeable if he waited with a chilled glass of lemonade. The chips clinked into the glass, and Nora slowly poured the last of the sunny yellow liquid from the pitcher.

In the parlor, she found her uncle as she'd predicted. Settled into her father's chair, the latest issue of *Wallace's American Trotting Register* open in his lap. He rose as she entered, setting the book on the side table near the hearth.

The parlor had once been home to ladies' knitting circles, friendly afternoon teas, and neighborly company. Nora remembered when every matching blue upholstered chair had held a lady of community standing.

But after several years of Nora refuting every one of Mother's friends' sons—or in some instances politely trying to discourage suitors by conveniently revealing snippets of her progressive thoughts and strong opinions—visitors had trickled to a halt.

At some point, Mother had simply stopped trying. Likely around the same time she'd determined Nora would become a spinster. Then Father had fallen ill, and every moment of their lives had revolved around his care.

Amos reached out for the glass, interrupting Nora's rambling thoughts. Why had she spent so much time pondering the past lately?

"Thank you, my dear." Amos offered a smile that reminded her of her father in his younger years. "A cool drink is most appreciated on a day such as today."

Pleased with her decision, Nora returned his smile and then bustled back to the kitchen. Now, what to prepare that wouldn't cost her an hour? She hadn't baked any bread, nor did she have any pies waiting on the counters. She surveyed the kitchen and spotted a basket holding a few sprouting onions and withered potatoes on the preparation table.

She diced the onions and potatoes, found a few carrots at the bottom of the basket, and unscrewed the zinc cap from two Mason jars holding garden peas Mother had preserved last fall.

Thankfully, the stove still held a few decent logs she had no trouble igniting. While she waited for the stove to heat, she pumped water into a stockpot and hefted it onto the cooktop. Salt, a few dried herbs, and a clove of garlic, and soon she'd have a base for a somewhat decent soup.

The vegetables plopped into the water, making tiny splashes. Nora frowned. She'd forgotten to use a little lard and flour to make a base. The soup would be thin at best. She added some salted pork and stirred the now bubbling pot. There. A light soup would work for a summer dinner. Who wanted a thick stew in this heat?

Nora busied herself cleaning up the mess she'd made and then returned to the stove to give the concoction a stir.

"At least you have the wherewithal to make an attempt at hosting."

Nora whirled at the sound of her mother's voice. Even dressed for deep mourning in an ebony gown trimmed heavily in crepe, Mother stood with the regal bearing of a queen entering her court. She crossed the floor on silent slippers and leaned over Nora's soup.

Though she couldn't see Mother's face through the thick veil draping down to her shoulders, Nora could have sensed Mother's disappointment in the concoction from as far as the stables.

Mother leaned back. "If he expected better, perhaps he shouldn't have arrived unannounced." She gave a small sniff. "Where is he?"

"He asked to wait in the parlor. He wanted to discuss something with us over the midday meal."

"I'll not suffer presiding over a dinner. He'll simply have to state his business and allow me to return to my chamber." She glided toward the door. "Join us, if you prefer."

Leaving the spoon in the pot, Nora scrambled after her mother. Even as a willowy shadow of her former bearing, Rebecca Fenton commanded any space with the force of her presence.

She strode into the parlor in a flurry of rustling ebony. "What news, Amos?"

Amos rose slowly. If he found Mother's lack of hospitality disturbing, he gave no indication. "Rebecca." He bent slightly at the waist, offering the smallest of bows. "Shall we discuss matters during our luncheon?"

Nora slipped in behind her mother, a shadow clinging to the far wall.

"As you are well aware, I'm in mourning. I've not the fortitude for company, yet my daughter insisted you have a matter of some importance to discuss." The icy words clung to the air, and Nora could almost swear she could see the shards of tension slicing through the space between them.

Lines at the sides of Amos's mouth tightened, but his voice remained smooth. "I met with the solicitor. The property is to fall under my management, as well as control of all assets, accounts, and men under the farm's employ."

The words hung on the air, the implications of the pronouncement hitting hard.

"I'd hoped to discuss the details of the arrangement, but I can see this is a discussion better left for another time." Amos plucked his bowler hat from the side table and tucked it under his arm. "When you're ready."

Father had left their farm to Amos. Why hadn't she seen this coming? She'd foolishly let herself foster a seed of hope that the property would fall to Mother, and Nora would then be able to live her life with a measure of freedom.

With Amos in charge, what would happen with Arrow? His training was progressing well. Given the time to work with him, she'd be able to enter him into a few small harness races. Starting with the local fair. Perhaps take him to Columbus in the fall for the large Mississippi and West Alabama Fair, where she could show his merit to breeders from across the country.

Arrow could run much faster than the necessary qualifiers, she was sure. The colt had speed. Might even be as fast as Dan Patch someday. Any horse that could come close to the famous bay's two-minute run would catch the eye of farms seeking stud rights or buyers looking for new colts.

Colts they'd gladly travel to Mississippi to purchase, paying prices that would lessen the threat of debtors and generate enough income for Nora to care for Mother and herself.

She'd never get the chance to prove her merit as a trainer in the world of men if she kept getting banished to the kitchen. Amos would allow Arrow to run, but not with her as trainer. And Arrow never ran for Roger like he did for her. With her, he came alive.

As she did with him.

Nora twisted her hands, her thoughts continuing to spiral the longer Mother stood like an ice sculpture.

"Hiram promised I'd never be destitute."

Did that reedy voice really emanate from her mother? The ice sculpture chipped, then shattered. The woman underneath suddenly appeared frail. Thin, stooping shoulders. Trembling hands clasped behind her back.

"And he has kept his promise by not leaving you the burden of management." Amos stepped closer, a tenderness in his eyes Nora had never seen before. "I will care for you, Rebecca. You have my word."

Something about the way he spoke made Nora feel as though she intruded on a private moment. Surely her father's brother only sought to put her mother at ease.

"And what of Nora?"

Amos glanced her way and their gazes locked. The look in his eyes cleared. He shifted slightly, seeming to pull back and become himself once more. "My dear niece may do as she wishes."

Hope leapt up from her chest and bloomed into a smile. He would give her freedom? Allow her to—

"Until such a time as you find her a proper husband, she will be cared for here."

A husband? Amos thought to marry her off? But he'd said—

Her throat constricted. Is that what Amos considered doing "as she wished"? Attending parties, flashing her eyes at men over a fan, hoping they saw her as a pretty bird to show off on their arms?

Mother offered a small nod, as though she expected nothing different. Even without her father, Nora's life would fall under the shadow of male control.

Resentment clawed up from her core and nestled in her heart.

They'd see about that.

chapter
FIVE

Philadelphia, Mississippi
June 1905

He'd never wanted to see this place again. Yet the need to find the truth pulled Silas into the town of Philadelphia, Mississippi, as though returning here might unfetter the need for justice that had long festered deep within him. Starlight plodded dutifully into the town center, her muzzle swaying near the muddy street. The evening cast shadows on the buildings, blanketing them in gray and softening their hard edges.

Choctaw men glanced at him from storefronts or lumbering wagons. He passed the mercantile, a few shops boasting various services, and a postal station. On the outskirts of town he came to the building that had often infected his nightmares.

It looked nothing like he remembered.

The inn was a squatty, unimpressive structure, its shutters sagging over more than one window, the whitewashed wood peeling in several places. Passing the hitching post in the front, Silas steered Starlight to the rear, where a stable hunched beneath the weight of a swaybacked roof.

Steeling himself, he dismounted and waited near the door. He wouldn't go in. Not yet.

An older man dressed in dungarees emerged from the side of the barn. He spotted Silas and veered his direction. "Evenin', sir. Planning to stay?" The man gestured to Starlight. "I'll see that she's properly tended."

Silas detached his saddlebags and hefted them over his shoulder before handing over the reins. He watched as the man led his horse away. Did she favor that left hind hoof a little? The old girl deserved a good brushing and a long rest. Maybe she'd feel comfortable enough in a stall to lie down tonight. He'd check later to make sure the groom had kept his word.

Even this late into the day, the blistering heat caused rivulets of sweat to snake down his spine. Silas rolled his neck, trying to release the tension of days spent in the saddle and stiff joints caused by nights on the hard ground. He did little more than cause a popping sound and a sharp stab of pain toward his left eye. A decent bed would do him wonders.

His fingers inched toward the pocket containing what little money he possessed. He could afford a few nights and a couple of meals at best. Then he'd have to see if he could earn his keep. Or move on.

He'd left everything, save his saddlebags and horse, to come here. To find the truth. What he intended to do after, he hadn't yet decided. Perhaps the truth would bring peace, and peace would open a path to a future. Doubtful, but the hope had been the only thing pushing him the long miles across the States.

Maybe he'd find work as a horse trainer. Or leave the profession altogether and join up with the railroad. Or take a ship and sail to his father's homeland to see what fortunes he could discover in Spain. The possibilities could prove endless, if he had any inclination what he wanted to do with his future.

In the meantime, he had to solve a murder left cold for fifteen years.

Teeth clenched, he strode to the dilapidated structure that scarcely resembled the establishment he remembered. The last place he'd seen his father alive.

The wood creaked beneath his boots as he mounted the steps. Inside, musty air clung to a smattering of mismatched chairs and tables, a long bar stocked with glass bottles, and men huddled around tables and decks of cards. Gas lights hung from the ceiling and along the back wall, casting wavering shadows one didn't get with the electric lights found in cities.

Not exactly the warm inn he remembered.

Spotting a balding man wrapped in a stained apron at the rear of the establishment, Silas moved in his direction. A few pairs of red-rimmed eyes followed his progress, but most dismissed him as just another dusty traveler. Not that he suspected many folks passed through this town. Most of these men probably had nearby families they should have been tending instead of filling their stomachs with whiskey and their fingers with cards.

The man in the apron, a stout fellow with a wide nose and a scraggly patch of whiskers, gave him a nod as he approached. "What can I get for you?"

Information. The truth. Relief from the questions that had long haunted him.

"A room, please. And a hot meal." What he needed would take at least the night. Most likely longer.

"Single room, or looking to share?"

"Private."

They agreed on the rate, and Silas settled on a stool, declining the man's offer of a drink. "This your establishment?" He propped the heel of his boot on the leg of the stool.

With a simple nod, the man resumed his previous task of wiping down the bar. He threw the rag over his shoulder. "What brings you into town?"

"Passing through. I take it you were here fifteen years ago?"

The man slowed his movements. "Why?"

"Stayed here with my father when I was a boy."

The fellow's features drew in, causing lines around his eyes and mouth that made him appear older than his probable fifty years. Silas searched the face, but couldn't bring up the features in his memories. If he'd worked here fifteen years ago, Silas hadn't noticed as a twelve-year old.

The man grunted. "Name's Joe Elroy." He thrust a beefy hand over the bar.

Silas shook it firmly. "Silas Cavallero."

Joe's face flickered with a look hinting that whatever he thought, he didn't want to share. Given the course of the conversation, the reaction likely had one cause.

"You remember my father?"

Joe sighed, a huff of breath that somehow conveyed both regret and frustration. "Bad business, that."

Fifteen years, and the wound still ached. Burned like something that festered under the skin, unreachable. "Do you remember anything from that night? Anything that might answer a few questions for me?"

"Been a long time." He drew the words out, as though speaking more slowly would make Silas realize he asked for the impossible.

Really, what did he think he would find here? The question had haunted him since crossing the Mississippi, but he'd forcefully kept the doubts at bay. He needed this sliver of hope. A chance to find an end to the questions. To close the chapter on his past so that he could make a fresh start. One he couldn't allow himself until he found justice for his father's death and vindication for his mother's pain.

A man called from across the room, wanting a bottle of whiskey for the card table. Joe mumbled something under his breath and scooted out from behind the bar. He approached the table, no doubt weighing the profits of another bottle against the risk of men becoming violent under his roof. If they were raucous this early in the evening, no telling how much worse they would get.

Two young serving women darted out from behind a swinging door near the bar, followed by a kindly older woman with dark hair and smile lines at the corner of her eyes. She spotted Silas and immediately veered his direction.

"I'm Myrtle, Joe's wife." Before Silas could answer, she gestured him toward a table. "I'll fetch you a plate while he's busy."

Joe still spoke with the men at the table. It wouldn't hurt for Silas to fill his stomach while he waited. He moved from the stool to the empty table near the staircase. Once Myrtle saw him seated, she bustled off again.

A few moments later he had a plate of roasted pork, salted greens, and lumpy potatoes in front of him. He thanked the woman, which sparked a grin before she disappeared once again. Silas ate quickly, hardly tasting the food that could use more seasoning.

"A good trotter is worth seven of your plow horses, you old fool," a man in a wide-brimmed hat shouted, tossing down his cards.

"And you ain't got a one of them to bet," laughed another, this one a skinny man with greasy hair and eyes too large for his gaunt face. "You don't own nothing more than the sweat off one of their backs."

Trotters. Interesting. Silas leaned back in his seat, but the men moved on to talking about other assets that didn't interest him. These men worked with horses. Standardbreds, if he met his guess.

His father had purchased an American Standardbred, though not for the purpose of the new trend of harness racing. He'd had other plans for a smooth-gaited, mild-mannered breed. Swarms of previously genteel Southerners had fled west after the war, and rather than building a ranch catering to cattle horses, Silas's father had planned to appeal to the fine ladies and gentlemen looking to regain their former soft lifestyles. Hackney horses, he'd said. In a world of cattle cutters, Papa wanted to breed trotters.

It had been a good plan. Might even have worked, given the time. But his father's death and the loss of their foundation stallion had left such notions to crumble to dust.

The chair across from him creaked, snatching Silas's thoughts from the past. Joe laced his fingers together on the wooden tabletop.

"That why you're here, son?" He picked up the previous conversation as though they'd never parted. "Looking for healing?"

Insightful question. "I was hoping you'd have a few answers for me. Things that never did quite line up."

Kind eyes searched Silas's face. "Sometimes we look for meaning in senseless loss. It's understandable. But I'm afraid I don't know much more than what you probably already do. The stallion spooked, trampled his owner, and fled. Never was found."

The same story he'd been told as a boy. But those men didn't know his father's uncanny ability with horses. Or the fact that he wouldn't have been so careless. "Do you remember anything unusual? Anything that stuck in your memory as peculiar?"

Joe regarded him with pity. "Everything I remember lined up with the sheriff's assessment."

Frustration bubbled like bile in his stomach, mingling with his tasteless supper and souring his senses.

"You're welcome to speak to him yourself. He usually comes in about this time each evening." Without waiting for an answer, Joe rose and returned to the bar, leaving Silas to his meal and contemplations.

True to his word, about a half hour later a weathered man with a tanned face and a hat slung low over his eyebrows entered and found a seat at the bar. No sooner had the man settled than Joe waved Silas over.

"This here's Marcus Henderson. Sheriff in these parts. Sheriff, this fellow is Mr. Cavallero."

The taller man's sandy hair curled out from underneath the brim of his hat as he nodded acknowledgment. A matching mustache drooped over the serious turn of his lips.

"Mr. Cavallero here has some questions about a case of yours from fifteen years ago."

Right to the point. Silas could appreciate a man of efficiency. Joe moved on to other duties, leaving the men alone to talk.

The sheriff regarded him evenly. Silas took the man's silence as invitation to ask what he would.

"My father died here when I was twelve. Never sat right with me as an accident. Thought I'd ask around, see if anyone remembered anything."

Henderson unbuttoned his coat and thanked a serving girl for the meal she placed in front of him. She smiled sweetly, then scurried off. "Fifteen years is a long time."

"Some things you don't forget. Like a skilled horseman mysteriously being trampled and a missing stallion no one ever recovered."

A flicker of recognition sparked in the sheriff's eyes. "I recall something about a case like that." He ran his fingers over his long mustache. "But what brings you here asking questions after so many years?"

Because at the time he'd been a boy easily ignored, his rants of injustice shooed away as a child's grief. "First time passing through since."

The sheriff chewed thoughtfully. "Not sure what else I can offer. Tragic, I recall. Traveler lost control of his horse. Suffered head trauma and multiple broken bones when the animal spooked in the stall. The horse escaped."

Indignation scorched through him at the callous words. "You had evidence the horse escaped and wasn't stolen?"

The sheriff paused with a forkful of potatoes partway to his mouth and his sandy mustache twitched.

Fool. No sense offending the man by implying he hadn't done his job. Silas forced calm into his voice. "That is, I always wondered why no one ever found the horse."

The fork resumed course. The sheriff took his time chewing. "Most likely, someone found a loose horse and claimed him."

Leave it to people to be dishonest whenever the opportunity arose. Henderson resumed eating, offering no other explanations for a missing horse. One who had in all likelihood been taken by some opportunistic local. With the owner dead and his son shipped back to his mother, who would care to find the horse's legal owners?

"Any signs of a struggle?" Silas pressed. "Evidence that someone else had been in the barn that night?"

"Lots of people came in and out. Stable hands, travelers, even local folks. All with legitimate reasons to be there."

Silas tried not to let disappointment surface. He'd known returning here likely wouldn't get him any answers. Not for a stranger who appeared to have been killed by his own stallion fifteen years ago. Silas was probably lucky they remembered Papa at all. He wouldn't get anything more from the sheriff.

Pushing aside his frustration, he thanked the man and returned to his solitary place at his table. Had he really expected to find anything useful the first night? He'd have to spend time here. Talk to locals. If he could find out who took the colt, maybe he could find his father's killer.

There had to be a murderer. Someone else who'd been there that night. Papa wouldn't have been careless enough for the tragedy to be an accident.

He tapped a finger on the table, food forgotten. *Foolish.*

He'd let his grief over his mother and the loss of their home drive him to grasp at shadows. The need to move, to find purpose— even one so far-fetched—had been the only thing keeping him from wallowing in destructive emotions that would honor neither of his parents. But now that he was here, facing the reality that he would probably never find the truth, the darkness threatened to overtake him.

What did he do now? A man with only one horse and a few changes of clothes? His mother had wanted him to find freedom. The emptiness offered only loneliness and destitution.

"Got the fastest horses this side of Kentucky!" a man shouted, drawing Silas's attention back to the boisterous card table.

A respectable looking couple edged their way around the table and headed upstairs to their room. If Joe wanted to rent rooms to decent folks, he should probably let the rabble find another place to drown in their drinks.

"That farm's falling to ruin and everyone knows it. Now that old Fenton is cold in the ground, I give the place half a year."

"Naw. Not now that the other Fenton has taken over. Heard him tell Walter we might get an increase in pay, once all that legal stuff is final."

Silas twisted in his chair, bits of the men's ongoing conversation clinging to his brain. Fast horses. Trotters. A farm that had gobbled up enough land in the county to rival one of the old plantations. Folks that had what was coming to them, thinking they were so uppity.

He found himself rising and hovering near the table.

"You need something, fella?" The man in the wide-brimmed hat eyed Silas with suspicion.

A thought occurred to him and he spoke before his better sense could stop him. "You work on a horse farm? I'm a trainer myself. Looking for work."

The man sneered. "Don't need no strangers at Emberwild."

Emberwild. He filed the name away for later. "Just asking." He shrugged and headed back toward his table.

"Wait."

Silas turned back to meet the brown eyes of another man at the table. "What kind of trainer?"

"Break colts, mostly."

The men exchanged a look, but the one in the hat shook his head.

The other one said something too low for Silas to hear and the man in the hat sneered. "Come to think of it, might be a spot for you after all, stranger. Come by Emberwild. Talk to Roger Reed."

Before Silas could respond, the men turned back to their cards and started up another argument over horses and this year's chances at some kind of harness competition.

He'd sooner swim in a river full of rattlesnakes than work with those idiots. But the prospect of a job could give him a few dollars in his pocket and a few weeks to see if he could find any answers.

Then he'd leave this backwater town and the painful memories behind him for good.

chapter
SIX

This was probably a terrible idea. Silas tugged his wide-brimmed Stetson low over his brows to keep the wind out of his eyes as he rode Starlight down the northeast road out of the small town of Philadelphia. The innkeeper had been able to point him in the general direction he needed to go, and once he stopped at a farmhouse on the outskirts of town to ask directions, all he had to do was continue down this road to find Emberwild.

After spending all of yesterday asking every person he could find if they remembered anything about that night fifteen years ago, he'd come to the inevitable conclusion that he'd find nothing other than the same story of a spooked stallion and an unfortunate stranger.

No sense hanging around letting memories eat at him. Papa had always said a man should take the first step in the right direction if he ever hoped to go anywhere useful, and so plodding along this deserted dirt road seemed like the best way to move forward.

On either side of the road, cornfields sprouted fat stalks that reached toward the sun. Drought had tipped their leaves brown, leaving them with crackling edges. He knew the feeling.

Hot summer wind toyed with his hat and played with the tips of his dark hair. He was weeks past needing another cut, and the ends

46

curled around his ears, tickling his skin. If he could find employment at this farm or another, maybe he'd head east.

But what then? He pushed the thought out of his mind. He'd worry about that once he had enough money to continue on his way.

True to the farmer's word, Silas soon came to the end of a sprawling cornfield and passed into pastureland. The fences, well-maintained as far as he could tell, enclosed flat pastureland rich with swaying green grass, their vibrancy hampered by the lack of rain. Sweeping ancient oaks and a few massive pines provided oases from the heat of the sun. Nothing like the dry and crumbling ground back home.

Starlight lifted her head and whinnied, ears perked. In the distance, a horse returned her call. She gave a shake of her mane and continued forward as though whatever question she'd asked had been answered to her satisfaction. Some time in the pasture with others of her kind would probably do her good.

He'd continued on this northeasterly road roughly eight miles out from town and hadn't seen another soul in at least the past three. How much of this land belonged to the Fenton family? Joe hadn't offered Silas much by way of information, only that the property had been the last vestiges of an estate owned by the late Mr. Fenton's father. Most of the acreage had been lost during the war. The Fentons had raised general stock until they'd taken an interest in racers.

Around the next bend, a pretentious house came into view, a spire at the front reaching heavenward. To the west sat a stone barn with several foaling paddocks. Foals pranced around their dams, their sleek coats shining in the sun.

Silas took his time approaching, analyzing the surroundings. How many of these horses were trotters? An interesting choice for an area known more for carriage or plow horses. And so close to where his father's stallion had gone missing.

The coincidence nagged at him.

Could his quest to find the missing horse be that simple?

He shook off a barrage of questions seeking to send his mind spinning and allowed Starlight to pass through the front gates. He gave her neck a fond pat. "Pretty place, ain't it, girl?" A far cry from the dilapidated cabin and crumbling barn he'd left behind.

Two men dressed in the sturdy clothing of farmhands eyed him as he approached the barn, but he didn't recognize either of them as the card players from town. He drew Starlight to a halt and she let out a snort, shifting her hooves. A moment later a lanky man with a saddle tossed over one shoulder exited the open doors of the large stable. He stopped when his gaze landed on Silas, a frown tugging at already angular features.

Silas dismounted as the man approached. The tall man dropped the saddle to the ground a few paces from Starlight, eyeing the two of them. Not the friendliest place.

"Mornin'." The man used the same drawn-out accent Silas had heard from the people in town. He spit a stream of amber liquid. "Can I help you, fella?"

"Looking for Roger Reed. Few men in town said Emberwild might have a place for a horse trainer."

The man raked a gaze over him. "You from around here?"

"Passing through on my way east. Looking for a bit of work to get me there."

The man reached for the saddle again. "Don't take drifters here. Best you move on."

Silas kept an easy hold on Starlight's reins, balancing his tone on the line of respectful and confident. "Just because a man is passing through doesn't make him a drifter. I'm good at breaking colts. Even the ones most men would have turned over to the bronc riders."

The man paused, his assessing gaze sweeping over Silas again. "How long you plan on staying in these parts?"

"Few weeks. Couple months at most."

A blur of movement caught his eye as a horse sped along the track to his left. A boy hung on as the horse took a breakneck turn around the corner. Fool kid. Too young to know he'd get himself killed on a run like that.

The man in front of him spit again and mumbled a curse. "Got one colt could use a firm hand." He glared at the boy holding tight enough onto the pommel to imprint the leather. "Boss insists we train him for the harness, but he ain't the sort. Too temperamental."

The red streak of horseflesh careened around the far side of the track, the boy nearly coming off the side of the saddle. Silas thrust his chin toward the churning dirt flying behind the horse's hooves. "That one?"

A lift of the man's eyebrow in a sun-lined face was the only answer Silas received. "What's your name, drifter?"

"Silas Cavallero."

The man grunted. "Mexican?"

Silas fought back annoyance at the sneer in the man's voice. "My father was Spanish."

He gave a nod as though the distinction meant little. "Roger Reed." No offer of a handshake. "I'll give you three days to see if you can do anything with that colt." He thumbed toward the stable. "Empty stall left rear. You can put your saddle in the tack room. I'll send a man to show you to the bunkhouse." He grunted as though he'd didn't expect Silas to make it long enough to need the bed. "You can start this afternoon."

Silas nodded in thanks, but Mr. Reed was already walking away. He watched the red colt fly around the track again, his gait swift, if a bit unsteady. He was fast, sure, but he needed more control. He could read the defiance in the set of the horse's ears. The barely contained energy would get that boy clinging to his saddle killed.

Shaking his head, Silas led Starlight into a well-ventilated barn. Sunlight poured down from upper windows and splashed across the cobbled floor underfoot. Starlight nickered, her hooves clicking softly down the aisle as a few mares poked their heads out in greeting.

They found the empty enclosure at the end of the long hallway. In addition to the four foaling stalls, he counted ten regular stalls down each side of the barn, two stallion stalls, a tack room, a feed room, and two other rooms with closed doors. He let Starlight into a clean stall, water bucket already filled. Silas quickly removed her saddle and blanket, pulled the bridle over her head, and rubbed her down with a handful of clean straw. He'd give her a good brushing later. Probably shouldn't keep the stable master waiting. He stored his equipment on an empty rack in the tack room and strode back outside.

A boy with a muck cart nodded at him in passing before hurrying along with his duty. Roger was nowhere in sight. While he waited, Silas approached the rail of the oval track. The colt had slowed, his flanks heaving. At the slower speed Silas could take stock of the young stallion. He had the high croup and low withers prized by all Hambletonian Standardbreds. Straight cannon bones, slightly narrow hooves. Something about the fiery red coat reminded him of the stallion that had supposedly taken his father's life.

Silas chided himself for grasping at every perceived coincidence. He'd need more than vague similarities if he ever thought to find the truth.

"You the new fellow?"

Silas turned and found the source of the rumbling voice to be a barrel-chested man with a deep complexion and an ebony beard that grazed the top of his blue shirt. An assessing gaze harbored hints of friendliness.

"Silas Cavallero." He stuck out a hand. "I'll be helping out for a few weeks." If he passed Roger Reed's assessment, at least.

Surprise lifted the man's features for an instant, then his face split into a grin, proving Silas's intuition. He enveloped Silas's hand in his larger, calloused one and gave a firm shake. "Asa." He glanced at the ground around Silas's boots. "I'm supposed to show you to the bunk. You got any saddlebags?"

"Left them with my tack in the barn."

The big man nodded. "I'll wait while you fetch them."

Silas gave a quick nod and trotted off to gather his belongings, casting one last glance at the boy on the tall stallion as they finally came to a stop on the track.

A good run. One of their best, actually. In the weeks since Amos's declaration that he would run the farm, her uncle had come by nearly every day around midmorning to conduct whatever business that he seemed to think necessary and try to get her mother to take his company. His tendency toward routine, however, had allowed Nora to continue her training with Arrow mostly out of his notice.

She slid down from Arrow's back and scratched the base of his mane. He lowered his head, becoming more complacent with each rub of her fingers. Silly boy. Even with all his bravado, he was still the sweet foal she'd loved since he took his first steps on spindly legs. They'd bonded during those times, and no matter what Roger said, Arrow would never hurt her.

Not intentionally, anyway.

"He's got nice form," a man's voice said from behind her, "though you could use a bit more caution on those turns, boy."

What? Nora whirled around to find a tall man casually leaning on the fence, watching her. "Who are you?"

Surprise flickered over his tanned features, deep brown eyes widening slightly before settling into a calm gaze once again. "Silas Cavallero."

He spoke with an easy cadence, his voice both deep and smooth. He watched her openly, as though trying to figure out all of her secrets. She bristled. "And what are you doing here, Mr. Cavallero?"

"Looking at your horse."

A buyer? She'd heard nothing about a buyer coming by today. This man in his dusty dungarees and once-white hat didn't look like the type, but appearances could be deceiving.

Satisfaction swelled as she ran a hand down Arrow's neck. "You won't find any better. He won't be ready for breeding until next year, but I hope to start putting him on the books soon. Are you looking for a new stud?"

The man stared at her, strong jaw set against a serious mouth. "I'm not here to secure stud services. Mr. Reed hired me to get a handle on this colt."

She couldn't possibly have heard him correctly. "Excuse me?"

He casually swung over the fence and landed next to her. Arrow tossed his head. Get a handle on him? Arrow would wipe the pride right off this fellow's face and leave him wishing he hadn't been so cavalier.

Withholding a smirk, she loosened her hold on the reins and let them slide through her fingers, giving Arrow his head. If this man wanted to pounce over the fence like some self-absorbed peacock, he could be her guest. Arrow would put him in his place and send him scrambling right back where he came from.

But rather than approaching Arrow, the stranger turned his shoulder to the horse and acted as though he couldn't care less about the threatening way Arrow had lowered his ears. Then just as casually as he'd entered their space, the man held out his hand to the side.

Nora grunted. Stupid man. Arrow didn't take to strangers, and he wasn't fond of men in general. They were too rough. Too demanding. And they always thought they could bully everyone into doing—

Arrow reached out and sniffed the cowboy's hand, puffs of air quivering his nostrils. Lulling him into a false security. One swift move and he'd take this man's fingers off at the knuckles.

Well, perhaps that was a bit of an exaggeration. Arrow didn't bite unless provoked, and this man was as still as a statue. He just stood there. Quiet. Unassuming. How could a man look both puffed with ego and calmly reassuring at the same time? The notion unsettled her. Arrow, however, seemed intrigued.

To her amazement, her horse took a tentative step forward and then nuzzled the man's upturned palm. She expected him to reach for Arrow then, but he merely smiled and lowered his hand, then turned his attention to Nora.

"There might be hope for him yet."

Her amazement melted under a surge of heat. Who did this man think he was? Coming onto her land, insulting her horse? "Sir, I don't know who told you that you could work here, but we don't need your services."

"That so?" He leaned back against the fence again, as though her words meant nothing. "Fellow named Roger Reed said he'd see how I did with this colt."

She opened her mouth to tell him he could keep right on moving, but paused. Roger had hired a trainer specifically for Arrow? Why? So Roger didn't have to work with the horse as Amos had directed or so that Nora would be pushed out by a stranger they both thought she wouldn't refute?

"Roger brought you here?"

Mr. Cavallero, whom she supposed most women would consider handsome with his wide shoulders and dark hair curling out from under his hat, maintained his infuriatingly arrogant casualness, in no hurry to answer her questions. Or even look her in the eyes. Arrow, now curious about this man who showed little interest in him, stepped forward. Mr. Cavallero offered him a slight smile before looking back at Nora.

"Heard some men in town talking about a horse farm. I'm a trainer. Figured this might be a good place to earn a wage." He smirked as Arrow bumped his shoulder. "For a time."

His explanation made even less sense than the one she'd assumed. Some drifter had shown up on their land and Roger thought he'd let this stranger work with Arrow? Indignation swelled. Did no one respect her enough to at least *ask* her opinion?

"I'm sorry to disappoint you, but your services won't be needed." Mr. Cavallero lifted his brows.

"You see, I'm not currently hiring any trainers. While your offer is appreciated, it's unneeded at this time." There. If Roger thought he could hire men without her input, then she could certainly dismiss them without his. No matter what Amos had decided, this was still her family's farm. She'd not be ousted by a stable master and some no-account drifter.

The cowboy, however, regarded her stoically, completely unperturbed by her statement. "You must be Miss Fenton."

She gave him a curt nod. "I am. Arrow is my horse, and I will decide who trains him."

The man cast another look at Arrow, who had now treasonously positioned himself next to the man's side and began nuzzling his arm. Nora snatched the reins, and the horse snorted.

"If you will excuse me, Arrow needs his cooldown. Tell Roger I said to give you a half-day's wages for your trouble, but you won't be staying."

She felt his eyes on her as she led Arrow away, but he never uttered a word.

chapter
SEVEN

What a spitfire. Silas held his tongue while the woman he'd mistaken for a boy led her nearly-as-temperamental stallion off the track and to a nearby corral. Once he'd gotten close, there could be no mistaking those delicate features as masculine.

She'd stuffed her thick braids—the color somewhere between that of a bay and a dun—beneath a floppy hat that shaded a straight nose, a smooth if somewhat tanned complexion, and large blue eyes that flashed hostility. The lady would probably be most fetching if she ever turned those peachy lips into a smile.

Silas eased closer to the corral, though not close enough to catch Miss Fenton's attention. He might as well observe the stallion while he waited to find Roger again. The colt she'd called Arrow pranced around, sweat frothing on his chest and shoulders.

Almost like a dance, Miss Fenton moved and the horse responded, turning one way for a few laps and then the other, his attention never leaving his mistress. Silas had only ever seen one other person dance with horses rather than command them.

His father.

Drawn to the way they responded to each other, Silas soon found himself leaning on the rail. Miss Fenton caught sight of him and scowled.

"Did you not hear what I said?"

"I'm waiting on Mr. Reed."

That brought another scowl.

Arrow tossed his mane and made a wide turn, hindquarters swinging dangerously close to Miss Fenton.

"Shouldn't you have a whip or some—"

She whirled on him. "Now you listen, sir. I won't have some stranger coming here telling me how to work with my horse. Don't you think I get enough of that already? I don't need you to add to what I'm . . ." She trailed off, cheeks growing red. Without another word, she turned on her heel and waved an arm at Arrow, but he ignored her command and tossed his head.

The stallion snorted, front hooves pounding on the dirt. A surge of panic had Silas leaping over the fence before he could think. He grabbed Miss Fenton's shoulder, hauled her against the rail, and shielded her with his body.

With a strangled squeak, she pushed against his back, but Silas kept his eyes on the horse. Arrow snorted, eyes rolling dangerously. Silas widened his stance, kept his hands spread to his sides, and waited.

Arrow pawed the ground. One wrong move and he'd—

"Will you get off me!" Miss Fenton shoved him hard enough that he had to take a step forward.

She bolted out from behind him, muttering something that he thought compared him to a pile of horse droppings. He reached to stop her, but she slipped out of his grasp and walked straight up to the horse. She slid her hand into his bridle and ran a hand down his muzzle, trying to shush a stallion like one might a yowling cat. This woman was going to get herself killed.

No wonder Roger was having a time with this pair. Afraid to make any moves to frighten the horse and make him trample Miss Fenton, Silas remained in his position.

Still holding the horse, she turned on him. "What do you think you're doing?"

"Saving you."

"Saving *me*? I don't need saving." The horse snorted again, and she lowered her voice, tone laced in steel. "Kindly take your leave."

"Everything all right over here?"

A man with dark hair approached, dressed in a well-made summer suit with the gold chain of a watch dangling from his vest pocket. The man swept an assessing gaze over Silas before it landed on Miss Fenton. Disapproval tightened his features.

"Nora, didn't we agree Roger would take up Arrow's training? Your mother needs you."

"I was only exercising him."

The timid voice made Silas turn back. What had happened to the prickly woman who'd only a moment ago been daggering him with harsh words? She'd nearly deflated, with downcast eyes and fingers that twisted in the horse's mane.

Arrow seemed to finally relax, lowering his head and nudging Miss Fenton with his big nose.

The large man sighed. "We've discussed this." He pulled the watch from his vest, checked the time, and then gave it a twirl before stuffing it back into his pocket. "It's past time you get cleaned up and help your mother. She'll be expecting you, and we wouldn't want to disappoint her, now would we?"

Miss Fenton said something under her breath Silas didn't catch as she turned to lead the horse away.

"Leave him. Someone will get him stalled."

Her shoulders tensed, but she released the horse's halter, draped a lead rope that had fallen to the ground on the corral fence, and quietly exited without sparing a look for either of them.

When she'd gone a few paces to the house, the man turned to Silas.

"Forgive my niece. I'm afraid my brother's death has been hard on her, and she's been acting out in some rather unusual ways."

He let the comment pass and instead extended a hand. "Silas Cavallero, sir. I spoke with Mr. Reed about doing some temporary training here. I break colts, and he offered to let me try a hand at that one." He nodded toward the stallion prancing at the edge of the corral, watching Miss Fenton retreat.

"Ah. Seems Roger made quick work of my suggestion to hire on a trainer. I didn't think he was interested." The man gave Silas's hand a firm shake. "Amos Fenton." He scrubbed his chin. "I must say, I don't know that he's worth the trouble, if not for keeping a lady appeased." He offered Silas a weary smile as though he would understand the sentiment.

When Silas didn't respond, Mr. Fenton gestured back to Arrow. "A fine-looking horse, and one we'd thought to sire out. But he's far too temperamental to take to trials, and without passing a standard run, we won't get him in the breed registry." He pulled the watch out again and spun it around his finger as he talked. "You have any experience with harness racers?"

"Nope."

The man regarded Silas with brows lifted in question. He would have had plenty of experience, had life gone differently. Not that he planned to explain that now.

"But I do have a lot of experience with breaking colts to ride, teaching them to respond to commands, and I have been successful in tempering their more aggressive tendencies."

"And you say Roger hired you?"

"More like a trial than hiring, sir. He gave me a couple of days to see what I could do with that colt, though Miss Fenton has already dismissed me."

Mr. Fenton chuckled. "Of course she did."

Not sure how to respond, Silas kept to the topic at hand. "I'm on my way east, and I'm looking for a short-term project to see me on the next leg of my journey. If you'll agree to the employment, that is."

The man considered, then gave a nod. "I'd like to see if you can do anything with him as well." He twirled the watch again, apparently a habit. "My niece is very fond of this horse." His tone implied more meaning than the words suggested. Was the man warning him he'd have trouble with Miss Fenton or warning him he'd best take the utmost care with her pet?

Either way, Silas took the words to heart. He nodded. "Yes, sir. I understand."

Mr. Fenton pocketed his watch. "Good. Then you might as well get started."

He strode toward the house, leaving Silas with the snorting stallion.

⁓

Why did men always think they could order women about? Nora fumed as she stalked across the yard and headed toward the house. Amos could claim some authority over her. And even Roger could voice concerns when it came to the horses. But who did that Silas Cavallero think he was? Waltzing onto her property and thinking he could take over training her horse?

What was worse, she hadn't even said anything when Amos arrived. She'd ducked her head and dutifully obeyed. Not that her uncle would listen to her, but she could have at least spoken up. Made some kind of case for herself. Instead, she'd been a coward. Again.

Nora pulled off her boots as she entered the house, then headed upstairs to change and get started on her duties for the day. Why hadn't she told her uncle Mr. Cavallero's presence was a bad idea? Not only because the cost of hiring him would further strain their accounts, but also because they simply didn't know anything about him.

He claimed to be a good trainer, but what proof did they have? The man could be down there mistreating Arrow and not a one of those men would take notice. Didn't they understand that force only made Arrow more resentful?

"Still ignoring your father's instructions, I see."

Nora whirled at the sound of her mother's quiet voice. She'd been so lost in thought she hadn't even heard the door open.

Mother sighed, a sound that ruffled the veil hanging over her face. "Did his wishes truly mean so little to you?"

The censure in Mother's tone rankled, and Nora struggled to keep the frustration from her face. "I mean no disrespect."

"Yet you continue to act as a man and have wasted your marrying years playing with horses." She shook her head, her voice laced with sadness. "I'd wanted so much more for you than the life of a spinster."

At twenty-eight Nora didn't consider herself too far into spinsterhood to necessarily be sealed to the fate. But better a spinster with freedom than a pretty rug to be wiped under a husband's boots.

Except freedom continued to elude her, no matter what path she chose.

Mother wanted Nora to promise she'd do better or offer an apology. But they'd danced to that tune far too many times, and she simply didn't have the energy.

At Nora's silence, Mother sniffed. "Did you finish darning those socks like I asked you?"

"No, but I thought . . ." She let the sentence dangle, unsure how to finish such a statement. Why darn her father's socks when he no longer had need of them?

Mother's chin notched a bit higher. "I've decided to give all of your father's things to the charity house, and I'll not have anyone say I sent inferior items."

Teeth clenched, Nora inclined her head in silent acceptance and hurried off to her room before a simple matter turned into another argument. Or before Mother thought to find any more tasks to heap on her head in a vain effort to keep Nora too busy to return to the stables.

Perhaps that *had* been Mother's plan all along. If she made life here miserable enough, then maybe Nora might find escaping to a husband and the command of her own household far more appealing.

A sharp pain radiated through her heart. Did Mother truly wish to be rid of her? They hadn't shared the most affectionate of relationships, but the idea of such a rejection wrapped cold fingers around her and solidified her resolve. The only person she could count on was herself. If she wanted any hope for a life of her choosing, then she'd have to make her own way.

An infuriatingly difficult thing for a single woman.

Nora hurried through the process of changing her more practical trousers for a serviceable black skirt and sturdy blouse. The hallway stood empty when she emerged from her room a few moments later, Mother's door firmly closed against the rest of the world.

Nora slipped inside a room at the far end of the hall that hadn't embraced a guest in years and quietly made her way past dusty furniture and a mattress that needed fluffing. She peeled back the heavy green curtain a fraction, creating a slit of sunlight that illuminated dust motes floating in the air. Below, Arrow stood in the center of the corral, ears pricked forward. She shifted to angle herself and caught sight of what—or rather, who—had caught her horse's rapt attention.

Mr. Cavallero stood a few paces away, his posture relaxed. He wore clothing that matched his bearing, work-worn yet comfortable. Unassuming. She allowed herself a moment to study him, though she couldn't see much more than the width of strong shoulders and the confident set of his scuffed boots from this distance.

Transfixed, Nora watched as Arrow's curiosity grew. This cowboy was nothing like the trainers she'd seen at Emberwild. Where Roger and his men puffed their chests and tried to make themselves seem larger, Mr. Cavallero moved with an easy grace that didn't need to challenge Arrow. He simply stood there, waiting with a quiet confidence that drew the horse in a way Nora had never seen.

He'd admonished her for not having a whip, yet he made no effort to follow Roger's method of stepping in and letting a horse know who had the upper hand. She had the strangest sensation of watching two stallions assess one another, looking for weaknesses while at the same time offering due respect to the other.

Would Arrow see Mr. Cavallero as a challenge? If the brazen horse asserted his will, would this cowboy try to bolster his reputation by breaking Arrow's spirit?

Arrow was like the wind. You didn't contain it so much as you worked with it.

Arrow took one small step, ears flicking to every sound around him but keeping his eyes focused on the man in front of him. Three more steps, then Arrow snorted, tossing his head.

Nora gripped the curtain, waiting for the horse to rear and the man in front of him to lash out. But despite Arrow's peacocking, Mr. Cavallero remained in his relaxed stance. She couldn't see his face from here. What was he doing? Talking to Arrow? What expression covered his features? Arrow had an uncanny way of sensing what a person was thinking, and whatever he saw in this man had enraptured him.

Slowly, Mr. Cavallero lifted a hand. Arrow came closer. One tiny step, then another. Nora held her breath. Then suddenly the horse wiggled his upper lip in a comical way and blinked his big eyes.

What in the heavens?

Nora leaned closer. Arrow's head lowered, and as though Mr. Cavallero had passed some kind of test, Arrow stepped up and placed the soft tip of his muzzle into the man's waiting hand, his body language submissive and friendly.

How had the cowboy done that?

Gently, Mr. Cavallero reached out with his other hand and stroked the horse's neck. He'd snatch his halter now, surely. But the man gave Arrow a fond pat and stepped away.

Astonished, Nora watched Mr. Cavallero place his hands in his pockets, turn his back, and walk away while Arrow followed placidly behind him.

What kind of man could endear Arrow so quickly? Nora dropped the curtain, her thoughts troubled. Arrow was *her* horse. Her responsibility.

Her friend.

She took a step back, feeling conflicted. Only one thing seemed certain.

Silas Cavallero was different from any trainer she'd ever met.

chapter

EIGHT

Maybe this wouldn't be as difficult of a challenge as he'd expected. Silas gave Arrow a good scratch and led him out of the corral, pleased with their progress. A little high-strung, especially for a Standardbred, but Arrow was intelligent and curious. Silas could work with qualities like that.

"You got enough energy out?" Silas asked the horse as they clopped down the barn's center aisle. They'd spent a good two hours getting to know each other while Silas tested out Arrow's various gaits. No matter how long the horse trotted, he always seemed to have more pent-up energy hankering for release.

In response to Silas's question, Arrow tossed his head and side-stepped, prancing close to the stalls on one side before swinging across to the other, showing off to the mares. Silas chuckled.

He opened the stallion stall opposite the currently empty foaling stalls and let the big horse inside. He waited at the threshold until Arrow swung around to face him. When the horse pricked his ears forward, Silas stepped inside. He'd found that offering the creatures a measure of respect went a long way to receiving it in return.

He held out the currycomb he'd pocketed from the tack room for Arrow to inspect. The horse snorted at the metal plate, then lowered his head. Taking that as permission to proceed, Silas set to work with a circular pattern following the direction of hair growth.

He lost himself in the simple motion, the smells of horseflesh and hay familiar comforts.

As he ran his hands down the horse's hind leg, Arrow shifted his weight and lifted his hoof, allowing Silas to remove dirt clods and check for rocks. This horse had been trained far better than Roger had let on. They repeated the ritual with each hoof and then Silas checked down each cannon bone for any signs of lameness.

Job completed, Silas stepped back and watched Arrow snatch mouthfuls of hay. A beautiful creature. And certainly not the terror the other men had made him seem.

"Well, look a' there." A man let out a low whistle. "If it ain't the drifter."

Silas looked over the stall gate to find one of the men he'd met at the inn—the fellow who had suggested Silas ask after employment.

The man grinned. "Bill owes me good. He said you wouldn't show, but I bet you would."

They'd bet on if he'd come for a job? Why?

Arrow snorted and the man eyed the horse, his expression somewhere between wary and disapproving. Arrow lifted his head as though sensing the man's study of him and responded with a backward tilt of his ears. These two obviously harbored little care for one another.

Silas stuck a hand over the gate. "Silas Cavallero. Don't think we've been officially introduced."

The man swung his gaze back to Silas. "Oscar Hardy." He stepped forward to offer a calloused hand. Arrow snorted and tossed his big head. Oscar pulled his hand back and instead spit a stream of amber tobacco liquid onto the stone floor, leaving a dark stain.

Silas exited the stall. "Who usually works with him? I'd like to talk to the man about what methods he's used."

"Mr. Fenton has Roger facing off with him these days." The man shook his head as though glad the task had been passed to anyone other than him. "Though before that he's been mostly left to the lady. That's why he's a nightmare."

Interesting. After watching Miss Fenton with the horse, he'd suspected she had a lot to do with his training. Might also explain her hostility, if she thought Silas had come to take over. He'd need to find an opportunity to speak with her.

"You play cards?" Oscar splayed his fingers as though holding an invisible deck.

"Not the gambling type."

Oscar sneered, clearly offended.

Before Silas could think up something to soothe the man's scowl, Roger sauntered down the aisle, drawing both men's attention.

"How'd it go?" He came to a stop at Arrow's stall and peered in at the horse.

As though taking his cue to leave, Oscar turned toward the tack room, his boots thudding across the stone.

"Better than I expected, truth be told." Silas turned his gaze back to the stable master. "He's got a solid foundation on his training."

A skeptical look crinkled the corners of Roger's eyes.

"Though he reminds me of a Thoroughbred more than a Standardbred. In temperament, anyway." Physically, Arrow perfectly demonstrated the breed's standards with a high croup and thick hindquarters. "Do you know his lineage?"

"Both parents are association registered. He was sired by Ember, our foundation stallion. His dam was Miss Mary, a racer we picked up in Illinois. She died of colic six months after she had a hard time foaling Arrow. Only colt we ever got out of her."

Silas filed away the names for later.

Roger shook his head. "The problem with this one is he's been treated like some kind of pet. Mr. Fenton was far too lenient with letting his daughter play with the stock, in my opinion. Then when he got sick, no one kept her under control."

Yet the horse responded better than a lot of colts Silas had seen at that age. "Mind if I have a look at the sire?"

"Out on breeding loan. Won't be back for a few weeks yet. Probably not until after you're gone." Roger sucked his teeth. "Think you'll be able to do anything with him?"

"I do, sir. You planning on racing him?"

"Miss Fenton has it in her head to send him to the track. Make a name for him so we can use him as a stud, now that old Ember is getting on in years. Can't say it's a bad idea. Mr. Fenton agreed, so he charged me with getting that stallion into a harness. Something I don't really have the time to devote myself to."

Hence Silas's opportunity. "Should be able to start on harness work in a day or two, if that works for you."

Roger gave a nod. "Walter serves supper at seven. Be in the bunk on time or risk going to bed on an empty stomach."

"Yes, sir."

Silas followed Roger from the barn and out into a sultry afternoon not tempered by the slightest breeze to cool the sweat gathering under his hat. Roger left to see to whatever duties occupied him, leaving Silas to contemplate what to do with the time remaining before he needed to head to the bunkhouse.

In the paddocks partitioned around the barn, mares grazed while spindly-legged foals played in the grass. The sun hung steady in the late-afternoon sky, casting long shadows.

With Arrow taken care of for the day, he could probably spend a little time with Starlight. Perhaps let the old girl meet a few of the mares without foals over the fence. He turned back toward the barn when movement caught his attention. Across the yard a woman stood on the ornate porch of the tall house, shaking out a rag.

Miss Fenton? There was no mistaking her womanly form. He felt a little foolish for having ever thought her a boy. Granted, he wasn't accustomed to seeing women riding barely trained colts in a man's shirt and trousers. An interesting lady, to be sure.

Perhaps her ire over his crass mistake had cooled enough that he could talk to her about Arrow's previous training. Silas moved toward the house, hoping the lady would become less thorny once she realized he had Arrow's best in mind.

∽

As busy of a bee as she'd been, Nora would have thought she'd have a whole pot of honey to show for her efforts. Instead, all she had was a bunch of wilted flowers and a fresh coat of pollen.

She laughed to herself at her silly metaphor and shook out the dusting rag, sending particles flying through the air and making her cough. She'd finished the laundry and the dusting, but she hadn't even started on the floors. And now it was nearly time to start working on their supper.

What did she have available? She mentally checked through the items in the pantry, trying to decide what meal might put a little weight back on Mother's frame.

Kneading the muscles in her lower back, Nora looked out over the paddocks and sighed. The horses grazed peacefully, only the occasional swish of their tails shooing flies to indicate there was anything amiss in their world. A moment or two to enjoy them wouldn't change anything. She'd always liked watching the foals play.

One little darling she'd named Sunshine bounded across the grass looking more akin to a deer than a horse. Nora couldn't help but chuckle. The filly's shiny bay coat glistened in the sunlight, her little mane fluttering in the wind.

A figure stepped into her line of sight and stole the peace of the moment. Mr. Cavallero. What did that man want now? He'd already disobeyed her orders to leave. Amos had clearly overruled her position, so perhaps she couldn't really blame him, but knowing that fact didn't make her any less angry.

She should probably go inside before he came close enough for her departure to be considered rude, but her curiosity over how he'd handled Arrow kept her lingering on the porch. Nora watched him approach, his tilted hat shading his face from the sun.

He caught her eye and dipped his chin, coming to a stop at the bottom of the porch. "Afternoon, Miss Fenton."

Nora stood with the commanding posture hammered into her

as a girl and offered a small nod of acknowledgment. He'd come to her, so she would wait for him to speak his business.

He removed his hat and wiped his brow with his sleeve, obviously in no rush to speak. Hair so deep a brown it bordered on black caught the sunlight for a moment before he replaced the hat.

"Arrow is a fine horse. It's obvious he's already benefited from some excellent training. Training, I believe, that came from you."

He was praising her work with Arrow? No one had ever praised her training before. Every effort on her part had been staunchly met with disapproval.

"You think he's been well trained?" As soon as the airy words left her lips she regretted them. She sounded like a ninny grasping for the first compliment thrown her way. Still, she couldn't deny the way the words warmed her.

A hint of a smile turned his lips at the corners, creating small lines at the edges of his mouth. "He's high energy and a bit temperamental, but he responds well to cues and is eager to learn. Once he's been shown his due respect, of course."

A laugh bubbled out of her. "Seems you've already discovered his secret." She quickly sobered. "After only a few hours."

The man regarded her with what appeared to be a mix of confusion and amusement. But she found nothing amusing about the way he'd been able to so easily bond with her horse. Though it was ridiculous, she felt betrayed.

"Hopefully I can help build on those foundations. With your permission, of course."

He was asking her permission, when he'd already taken the job from her uncle? After she'd told him to leave?

Men. If he thought he would placate her by this pandering, he was wrong. "Since you've already accepted a position from my uncle that hardly seems necessary."

Mr. Cavallero had the decency to look sheepish. He cleared his throat. "Yes, ma'am. I did accept the trial position."

He gazed at her, nothing but sincerity on his face. Perhaps she could give him a bit more credit. He'd been looking for a job, and the men supposedly in charge had hired him. He didn't have to offer her any compliments or ask her for anything.

She crossed her arms and leaned against the porch, all former thoughts of maintaining a lady's bearing forgotten.

"Forgive me for saying so." He rubbed the back of his neck, looking as out of place as a carrot in a bushel of peas. "But knowing who is in charge around here is a bit difficult."

Perhaps he had a point.

"However," Mr. Cavallero said when Nora still didn't respond, "since you're responsible for the colt's foundational work, I'd like to understand your methods. And proceed with your blessing."

"And if I refuse?"

He hesitated a moment. "Then I will be on my way."

Did he really mean that? She was tempted to send him away that very moment, but the way he'd interacted with Arrow gave her pause.

"What training methods do you plan to use?"

"I was hoping we could discuss a plan based on what methods he's accustomed to."

He wanted to include her in working out a training program? She twisted her fingers together. Amos could hardly fault her if his new trainer asked for her help, could he? This arrangement might at least prove better than leaving Arrow to Roger.

If she was going to be stuck with a man working with her horse, then one who at least requested her input was better than the alternatives.

"I accept your offer. Still on a trial basis, of course. Shall we plan to meet in the stables in the morning?"

Tipping his hat as his only response, Mr. Cavallero turned and walked back toward the barn, leaving her to stare after him.

What a strange man. She watched his broad shoulders retreat, legs swinging in an easy gait that neither hurried nor tarried.

Perhaps it was no wonder after all why Arrow's curiosity about this man had gotten the better of him. The same could probably be said of her.

chapter
NINE

The first rays of light caressed the sky with streaks of pink and orange. Nora drew a deep breath of clear air, relishing the freshness of morning, those precious few moments before the taint of worries or problems.

She made her way across the yard, collecting dew on her boots from the glistening stalks of grass. One of Roger's scruffy dogs stretched underneath the towering oak, his shaggy brown fur throwing off water droplets as he shook. The sound of clicks and scraping wood preceded the release of the mares and their foals into the attached paddocks.

Grabbing a flake of alfalfa from a bale in the feed room, Nora shooed a barn cat out before closing the door behind her. The yellow tabby meowed his offense, but he would simply have to seek out his rodents elsewhere.

Arrow stood in the stallion stall in the center of the barn, just to the left of the tack and feed rooms. He poked his nose over the gate and nickered to her. The sound brought a smile to her face. Sweet Arrow. He acted tough with all these men, but to her he'd always be the sweet foal who had nuzzled her shoulder as she'd cried and let her bury her sorrows in the soft down of his mane.

She let him sniff her hand before she scratched between his ears, then waited for him to step back from the gate so she could enter. Shifting the flake of hay away from his searching lips, Nora laughed as she hefted the green hay into his rack. "Greedy boy."

While he attacked his breakfast with gusto, she forked out the sullied straw from his stall and dumped it into the wheelbarrow just outside of the gate. As soon as he finished they would move outside for training and exercising, then conclude with a good brush down.

Nora moved through the chore with quiet efficiency, and by the time Arrow finished his hay she'd cleaned out his stall, left the full wheelbarrow in the hall for a stable boy, and refilled his water bucket. While they were out, someone would put down fresh straw on the floor.

She wiped her hands on her trousers. "Ready to get started?"

"I am."

Startled, Nora whirled around to face Mr. Cavallero. She tried to school her embarrassment, but from the uptick of his full lips, she'd failed.

"Mr. Cavallero. I didn't see you standing there." How had she forgotten? She'd thought about how she would explain Arrow's training, and she'd even stayed up late into the night with her copy of *Gleason's Horse Book*, going over different terminologies and the proper phrasings of different methods.

She sighed. "I suppose you can accompany me to the corral." So much for her morning ride. She wasn't about to suggest he saddle up another horse and go with them. Rides were too precious to be spoiled with company.

Dressed in clothing similar to yesterday's dungarees and heavy work shirt, Mr. Cavallero stepped back as Nora exited Arrow's stall, then silently followed her to the tack room. Nora fumbled with the halters hanging on the hooks on the left wall, dropping two before she pulled Arrow's free. Heat scorched up her neck. She must look like a bumbling fool.

He waited patiently as she entered Arrow's stall and held the halter out to him. He sniffed it and snorted, tossing his head. Nora pressed her lips together. Most mornings he lowered his head and waited for her to slide the rope halter over his nose, but of course with Mr. Cavallero watching, Arrow took the opportunity to be obstinate. She was nearly tempted to force the tack on anyway, but she wouldn't undo all she'd accomplished in Arrow's training because of her own wounded pride.

She needed to work through her routines regardless of the man watching over her shoulder.

Making her nervous.

Nora drew in a deep breath and purposely forced her shoulders to relax. She'd pretend Mr. Cavallero wasn't standing there judging every move she made or noting every failure. Arrow nudged her shoulder and doe eyes blinked at her, seeming to say he was sorry for upsetting her. Sweet boy. A little laugh bubbled out of her and he pressed his big forehead against her.

"Thank you," she whispered. She held out the halter for him to inspect again. He lowered his nose and allowed her to slip the halter up his face and tie it behind his ears. She snapped on the lead beneath his chin and patted his neck. "Ready?"

She opened the gate and stepped out, the big horse close behind. He sidestepped Mr. Cavallero and rolled his eyes at the man defiantly. The cowboy might have entranced her horse while he'd had Arrow alone, but with Nora at his side Arrow resumed his usual haughty air. The click of his hooves echoed in the barn as they made their way out into a day already growing thick with heat.

Mr. Cavallero followed as she opened the gate and motioned Arrow forward. Nora glanced back at the new trainer, expecting him to enter the corral as well, but he stood waiting at the gate as though also seeking her permission to enter.

Nora inwardly cringed. Maybe Mother was right. She needed more human interaction. She turned up a palm. "Are you coming?"

He gave a nod and stepped just inside the gate. Rather than launching into a tirade of questions or taking over with the horse,

Mr. Cavallero leaned casually against the railing and merely watched as Arrow pranced at the end of his rope, eager to begin.

After another few heartbeats Nora's impatience got the better of her. Didn't he want to talk to her about the training? Perhaps he wanted to watch her instead.

Fine. She wouldn't let him see how his presence unnerved her. If he wanted to stand there silently, she could ignore him more easily.

Drawing in a deep breath, Nora moved to the center of the corral. Lifting the crop out to her side, she gestured for Arrow to begin his circles.

☙

Miss Fenton moved with a grace that rivaled the stallion's. Silas watched as the lithe woman's gaze never left the horse, seeming to assess his every movement, every placement of his hooves. Arrow stepped out to the full length of his long lead while Nora remained in the center of the corral, turning with him to keep him on a circle.

The horse moved with qualities that would make him a good racer. His pace was even, his hooves moving in concise beats, his back level. Arrow responded to commands, trotted with the proper gaits, and demonstrated the necessary speed. Silas had seen nothing that warranted a new trainer.

Maybe Arrow refused the harness. Or perhaps he wouldn't perform for anyone other than Miss Fenton. That could prove to be a challenge.

Miss Fenton stepped forward slightly and the horse slowed to an easy trot. She lifted the crop again and he spun on his hindquarters and turned the opposite direction. He snorted as she waved him back to the full length of his lead when he'd decided to make his circles too close. Silas made sure to stay up next to the rail and out of their way.

He watched Arrow make a few more circles before Miss Fenton turned him, and then he completed only half of a circle before she sent him the opposite direction. Clever. She was teaching him to keep an eye on his trainer rather than simply falling into a routine.

Movement caught the corner of Silas's eye. Mr. Fenton, dressed in a coat and tie and with the brim of a straw hat tipped up on his head, approached with a determined look plastered on his face. He came to stand next to Silas at the rail, lips downturned.

"Morning, sir." Silas nodded toward the colt. "Good horse you've got there."

Mr. Fenton removed the gold watch from his pocket and swung it around absentmindedly, his gaze riveted on his niece. "Didn't we hire you to work with this horse?"

"I'm assessing his current training and observing the methods he's used to."

Mr. Fenton grunted. "If I wanted my niece to be in the dust with the horses, I wouldn't have agreed for you to stay." He clutched the watch and stuffed it back into his pocket.

Not sure how to respond, Silas glanced back at Miss Fenton, only to find she'd stopped the circles and now held the horse by the halter.

She approached, keeping a firm hand beneath Arrow's chin. "Good morning, Uncle."

"Nora, what did I tell you about helping your mother and giving up these foolish notions of becoming a stable boy?"

Miss Fenton darted a look at Silas and her cheeks reddened. She tightened her grip on the horse's halter, and Arrow pawed the ground. "Arrow is mine." The words came out softly, as though Miss Fenton feared losing the claim even as she asserted it.

The man beside him grew rigid. Silas shifted, not wanting to be in the middle of a family argument.

"Please return to the house, my dear." The steely words were hardly softened with the added endearment. "We'll discuss the matter once you're properly dressed."

Silas winced. The bite in Mr. Fenton's tone left no room for argument, but the woman in front of him stood stock-still. Yesterday she had deflated under her uncle's commands, but this morning she notched her chin higher.

"I've cared for and taught this horse since he was six months old. If you think some stranger can come in here and take him from me, you are—" She stopped short and the muscles in her neck constricted with a deep swallow.

If he didn't need the money, he'd leave these people to their squabbles.

"Respectfully, Uncle," Miss Fenton continued more genteelly, "I ask that you consider Arrow and his temperament. He's used to me and my methods. I believe Mr. Cavallero will have more success if he's familiar with how the horse has been handled."

Mr. Fenton remained quiet for several moments, spinning the timepiece again like a little golden moon on an orbit around the man's fist. Miss Fenton stood stoically, her fingers clutching the lead in a stranglehold. Arrow, apparently sensing his mistress's distress, watched the men with large eyes and twitching ears.

"You're no longer a girl, but a woman in need of a husband. And no husband is going to take kindly to a wife who likes to play the stable boy."

The man spoke gently, though Silas doubted Miss Fenton found anything other than insult in his statement. This lady was a contradiction to everything he thought he knew about women.

A budding respect for this wealthy lady in trousers caused words to come out of his mouth before he could stop them. "Working against a horse, especially a young stallion, will only cause more trouble for everyone. I can train this colt for you, sir, but it would be wise to first understand his background before implementing a new program. Her being here is my fault. I apologize for asking Miss Fenton to show me her methods."

The gold watch stopped spinning and hung limp from the chain as Mr. Fenton regarded Silas with a blend of surprise and indignation. He broke the uncomfortable eye contact and focused on the watch to give the man a chance to compose himself. Something about the swirled pattern on the gold face tickled Silas's memory.

Mr. Fenton grunted and pocketed the watch. "There's a harness race at the county fair this year. Seems the local gents are picking up on the trend, likely something to do with the sensation of Dan Patch."

Why the sudden change of subject? "Um, that's good, sir." He'd heard of the horse that had set records at the Illinois State Fair and had made his owner a nice sum of profits.

"If you think you can have him ready to run by then, we can clock his times and get him qualified."

"When's the fair?"

"Last week of July."

Only a month. "Depends on how he responds to the harness. From what I've seen of his foundational training, however, Miss Fenton has done well preparing him. We might have enough time."

A scowl crossed Mr. Fenton's face but he quickly smoothed it away. He opened his watch again, checked the time, and snapped it closed.

"If I may ask, where did you get that watch?"

Mr. Fenton looked back to Silas. "I won it in a wager." His eyes narrowed. "Why?"

Silas shrugged. "Fine piece. Once Miss Fenton finishes her demonstration, I won't take up any more of her time."

Mr. Fenton eyed Silas skeptically for a moment, then gave a small nod. "Very well. I have business here for a few hours, if you have need of me." He cast one more disappointed look at his niece, then turned and headed toward the house.

Miss Fenton twisted her fingers through the horse's mane. "Did you mean what you said?"

About the fair? "It's possible. But I won't know how well his speed will transition to the harness until I see him in it."

Confusion crinkled her thin eyebrows for an instant before her expression cleared. "A reasonable assessment." She straightened her shoulders. "Shall we fetch the harness, then?"

"Not yet. I'd like you to finish showing me your routine, if you don't mind."

Those bright blue eyes narrowed on him again, though Silas couldn't begin to guess what thoughts churned behind them. With a shrug she made a clicking noise to Arrow.

The horse bounded forward, forcing Silas to scramble out of the way.

As he clambered up the rail, he could have sworn he heard the woman chuckle.

chapter
TEN

Why was everything she did wrong? Nora heaved a breath and set to scrubbing the blackened crud in the bottom of the pot with more gusto. She'd managed to burn their soup, too busy reading her copy of Gleason's horse training manual to notice she'd let the base thicken too long. Oddly, Mother hadn't cared she'd served such a terrible noonday dinner to Amos.

Perhaps Mother simply didn't notice. She'd hardly taken two bites. She appeared gaunt. A shell of the woman she had once been. A part of Nora longed to reach out to her. Offer comfort in some way. But what could she do? She didn't grieve as Mother did.

But Mother *had* come down to eat, and she'd removed her full-mourning veil. That was something. Perhaps a good sign.

Maybe. She huffed and scrubbed harder.

Fine. Probably not good. Suspicious, actually. Mother was usually a strict adherer to all manner of correct social usage, and a widow should remain in seclusion for a few more weeks. Mother had always been reserved, mostly keeping to herself the past few years—and even more so once Father fell ill—so Nora had expected her to stay in a widow's full mourning for an entire year. It had only been three months.

Nora sighed. Three months felt both like ages ago and only yesterday. So much had changed in that time. Including the way her uncle had continued to insert himself into their daily lives.

One particularly nasty place on the edge of the pot resisted her efforts, and Nora grunted as she worked the rag. If she lived in a big city, she'd eat at a restaurant every day and never have to scrub pots.

Or you could marry a man of means who would provide you with a cook and kitchen staff.

Nora shoved the thought aside. A few dishes weren't worth the price of freedom.

Freedom she was about to lose anyway. Once Mother started coming out of her room, she'd noticed Nora had been spending longer and longer each morning in the barn. Then she'd found more duties to occupy Nora's "idle time." Mother probably meant well, but Nora didn't spend her time in the barn because she was bored.

Except now that Mr. Cavallero had arrived, she wouldn't be doing any of the training. She ground her molars. On one hand, he'd stolen her only joy from her. On the other, he was certainly better than Roger.

At least he'd tried to stand up for her against Amos. Not a trait to be dismissed lightly.

Why couldn't she have been born a boy? Then the farm would be hers, she could do as she pleased, and no one would expect her to jump into a marriage if she didn't want one.

Nora blew a strand of damp hair up her face and leaned away from the sink. Done. Finally. The interior of the copper pot gleamed. Gracious sakes. She'd rather muck the entire barn than scrub pots. She rolled her shoulders to release the tension and worked the foot pump under the cast-iron sink to start a stream of fresh water. Once she'd finished rinsing the dishes, she leaned back against the sink and closed her eyes. Just a moment to rest. Then she'd need to get to work on—

"Daydreaming?"

Nora startled at the sound of her uncle's voice and lurched forward. "Oh!"

He chuckled. "Forgive me. I didn't mean to give you a fright."

Wiping her hands on a clean towel, she offered him a tenuous smile. She wasn't accustomed to men intruding upon the women's domain, much less one who didn't even live here. She twisted the towel in her hands. "Are you thirsty?"

"I was wondering if you and I could talk."

In the kitchen? She untied her apron and hung it on a hook on the wall. What else could she do but agree? It wasn't as though she could ask him what gave him the right to think he could institute authority not only over the farm's operations but over the household as well.

"I'll be in the parlor."

Did that mean he wanted a tea service this soon after the midday meal? Best err on the side of hospitality even if male relatives paid no mind to proper visiting hours.

Nora filled two glasses with leftover tea from the meal, then dropped an extra sugar cube into each. Plastering on her best smile, she entered the parlor with a lady's graceful movements and gently lowered the silver tray to the serving table in the center of the room.

Amos rose as she entered, a pleased expression gracing his tanned features. "So lovely to see you acting as a lady should."

Nora cringed. How she hated insults dipped in sweetness.

"Come, sit." Amos gestured toward the settee.

The windows in the parlor had been opened, leaving only the thin lace curtains to keep out the summer bugs. Nora wished she had a fan to cool her face. The thick coils of her braids were making her neck sweat. She perched on the edge of the settee and waited patiently while her uncle collected his glass, settled in her father's favorite chair, and set his dark eyes on her.

She braced herself for a lecture. This time, however, she had a plan. Some logical arguments to make Amos see that she—

"I plan to marry your mother."

All thoughts fled.

She couldn't have heard correctly. The heat must have muddled her brain. Nora tried to blink away the fog. "You—? I'm sorry. What?"

Amos regarded her with a patient expression as though he hadn't just said something unthinkable. "I've long cared for Rebecca." When Nora gave no response, he cleared his throat and continued. "It's a reasonable arrangement, as I'm sure you're aware."

As she was aware? He thought marrying his brother's widow—who was in mourning—was a reasonable arrangement?

Amos watched her, waiting. Nora managed to keep both her features and her voice calm. "My mother is in mourning."

"Of course." He chuckled. "Do you think me crass? I'll bring up the matter when she's ready, and of course we wouldn't take vows until she's out of blacks."

But why? Did Amos want to marry her mother to solidify his claim on the farm?

The idea didn't make sense, not when he'd already been granted ownership in her father's will. But she had no other ideas as to why he'd even mention such a thing.

Come to think of it, Nora hadn't seen any evidence that her father *had* left Emberwild to Amos. Nothing more than his word, though she shouldn't have to doubt Uncle's honor. Still. Did the reason he wanted to marry her mother stem from robbing a widow of her inheritance?

Surely not.

"I'd like to know your thoughts on the matter," Amos said slowly, pulling Nora from her spiraling contemplations.

Her thoughts? Since when had her thoughts mattered? She spoke carefully. "I'm sure eventually Mother will want to seek companionship and security." Eventually. But then, that didn't make sense either. If Amos ran Emberwild in her father's stead, wouldn't Mother be secure here without a marriage?

"Then there is the matter of your dowry, of course," Amos continued as though Nora hadn't spoken at all. "I'll provide you a substantial endowment to aid you in finding a husband."

81

The words soured her stomach. Just what she wanted. A sum of money to convince some old geezer to take her off Amos's hands.

Nora frowned. "And if I don't wish to marry?"

Amos's eyes turned cold. "You would put that burden on your mother?"

Burden. How she hated that word. "I intend to work and earn my way, providing for the both of us."

Amos tilted his head back and roared with laughter. Indignation lit a fire in her center, and it took every ounce of her willpower to keep her features serene.

He shifted in his chair and tapped a finger on his glass. "I can appreciate your ambitions, child, but you know nothing about running this farm. A few mornings playing with the stock won't change that."

Bile crept up her throat and Nora took a sip of her tea to hide her discomfort. He had a point. But she could learn. Nora had always been quick with figures and could surely take over ordering supplies and handling inventory. She could learn all she needed to know. If only someone was willing to teach her.

An idea formed. "Uncle, what if I were to have my dowry instead?" Could she use the funds to purchase a few horses of her own? Perhaps buy Arrow away from Emberwild and start servicing him? There would be the costs of his feed and boarding to consider if she was looking to separate herself from the farm. But with his stud fees she could probably even pay to rent a room, so as not to be a burden to anyone. She parted her lips to say so when Amos shook his head.

"A dowry isn't going to provide you a life of spinsterhood for long. You'll need a husband to care for you. It's unfair for you to expect your mother and me to do so. Think of your duties to your family."

"May I ask what you intend to offer?"

Amos scowled. "That will be a discussion I'll have with your suitors." A curt nod. "We'll invite Mr. Dale for supper tomorrow. I suggest your mother's famous pork with parsnips."

"Parsnips aren't in season," Nora snapped. Who did he think he was, inviting people to supper at *her* house? Before their mourning was complete, no less. She squared her shoulders. "I'm afraid that is quite impossible. Not only have you not given me enough notice to properly prepare a meal for company, but in case you have forgotten, my family is in mourning. It would not only be entirely improper to entertain a suitor, but I fear he would be most displeased with my lack of proper provisions and my less-than-complimentary company. Given my grief, of course."

Amos narrowed his eyes. "Of course." He cleared his throat. "You are right. I suppose I thought you in a line with your mother." He smiled fondly. "I remember how Rebecca always had her home ready to offer hospitality at a moment's notice."

That had been when Mother had both a maid and a cook. And never while in mourning. Nora's cheeks burned.

She had to figure out something soon.

Or risk her uncle selling her off like a filly to the highest bidder.

⌁

Four days into his employment and Silas still hadn't gotten used to sleeping in a bunkhouse. Each night he'd listened to men snoring more than he'd slept, and that only after they'd stayed up well into the night arguing over cards.

How did they ever get enough rest to do their jobs well? Though to be honest, he hadn't seen the men doing all that much. In his opinion, the Fentons could shut down the bunkhouse and get rid of Oscar, Bill, and Jonas entirely. They did more loafing than working and he didn't see why the operation of Emberwild required so many live-in hands. They could save a lot of expenses by not maintaining so many workers.

As the last light of the day began to fade, Silas made his way to Starlight's stall for her evening brushing. The simple ritual reminded him of home. He passed Arrow's stall and the stallion poked his big head over the gate.

Silas paused. "Good day today, big fella."

Arrow wriggled his lip and stretched toward Silas, so Silas chuckled and stepped closer to scratch his ears.

They'd been making good progress the past few days. He hadn't gotten any farther than where Miss Fenton had shown him that first day, but he had to first establish trust before moving on to new exercises.

The horse lowered his head into Silas's fingers, seeming content. Silas scratched, noticing a few white hairs interspersed in the sorrel red. Interesting. Would this colt turn gray? Rare for a trotter. They usually came as bays or chestnuts. At least to his knowledge.

He gave Arrow a pat and continued to Starlight's stall, his thoughts far from his task. He hadn't seen Miss Fenton again. He hoped she wasn't ill. He'd expected to see her standing at the corral railing every morning, her keen eyes dissecting his every move. But as far as he could tell, she hadn't left the house.

Arrow had watched for her each morning, and Silas had to give the horse time to realize his mistress wasn't coming.

He couldn't help but feel guilty. The woman obviously loved her horse, and he had no desire to sever such a relationship. Clearly, however, Mr. Fenton did not want his niece to work with the colt. Silas couldn't change that. Best he could do was train the horse well so that once he left, Miss Fenton would have a horse her uncle no longer believed might harm her.

Finished with Starlight's grooming, Silas gave the old mare a fond pat and made his way to the bunkhouse. Probably to another meal of salt pork, beans, and crusty bread. Did Walter know how to make anything else? Not that he should complain. A full stomach was all a man could ask for.

Fireflies twinkled in the twilight outside the barn, giving the fields the look of a sparkling sky. Two hounds scurried out of his way as he neared the long structure of the bunkhouse, and the mangy one on the porch growled at him before slinking away.

Silas removed his hat and stepped inside, the scent of beans and unwashed men hitting him in the face. Four of the five hands had gathered around the card table. Oscar Hardy and Bill Alden, the two men he'd met at the inn in Philadelphia, Walter Griswold, the cook who looked near on eighty, and Jonas Pickens. None of them paid him any mind as he made his way through the small common area and to the rear of the building.

The only man he would have been glad to have as company spent his nights at home with his own family. Not that Silas would begrudge Asa that privilege. He'd certainly take evenings in a quiet, cozy home over a packed bunkhouse with this feckless crew.

Six single-man bunks crowded the back of the cabin, two sets on either wall and one on the back. Silas dropped his hat on the bottom left bunk, his for the duration of his stay, and changed out of his sweaty shirt.

Raucous laughter filled the space, the men already indulging in their evening vices. Two more days, and the men would get leave to go into town. Maybe then he'd get a few nights of peace.

Perhaps he'd been moving in the wrong direction. He'd set out east as an opposite for everything he left behind. But going east would only mean more people, crowded cities, and fewer open skies. Why hadn't he thought of that before? He should go farther west, past Texas. Out to the open lands of Oregon or Utah. Places where a man could still breathe.

"Hey, Mex, come join us!" Bill called.

Silas clenched his teeth. He'd informed the men more than once that he wasn't from Mexico, and therefore the nickname didn't fit, but the more he'd protested, the more they enjoyed their joke.

"No thanks."

One of them grumbled something about how Silas thought he was too good for the likes of them. Ignoring the barb, he pulled a worn Bible from his bag and settled down on his bunk to read. He'd barely read two lines when Walter plopped down on the bunk across from him, knees creaking.

"Is it the cards you don't like, or the company?"

Silas looked at him over the top of the Psalms. "Don't care for gambling or the effect it has on men's temperaments."

Walter grinned. "So, both." He chuckled. "Don't look so guilty, boy. Ain't no shame in that." He put his hands on his knees, face thoughtful. "I been wondering. What brings you to Emberwild?"

"Need to make a little money before moving on." He closed the book and sat up.

"Where you headed, if you don't mind my asking?"

"Lately I've been considering Wyoming or Montana."

"Good land, from what I've heard." Deep brown eyes studied Silas from a weathered face that had seen its share of wind and sun. "So why come through Mississippi? Neshoba County ain't really on anyone's travel plans."

He considered shrugging the man's probing aside, but decided on honesty instead. "Philadelphia is the last place I saw my father alive."

The statement didn't seem to surprise the old man. "Figured there must be a reason. No one comes through these parts unless he has something drawing him." He pushed up on his knees and stood, stretching his back. "Welp, good talkin' to ya." Walter wandered off, conversation apparently finished, then flung over his shoulder as an afterthought, "Come get your grub before it gets cold."

Silas shook his head and followed the man to the table, where he mostly ignored the others as they scarfed down the evening meal. After handing his bowl over to Walter with a nod, Silas made his way outside into the relative cool—and quiet—of the evening.

He settled on the steps of the bunkhouse and propped his back against the railing. Past the barn and the paddocks, the large estate house glowed with warm lights in the upper windows.

A sudden dot of brightness appeared in the shadows by the side of the house, then quickly disappeared. Silas frowned. What was that?

It appeared again, a few steps from the front porch, bobbing a few feet off the ground.

The light stole across the yard, mostly keeping to the shadows. Why would anyone be creeping around in the dark?

The light drifted from tree to tree, held too low for Silas to get a look at the person's face. When the lantern moved around the back of the barn, he rose.

Should he get the others? He waffled a moment, then stepped off the porch and headed toward the barn.

He'd alert the men if he needed to. But first, he intended to see for himself.

chapter
ELEVEN

This was ridiculous. Nora picked her way across the yard, holding the lantern low so she could see where she stepped. She hadn't seen Arrow in days. Poor horse must think she'd abandoned him. Left him to a strange man. Had he been worried about her?

Did horses worry?

Nora shook her head at her own foolishness. Mother was right. She really needed to find some friends other than animals. She'd just always found horses more accepting than people. Easier to understand.

She cast a glance at the second floor. Mother had retired to her room. Light glowed faintly through the lace curtains, open to let in the summer breeze. Nothing stirred on the other side.

Nora struck out across the yard, choosing the most direct path to the barn. Mother might insist she spend her days doing "more productive" activities than playing with horses, but she hadn't said anything about the evenings.

Mosquitoes hovered around her light, their nasty little wings buzzing furiously. Why had God created such horrid beings? They existed only to bring others misery.

The barn loomed up ahead, a deep shadow silhouetted against

an inky sky. Behind the barn, the bunkhouse glowed softly, the men out of her way for the evening. She opened the end door quietly and slipped inside.

Several mares poked their heads over the stall gates, wide eyes reflecting in the light. She cooed softly to them, trying to let the mothers know their foals weren't in any danger. A few nickered, but most returned to the shadowy recesses of their stalls. She made her way past the tack and feed rooms and to the stallion stalls.

One stood empty now, with their only other stallion, Arrow's sire, out on breeding loan. They kept Arrow safely in the middle of the barn, though none of the mares were currently in season.

She held the lantern up over his gate. His big head bobbed up from where he'd been sleeping.

"Miss me?"

Arrow remained in the center of the stall, left hind hoof cocked. He lowered his head and sighed. Was he pouting, or did her presence simply not interest him? She knew she shouldn't feel a stab of hurt at his dismissal. Being rejected by an animal made her feel more pathetic than she cared to admit.

Maybe this was a bad idea. What did she really think was going to happen out here anyway? Some kind of joyous reunion?

Arrow looked fine. She needed to go back to the house and forget these girlish notions about—

A scraping sound sent her heart into a reckless gallop. Nora snatched the lantern as she spun around, but nothing revealed itself in the light's reach. She peered toward the door, watching. The hallway remained empty.

Probably a cat after its supper.

Nora stalked to the tack room. She'd come out here in the dark. Arrow would get a brushing whether he wanted one or not. After gathering both a stiff and a soft brush, a hoof pick, and a comb for his mane, Nora awkwardly closed the door while trying to balance the tools and the lantern. How long would it take for the convenience of electric lights to be available here as in the big cities?

Perhaps she should set the lantern down. She dropped the brushes, set the lantern in the hallway, then gathered her supplies and closed the door to the tack room. The scent of fresh hay brought a familiar comfort.

She left the light in the hallway while she opened Arrow's stall. He regarded her with a flat stare.

"What?"

He snorted, an answer she imagined said he'd rather she left him to his sleeping. She stepped inside and felt her way around with her toe, hoping she didn't find any fresh piles of manure.

The cloudy night didn't offer even a hint of starlight through the upper windows of the barn, and the dim atmosphere sent tingles along her skin. She balanced the brushes along the ledge by the feed trough and stepped out to retrieve her lantern.

After placing the lantern safely away from the straw on the floor, Nora left the stall door ajar and plucked the stiff brush from the ledge. She held the bristles out to Arrow, who bobbed his head with annoyance.

She put her hands on her hips. Now what in the world had Mr. Cavallero done to her horse to make him so—

A scraping sound came again, a sound like the scuff of boots on stone. Her breath caught. She clutched the brush against her chest and peered out into the hallway. Outside the circle of light, darkness stretched in both directions down to the ends of the barn. Cats didn't make noises like that, did they?

Her pulse skittered.

"Hello?" Infusing as much confidence into her tone as she could muster, Nora called out, "I know you're there. Best be a man about it and step out of the shadows."

A man barked an incoherent reply.

Nora jumped back, not really expecting anyone to be there. Her legs tangled in her long skirt and she stumbled against Arrow. The horse squealed. Nora scrambled, her boots slipping in the hay. She caught herself and managed to get her feet under her.

"Easy, boy, I—"

Hands suddenly grabbed her waist and she screamed. Arrow reared. The assailant hauled her backward. Arrow shrieked, his hooves thumping against the stall floor as he stomped.

Panic gripped her throat, choking off her ability to scream again. She twisted, but the hands held firm, pulling her through the stall door and out into the hallway. Nora kicked backward and her boot met something solid.

The man grunted. "Miss Fenton! Please."

The hands released her.

Nora lurched away, breathing hard. She whirled, every muscle in her body poised to fight or run. Mr. Cavallero stood in the ring of lantern light, his features a mix of wariness and apology.

He held up his hands. "Miss Fenton. Forgive me. I didn't mean to—"

"How dare you take ahold of me like that!" She took a step away from him, pulse thrumming in her ears. She drew in a deep breath to try to steady herself, her senses muddled. "You . . . you . . . *what* are you doing in here?"

He regarded her evenly, not at all abashed as a man who'd been caught assailing a woman ought to look. Despite the fact that he'd grabbed her, however, she didn't see the first trace of malice or even lecherousness on his stoic features. He stood quietly, palms lifted, waiting.

Fear gave way to anger. Didn't he realize the danger he'd caused by spooking a horse in the dark? She crossed her arms and gave him a pointed stare. Maybe he hadn't really meant her any harm. But he could have caused it by his rash actions.

"Forgive me, ma'am." Mr. Cavallero spoke with a slow, calming voice, as though she was the spooked horse. "I saw a light and came to investigate. Once I saw you, I aimed to give you a little privacy. Then you called out, so I came forward."

She glared at him. "And how does that explain why you grabbed me?"

Rather than looking apologetic for his idiocy, however, the man's already stony face hardened. Nora resisted the urge to look away under his scrutiny. How had he managed to make her feel like the one who'd done something wrong?

He cleared his throat. "It isn't safe to be in a stall with a spooked stallion."

The man spoke as though she had no sense at all. "I'm aware. Which is why *you* shouldn't have been sneaking around." She knew how to handle herself with horses. This man had no right to—

"My father died in a similar situation."

All the fire went out of her accusations. "Oh." She glanced back at Arrow. "He would never hurt me."

Mr. Cavallero's expression radiated disagreement. "I'm sorry for intruding on you, Miss Fenton." He dipped his chin. "Good night."

"Nora," she said on a sigh. "Just Nora is fine." She hadn't been fair. He'd only been trying to keep her from sharing his father's fate, and she'd been treating him like a cad.

The side of his mouth lifted slightly, but he gave no other indication he appreciated her offer of familiarity. An olive branch of sorts, to soothe a bit of the awkwardness surrounding them.

"Yes, ma'am. Good night."

"How's he been doing?" she called after the cowboy's retreating back, not entirely sure why she sought to prolong his company.

The question seemed to relax him, because Silas—she figured since she'd given him permission to use her given name, she could use his as well—brightened as he turned back to her. "I've been able to get him to move through the exercises you showed me."

He'd imitated her exercises? "And your assessment?"

Silas thought a moment. "He's temperamental, which is normal for a stallion. He also tests commands at times. But I don't see any of the issues your stable master implied."

Nora grinned. Ha! Wouldn't Roger love that. He couldn't get a more objective opinion than one from a stranger. "Once he qualifies at the fair, I'll be able to start setting up stud services for him."

"A fine horse, Miss Fenton, to be sure." His dark brows pulled together. "He reminds me a lot of a horse my father had, actually. The one they say killed him."

Nora's sense of satisfaction faded away, leaving a cold unease in its wake. He thought Arrow was like the horse that had killed his father?

"We were traveling through Philadelphia about fifteen years ago." His words laced with regret. The kind of pain that had long since scabbed over, but the wound remained underneath. "They say the horse spooked and trampled my father in the stall."

No wonder he'd reacted as he had. Sympathy bloomed in her heart. She also knew a small measure of what it had been like to lose a parent at that age. Not to death, as he had, but to lose someone you loved, to watch them transform into someone cold, distant, and . . . well, she could still sympathize with his grief.

"How terrible." Nora glanced at Arrow, who had lowered his head again, though his eyes watched them. "I'm so sorry to hear of your loss." He'd come back to this town, where his father had died? Why? Wasn't he supposed to be traveling somewhere east?

Unease tingled along her arms, though she couldn't exactly say why. Perhaps it had something to do with the strange way he was looking at her. As though expecting her to say something more. But what?

Nora cleared her throat. "When do you think you'll get him in the harness?"

Silas allowed the change of subject, the momentary thoughtfulness on his features fading. "I'd planned on trying in the morning. Would you like to be there?"

Of course she would. But Mother had set the two of them to cleaning the house as though it would dispel every bad memory along with the dust. She had to dust all of the curtains and scrub the—

No. She would help Mother and care for the house, but not at the expense of all the effort she'd put into Arrow. Not to the detriment of the key to her future. Dust could wait.

As though sensing the shift in her mood, a hint of mischief entered Silas's brown eyes. The look flickered away so quickly, however, she might have imagined it.

"What time?"

"I'll wait on your convenience, Miss Fenton."

"Nora."

"Yes, ma'am." He dipped his chin and turned, striding into the darkness.

She watched him until he melded into the shadows and listened to the barn door slide into place. Only then did she allow her shoulders to sag and the breath to leak out of her.

What was it about that man that had her feeling like a sailboat in a hurricane? Nora turned back to look at Arrow.

He regarded her with flat ears, looking not at all interested in her company. She closed the stall door, gathered her lantern, and left the ornery creature to his mood.

Males. No matter the species, she feared she'd never understand them.

chapter
TWELVE

Maybe this horse really was mad. Silas held out the breast collar for the training harness. While he waited for Arrow to sniff the next piece of equipment, he checked the sun. More than two hours to get this colt fitted in a halter, surcingle, and back pad. At least another to fit him into the breeching and back straps, as Arrow had shown no interest in standing still for those.

The belly and hold-back straps had nearly caused Silas to lose any hope for the colt at all. The training harness came in individual pieces, so he didn't have to attempt to put so much on the horse at once. However, Arrow had not cared for the sound of the snaps and had made his displeasure known in no uncertain terms.

At the moment, the stallion flattened his ears and regarded Silas with what could only be called disdain. Silas took a patient step forward and presented the bridle again, earning a snort and pinned-back ears that warned Arrow would give no more. Silas sighed and stepped back.

Only two options remained. Unhook the horse, allow him to calm, and try again, or . . . approach this problem in a different manner. Silas turned on his heel, dropped the bridle in the dirt, and strode for the fence. He hopped over the rail and walked away.

Hopefully the fool creature wouldn't maim himself while Silas fetched Miss Fenton. He'd waited on her in the stall this morning, then for a while longer while exercising Arrow, and had finally decided the woman had changed her mind. Regardless, he had the suspicion that her presence would help with Arrow's attitude. He simply had to be certain he kept her out of harm's way.

He jogged across the yard, mounted the porch steps on the large house, and hesitated beneath the decorative eaves. Mr. Fenton wouldn't take kindly to Silas seeking help from Miss Fenton, and the act might even get him dismissed. But if they wanted that horse to make time trials in a matter of weeks, then Silas needed a little assistance.

He knocked firmly on the door and stepped back to wait. A few moments later, a stately woman dressed head to toe in black regarded him with a pinched expression. She waited, obviously expecting he should speak first.

Silas swiped off his hat and tucked it under his arm. "Good morning, ma'am. May I ask if I could borrow a moment of Miss Fenton's time?"

The woman's pale features somewhat resembled Nora's. Though where the older lady had refined, angular features, her daughter's face was softer, more inviting. Silas found himself wanting to step back from the starchy woman's scrutiny.

"You're that trainer, I presume?" Mrs. Fenton spoke with a genteel accent peppered with the drawn-out syllables of Southerners, far more pronounced than the way her daughter spoke. Did she do that on purpose?

"Yes, ma'am. I have a question for her, if she's available."

Mrs. Fenton lifted her nose in a haughty way that had Silas's jaw clenching. "My daughter is not to be involved in horse work. Such things are for the hired hands. Good day to you." She started to close the door when another voice came from inside.

"Wait!"

A crack remained in the door, allowing harsh whispers to slip

96

through. He caught something about "improper behavior" and some kind of argument about "managing the people." A moment later Miss Fenton slipped out and pulled the door closed behind her. Dressed in a long black frock made from dull cotton, she appeared somehow diminished from the vibrant woman he'd caught in the barn.

"May I help you?"

Silas scratched the back of his head where caked sweat started to itch. Maybe this wasn't the best idea. "I'm having a bit of trouble with your training harness."

Her eyes widened. "Is Arrow hurt?"

He shook his head, the strange desire to comfort her causing a quick response. "He's perfectly fine. Merely stubborn."

"Oh." She cast a glance at the door behind her. Had she forgotten about coming out this morning? Or had her mother not allowed her?

"I've had no problems saddling him," Silas continued. "But every time I try to fit him with the harness for the breaking sulky, he becomes a bit . . . obstinate."

The corner of her mouth twitched as though she found the situation amusing but didn't want to let him know. "He does have that tendency. Have you tried offering each piece for his inspection prior to trying to put it on him?" At Silas's nod, she scrunched her brows in a moment of thought. "And you've given him time to move around in each piece before donning the next?" At his next nod, she pursed her lips. "Perhaps he merely objects to you training him."

Silas gave her a questioning look. Did she really believe that, or had he detected a warble of jealousy in her voice?

"Gleason says most of a horse's faults are a direct result of vicious training."

She was accusing him of vicious treatment? With what evidence? "Gleason also said that sorrel horses are generally of a mean disposition and stubborn will."

She opened her mouth, then closed it again and pressed her lips into a thoughtful line. "You've studied Gleason's methods?"

"As you have, I gather."

Glancing away from him, she twisted her fingers, seeming to undulate between a thorny woman intent on insulting him and one who more resembled a nervous filly. He had to admit the woman intrigued him, caused him to act impulsively just so he could find himself in her company. But he should know better than to risk his entire purpose for coming to this place because he'd been captivated by a pretty face and a glimpse of a kindred spirit.

"Forgive me for intruding on your morning." He pulled his hat over sweaty hair and turned to leave.

"Wait. I'm sorry." The words came out in a rush, and before he could react, she'd hurried past him and out into the yard.

What was she doing?

Having no choice but to follow her, Silas watched her long skirts drag across the ground in a brisk swish.

She came to a halt in front of the corral and placed both hands on the railing. "What in the heavens?"

Silas withheld a chuckle. Arrow stood in the center of the corral, the bridle he'd refused now gripped between his teeth, looking as forlorn as a boy who had a wooden sword but no fellows to play with. A laugh burst out of Miss Fenton, and she turned sparkling eyes on him.

"Looks like he changed his mind." She put a foot on the rail as though to climb over, then dropped back to the ground. She brushed her hands down her skirt, gave him a tight smile, and then started to stride away.

Baffled, Silas caught up to her. "Where are you going?"

"You don't need me." Her tone warbled between dejected and annoyed.

Something must have happened between Miss Fenton and her mother that had her acting as moody as Arrow.

He lengthened his stride to keep up with her. How did she move so quickly in that dress? "But I didn't get a chance to ask you anything."

She came to a sudden halt. Her eyes, a deep blue that reminded him of Papa's description of the ocean, searched his face.

Silas grabbed for words that had decided to disintegrate. "Miss Fenton, I—"

"Didn't I already give you leave to call me Nora?"

"Yes, ma'am, but—"

"But what? You decided to continue an act of formality after you frightened me near to death?" The humor crackling through the words belied their bite.

Odd woman. Silas had not often felt at a loss when speaking to people, but this lady—with her flashing moods and unusual mannerisms—had him floundering.

A chuckle bubbled in his chest. "My apologies."

She tilted her head. Waiting for . . . ? What else did she want him to say?

"And . . . thank you for the invitation."

Still no response. Just that unnerving expression of a schoolmarm expectantly waiting until her pupil stumbled his way to the right answer. She lifted her already arched brows, as though hoping to hurry him along. If not for the humor sparkling in her eyes, he'd think her a shrew.

Perhaps Arrow's obstinance was learned behavior.

"Thank you for the invitation, Nora."

She flashed him a smile, one that lit her features and gave him a glimpse of her true beauty, less the cactus and more the sunflower turning to—

"Is something funny, Mr. Cavallero?"

His grin widened. "Silas. As I recall, we agreed on given names." They had, hadn't they? Surely he'd remembered enough of his manners to offer his as she'd offered hers.

She smirked. "You had something to ask?"

Suddenly forgetting anything relevant to Arrow, Silas blurted out the first thing that came to mind. "Did you ever hear about anyone local finding a stallion that appeared out of nowhere, about fifteen years ago?"

Nora blinked, her hand coming to her throat. "What does that have to do with Arrow's training?"

She looked decidedly pale. Had the question upset her, or merely left her confused?

"Nothing. Just . . . been meaning to ask you. Since I told you about my father."

Idiot. He sounded like a loon. No wonder she gazed at him with a guarded expression.

"No, I'm sorry." She pinched her lips together, and he gave her a moment to ponder. She had to have been Silas's own age or perhaps a bit younger when his father had died.

"What kind of stallion?"

Hope fluttered in his chest. "A bright sorrel, nearly fiery red. Tall, probably already fourteen hands, though he was barely two."

"Any distinguishing markings?"

Papa might have mentioned something about a spot inside his lower lip, but . . . He shook his head. "The only thing would be a stark white spot, about the size of a man's thumbnail. An oddity on a horse so bright of a sorrel."

Nora frowned.

"Do you know him?"

Her features tightened, and she shook her head. "I wish I could help you." She fanned cheeks that had turned a strawberry red. The heat in that garb must be getting to her. "I should be going."

Silas watched her hurry away, feeling a little foolish. He hadn't expected her to know anything about the stallion. He'd simply kept talking to keep her company. That woman had a decidedly unnerving effect on him.

He found Arrow still standing in the center of the corral, hind hoof propped in a lazy stance. He'd dropped the bridle. A sullen gaze met Silas as he scaled the fence. As soon as his boots hit the dust, however, Arrow tossed his head, whirled his hindquarters around, and bolted in the other direction.

As he'd suspected. Purposely cantankerous.

Just like his mistress.

❧

A coincidence. It had to be. Nora hurried toward the house, her stomach knotting with every stride. What had her father said? A stolen horse?

Secret. A secret horse. No. A lie.

Everything we have was built on a lie.

Her father's words echoed in her mind, bouncing off unanswered questions.

"Four half-starved mares and a floundering stallion that wasn't worth his weight in manure."

No. Couldn't be. Just because Silas's father had lost a horse around roughly the same time her own father had purchased their foundation stallion didn't mean . . . did it?

"All these years . . . didn't say anything."

Hot. Much too hot. She scrambled inside the house and bolted the door, breathing hard. She felt as though she'd just run a lap around the track. A hundred questions darted through her mind. A secret. A lie her father had kept from her mother.

A horse . . . a fiery sorrel.

They could be connected. Possibly. But more than likely not. The odds were too small. And she couldn't risk rumors saying otherwise. Not if she hoped to make Arrow their next stallion. Not if she hoped to forge a new path for herself.

But maybe the lie was that he'd found the horse. Not stolen. Her heart wrenched. Possibly no better. Her mouth dried, connections and implications falling into place.

If Father had found Ember, then he wouldn't have known the horse's bloodlines. Which meant he didn't have a proper registration.

Ice flooded her veins, causing the heat radiating through her to sputter into steam.

Without the proper bloodlines, then every foal they'd ever produced would be called into question. Their registrations revoked. Over a decade of breeding. Hundreds of foals. All dismissed.

They would be ruined. They would lose—

"Are you all right?" Mother hurried toward her, concern crinkling her features. "Did something happen with that man?"

Nora placed a hand to her pounding chest. Mother would need to know if everything they had was in jeopardy. If their reputation was on the brink of destruction. And Amos. He would have to know. Would have to deal with—

"Nora?" Mother gripped her shoulder. "What happened?"

Father had wanted to keep the secret from her. The tarnished reputation would cause as much harm to Mother as financial ruin. Despite the distance growing between them these past years, Nora still loved Mother. She wouldn't add any more to her than life had already. Especially not without proof.

Amos's words found purchase in her scrambling thoughts.

"No sense causing your mother heartache over wagging tongues."

"Nothing. I was . . . I was just thinking about Father." Truthful, though probably not in the way her mother expected. Her voice cracked at the end, weighing the statement with even more grief. Mourning over what the secret could cost them more than the man who had bequeathed the burden.

Without any warning, the rigid statue Mother had become crumbled. Her shoulders drooped and the icy walls that had stood between them for years seemed to shatter.

Before Nora could move, Mother wrapped her in a tight embrace. "Oh, my dear girl. I'm so sorry." Tears thickened her voice as she settled Nora's face in the crook of her neck. "I've spent so long wrapped up in my own grief that I hardly considered yours."

Nora stood stiff, shocked. Then a feeling, one she'd long ago dismissed as extinct, welled in her center. She wrapped her arms around Mother's waist like she'd done as a child and clung to her. Hurt, fears, and anger swirled through her, but for a moment she was a girl again. One in need of her mother's comfort.

They stood there for a time, each clinging to the other. How many years had it been since she'd enjoyed her mother's embrace? Before their arguments over suitors had caused a rift between them. Before illness turned Father's bitterness into cruelty and Mother had withdrawn a little more each passing month.

In the time since, Nora had forgotten what it felt like to be held by another, to be comforted.

After a few moments Mother pulled back, her eyes glistening. "Come, let's have an afternoon together, shall we? I've been trying to keep us busy, and I thought that occupying your time would . . ." She waved the rest of the words away. "Never mind. I was wrong. Let's forget duties for today. We'll share fond memories and have tea. Won't that be nice?"

Mother wanted to have tea together? To reminisce and enjoy one another's company? "I'd . . . like that."

"Good." She gave Nora's shoulder a fond pat. "Why don't you have a seat while I fix our refreshments?"

With a rustle of black crepe, she swished away, leaving Nora to stare after her. Numb, she wandered into the parlor and took a prim seat on a blue cushion to wait.

A dangerous thought struggled to break free of the confines of her conscience.

What if she kept Father's secret? Would it matter, truly, after so long? The horses had all proven themselves. Been sound purchases for their buyers. Why cause an upheaval in so many lives?

And what of Mother? What good would solving an old mystery do? Even if Ember had once been Mr. Cavallero's horse, they had no proof her father had done anything wrong. Maybe he had found a lost horse, not a stolen one. Was that so bad?

The idea sent snaking roots to fill crevices in her heart. Keeping the secret gave her a chance at the life she wanted. She'd heard of widows who managed their late husbands' assets before. She and Mother could succeed without Amos. They could care for themselves.

Be free.

Mother would have parties again. Smile more often. Laugh, like she used to. The house could be filled with friendship and joy. Nora could manage the farmhands and order the breeding programs while Mother managed the house. If she did well enough with Arrow's stud contracts, they could hire helpers to cook and clean.

Excitement filled her as Mother entered the room wearing the first smile Nora had seen in months, and those little roots sank deeper. It *could* work.

All she had to do was keep Silas Cavallero from asking too many questions that could dig up secrets better left entombed.

chapter

THIRTEEN

Silas shook off his annoyance as he pulled on his boots before daylight had even poked the first sleepy rays through the open windows of the bunkhouse. The inviting scent of coffee lingered in the air, promising a jolt of energy to counteract his sleepless night. Walter must not have slept either.

Snores emitted from three of the other bunks, though Silas didn't bother trying to remain quiet. It would serve them right if they felt groggy after a night of cards, whiskey, and two separate fights Silas had needed to help Walter break up. He had half a mind to dump all three of them out onto the floor.

Instead, he stomped to the front of the bunkhouse and accepted a steaming mug from Walter before he stepped out onto the front porch to watch the sun chase the gray out of the sky. His favorite time of the day. Silas drew a long breath of humid air too hot for the warm drink he held. He took a sip anyway and smacked his lips against the bitterness.

Today he would start the long lines on Arrow. They'd finally made it through harnessing, and now Silas could get the horse into all of the equipment in under twenty minutes. A far cry from where he'd been a week ago, and yet he still felt too far behind. They needed to make better progress. He had to get this horse prepared for the fair, though he doubted Arrow would make a good run. He had the speed, just not the inclination. They would do better to give him a few more months.

But that wasn't his call.

Silas blew on his coffee and listened to the birds as they welcomed the new day. He lingered a moment longer, then came to a decision. His main reason for coming here had been to discover the truth. And he didn't want to leave Mississippi without having first put his every effort into settling his doubts about Papa's death.

He owed his father that much.

Regardless of what the others thought about his questions, he *would* ask. Starting with Walter.

Inside, he found the old cook poking at a skillet filled with sizzling sausages. The grizzled man cast a glance at Silas.

"Be ready in a few."

"Wondering if I could ask you a few questions. May seem a little odd."

Walter stopped pushing the sausages and looked at Silas expectantly.

"How long have you worked for the Fentons?"

"Eight years."

Not long enough. "How long have you lived in these parts?"

"Born and raised." Walter continued to poke at the sausages, though two had already charred along one side.

"Do you remember anything about a man that died at the inn in Philadelphia fifteen years back? Trampled by a horse?"

Walter stirred slowly, his eyes on the skillet. "I remember something about that." He flipped one sausage with the spatula, then two more. "That your pa? Makes sense. You coming here and all."

Here? As in this farm? "Why's that?"

"Philadelphia was the last place you saw your pa. If he was the man killed by that horse, I can see why a fellow might come looking to put his past to rest."

Silas leaned against the counter. Though he didn't know why he would care one way or the other, Walter's reassurance set him at ease. "I know it seems foolish, after all these years. But I feel like I should at least try to find answers before moving on with my life."

Walter nodded as though that made perfect sense to him, and Silas couldn't help but appreciate the man.

"Wish I could tell you something to help." He scooped the sausages out and plopped them on a tin plate. "But all I heard was stories and rumors. Horse spooked and trampled a traveler. Afraid I don't know any more than you do." He cut a quick look at Silas. "Sure you've probably heard the same already from anyone else you've asked."

And he wasn't likely to get more. "Never sat right with me. My father was better with horses than any man I've ever seen."

Walter gave him a sympathetic look. "Accidents happen to the best of men."

And death knocked on every man's door. All things he'd heard before. "I wonder about the horse, though," Silas said, shifting the topic away from his father. "No one ever found him? Seems odd, don't you think?"

"Naw. Horses run. Miles, sometimes, if they're spooked enough. Could have ended up anywhere. Or been killed by coyotes in the woods."

Possibly. Logical answers, and probably likely. "Do you know anything about Ember, the stallion here?"

Walter paused on his way to the table with a stack of half-burned flapjacks. "Big stallion. Throws good colts." He plopped the plate down. "Get your grub!" His shout nearly rattled the rafters.

Grumbles followed a moment later. Walter eyed Silas thoughtfully. "Why you askin'? You think your father's horse ended up here? That he's the Fentons' breed-registered stallion, purchased from a farm in Indiana and sporting fancy paperwork officially stamped by the registry?"

The more Walter talked, the more ridiculous Silas felt. "Of course not."

Walter gave a small nod toward the round table crowded with mismatched chairs. "Best get your feed before the wolves slobber all over it."

"I'm good, thanks." Coffee would do. "I want to get an early start."

He dropped his mug in the sink and ducked out as the stable hands meandered into the room. Outside, the Mississippi humidity rose with the sun, blanketing him in suffocating moisture. Texas air had been dry, sucking the life out of the marrow. But here, the air felt heavy, as though at any moment it would gather and condense on his skin.

Today he needed to introduce Arrow to various objects that could spook the horse on the track. Even mellow horses would bolt at unfamiliar items such as blowing paper sacks, the pop of a firecracker, or the shouts of a crowd if they hadn't been taught such things wouldn't harm them.

Shooing a cat out of his way, Silas stepped into the room nearest Arrow's stall. The scent of leather hung heavily in the air. The saddles and equipment must have been worked by one of the boys recently. Leather oil gleamed on the saddles from where they hung on the walls or sat draped across stands. Silas selected the training harness and located the long lead lines.

"Plan on hitching him today?"

Asa's deep voice rumbled behind him and Silas turned. "Not yet. Need to work on the leads first."

The big man leaned against the doorway. "Seems like he's taking to you."

Silas didn't know about that. Tolerating him in Nora's stead, more likely. As though sensing his thoughts, Asa laughed.

"Course he prefers that little lady to any of us."

"Seems that way." Silas looped the long lines into a circle and draped them over his elbow. "Don't know why they don't just let her finish with him. They both prefer it."

Asa looked at him thoughtfully. "Not many men would say so. Even my Emma thinks it's odd Miss Fenton goes about in trousers training horses like a man." As though realizing he'd said something he shouldn't, Asa's eyes widened. "Course, ain't none of my affair, I only mentioned it to her a time or two." He shifted his feet. "Ain't my affair."

Silas chuckled. "You don't have to filter your thoughts on my account, Asa. If I had a wife waiting on me at home, I'd share my day with her too. And my thoughts on the unusual behaviors of others."

Asa tipped his head back and roared with laughter. "I like you, Mr. Cavallero."

Silas grinned. "Just Silas."

Asa returned the smile, and together they moved into the hall.

Silas paused. "How long have you worked here?"

"My pop worked here, long before this was a horse farm. Back when these were still plantation fields." Asa shrugged, his mannerism speaking more than his words about what kind of life that must have been. "I've been working in these parts most of my life."

"So were you here when they first started?"

"Not much in those days. We mostly kept to the smith, but I was around. Why?"

"From what I hear, Arrow got a lot of his temperament from his sire. I wondered if anyone knew what the stallion was like as a colt."

A shrill cry split the air, startling both men.

Arrow.

Silas dropped the tack and dashed toward the colt's stall. He'd heard that harrowing sound before. The eerie shriek of a horse in pain. Both men darted toward the sound, boots pounding on the paving stones.

Arrow thrashed, hooves flying wildly. Silas thrust open the stall. Arrow reared. A blur streaked out past Silas's feet, causing him to stumble. Asa shouted something Silas couldn't make out over Arrow's snorts.

What was that? A blur of fur streaked down the aisle. A cat? Silas ignored the frightened creature and stepped into the stall to calm the horse. Arrow snorted, but allowed Silas to stroke his neck.

"Easy, boy. Easy."

Lines of thin scratches streaked down the horse's withers at the base of his mane and trailed in little lines down his front shoulder. Silas frowned. "Looks like that cat jumped on his back and then tried to hold on as he fell to the floor."

Asa looked over the gate. "What was that cat doing in here?"

Silas studied the stall. A large twelve by twelve square, the enclosure had solid wooden walls about chest high, topped with a line of bars that reached several feet taller. The bars were encased with another beam along the top. Above that, the barn's high ceiling rose to a point at the center, where windows let in the light.

"I suppose the cat was walking along the top here. Guess he fell in."

Asa shook his head. "I say that fellow there just used up one of his nine lives and was lucky it wasn't his last."

Arrow began to calm, so Silas led him to the food trough and encouraged him to continue eating. He snatched at his oats sullenly, the skin on his side twitching.

"Probably ought to put a little poultice on that." Asa eyed the scratches. "You wait here while I fetch us some from my bag."

A half hour later, they had the thick yellow substance smeared on Arrow's side and Silas brought him out of the barn, keeping a watchful eye for cats. The cuts weren't deep, but the horse could have injured himself in the commotion. It was a wonder the cat had survived the colt's hooves. Might not have, if Silas hadn't opened the door.

Maybe they would try a different plan today. One that didn't involve putting equipment on top of the fresh scratches.

Silas worked with Arrow until noon, focusing on trust maneuvers and introducing various objects for inspection. As with everything else he'd tried with this colt, the lesson required a hefty dose of patience and more calm than he could muster. But by the time Walter clanged the bell for dinner, he'd made decent progress.

He stalled Arrow rather than turning him out in a paddock. The scratches looked fine, and he wanted to work on the harness again after the noon meal. He refilled Arrow's water bucket, then went to the tack room to gather his equipment. Best to have everything ready to go. He'd just grab a few bites from the bunk and head back out to the barn.

He found the equipment dumped in the middle of the tack room. Asa must have picked it up off the floor when he'd gone to get the poultice, but he hadn't bothered with putting the tack back on the pegs where it belonged. Odd. He would have thought the man to be the more organized sort. But then, he hardly knew the fellow.

Scooping up the long lines, Silas looped them over his arm and bent to gather the rest. He hesitated, running his thumb along a smooth cut in the thick leather of the harness strap. Had that been there before? If he hadn't been paying attention, he might not have noticed it. But if he had put this on Arrow and the horse had spooked or Silas had pulled hard on the lead lines, then the harness could have snapped.

How had that happened? He turned the strap over and examined the other side. The threads where the top piece that went over the withers connected to the breast piece looked frayed, barely holding together. He angled the piece toward the light streaming through the doorway.

The threads hadn't frayed. They were cut. He sat back on his haunches. That couldn't be right. Surely one of the boys hadn't been fooling with any knives while he was polishing. He'd need to have a word with the young fellows. They couldn't be careless with equipment. Not when they could put animals and men in danger.

A scuffing sound made Silas turn.

Roger stood in the aisle, watching him. Their eyes met and a strange gleam flickered briefly in Roger's eyes before it quickly evaporated. He flashed a smile, dipped his chin, and walked away.

Silas stared after him.

Something about that man didn't sit right.

chapter

FOURTEEN

The next morning, Silas still hadn't come up with any answers. Any questions he'd posed about Roger were met with distrustful glances, so he'd left it alone. He made his way to the barn, determined to focus on the job at hand.

And keep a keen eye on the equipment.

He found Nora in Arrow's stall. What was she doing mucking manure? Silas approached slowly and paused to watch Nora pitch another forkful of straw through the open gate. Arrow flicked his ears toward Silas but continued eating his hay, content.

"Don't you have stable hands for that, Miss Fenton?"

Nora paused and put a hand to her hip. A shapely hip, one encased in strange trousers that no man would wear. No, on closer inspection they weren't trousers at all. Slim at the waist, the single divided skirt then flared out into bellows that fell to the top of her boots. And she wore a shirtwaist, belted neatly, along with a lady's riding jacket and suitable hat. Utilitarian, perhaps. Something about her hair looked different, but—

His gaze rammed into hers.

A tinge of color painted her smooth cheeks at his inspection. She held his look with a gleam in her eyes that hinted at embarrassment, defiance, and . . . a little satisfaction? He forced himself to break eye contact and nod toward the wheelbarrow.

"As I understand it, Emberwild employs hands for that kind of labor."

She blew a strand of hair up her face, already a bit dewy from the humidity, even this early. "I don't mind. It gives me something to do while I wait for him to finish. I don't dump it," she hurried to add, as though that made a difference.

He waited, not sure what else to do. What did a man say when a woman insisted on doing such a task? His discomfort grew the longer he stood there until he nearly hopped over the wheelbarrow and plucked the pitchfork from her fingers. He made a move in that direction when she dropped the fork on the mound heaped in the wheelbarrow, flashed him a brilliant smile, and then gave Arrow a pat.

"I thought we would attach him to the sulky today." Nora slid a halter onto Arrow's nose, as commanding with the colt as her tone indicated.

Silas snagged on the "we" part. He hadn't seen a glimpse of her in days, and suddenly she wanted to get in the middle of his training? She buckled the clasp on the halter and turned expectant eyes on him. What did she want him to say? Rather than saying anything she might find offensive—like asking what she was doing out here and why she was taking over—he simply nodded.

Her lips pressed together in a pucker of annoyance.

He tried for confirmation instead. "He should be ready for it."

Nora attached a lead rope under Arrow's chin without a word. Had she wanted him to refute her?

She stood there, waiting. It took Silas a moment to realize he was supposed to move the wheelbarrow out of her way. For some reason, he found himself jumping to her unspoken command. He lifted the rear wheels and pushed the cart clear of the door, but he had no intention of dumping it.

Arrow's hooves clopped down the aisle as Nora walked past, her divided skirt making a whisk-whisk sound. Where had she gotten that outfit? It seemed as though she had taken a dress, split it up the middle, and sewed each half into a voluminous pant leg.

Maybe she had.

Transfixed, he watched her sway out of the barn. She'd reached the door before he gained his senses enough to follow after her.

Nora let the colt into the corral and then turned to face Silas, her expression holding a question. "The sulky?"

Of course. She expected him to fetch it for her. As he turned to do her bidding, he caught a slight smile bloom on her face. Had she purposely planned to make sure he remembered his place?

Women and their schemes. He had a mind to—

He stopped short. In the shock of seeing her this morning, he'd forgotten to check the equipment. He had questioned the stable boys about the damage to the harness, but neither admitted to cutting it.

His mind had run to other possibilities. Had someone cut it intentionally to sabotage his work with Arrow? Roger had been watching him in the tack room. But if the stable master wanted Silas gone, he could simply dismiss him. Which left the gambling stable hands. He could handle himself with them, but if anything caused injury to Nora . . .

"Did you forget something?" Nora sent him a mischievous smile, once again derailing his line of thought.

How did she do that? Jumping from a prickly cactus to a playful minx in less time than it took for a horse to swish his tail? Ignoring her, Silas hopped the fence.

Her smile disintegrated and she drew herself up. "What are you doing?"

He took the lead from her and turned it over in his hand, but saw no damage to the fibers. He checked the clasp under Arrow's chin, and the horse bobbed his head, clearly sensing Silas's unease. Arrow's halter appeared intact.

"Yesterday I found a cut in the harness."

The small brim on her hat barely shaded her scowl. "Cut?" Her eyes flashed. "You think someone is purposely damaging our equipment?"

He hadn't said that, exactly, since he couldn't prove anything. He offered a noncommittal shrug.

"Why?"

Because men with too much pride and a gut full of whiskey did stupid things. Likely they thought to embarrass Silas. Not that he would tell her any of that.

"I don't know, but everything here looks fine. I'll check the sulky." He turned and scaled the fence before she could say anything more. Better to not get into a conversation about his thoughts on her employees.

A short distance from the corral, Roger stood under the oak watching Nora with narrowed eyes. Silas steered clear of him. No sense giving the man a reason to tell him to make Nora leave. If Roger wanted to oust the woman from the corral, he'd have to do it himself.

Oscar led one of the mares out of the barn with a frisky foal bounding along behind her. A shaggy-coated brown dog pricked his ears their direction, but wisely left the spindly-legged colt alone. Behind Oscar, Bill carried saddlebags filled with tools and a coiled length of wire. He showed none of the effects of his late night with a whiskey bottle. He met Silas's gaze with a hard stare.

Silas rounded the western side of the barn and headed up the curved path to the carriage shed. Smaller by far than the barn, the wooden structure housed two buckboards, a rockaway carriage, a four-wheeled coach, a one-horse buggy, and two racing sulkies.

For people who lived out in the country, the Fentons had plenty of conveyances. He supposed as one of the wealthiest families in the county, they could afford such luxuries. Maybe they used to travel a lot before the late Mr. Fenton grew ill.

Sunlight filtered through uncovered glass windows set in the plank walls, illuminating the dust that stirred with his steps. Overhead, the second floor of the carriage house served as an office and living quarters for Roger. The place smelled of disuse, and a rat scurried out of the corner as Silas made his way to the racing cart.

He painstakingly ran his hand over the u-shaped metal of the sulky. The small seat held firm to the metal frame as he wiggled it, and none of the spokes on the high wheels appeared loose. No issues with the frame or the axle, as far as he could tell.

An older-model sulky, heavier and taller than modern versions. He'd heard mention of a new design, something about pneumatic-tired bicycle wheels on a high-wheeled sulky frame. What the racers were calling a bike sulky. The newer models apparently had more stability than these older models, which were prone to tip around tight curves if not handled properly.

Silas lifted the cart, only about sixty pounds, and rolled it out of the carriage shed, pleased to note the wheels rotated easily. The shaggy dog ran up to sniff the spokes as they rolled past his shady spot, but the furry fellow lost interest after a few moments and trotted back to the hole he'd dug to cool himself.

In the corral, Nora had Arrow practicing backing up and coming forward on command. Arrow watched her with intelligent eyes, ready to respond to her slightest movement. Silas had to admit, the lady had a way with horses. Arrow relaxed in her presence, almost eager to please.

Both stopped to look at him as he maneuvered the contraption through the gate. He dropped the shaft into the dirt.

"Where is the harness?"

Still in the barn. Where she'd left it. Keeping his thoughts to himself, Silas left the sulky in the corral and headed back to the tack room. He repeated his inspection process for each piece of the sulky harness, including the patch job he'd seen to himself, and gathered the long lead lines.

Roger stood in the barn doorway, a wad of tobacco stuffed in his scruffy cheek. "Mr. Fenton don't like her out there with the colts. You know that, right?"

Silas slowed. "Sounds like an issue between the Fentons."

Roger's scowl deepened. "Look here, ain't your place to go around causing problems. Asking a bunch of questions, making eyes at the boss's niece. You hear?"

The muscles in Silas's shoulders tensed and he had to force his grip on the breast collar to relax before the leather left marks in his palm. "It's also not my place to tell Miss Fenton where she can or cannot be. I'm simply following the lady's orders, as is fitting for a hired hand."

Roger sniffed at the snide tone. "Don't say I didn't give you fair warning. Mr. Fenton may have your hide before he sends you packing."

The man stalked away, spitting an amber stream of liquid into grass wilting under the summer heat. Silas shook his head. Roger didn't seem to care for Silas, yet hadn't ousted him. Maybe only Mr. Fenton could terminate employees.

He found Arrow sniffing the sulky in the center of the corral. Both horse and woman ignored him as he entered and put down the harnessing equipment. He waited while Arrow snorted, pawed the ground, tossed his head, and finally decided the little cart wasn't going to attack him.

Nora grinned as the horse, now settled, nuzzled against her. A glimmer of sweat snaked down the side of her cheek, but she didn't seem to notice the heat. The smile softened her features, making her even more fetching.

"Once we get him strapped in"—Nora scratched behind Arrow's ears—"I'll take him around a few circles in here before we try the track."

The track? She thought she was going to drive this colt on the track? Silas shook his head. "No, ma'am. I don't think that's a good idea."

She popped a fist on her hip and resumed that demanding stance he'd come to recognize meant she wouldn't tolerate him arguing. "Is that so, Mr. Cavallero? Well then." Her chin lifted another notch. "What exactly do you plan to do to stop me?"

Palms slick with sweat she tried to inconspicuously wipe on her skirt, Nora nudged Arrow to stand straight and wait for harnessing. Had she really just gotten a man to back down? To consider and then concede to her logic? Silas had listened thoughtfully when she'd argued Arrow had been on the track before and it would be the best place to allow the horse to feel the straps and cart weight at a full trot. He hadn't berated her or called her ideas "the foolish notions of an addle-minded female" as her father had often done.

After a brief consideration Silas had agreed, and now they were moving forward as a team. A tiny sense of victory swelled in her center. She'd held firm and earned his compliance. And not by brow-beating him either.

Oddly, the man appeared content to treat her both with deference and yet still maintain an egalitarian partnership. She'd never encountered a man like him. The idea brought an unfamiliar warmth she didn't dare consider. He was her employee, after all.

Maybe battling her cowardice and attempting to speak with more authority had simply earned her a measure of respect. Or perhaps the sudden return of the mother she had thought lost to memories had somehow emboldened her.

She could still scarcely believe she'd actually succeeded in convincing Mother to let her train Arrow. With a myriad of stipulations, of course. The primary of which had been that Nora could no longer dress in trousers and must wear a proper riding habit.

Mother had not, however, forbidden alterations to said attire. Nora had been able to take a deep gray riding habit—a suitable color, Mother had conceded—and split the skirt in two, making movement much easier while still maintaining modesty.

A good balance.

Arrow stiffened, drawing her attention back to the task at hand. Silas had approached with the sulky. Without her having to say anything, he backed up a small step and waited for the colt to relax once more.

Not only was he an egalitarian gentleman with a soft spot for a difficult colt, but a wise and perceptive one as well. If any of her suitors had been like this man, she might not have balked at the idea of marriage.

She had not anticipated the effect Silas would produce. She'd often found herself musing over his serious demeanor that would abruptly shift into a casual confidence.

If he wondered why she'd returned to the stable this morning after several days absent, he hadn't asked. She wasn't sure if she should give him credit for that or not.

Silas gave a nod that he was ready for Arrow to back into the waiting shaft of the sulky so he could attach the cart to the harness. Nora gently touched her fingers to Arrow's chest and asked him to step back. Arrow complied, one tiny step at a time. Painstakingly slow, but at least he didn't refuse. Finally, she had the colt in position. Behind him, Silas set to work connecting the lines.

"Please, Arrow," she whispered in his fuzzy ear. "I only need this one race." Perhaps one or two more.

She needed the time trials in order for him to be listed in the registry. Then he'd need several more to gain the attention of breeders and buyers. She wasn't callow enough to think that one good run would allow Arrow to ride on Ember's coattails as their foundation stallion. He'd need to prove himself in order to secure stud contracts and sell foals.

Mother had listened to that much, at least. Whatever had caused Mother's sudden change of perspective, Nora didn't want to look a gift horse in the mouth. Still, one did have to wonder why—

"Nora?"

She snapped out of her thoughts to find Silas staring at her, a crease between his dark brows. Heat scorched up her neck. "Yes?"

"Do you?"

"Do I what?"

"Agree to my suggestion?"

How lost in thought had she been? "What suggestion?"

The small muscles at the sides of his jaw twitched. A sudden sourness crept into her stomach. Her father had that same expression whenever he started to get angry but didn't want to show it. Nora tightened her grip on the lead. Her distraction must have been a drain on his patience.

"May I ask—just for this first run—that I be the one to take him onto the track." The way he phrased the question and the tightness in his tone left no room for argument. In this instance, he looked like a mule who had pinned his ears and anchored his hooves.

She had no intention of losing her ground now. She was perfectly capable of handling Arrow, and the sooner Silas understood that the better. She opened her mouth to set him to rights, but he spoke before she had the chance.

"Solely out of concern for your safety, of course, and not because I don't think that you're capable."

Nora snapped her mouth shut. Trying to protect her by not letting her do anything while at the same time conceding that he knew she was indeed capable? What did one say to that?

He gripped the back of his neck, his dark eyes intense. "If anyone's going to take a tumble getting a feel for those first turns, it should probably be the hired hand and not the lady of the house." His wide mouth pulled into a smile that was somehow both imploring and slightly mischievous.

Perhaps he had a point. Mother would certainly forbid Nora's forays to the barn if she broke her arm the first day into their new understanding. She tapped a finger on her chin, thinking out loud. "We won't run him. Only take him around the track with the weight of a rider. And you're too heavy."

The edges of his mouth twitched into what she thought might be a smile denied full bloom. "Wise idea. I'll lead him at a walk." He gave Arrow a fond pat. "And we'll put one of the boys in the seat to give Arrow a little weight, but not too much."

That's not what she'd meant at all.

"And of course you'll be watching his gait and judging his reactions so that we can proceed to the next step," he added.

Oh, fiddle-faddle. She couldn't very well contest his logic without making herself seem useless. Any boy could sit the seat at a slow walk. The more important person would be the one watching and assessing. Not the ones riding or leading. At least, not in this instance.

And just like that, he had her. They both knew it. She could tell by the way he tried to hide the satisfaction on his face under the brim of his cowboy hat.

Arrow bobbed his head, watching her. He really had done quite well with all the tugging and whatnot Silas was doing back there with the sulky, testing the colt's reactions. He should take the track fine. She tangled her fingers in Arrow's mane, denying Silas the vindication of a response.

Satisfied after another few moments of jostling, Silas reached to take the lead from Nora. Arrow snorted and shied away.

Silas rocked back on his heels. "Wonder what's gotten into him?"

Nora stroked the colt's nose. "Maybe I need to hand him over, rather than you taking him?"

She extended the lead rope out to Silas. Arrow watched calmly, but as soon as Silas put pressure on the line and Nora stepped back, he tossed his head.

Silas grunted.

Had her presence interfered with the relationship these two started? They couldn't be more dissimilar. Where Arrow flashed hot, Silas remained cool. Where Arrow skittered and jumped, Silas remained as steady as an old gelding. Not that he was old. Or gelded. Certainly not that.

Her face scorched. Her mother would skin her alive if she ever suspected Nora had thought such an indecent thing.

Silas was staring at her. She forced herself to maintain a serene expression despite the embarrassment making her neck itch. "Perhaps I should lead him."

Finally, after an excruciating moment under his gaze, he nodded. "I'll fetch Pete."

While she waited for Silas to find the skinny youth, Nora led Arrow in a slow walk around the corral. He didn't seem in the least concerned with the sulky trundling along behind him. She let the lead slip through her hands, giving more distance between them. He could probably make a good circle, like he usually did with his exercises.

Nora took her place in the center of the corral and let the line all the way out. Arrow kept one eye on her, his head bobbing. She lifted her free hand to signal the trot.

Arrow lurched, bounding forward, then settled into the smooth diagonal swing of his hooves. Perfect. He was moving nicely, gait even and—

Why was he pinning his ears?

Arrow tossed his head, his speed increasing. He leaned his shoulder, bending into a tighter turn. Nora raised her hand to signal him to slow but he only increased his pace.

Tighter.

Closer.

She tugged the line, trying to get his attention. Arrow lowered his head and barreled forward, trapping her in the center of the narrowing circle, the sulky careening closer.

Tilting.

The cart tipped up on one side, the outer wheel lifting off the dirt. A scream lodged in her throat.

Arrow's circle tightened. The cart teetered precariously.

Someone shouted.

The balance shattered, and time ripped from an unnatural slow motion to slam into a reckless speed.

Arrow squealed and snatched the rope through Nora's palm. The sulky crashed to the dirt. Arrow bolted, fighting against the weight holding him.

The sulky twisted against the horse's hind legs. Cart and animal blurred together, creating a sickening jumble that was coming straight toward her.

chapter

FIFTEEN

Run! Silas's feet churned up red dirt before he could think further. Nora stood petrified in the center of the corral, horse and tangled cart sliding toward her. He launched himself over the rail and rolled as he hit the ground, leaping to his feet in one fluid motion.

Pete shouted, but Silas's focus pinned on the paralyzed woman in front of him.

"Nora!" Her name wrenched from his throat.

As though hearing him had awakened her from a trance, Nora screamed and stumbled backward. The horse shrieked, the tipped sulky throwing the animal off-balance. He kicked out with his hind hooves, but the rear harness straps kept him confined. His large body swung dangerously close to Nora.

Silas reached her just in time to wrap an arm around her waist and yank her backward. She screeched.

The colt reared.

Silas snatched Nora from the center of the corral, putting distance between her and the frightened animal.

Another stride backward and he slammed into the rail. He pulled her against him, her back pressed firmly into his chest. Her hat had come unpinned, and strands of honey-brown hair whipped into his eyes.

"Arrow!" Nora pulled against him, struggling to cast herself into the danger he'd only just saved her from.

"I've got him." The words scratched out of his throat in a growl.

He thrust her behind him and eased toward the spooked colt, carefully speaking in low yet commanding tones. The frantic horse had kept his feet, the twisted sulky toppled behind him.

"He's frightened," Nora called behind him, as though Silas didn't know that already. He ignored her and continued his slow approach. The last thing he needed was to further spook the horse and cause injury.

"Easy, boy. Whoa, now." Silas approached, and Arrow shied back. Fool horse would get them both killed. Shoving his anxiety as deeply down as he could, Silas pushed his lips into a false smile. "Got yourself in a tangle, didn't you?" He forced a chuckle. Behind him, Nora mumbled something unintelligible.

Arrow flicked his ears toward Silas, front hoof still pawing.

"Bet you'd like me to get that thing off, wouldn't you?" He took slow steps forward, trying to appear casual. Arrow, however, didn't seem fooled. He tossed his head and snorted as though to inform Silas that the situation fell far short of ideal.

"Can't get it off if you spook." Not that he thought the horse understood his words. "You've got to let me help." Hopefully, however, his tone would convince the animal to relax. At least a little.

Arrow whinnied and pawed the ground, digging up the soft earth.

Silas reached out. "Easy, boy. I'm trying."

Arrow thrust his muzzle toward the harness in a way Silas might have found comical in any other situation. The gesture seemed to point out the severity of Arrow's predicament and indicate that Silas's lack of concern was shameful.

A genuine smile lifted his lips. "Yep. Got to get you untangled, big fellow."

He reached the horse without Arrow bolting and quickly unhooked the coupling. Arrow's skin along his haunches quivered, but the colt remained still. Silas spoke soothingly to him, keeping his palm along the horse's body as he worked his way around Arrow's wide chest to the other side to fully release the sulky.

The metal hit the ground with a clang and the horse bolted forward. He pranced away, harness jingling. As far as Silas could tell, he didn't look injured.

"We'll never make the trials now." Disappointment weighted Nora's words, as though making the trials at a local county fair had been the pinnacle of her life's goals.

Silas stared at her, incredulous. "At least you still have a horse capable of running. A wreck like that could have broken a leg. Might have even caused the horse to have to be put down." What had she been thinking, making him run tight turns like that?

She blinked. "Of course. And I am thankful, certainly."

The fact that she could have gotten herself killed with such a foolish stunt leapt to the tip of his tongue, but he bit the words back.

"What's going on here?" Amos Fenton's voice boomed across the yard, followed quickly by the voices of others. Apparently Pete had scrambled for help while Silas had gone after Nora.

In a matter of two more heartbeats, nearly every man on the farm gathered around the railing. Silas filled his lungs with dusty air and released his breath slowly. How did he explain that he'd let Nora do something so stupid? Well, he hadn't *let* her. The woman had a way of taking off without him before he even knew which way she wanted to go.

"The sulky turned over, Uncle. It happens." Nora's voice rang out over the gathering, commanding and in control.

Silas turned to stare at her. Still poised at the edge of the rail, she brushed a hand down her skirt and leveled cold blue eyes on her relative as though he had interrupted a women's gathering uninvited.

Amos started to sputter, but Nora cut him off. "The newer carts are far less likely to overturn than these old ones. I'll purchase us a better racing harness for his events, but for now this one will teach him not to cut turns too sharply."

Every man present stared at her as openly as Silas. She tugged two black gloves over her long fingers, produced from somewhere in her hidden pockets, then strode toward the stallion as though so many pairs of eyes assessing her had no effect whatsoever. No one stopped her. Perhaps they were all simply stunned.

Regaining his senses, Silas scrambled after her and took Nora by the elbow two paces from the horse.

"Unhand me," she seethed. "I cannot let my uncle see my weakness."

The words stilled him. Filled with both desperation and thinly masked pleading, he let her slip from his grasp. She cast him a heap of gratitude in one meaningful glance, and he found himself respecting her all the more. Regardless of her fear, she wouldn't let the situation undo her. She approached the horse with a hesitation he suspected only he noticed, slight as her pause had been.

Arrow rolled his eye at her, nostrils quivering. She held out a gloved hand to him, her shoulder set in staunch determination. Either the horse would yield to her, or he would balk against the direct approach. With this stallion, a man could bet either way and find himself a loser half the time. Arrow tossed his head.

"Arrow. Come," Nora commanded, the slight tremble in her hand barely noticeable.

Please, boy. Give her this.

The stallion snorted, then stepped forward and placed his muzzle into Nora's palm. She took hold of the horse's bridle, leading him farther away from the men gathered at the fence. He couldn't be sure, but her steps didn't look as steady as they should.

"Cavallero!" Amos's barked command left no doubt Silas had reached the end of his employment at the Emberwild farm.

"Sir?" He turned to find the man had entered the corral and that the others, save Roger, had started to scatter and head back to their work. Asa gave him an approving nod before tucking his farrier's hammer into the loop on his apron and striding back to the barn.

"Explain."

"These high-wheeled sulkies tend to flip on tight turns."

Amos glared at him, the pomade in his hair glistening nearly as brightly as his eyes. "And my niece?"

Nothing for that but the truth. "Miss Fenton and I were working together."

"Did I not make myself clear about my wishes regarding Miss Fenton and the horses?"

He had, in no uncertain terms. Why the men around here thought it fell to Silas to tell the lady otherwise, he hadn't a clue. "You did, sir. And Miss Fenton made her wishes equally clear."

The words hovered between them. Finally, the man let out a puff of air. "That I don't doubt." He grunted. "Well, can't say as I blame you for not being able to put her in her place. I find the task difficult myself."

Across the corral, Nora's shoulders tightened and she jerked on Arrow's reins. The horse snorted and tossed his head. She moved to release him from the harness.

"With respect, sir." Silas separated teeth that wanted to clench. "I believe Miss Fenton is in her place already."

Amos rounded on him. "Watch yourself, boy. We aren't in such a need that you won't find yourself out on your ear."

The threat slid off him. The man could dismiss him if he wanted. It wasn't as though he'd ever planned to stay long. But the thought of leaving Nora alone to face the odds stacked against her immediately sent a strange tingle through him. Didn't her uncle see that forcing Nora into a mold that didn't suit would only diminish her?

True, this woman who had captivated him was as high-strung as a wild filly and he would do better to keep clear of her. Yet his admiration and desire to see her dreams fulfilled had him mustering up a respectful tone when his better judgment warned he should walk away. "Forgive me, Mr. Fenton. I don't mean any offense. Simply that the horse is exceedingly fond of the lady, and she succeeds where many of us have failed."

Amos considered him a moment, taking out the gold watch from his vest pocket and spinning the chain around his finger. The familiar pattern on the timepiece caught Silas's eye again. Where had he seen it before?

"You're telling me you need a woman to help you break that colt?" Silas flexed his fingers at the man's tone. "Yes."

Amos snorted.

"Mother and I have spoken at length." Nora appeared beside them. How had she gotten that close without either man noticing? "I'll be preparing Arrow to become the foundation stallion for this farm."

Surprise shrouded Amos's face. "Rebecca has allowed this?"

A spark of satisfaction crossed Nora's features. "We've agreed that I'll continue with Arrow's training and procurement of stud services."

The watch made another rotation, and Silas focused on the face. Something tickled the back of his mind. A wisp of a memory too hazy to grasp.

"Thank you." Nora's caustic tone snapped his attention back to the Fentons still squaring off with one another.

The two stubborn relatives had reached an apparent stalemate. Uncle stared down his niece—who showed no indications of being cowed. Silas silently cheered Nora on.

Amos stuffed the watch back in his pocket and cleared his throat. "A word, Mr. Cavallero?"

The slightest upturn of Nora's lips before she turned away was the only indication of her victory.

Silas followed Amos from the corral and to the shade of the large nearby oak. They stood there for a moment, both watching as Nora finished removing all the harnessing from Arrow and then led him over to inspect the overturned cart.

"My better judgment says to send you on your way."

Silas waited, sensing an unspoken "yet" in Amos's tone.

"But I fear for my niece's safety without someone to keep a close eye on her." Hard brown eyes raked over Silas.

He'd signed up to break a colt, not watch over a woman. Besides, there were others who had known Nora far longer. Not to mention Amos could take up the task himself.

As though reading his thoughts, Amos continued. "As I'm sure you have realized by now, my niece is an uncommon woman. Most men find her . . . off-putting." He hooked his thumbs through his bracers. "Yet she seems to tolerate you."

The thought almost made Silas chuckle. Nothing like being told a beautiful woman tolerated you more than she did most men. Amos's next words, however, doused the humor before it had a chance to spark.

"Something I'll need to remember when negotiating with suitors."

Negotiating with suitors? The way the man phrased courtship made marriage sound like a business deal. He'd been under the impression people married more for love than practical arrangement these days. Regardless, he suspected that even if Amos saw matrimony in that light, Nora wouldn't agree. Could that be why she'd remained unwed?

"Wouldn't want to burden her with a man she couldn't come to love. Wouldn't you agree?"

The muscle in the side of Silas's jaw quivered. "I couldn't say, sir. That's none of my affair."

"Quite right." Amos chuckled. "Walter tells me you've been asking around about your father."

The sudden change in topic caught him by surprise. When had Mr. Fenton talked to Walter? And why about him? Silas pushed the brim of his hat back, senses on edge. "He died in Philadelphia when I was a boy."

"Long time. Why come here now?"

The timepiece came out again, snagging his thoughts. "Where'd you say you got that again?" The spinning stopped, and the watch dangled from its chain. Silas tried to force his memory beyond shadows of recognition.

Amos bristled and stuffed the gold piece back in his pocket. "It was a gift."

Earlier he'd said he won it in a wager.

They studied each other a moment, both apparently uninterested in answering the other's questions. Why that bothered Silas, he wasn't entirely sure. He had nothing to hide. Perhaps he'd only gotten his hackles up against the man because of how Amos treated Nora.

In the corral, Nora stroked Arrow's neck as the horse nuzzled her arm, clearly over his debacle with the sulky.

"What happened to your father?" Amos drew Silas back into their peculiar conversation.

"Horse spooked in the stall with him. He was trampled." The words came out wooden, years of familiarity with their pain having sanded the splinters smooth.

The lines around Amos's eyes crinkled. "Bad luck, that."

The statement required no response, so Silas turned his attention back to watching Nora rub her gloved hands over the sulky and try to convince Arrow that the contraption was nothing to worry about.

"Does it help you put the past behind you, coming here?" Kindness filled the other man's voice. The kind of empathy that came with understanding from experience.

Silas turned back to face him, finding all earlier evidence of hostility wiped from Amos's features. "I suppose. I wanted to find answers to a few things that had always bothered me. Things I felt were unresolved as a boy."

"Like what?"

A fly buzzed around his head and Silas shooed the nuisance away. "Just questions no one could answer. Why was he out in the barn late at night? Why would a man characteristically careful and methodical have left both the stall gate and the barn door open? Not to mention wondering whatever happened to the horse he'd gone to Tennessee to purchase."

Amos gave a slow nod. "Hardest parts of life can often be questions a man has no answer to. Lost my own father when I was a boy. He was felling logs when a tree took a bad turn on the way down."

Something passed between them. The shared grief of losing a

father—the man who was supposed to teach you the ways of the world. Someone you expected to see you into your manhood with wisdom and encouragement.

"I hope you find the answers you're looking for." Amos clapped him on the shoulder. "In the meantime, I'd like to ask a favor of you." He nodded to where Nora had her hands on her hips, her frustration with Arrow's refusal clearly getting the better of her. "Keep her safe. Her mother has already lost so much. I'd hate for Rebecca to lose the last family she has."

He squeezed Silas's shoulder. "Can you do that for me? Protect her no matter what?"

Silas found himself nodding, though the words carried an odd weight that he didn't think should rest on his shoulders. He wasn't this woman's kin, nor her intended. He was merely the horse trainer who hadn't planned to be here long.

"She'll want to race him, but there's good reason women aren't allowed on the tracks. She's too precious to risk."

Too precious to risk.

The truth of the words coiled inside him. "Yes, sir. I know."

SIXTEEN

Victory. Nora couldn't withhold her grin. She'd done it. Held her ground and earned her place.

She hadn't let herself quit. Or complain. Or let anyone see her falter. She could take pride in herself. She'd been terrified. Humiliated. But she'd held herself together. For the most part, at least.

Thanks to Silas.

He hadn't berated her or insisted she leave. He'd even let her go when she needed to get Arrow in hand and prove herself in front of her uncle. He'd understood that she had to stay in command. That she couldn't show weakness even when her knees had threatened to buckle underneath her.

She owed him for that.

The men finished their discussion, and Amos shook Silas's hand.

"Come to the house for dinner with us?" The words galloped out of her mouth and across the yard before she could think better of them and all the invitation implied.

Both men turned to stare at her. Surprise lifted Silas's eyebrows.

Her and her big mouth.

A stupid thing to ask, certainly. Mother wouldn't be pleased. But she could hardly call the words back now. She straightened her shoulders. Silas shared a look with Amos.

"Thank you kindly, Miss Fenton." The words came slowly. "But I should be getting on with my duties."

Of course. He could answer no other way to a question she shouldn't have asked.

"Very hospitable of you, dear." Amos watched Silas walk away. "I shall be along shortly." His voice held a note to it Nora couldn't place.

She wouldn't let herself reveal her disappointment in her courteous nod. Dignity intact, she led Arrow from the corral and back to his stall.

Now she had to get a meal together. Really. What had she been thinking?

After tending to the horse, Nora hurried to the house and scrambled upstairs and out of her dirty riding dress. A black skirt and thin summer shirtwaist in a light dove gray felt much cooler by far than the thick riding habit. She ran a hand over her hair. Between the heat and her elation over her and Mother's compromise, she'd done something a bit drastic last night.

The scissors and at least eighteen inches of hair still lay on her dresser.

Nora coiled the much shorter—and decidedly lighter—strands into a small twist at the nape of her neck and replaced the pins before rushing downstairs again.

Mother would never know she'd had a brush with death this morning.

At least, it had felt that way. Until she'd found herself encased in Silas's strong arms. Saving her—yet again—from a situation she should have been able to handle.

The fact that her mind kept returning to how she'd felt protected and safe with him was indication enough that she needed to be more careful. Her loneliness was getting the better of her.

Something else she did not need Mother knowing. They'd have her wed to the next available bachelor.

She found her mother in the kitchen, staring down into the icebox. Dressed in black cotton, she wore a single strand of pearls around her throat, the bright white beads nestled at the top of the delicate lace collar. Yet another subtle shift in the mourning attire.

She turned to Nora with a soft smile. "I baked bread." She pulled a clean towel from the stack by the sink and opened the oven door. The rich aroma of yeast permeated the room and roused Nora's hunger. "Shall we eat it with jam and pears on the porch today?"

"I invited Uncle to eat with us." The words darted out before she could catch them. Mother had to know, of course. Only the plan had been to tell her in a more . . . sophisticated way. If such a thing were possible.

Mother paused and then removed the loaf from the oven without comment.

"He was here." Nora shrugged. "Again. Seemed the polite thing to do."

Mother nodded as she set the steaming loaf on the stovetop. "He'll want to eat in the dining room, I'm sure. We'll need to find something more suitable than bread and pears."

Bread and pears sounded heavenly. Along with some iced lemonade and a nice breeze on the porch. She wished she hadn't been so hasty in her invitation. Life with Mother kept growing steadily more comfortable without the pressures placed upon them by catering to the needs of men.

Yet another reason to remain free of them as much as possible.

Mother seemed to have turned a corner of sorts. As two women unconstrained by expectations, they had allowed themselves a few more liberties. Freedoms that Nora suspected had a lot to do with the smiles tugging at Mother's lips a bit more often as June slipped into July. By Christmas, Mother might even laugh again.

"I'm sorry. I shouldn't have asked."

"Nonsense. What else could you do? Anything less would have been improper."

Nora crossed the wood floor that still gleamed from yesterday's scrubbing and opened the salt box. "We're nearly out of ham."

"We're low on plenty of other things as well. You and I should take a trip to town and put in an order with the butcher." Mother tapped a finger on her chin. "The grocer as well." She gave a nod. "I'll make a list."

A sense of relief swelled at Mother returning to thinking about such necessities.

"Didn't I can squash last summer?" Mother asked, poking her head into the pantry.

"Yes, ma'am. I believe there's a jar or two remaining in the cellar."

"Fetch them. We'll have squash and potatoes."

Nora descended into the cool of the cellar and retrieved the jars, her eyes scanning the nearly empty shelves. They'd always had preserves stocked down here for the winter. What would they do this fall without the produce from the garden they hadn't planted this year?

A question for another time. For now, Nora settled into an easy conversation with Mother about what items they needed from town while they worked together chopping potatoes and heating stewed squash. By the time they finished, Nora's stomach growled.

Nora carried the covered dishes to the dining room and placed them in the center of the table while Mother brought in glasses of lemonade. Not a moment later, a knock sounded at the door.

"Always on time," Mother muttered as she went to answer it.

Amos entered with a smile. "Afternoon, ladies. A pleasure to spend it in such fine company."

They settled, with Amos taking Father's place at the head of the table and Nora and Mother sitting on either side.

"So, Nora. Mr. Cavallero tells me Arrow will be ready to run at this year's fair."

Nora paused with a slice of bread hovering over her plate. Amos never spoke of horse training at the table. She gently set the slice on her plate and glanced at Mother, but Mother focused on spooning a tiny portion of squash onto her grandmother's hand-painted china.

"Yes, I believe he will," Nora said carefully. What game did he intend to play?

"Given today's mishap, I feared we'd need to wait until the fair in October, though I suspect we can still make a few good runs there as well."

He wanted to take Arrow all the way to Columbus to the Mississippi and West Alabama Fair? Excitement tingled along her skin. There would be far more buyers and breeders there than at the local Neshoba County Fair.

"Mishap? What mishap?" Mother's sharp eyes landed on Nora.

"The sulky turned over." Amos casually waved his fork. "Made quite a mess. Bent the frame, I believe. We'll need Asa to make repairs before we can use it again."

Mother set her napkin on the table, the linen crinkling in her fist. "Where were you when this happened?" Her gaze bore into Nora as though mining the truth straight from her core.

"In the corral." Amos lifted his eyebrows. "Didn't you give her permission to be there?"

Nora clenched her hands under the table. Mother would recant if Nora didn't speak up, defend herself in some way. But the words stuck in her throat under her mother's penetrating stare.

"Thankfully, Mr. Cavallero was able to keep Nora from any real danger," Amos continued, stabbing a slice of stewed squash.

A line formed between Mother's brows.

"Good hand, that boy. He keeps a very close eye on her. Nora invited him to dine with us, but of course he had duties to see to."

The man was going to give Mother an apoplexy if he didn't stop. Perhaps that was his intention. That, or make sure Nora never left the house again.

What in heaven's name had turned her once favored uncle against her?

The line between Mother's brows deepened. "Of course."

Nora's shoulders hunched. Too bad she couldn't sink beneath the table and disappear. Mother continued to study her, and then suddenly, as if shaking herself free of something, she straightened and picked up her fork again.

"I'm glad to hear no one was hurt. You'll be diligent in keeping yourself out of any situations that could compromise your safety from now on, I'm sure."

Nora eyed Mother cautiously, trying to decipher the deeper meaning behind her words. She shifted her scrutiny to her uncle. Something about the way he and her mother looked at each other gave her pause. Almost as though the two played some game they didn't wish her to understand—and were using her as a pawn in their match.

Amos chewed thoughtfully, then wiped his mouth. "If you find it agreeable, Rebecca, I'd like to invite Mr. Dale as we discussed."

Mr. Dale?

Mother cut a glance at Nora and then back to Amos. "Perhaps. In a few weeks' time."

"I believe he will be traveling to Atlanta for business soon and doesn't expect to return until spring."

Mother set her fork down again, still not having taken a single bite. Who was Mr. Dale? Nora knew every family in the county and didn't recognize the name. Her mother and uncle had been spending a lot of time together lately, but she hadn't realized their discussions had strayed past managing the farm.

Mother finally met Nora's gaze. "Mr. Dale is an associate of your uncle's. He lives in Jackson, but has been visiting family near Philadelphia."

A friend of Amos's, then. So why not invite the man to his own house? Her uncle owned a nice two-story town home in Philadelphia and had both a cook and a maid. Why he wanted to invite his company out here made no sense.

Oh no. Recollection surfaced. The man Amos had tried to invite weeks ago when he'd wanted her to live up to Mother's famed hospitality in the middle of their deep mourning period. A tingle snaked through her belly and soured her appetite. He meant for this man to come here to meet her.

They'd have her input in this little game whether they wanted it or not. "May I inquire about this new gentleman and the nature of his visit?"

Mother shared a look with Amos. After a moment of what appeared to be a silent debate, her uncle finally spoke.

"Mr. Dale is a wealthy man, well respected in Jackson. He owns an iron and steel company that is soon expanding to Atlanta and Memphis."

She waited, hoping he would provide more than the man's business ventures. Amos resumed eating, apparently finding the information sufficient.

"He's only a few years older than you, Nora," Mother said. "Forty-five, isn't it?" She directed the question to the head of the table, where the current king had set up his reign in this rapidly deteriorating match.

A *few*? Seventeen years was far more than a few. What was Mother thinking?

Amos nodded. "And in good health. George has one son. Fine lad."

Son? Moisture drained from Nora's mouth so quickly she could scarcely swallow.

"The boy's mother died three years ago. He would do well with a woman's attention."

A man seventeen years older than her with a son. Nora picked up her fork and stabbed a diced potato she was no longer interested in eating.

"As a man with ample property of his own," Amos continued, as though he weren't currently conspiring to upend her entire life, "he's more interested in finding a good match than a dowry, which I believe will please you."

Heat crawled up her neck and she had to resist the urge to scratch. Pleased? He thought she'd be *pleased* that Amos had found a man to take her without him having to spend a cent? Bitterness swelled and she looked at Mother, finding the older woman's expression unreadable.

"A supper only, of course. There can be little harm in that, can there?" Hope laced Mother's tone, and Nora's mouth went dry.

After their talks of the future and the farm, Mother still wanted to be rid of her? Tears burned at the back of her eyes and she fought to keep them at bay. Her stomach clenched.

Nora placed her napkin on the table. "If I may be excused, I'm not feeling well."

Amos looked up, surprised. "Are you hurt after your episode with the horse?"

Fury warred with the burning tears, and to her horror, wetness swelled and leaked out of her left eye. Refusing to swipe at it, she rose. "If you'll excuse me."

She scrambled out of the room, feeling their eyes boring into her. Another match lost.

A lady had invited him to dinner. Silas couldn't remember the last time he'd been invited anywhere. Church socials didn't count. Everyone had been expected to attend those. He'd even danced with a few women a time or two at wedding celebrations. But one had never invited him into her home.

He'd had to refuse. That had been the right response, of course, but as he sat at the table surrounded by sour-smelling men and holding a plate of half-burnt pork and boiled beans, he wished things could have been different.

"What you smiling about, Mex?" Jonas gestured at Silas with his fork, his tone teasing.

Silas let a smile he didn't know he had fall from his lips. "Horse did well."

"Horse, or the lady?" Bill chuckled. "Beat all I ever saw."

"You boys leave him be." Walter dropped a basket of rolls on the table. "Ain't no call for talking about Miss Fenton."

The men grumbled but stabbed at their meals and let the matter lie. For a moment, at least.

"You see her march right out there and grab that stallion like he weren't nothing but an old plow mule?" Oscar's brow wrinkled. Silas hadn't missed the looks the man had given Nora. Not that he could fault the admiration.

"Sure enough." Bill let out a low whistle. "Thought for sure she'd get herself trampled."

None of them had seen how close she'd come. Or how terrified she'd really been. Amos's words repeated in Silas's head.

"Too precious to risk."

Of course the man would care for his relative, but there'd been an underlying current to the conversation he'd had with Amos. What exactly did the boss mean? Other than getting Silas to agree to watch out for Nora? To let her help without allowing her to be in harm's way. Tempering, Amos had called it. Letting a woman have her way but doing so in a manner that a man could control. Made sense, he supposed, though he had to wonder if Nora would object if she knew about their conversation. How in the heavens had he allowed himself to land in the sticky ground of their battlefield?

A ball of dread formed in the pit of his stomach. What if he couldn't protect her? A person could never grow complacent with horses, especially young stallions, no matter how many years of experience a trainer had. There were simply too many things that could go wrong.

Like today.

A thought occurred. "Any of you men had any problems with the tack?"

Conversation that had turned to how Miss Fenton looked in her riding attire came to a halt.

"What kind of trouble?" Walter asked around a too-large bite of pork chop.

"Frayed stitching, cracks in the leather."

The men looked at each other, all seeming confused.

"No." Bill scratched his greasy head. "But we don't do too much with all that stuff. You ask Pete?" At Silas's nod, he said, "Then I'd tell Roger to make sure them boys is getting their work done. They're supposed to keep all that stuff oiled."

The other men shared nods. Mostly they moved horses from one place to another, ran the farm's steam tractor, mended fences, and did other work typical for farmhands. The horses, it seemed, received little attention beyond feeding and care once the mares had all foaled.

"Don't need either of those boys, if you ask me." Bill punctuated his words with a forkful of beans. "Roger just keeps them around to get more pay."

Both boys were nephews of Roger, Silas had learned, and lived with their mother in a small cabin about two miles down the road. He didn't know what had happened to their father, but he suspected their mother needed whatever income the boys brought home.

"Boys do a good job. Work hard." Silas spoke up for the lads, not wanting to put a widowed mother in worse circumstances by setting these men on a path to get rid of the boys. "Least as far as I can tell. I don't think the equipment problem is their fault."

Oscar shrugged. "Probably just old. This place ain't what it was. Don't think they've gotten anything new in years."

"Don't need to." Jonas shrugged. "Don't race anymore, just breed mares. And mares don't need all that tack." He looked at Silas. "Before Mr. Fenton came down with the wasting disease, he used to have several racers. Would be gone months at a time, him and his brother, taking those horses all over the States to race. Did well enough, till he got sick and the money started to dry up. Turns out folks ain't as interested in foals from an old stallion who *used* to run. Getting fewer and fewer buyers every year. No one seems to remember this place, so far from where all the action is."

That answered a few questions Silas had about the farm and the racing. Why hadn't Amos continued? Didn't the two brothers have a partnership?

None of his affair. Except that Nora had plans to revive the racing enterprise, starting with Arrow. Something he still wasn't sure would be successful in Mississippi.

They finished the meal talking about fences that needed mending, Jonas's sweetheart in Philadelphia, and who needed to tell Asa that he'd forgotten to trim one of the mares. Silas volunteered for that, which pleased the others.

After handing his scraped-clean plate over to Walter, Silas returned outside.

The sulky still lay on its side in the center of the corral, one wheel pointed toward the sky. How close had Nora come to being tangled underneath it? Silas stared at the contraption a moment, a strange sense of unease snaking under his collar.

The gate squeaked and he turned to find Nora entering the corral, her face red. She had changed into a black skirt and gray blouse, but still had to be hot in the midday sun. Hadn't his mother once said refined women stayed indoors and out of the sun during the hottest parts of the day? Not that Nora could be classed with any type of woman, he supposed. The ribbons of her straw bonnet danced on the wind, playing chase beneath her chin.

"I was foolish, I know," she announced as soon as she gained his side. "Thank you for not saying so in front of Amos."

Silas rose from where he'd knelt to examine the frame, not sure how she expected him to answer. "You're welcome" seemed an insufficient response to the gravity in her tone. She spoke as though he'd saved her more by his silence than he had from pulling her from Arrow's path. Nora gazed at him expectantly, clearly wanting him to say something.

"Accidents happen, especially with young stallions. I'm only glad you weren't harmed."

She offered a small smile that didn't reach her eyes then gestured toward the sulky. "How bad is it?"

He tugged on the wheel, pulling the cart back to rights. "Looks no worse for wear." He dusted his hands on his dungarees. "Should work just fine if you want to try him on the track."

She made a small squeak she quickly smothered beneath a stoic scowl. "Today?"

He couldn't help a chuckle. "I think Arrow's had enough for today." As had she, if he were to guess. "Want to walk with me while I take it back to the carriage house?"

Nora blinked and glanced back at the house. She straightened her spine and gave the slightest nod of acquiescence.

He hefted the frame and took the place where a horse would be hitched. The sulky rolled unevenly behind him.

Nora sighed. "Looks like it needs some work after all."

The wheels wobbled behind him, one lurching out of rhythm with the other. "I'll talk to Asa about that when I tell him he forgot to trim one of the mares."

"Oh, he didn't forget." Nora waved an ungloved hand dismissively. "I told him to come back in a week or two for Mayflower. She's been a bit tender on her left hind hoof, and she gets testy when she has a nursing foal. Better to give her a little time than fight with her. The hoof trimming can wait."

How did she know that? The woman obviously paid more attention to the stock than he realized. "You would do better running this place than Roger."

He hadn't meant to say that out loud, but the look of surprised delight that crossed her face made him glad he had.

"You think so?" She hurried ahead of him to open the corral gate. "There's so many things I need to learn, but I feel with some instruction, I could be up to the task."

She'd thought about running the farm? Amos probably wasn't keen on the idea. A sentiment that he assumed had been shared by her late father.

Silas paused at the gate and held Nora's gaze. "Miss Fenton, I have the feeling you could take over the world if the notion suited you."

Her blue eyes sparkled and something in him yearned to draw closer to their light. "Good thing I don't have such notions." She laughed. "I'd settle for Emberwild."

"Why don't you, then? Run things, I mean?"

The smile slipped from her lips. "My uncle believes such tasks aren't for a lady." She searched his face, as though looking for any hint he agreed.

Instead, Silas shook his head. "My mother was a capable woman. Intelligent and determined. You remind me of her, actually." He cleared his throat. "Anyway, she and my father didn't have much, but they worked together on everything. He always said only a foolish man disregarded the good sense God gave women. Said they see things differently than men, and that's why God said Adam needed a helper."

Nora regarded him thoughtfully, a hint of hope in her eyes. "You are an interesting man, Mr. Cavallero."

He wasn't sure if that was a compliment or an insult.

"What are your thoughts on women's right to vote?"

"Same as they are for a woman to own property." At her lifted eyebrows, he continued. "Rights that should be granted."

She rewarded him with a smile, and the day suddenly felt all the brighter.

SEVENTEEN

Why did her heart feel like it wanted to flutter out of her chest? Nora cast a glance at Silas, tipping her hat to shield her face. He was certainly more intriguing than Mr. Dale sounded.

Nora slowed to follow behind Silas as he trundled the cart toward the carriage shed and forced herself to dismiss the thought. She had no intentions of marrying any man, progressive types included.

Not that Silas had any thoughts on marrying her. She was being ridiculous. She snorted at herself and her cheeks heated when Silas turned to look at her.

Still, she couldn't deny the way his words had watered her heart, seeping down into the parched places she tried to ignore.

He thought her capable.

If only Amos did as well.

They passed into the carriage shed and Silas backed the sulky between conveyances her family hadn't used in ages. How long had it been since they'd taken trips to Philadelphia or traveled to see friends?

She scarcely remembered those days when they'd attended church services regularly and spent many afternoons and evenings at social gatherings. What would life have been like if she'd taken to a suitor? Would anything have been different?

"Nora?"

She snapped out of her contemplations, realizing she'd been staring at the family carriage that had taken them to that disastrous evening at the Cromwell house, the start of her father's meanness toward her.

"I'm sorry. What did you say?"

"I asked if—"

Something creaked overhead. Silas looked toward the rafters, and Nora followed his gaze. Plow yokes, farming implements, and other contraptions swung from chains overhead. She frowned. "What was that?"

Silas shook his head. "Must have been something shifting." He took a step closer, and her throat constricted.

His eyes searched her face. "I asked you about your uncle and the ownership of this farm."

What? Oh, right. They had been talking about her running things here. She blinked, trying to gather herself. Why did her head suddenly feel stuffed with wool? He was looking at her like that again. With those intense brown eyes.

"My father's will left the estate to my uncle, though I had thought it would be left to my mother." She took a breath and some of the fog cleared. "I never did see anything from the solicitor, but of course it makes sense he would want his brother to care for us." Had he moved closer? She clasped her hands. "It makes sense," she repeated when he continued to look into her eyes as though searching for something.

A dusting of stubble along his jawline darkened his already tanned complexion. The man was handsome. In a rough sort of way. And with that hat pulled low on his brow and those eyes delving into her . . .

Nora took a step back and straightened herself. "Anyway, that's the way of the world. I'd hoped not to marry, but Uncle seems determined otherwise."

"You don't want to marry?" His voice held no condemnation, no judgment. Just simple curiosity.

"It's not that I don't necessarily want to marry. I don't despise men, despite what my father said."

He lifted an eyebrow in question.

"I simply don't wish to enter into an arrangement in which everything that once belonged to me now belongs to someone else by right. Especially not as a business arrangement in which neither of us holds much affection for the other."

Why in heaven's sakes were they even having this conversation? A whoosh of dusty air clogged her lungs, bringing on a cough.

Silas stepped closer and put a hand on her elbow. "Are you all right?"

"Yes, I'm . . ." She held his gaze, the words flitting right out of her.

Something changed in his eyes. He dipped his head lower, studying her. Alarm bells clanged in her mind, and she told herself to step away. They shouldn't be here alone like this. Standing so close.

But she was tired of keeping track of all the things that she should and shouldn't be doing. She allowed herself to tilt her head back a fraction more, setting her senses alive.

If she moved closer, would he kiss her?

Would she want him to?

Pulse pounding, she leaned in. Just a taste. A sip to see if all this lightning coursing through her would find its match.

His eyes darkened, staring down at her lips.

Beckoning.

Something snapped. Silas dove into her, throwing her to the ground. A shadow passed over them, followed by a sickening crash.

Nora screamed.

Silas covered her, pressing her back into the dirt. What in the heavens?

In an instant he bounded up, pulling her to her feet. She stumbled, stunned. What had happened?

A low sound emanated from Silas, something Nora could only

describe as a mixture between a groan and a growl. "This time there's no mistaking."

Nora clutched his arm, pressing herself into his side. Her lungs pulled for air that had been knocked out of them.

The farming plow she'd seen overhead earlier now lay on top of the sulky, its slim metal frame bent and mangled beneath the heavy plow. The muscles under Silas's shirtsleeve were tight.

"No mistaking what?" she asked on a shuddering breath.

The muscles bunched as he flexed his fist. "First the harness. Now this." Silas looked down at her, all traces of the warmth gone from his eyes. "There's something very wrong at Emberwild."

"I'm serious, Mother. What if it wasn't an accident?" Nora held her teacup to keep her hands from fidgeting, though she'd yet to take a sip.

Mother set her knitting in the basket by her chair in the library and regarded Nora with concern. "First this mishap with the horse and now you say you were nearly crushed by a falling plow?"

It sounded a bit ridiculous when Mother said it that way. "Yes. It fell."

"And what were you doing in the carriage shed?"

"We were putting the sulky back."

"We?"

There was no mistaking the implications in that single word. Nora tried not to let her discomfort show. "I was speaking with Mr. Cavallero while he returned the cart."

Mother sighed, disappointment etching lines along the sides of her mouth. "Surely you know by now that it's improper for you to be alone with one of the hands."

That's what she worried about? Never mind that she had every reason to worry. Nora had all but presented herself to the man as a willing recipient for his advance. Would he have taken what she offered if the plow hadn't fallen?

Deciding the conversation needed to take a different turn before she gave anything away, Nora nodded. "I'm concerned about what Mr. Cavallero said afterward. First there was a harness deliberately cut and now this. He believes there's someone with ill intent at Emberwild."

Something niggled at her memory. The morning her father died, on that first ride with Arrow, her girth strap had snapped. Had that been an accident as she'd presumed?

"Why would anyone have ill intent here?" A crease brought Mother's eyebrows low. "Nothing unusual has ever happened here before."

The implication in her tone clearly meant before Silas had come to Emberwild. Mother didn't know about her girth strap the day Father had died. Nor did she know anything about the questions Silas had been asking about a missing horse. Maybe her faulty girth strap was an accident. Perhaps the other incidents were as well, but there were too many to be completely coincidental.

Could Silas asking questions and his string of bad luck be connected?

"Perhaps it's better if you stay away from the man."

Nora opened her mouth to formulate a reply, but Mother grabbed her knitting again and launched into another topic. "I've agreed for Mr. Dale to come."

"Why?" The word leapt out of Nora before she could call it back.

Mother never looked up. "You know why. It's far past time we stopped pretending. You're getting old, Nora, and I won't be around forever. What will happen to you when I'm gone? Do you want to be alone in this world?"

No, she didn't want to be alone. But that didn't mean she wanted a life of confinement, either.

"And what about me? Don't you think I'd love to play with grandchildren? Find joy in them before I'm gone? Do you really want us to spend the rest of our days without the laughter of family filling our home?"

Was she being selfish, denying her mother the hope of family? Guilt weaseled in and settled like a weight. Perhaps Mother wasn't looking to be rid of her so much as wanting to be sure Nora didn't face the world alone. The idea lessened some of the ache in her chest.

But Mr. Dale?

Why this sudden insistence on a suitor? Had Amos been needling Mother in this direction or had she simply decided that with Father gone she must take up arguments Nora had thought they'd left behind?

"He's much older than I. And a child? Do you truly think me ready to be a mother?"

A small laugh escaped Mother's lips. "No woman is really ready to be a mother, despite what she may think. You will adjust. Then you will have children of your own and find yourself more prepared." Her eyes sought Nora's and held on with an iron grasp. "Don't you want someone in this world who will care for you when you're old? Who will, if not your own children?"

As Nora should be doing for her? She was trying, but not in the way Mother wanted. Mother wanted Nora safely tucked away into a family with children clinging to her skirts and a man to look after all of them.

Maybe it wouldn't be a bad life. She hadn't even given this Mr. Dale an opportunity. "What's he like?"

Mother's features softened and her knitting needles started clacking again. "A tall man, I hear. Fair in his dealings and respected in the community. He isn't known as a man of quick temper."

A comfort of sorts, given her father's disposition. Perhaps why Mother thought to include such a description. But would he make her heart feel electrified? Would she ever find herself leaning toward him, hoping to find out what his lips felt like against hers?

The thought brought a flush. No wonder Mother said she needed to stop pretending. Stop thinking like a girl. She was a woman with responsibilities.

"I will meet this man, Mother. Though I ask you to answer something for me in return."

The knitting needles stopped.

"Given the option, would you choose to marry again and step under another husband's provision and authority, or would you live out the remainder of your days as the keeper of your own property, doing as you alone see fit?"

Mother studied her so long Nora wondered if Amos had already shared his plans to ask for Rebecca's hand.

Finally, she gave a little sniff and started the needles again. "Don't be silly. No woman ever has that choice."

Some did. Mother might.

"Besides, who in this world really gets to do solely as they wish?" Mother's fingers moved furiously. "Do we not have responsibilities to those we love? Do we not have others to consider?"

Guilt needled Nora again.

"If it came to choosing between losing all that we have here and my independence, then yes. I would put our family, our legacy, first."

Nora sank farther into her chair. "But what if you could have your freedom *and* your home? Why not choose that?"

Mother barked a laugh. "For all your years, girl, you're still a child. Life isn't that simple."

But could it be?

"Be careful, Nora." Mother's voice held an eerie calm as her needles clicked. "Don't risk losing all the things that others have sacrificed to give you. You never know what's real, and what's merely smoke and wishes."

The words hung between them, haunting. Her father's secret. The questions brought up by a stranger. Did Mother know?

"Sometimes," Mother said softly, "a woman has the most power by influencing the men who think they hold it over her."

Their eyes met in the flickering lamplight, and something passed between them.

Nora's pulse skittered. Her father's secret pressed down on her.

The deception. The lie that could break their family and ruin their farm if proven true. Mother couldn't know that, could she?

What of Amos? Was Mother trying to tell Nora she knew about her brother-in-law's plans? Or something else entirely? Why not speak plainly?

Probably for the same reason Nora couldn't ask directly.

Fear of saying too much and tipping the delicate balance that kept them all pirouetting around one another like dancers on the ballroom floor.

Mother continued her knitting, the needles clacking tirelessly as Nora's thoughts swirled. Too many secrets. Too many meaningful glances and weighted words that she couldn't decipher. She rubbed her temples.

Sooner or later, one of them would trip and the lies—or perhaps the truth—would spill.

Then she could only pray the secrets of Emberwild wouldn't leave them all with broken hearts and shattered hopes.

EIGHTEEN

Nora wasn't going to like this.

Silas held Amos's gaze as the older man leveled a stare as hard as any good horseshoe, his downturned lips only adding to the effect.

"She will *not* and that's final." Amos twirled the watch at a near hazardous speed, then shoved the timepiece into his vest pocket with such force Silas wondered if he'd ripped the stitching.

"I understand," Silas repeated, as the man hadn't seemed to have heard him the first time. "But I don't see as where I have any authority to stop her."

Amos grumbled, muttering something about Rebecca and women's schemes under his breath. Whatever had happened in the Fenton house two days ago had put the man in a sour mood.

"You run that horse at the fair." Amos pointed a finger at him. "Get the colt's times clocked for registration. Then I will see you off with a good bonus for your efforts."

So he'd outlived his welcome at Emberwild. Silas acknowledged the statement with a nod. They'd leave for the Neshoba County Fair by the end of the week. Giving him only a few more days to spend with the most fascinating woman he'd ever encountered.

"Nora is under no circumstances allowed anywhere near the

stables or the track, or you'll forfeit my generosity." Amos wagged the finger he still pointed at Silas for added effect. "Don't try me."

Silas removed his hat and ran his fingers through hair long due for a trim. No, Nora wouldn't like that at all, but Silas couldn't see where she'd have an option. Amos set the rules, not him. Besides, he didn't think women were allowed to race at any track regardless of Amos's pronouncement.

Maybe she wasn't planning on being there anyway.

He let the ridiculous thought dissipate like fog under the light of reason. Nora Fenton would do as she liked, and she liked nothing more than to insert herself into the middle of all things having to do with Arrow.

Movement caught his attention and he flicked a glance toward the house. As though to prove his point, the lady in question stalked their way.

Amos snatched out the watch again, this time rubbing the face with his thumb. The man did have an odd attachment to the thing. He caught Silas looking at him and jabbed the timepiece into his pocket once more.

"I'll not have Rebecca suffer the shame that girl seems intent on thrusting upon her. Nor the stress she causes Rebecca's delicate sensibilities. I don't care what you have to say, she stays away from that track."

Without waiting for his niece to come close enough to speak to him, Amos tugged on the hem of his fine linen jacket and spun away. Silas watched him stride to a sleek bay tied to the post outside the front of the barn, mount, and nudge the creature into a brisk trot.

Apparently, he didn't plan to stay around today. Had he come all the way out here this early merely to cajole—or threaten, depending on one's perspective—Silas into keeping Nora away from the track?

Dressed in her riding outfit with the split skirt and fitted jacket, Nora made her way across the yard, stopping to stroke the fur of a scruffy yellow cat.

He waited for her to approach and was rewarded with a smile that warmed her eyes. "Good morning, Silas."

He dipped his chin. "Nora."

"Everything all right? Seems my uncle was in a hurry to leave." If she knew the reason for the man's strange behavior, she didn't share.

"He wanted to tell me to make sure you stayed away from the track at the fair." He hadn't meant to speak so bluntly, but truth was best spoken clearly and succinctly.

Nora arched an eyebrow, her expression more defiant than annoyed. Precisely as he'd expected.

"I'm sure he did." She watched him, as though waiting for his response. When he gave none, her eyes narrowed. "And what did you tell him?"

"That I didn't see where I'd be able to tell you otherwise."

Again, the simple truth. This time, however, his words elicited a smile. One that balanced an odd mixture of coy and . . . sly. "Did you?" She drew out the words longer than necessary.

Before he could get drawn in further, Silas hurried into the barn and to the stallion's stall. He had the horse haltered and in the hallway before she caught up.

"What are you doing? He gets his oats before exercise."

"He does with you. With me, he earns his feed." Silas led the horse around her, glad the creature hadn't balked and made a fool of him.

The stallion had come to realize the sooner he did as Silas wished, the sooner he could get back to his oats. They clopped down the hall and out into the sunshine, the relentless humidity already thickening the air.

Silas moved Arrow through his routine, ignoring the way Nora clung to the rail, scrutinizing him. He had a job to do, and he couldn't let her distract him.

Like she'd done that day in the carriage shed.

No. He didn't need to think about that now. He couldn't afford to remember the way her eyes had glittered or the way she'd tilted her head up to him. Tempting.

If the plow hadn't fallen, he would have kissed her. She probably would have let him. The thought of her in his arms sent a wave of heat through him that had nothing to do with the July temperatures.

His hands worked through the task of fitting Arrow into the harness and attaching the repaired sulky behind him without need for much of his attention, allowing his thoughts to wander. Ever since the crash, the horse had been more compliant. Another confounding aspect of his personality. Silas had expected Arrow to be more skittish than ever, but the debacle had instead proven to the horse that the annoying contraption he pulled behind him didn't cause him any actual harm.

With the horse fully harnessed and fitted to the sulky in the fastest time yet, Silas led Arrow toward the corral gate. Nora opened the latch for them to pass through. He offered a nod of thanks, meeting her eyes only briefly. Did she think about what had almost happened between them?

He hadn't seen her since he'd returned her to the house, both of their nerves a bit shaken. If anything had happened to her . . .

He didn't finish the thought.

As long as she stayed away from him, she'd be safe. He'd spent hours thinking about how the plow had fallen. Despite his suspicions, he couldn't figure out how anyone would have rigged the contraption to fall on cue. Someone had to have known he would be the one to return the sulky to the shed, but not when. Perhaps it truly had been an accident. The link of chain that had once held it to the ceiling had completely rusted through.

Harnessing complete, he led Arrow onto the track. The horse remained calm. No need to lead him around again today. They could probably move on to a weighted run.

"I'm much lighter than you, you know." Nora's voice right behind his shoulder startled him. When had she gotten that close?

"Doesn't mean you need to be in the sulky." He refused to meet her gaze, but he hoped his voice conveyed all the expression he needed.

"I don't see how you intend to stop me."

Her voice held a hint of teasing, but Silas was in no mood for games. He turned to face her and her expression shifted.

"If I need to hoist you over my shoulder, Miss Fenton, don't believe I'm above doing so."

Blue eyes widened in shock. "You would do no such thing."

"I would, and more, if I thought it would keep you from harm's way."

She blinked at him a moment before her cheeks flushed. "I'm not in harm's way."

"As you weren't when he reared on you in his stall or when you were nearly overrun in the corral? Or how about when you were almost crushed in the carriage shed?" He hadn't meant for his voice to gain steam as he listed each nearly disastrous incident, but when she took a step back, he realized he'd gotten more emotional than he'd intended.

Nora searched his face. "You saved me." Her tone held threads of both defiance and appreciation, woven together too tightly to separate one from the other.

The declaration searched for a hold on him, seeking to set roots into a heart already becoming too fertile. He shook his head. "I don't want you in danger."

Arrow pawed at the ground, his patience wearing thin.

Nora moved closer, an arm's length from his side. She held his gaze. "I'm not in any danger." A quick breath lifted her shoulders. "At least, not in the way you suggest." The last words were muttered so softly he almost missed them.

What did she mean?

She stepped away, shoulders tightening into a perfect posture. "If you don't mind, I'd like to see how he makes the turns."

At least she hadn't insisted on getting on the sulky. A small victory in his favor.

He should probably get one of the boys to make the ride, but he didn't want to put anyone else at risk. Silas gathered the reins and swung up into the small seat.

Arrow's withers flinched. He nodded to Nora to step back, and she marched to the rail.

They'd take this first lap slowly. Ease into the feel of things.

Silas gathered the reins and flicked them lightly across the colt's back.

Arrow pinned his ears.

"Easy now, boy. You don't—"

The horse bolted.

❦

Arrow lurched forward and Silas let out a startled yell. Nora grabbed her skirt, ready to run to his rescue.

Silas reseated himself and took a full grip on the reins, his feet secure in the raised stirrups. Before she'd even taken a step, Arrow started the first turn.

Alarm morphed into surprise. If he ran that fast carrying Silas's heavier frame, what more could he do with only her weight? She wasn't considered a slight or petite woman, but she certainly weighed less than the bulky man hunkering on the sulky.

Arrow gained speed in the straightaway. Nora leaned forward. Impossible. His gait was perfect. His graceful neck arched as he trotted, still gaining speed.

If only she had a watch! Where was Amos when she needed him? She hadn't thought to get her own timepiece. Arrow could be breaking records on his very first run.

Implications swarmed through her mind. If he broke a record at his qualifier, there'd be an immediate interest in Emberwild. Enough for her to start booking Arrow's services during the week of the fair. Excitement built. She would need to figure out how to gain legal control of the horse. Soon. Otherwise all of her work would do nothing but benefit an uncle who would ship her off to be an old man's second wife.

Nora scrambled over the railing to get out of the way as they made the final turn and headed back toward her. Arrow had settled into his element, hooves flying. He was always at his best when given the chance to run, and even with the restrictions of the harness and sulky, he appeared to be enjoying himself.

If he'd been a Thoroughbred, Nora had no doubt Arrow would have loved to run in the derby. His hooves churned up the soft dirt on the track, and in another instant, horse and driver sped past.

Nora pressed her hands to her cheeks. If he could run like that at the fair, she'd have no problem rejuvenating Emberwild. Heart swelling with possibilities, she watched them make another lap before Silas brought Arrow to a halt in front of her.

He leapt from the seat. "Did you see that?"

She couldn't help grinning at his excitement. "He's got to be the fastest horse in the state." She rushed to him and grabbed his arms. "I'll have no trouble finding him breeders now."

"He's certainly special." Silas's voice deepened, sending her pulse into a gallop.

Then he stepped back, breaking the intensity of the moment. He looked over his shoulder and chuckled. "Think I lost my hat."

"You did indeed." Nora laughed as she walked up to Arrow and stroked his neck. "Look at you. I always knew you'd fly like an arrow."

Arrow bobbed his head, seeming pleased with the attention.

"How about we get those oats now, boy?"

Arrow nickered as though he understood exactly what Silas had said. She tilted her head. "Hmm. Seems making him work for his breakfast wasn't such a bad idea after all."

"You thought it was a bad idea?" He cocked a mischievous brow.

"Not now."

Silas chuckled again and took Arrow's halter. "I'll get him unhooked, then I need to find my hat."

Following along behind him, Nora watched as Silas dropped the sulky in the corral and unhitched the horse, feeling a bit unneeded. She tried not to let the notion bother her. Today had been a great success, and Silas deserved credit for all he'd accomplished.

"Shall we, Miss Fenton?" Silas stood at the corral gate, arm extended. The levity in his tone surprised her, and she couldn't help but play along.

"Why certainly, Mr. Cavallero. I'd be most pleased to accompany you and your handsome companion." She looped her hand through his elbow and settled at his side.

There was something oddly comfortable about the gesture, as though she belonged on his arm. She quickly dismissed the feeling. No sense in ruining the fun of the moment.

"I do believe this particular establishment is rather limited in their selections, but I hear the locals love it." He wiggled his eyebrows at her.

She did her best to keep a straight face and failed. "Do they now? Must be some quality oats."

He gave a serious nod. "So I hear. Though they say there's no accounting for taste."

Nora leaned into his side as they walked back toward the barn. When had she ever felt so at ease with a man escorting her?

Somehow, walking with Silas at her side, her beloved colt trailing placidly behind them and the smells of hay and horseflesh in the air, everything felt right with the world.

And that was a serious problem.

chapter
NINETEEN

She needed to tell him. Nora paced in her room, her fingers fidgeting in the folds of the gray dress she'd chosen to wear to tonight's supper with Mr. Dale. The implications of the meeting sent a wave of unease through her middle.

First she had to do right by Silas. Then she could deal with her uncle and mother's plans.

She'd meant to tell Silas the truth. Instead she'd let herself get swept away in the pleasure of his company. She'd found too much joy laughing as he'd escorted her across the yard as though they were a couple on their way to a big-city restaurant and not two dirty horse trainers headed into the barn.

If she let herself be honest, she'd enjoyed the appreciation in his gaze as they shared the joy of Arrow's success. She couldn't stand to turn that look of admiration into distrust.

The moment hadn't been right.

Like it hadn't been right any time in the two days since.

Nora clamped her fists together. In two days he would leave for the fair. She had to tell him she suspected her father had stolen the Cavalleros' horse. Tonight. As soon as she suffered through the meal and completed her duty to her mother of at least trying to entertain a possible suitor, she'd tell Silas. If there was any chance her family and his could be connected by a terrible tragedy, then they both deserved to know the truth.

Because the more she grew to care for Silas, the heavier the weight of her suspicions pressed on her.

Nora rubbed her temples to ward off a headache. She had to tell him before he returned from the Neshoba County Fair and found Ember returned from stud loan. With Arrow showing such promise, Silas would of course want to see Arrow's sire. Would Silas recognize the stallion as his father's lost colt? Would he publicly accuse her family?

He couldn't prove anything if he did.

The thought brought an immediate wave of guilt. He shouldn't *have* to prove anything. If Nora dug through her father's office and discovered Ember had belonged to Silas's family, she'd need to give him back. It was the right thing to do.

So why was doing the right thing so hard?

Questions dug claws into her composure, causing her to pace faster and her head to pound more furiously.

What would that mean for Arrow? Or any of the other colts he'd sired? Would Silas seek retribution from all they'd gained from Ember?

Nora made another lap past her dressing table, the writing desk, her washbasin, and back in front of the hearth. Her stomach clenched, making her feel nauseated.

She needed to force herself to think of something else.

The only thing that came to mind was Mr. Dale.

Her unwanted suitor. Not something she really wanted to consider, but yet, she couldn't help but wonder. What would the man her uncle had invited to supper be like? Fat and balding, she was sure. A man in search of a nursemaid for his son. She could refuse him. Certainly Amos couldn't force her into a convenient marriage. Could he?

She twisted her fingers. This line of thinking wasn't helping the condition of her stomach.

If Silas ever found out she'd harbored suspicions her father could have been involved in what had happened and yet never told him, he might never forgive her.

Yet by telling him, she'd be putting her family, her home, and her entire future at risk.

Why had Father cursed her with this burden? Ignorance would have spared her the dilemma over lying. Or ruining her family.

Guilt tugged at her. Was she really willing to keep secrets to maintain her family's reputation and livelihood? Like her father?

Nora rubbed the tight muscles in her neck and pulled in a calming breath. Then another. There was only one way to know the truth and stop these cyclical questions. She would find her father's paperwork on Ember and set her mind at ease. Once she knew her father had nothing to do with the misfortune that had befallen Silas, then she could put the nagging voice to rest.

A weight lifted and she stopped pacing. A good plan. Sensible. Unless of course she discovered that Father had been involved after all.

Then what?

She'd worry about that later. First, the truth.

Truth, however, seemed to be lacking in the Fenton house these days. Not only were Mother and Uncle Amos continuing their match of undertones and guarded glances, but Mother had grown increasingly more evasive. As though she kept trying to tell Nora things without actually telling her anything. Leaving her daughter to sort out riddles.

Her guilty conscience had led her to believe that maybe Mother knew Father's secret all along, but none of Nora's subtle queries or hints in that direction brought any revelations.

Either Mother had been meant for the stage or she truly believed there was nothing suspicious about Ember and how he'd come to the farm.

Nora's own worries had made her see ghosts where none existed.

The specters her mother feared were perhaps more worrisome. Father's secrets tainted the past. Mother's could hinder the future.

In a way, Silas had been right. Something was wrong at Emberwild. It stirred beneath the surface like a monster slowly rising from the depths. Indistinguishable yet dangerous.

A knock sounded at the door, startling her. She swallowed bitterness that gathered in the back of her throat. She could get through this evening. Be the well-mannered daughter Mother wanted her to be.

At least for tonight. In the morning, she'd do her best to set everything to rights.

Nora fortified herself and opened the door to find her mother dressed in a high-necked black dress with lace trim and two layers of pearls. When had she gotten that dress?

Mother frowned. "You look terrible."

"I have a headache."

"Of course you do." Mother sighed as she bustled in and shut the door. "But that won't get you out of supper with Mr. Dale. He's already arrived."

Her stomach fluttered again, threatening to heave up what little she'd eaten earlier in the day. Maybe it wouldn't be all bad if her family name was ruined. At least then she wouldn't have to entertain suitors nearly old enough to be her father.

"Sit." Mother pointed to her dressing chair. Her assessing gaze swept over the room Nora had failed to keep tidy but thankfully she withheld a comment on Nora's sloppiness.

Nora plopped onto the delicate chair and studied herself in the mirror. Perhaps she hadn't tried to look her best, but "terrible" might be a bit of an overstatement.

Mother gasped. "Nora! What have you done to your hair?"

Nora's fingers immediately darted to the shortened length she'd thus far managed to keep from Mother's notice.

Mother tugged pins from Nora's hair and released the damp strands that now reached just past her shoulders rather than to the small of her back.

"It was hot, and all that hair . . ." Nora let the rest of the excuse fall away. It had been hot, yes, but she'd also taken the opportunity to exert her independence over custom. The shorter hair had seemed to go perfectly with the divided skirt.

Shaking her head, Mother managed to braid, twist, and pin Nora's hair into a surprisingly fashionable design, then gave her shoulder a pat.

No lecture? Nora stared at her mother a moment. She must be more nervous about this supper than she let on if she wasn't going to admonish Nora for cutting her hair.

"I know you chose that dress out of spite. It won't work." Mother flung open the wardrobe. "I'll take tardiness over dowdiness."

Spite? She'd not chosen a dress out of spite. She'd worn this same one several times in the past weeks and Mother hadn't minded.

Mother riffled through the clothes hanging in Nora's wardrobe. "Where's that green dress I bought you a few summers ago?"

Nora frowned. "We're still in mourning."

Mother located the sage gown and shook out the fabric. "This deep color is suitable for a daughter half a year after her father's passing. Especially one entertaining a suitor."

Half a year? They'd scarcely passed into the fourth month. Not that she would mention Mother's miscalculation.

Just as her heart had changed in the months she'd been working with Silas. Strange how life could upend in ways one never—

"Nora Marie Fenton, are you ignoring me?" Mother stood with her hand on her hip, her foot tapping impatiently.

Nora shot to her feet and took the dress from Mother's fingers. If Mother wanted her to wear green instead of gray, then she'd wear green. What would her dress color matter if the man found her as unpleasant as most men did?

Except for Silas. He seemed to genuinely enjoy her presence.

She stepped behind the dressing screen, pulled the gray dress over her head, and swapped it for the other, trying not to muss Mother's efforts with her hair. Now wasn't the time to think about Silas. But she had to admit she hadn't even tried to hide her quirks or her opinions and he still smiled warmly at her.

She stepped out from behind the screen and waited as Mother tugged and situated until the green gown fell in the correct folds.

"A few years out of fashion, but it will do." Mother pinched at the puffed sleeves as though she could deflate them. Then she narrowed her eyes at Nora's middle. "Did you tighten your stays well enough?"

She thought she had. "Does the dress not fit properly?"

Mother waved the question away. "Nothing more I can do. We need to hurry." She opened the door and gestured Nora into the hall. "Remember your manners. Speak when addressed to, and if the opportunity presents itself, be sure to assert your attributes."

"Like what?" She'd heard a great deal about her faults over the years. She'd like to know what Mother considered her attributes. She suspected Mr. Dale wouldn't consider her work with horses to be one of her better qualities. She couldn't cook and didn't care much for housework.

Mother shook her head, declining to answer that question as well.

Nora worried her upper lip between her teeth. She had always been quick with figures. Perhaps that would count.

She chided herself. She had no interest in spouting off her qualities like an auctioneer showing a filly. What did she care if the man found her appealing? She rather wanted him not to.

They descended the stairway, male voices drifting up from below. Had Mr. Dale brought his son? "How old is the boy?" Might as well prepare herself if she'd be expected to entertain a toddler. He wouldn't bring a child that young to supper, would he?

"Young Michael is eight, and staying with his aunt," Mother whispered as they reached the first floor.

They entered the parlor to find Amos laughing with a tall man over by the cold hearth. Before he could notice her, Nora took the chance to assess the fellow Amos—and apparently Mother, by the way she kept patting Nora's arm encouragingly—considered a match for her.

Dressed in a fine suit, Mr. Dale wasn't at all the balding, pudgy man she'd envisioned. Not even a smattering of gray lightened his full, dark hair. As though feeling her eyes on him, he shifted his gaze to meet hers. Dark eyes lit with a smile that spread over what Nora had to admit was a pleasing face.

His smile widened and her cheeks heated. Had he guessed her thoughts?

Mother obviously had because she squeezed Nora's arm and wore the largest smile Nora had seen in months. Amos practically beamed. If he grinned any wider they wouldn't need to burn the gas lamps.

Lovely. Nora withheld a groan. She really needed to get better at shielding her thoughts from others.

Amos stepped forward, chest puffed like a rooster. "Let me introduce my niece, Miss Nora Fenton."

Nora held out her hand.

"George Dale." The man bowed over their clasped hands. "A pleasure to make your acquaintance."

She inclined her head, but found her mouth incapable of forming words. Amos gestured toward the seating area while Mother excused herself to move the meal she'd spent all afternoon preparing to the dining room.

After so long eating simply, Nora couldn't imagine what specialties Mother had prepared. Especially since she'd been banished from the kitchen in order to make sure the dining room, the library, and the parlor were all in pristine condition for their company.

Nora took a seat, and Mr. Dale settled on the opposite end of the settee while Amos took a gentleman's chair.

"Your uncle tells me you favor horses." Mr. Dale smiled as he practically lounged on the settee.

His statement astonished her as much as his relaxed demeanor. Though of course something like this wouldn't make him nervous. He'd been married before. Probably courted plenty of women.

Nora had been socially outcast since she'd insulted the Cromwell family in front of all the people of standing in the county. She could do this. For Mother's sake, at least.

"I favor horses a great deal." Not surprising since she lived on a horse farm. Nora did, however, wonder why Mother or Amos had mentioned Nora's love of horses given the inevitable direction of the conversation. Did Mother think Nora would let the man believe she only enjoyed the occasional sidesaddle ride?

"As do I. I'm thinking of purchasing a few Thoroughbreds and trying my hand at racing."

She couldn't help the spark of interest that coursed through her. "I'm sure that would be an exciting venture." She smiled brightly. "I have a bit of experience at race training myself, though trotters are different, of course."

Heavens. She sounded like a fool. At least now the man knew she both enjoyed working with horses and had no qualms about sharing her opinions.

Besides, this would be the last evening she'd have to share his company.

Mr. Dale smiled just as brightly, the crinkles at the corners of his eyes remarkably attractive. "I look forward to hearing your ideas. Perhaps you'll even have a few on how I can keep Michael from trying to jockey them. I can scarcely keep the boy from riding off during his lessons."

Amos gestured at Nora fondly. "Perhaps the boy has something in common with Nora. She always did prefer riding to studying."

"You'll have plenty of time for riding at Oakwood, Miss Fenton." Mr. Dale's expression seemed open and honest. "If the notion suits you."

The man spoke as though her coming to his new home in Georgia had already been decided. Heat wormed through her middle.

"Mr. Dale's late wife—a fine lady I had the pleasure of meeting only once, I'm afraid—enjoyed spending her time out of doors as well." Amos flicked his gaze to the man sharing her couch. "Isn't that correct?"

"Painting and tending her garden, mostly." He chuckled fondly. "I told her we had plenty of gardeners, but she always found such pleasure in tending her flowers herself that I couldn't deny her wishes."

Would he let her enjoy horses the same way?

The traitorous thought pounced on her out of nowhere. Certainly she couldn't be considering this man she'd only just met simply because he'd let his late wife garden?

What had gotten into her? Nora straightened, her discomfort growing. Had Amos told Mr. Dale to say those things? Had they planned ways to try to manipulate her into liking this stranger who her mother knew nothing about?

Now she was being silly. Her uncle would never do such a thing. Had she truly become that cynical?

Both men were looking at her.

Nora's face heated. "I'm sure she appreciated that."

Amos looked at her, assessing. "Certainly."

"If you will join me," Mother called from the doorway, "the dining room is prepared."

Glad for a moment to gather her thoughts, Nora accepted Mr. Dale's offered arm and allowed him to guide her from the parlor. Amos offered to escort Mother, and after only a slight hesitation, she slipped her hand through the crook of his arm.

Mr. Dale kept an easy pace as they followed the other two into the dining room where he pulled out a chair for her. Mother had chosen to leave Father's place at the head of the table empty, instead situating four sets of china and silverware in pairs facing one another.

Nora expected Mr. Dale to sit at her side, but he rounded the table and sat across from her instead. She fidgeted under the table as Amos held out the seat next to her for Mother. With the man across from her, he'd be better able to keep her in his direct gaze and thus notice any flaws in her manners.

At least he wouldn't be too close.

They settled in their places and Amos asked grace over the food in the most longwinded prayer Nora had ever heard.

Once she lifted her head, she got a good look at the source of the scents that had been enticing her stomach the entire time she'd been waiting for Amos to finish. Glazed ham, squash, peas, butterbeans, cornbread, and Mother's biscuits graced the table. They hadn't had a spread like this since Mother had hosted Christmas two years ago.

Did she feel she had something to prove to Mr. Dale? Nora brushed the notion aside. Mother had always enjoyed cooking. Perhaps she missed preparing large meals or had overplanned. At least they'd gone to the butcher and grocer this week. She couldn't imagine serving Mr. Dale salt pork and canned squash.

Nora forked a slice of ham from the plate Mr. Dale held out for her. Plates filled, they began the meal with the mundane topics usually covered in polite company. Until Amos shattered all pleasantries.

"Nora will be quite happy serving as your wife, George." Amos smiled amicably.

A chunk of cornbread lodged in Nora's throat and she gagged. Her eyes watered as she struggled to swallow.

"She isn't much use in the kitchen, I'm afraid," Amos continued, ignoring Nora. "But as you're a man of means, I suppose that wouldn't cause a hindrance for you."

Nora forced the food down and dabbed the corner of her mouth with her napkin, unable to keep her eyes from darting to Mr. Dale.

Mr. Dale nodded along, his expression unreadable as he kept his focus on his plate.

Nora turned to her mother, who chewed thoughtfully. Not even the first hint of outrage at such an improper statement marred Mother's features.

Amos smiled warmly at Mother. "Her mother and I are prepared to send her to you in a matter of weeks, should you so desire."

Send her?

Weeks?

He chuckled. "Though if you're inclined to tarry here a few days longer, I'm sure we can send for the preacher and she can accompany you home, saving you the trouble of returning later."

He couldn't be serious! Fire raced up Nora's neck and over her cheeks. Mr. Dale must have noticed because he cleared his throat.

"All things to discuss in due time, yes?" He cast Nora an apologetic smile. "The lady and I should get to know one another a little first."

Nora let out a relieved breath even as Amos tried to stop a frown from turning down his lips. Mother remained infuriatingly calm. Did she have nothing to say on the matter?

"Though I will say, Miss Fenton"—Mr. Dale straightened his black necktie—"I'm known as a man prone to direct speaking." He set his fork on the table. "Therefore, I believe I should make my intentions clear so that you may be well informed when making a decision."

Nora blinked, unsure how to respond to such a statement.

"I'm looking for a woman who's interested in helping me with my son, managing the employees of my household, and providing me with amicable companionship. I'm not looking for a long courtship, but rather for a lady I believe I can form a friendship with based on mutual interests and personalities. From what your uncle has told me, I believe you and I could be such a match."

Nora's mind whirled. He wanted a friend to run his house and help with his son. And in exchange he would offer her freedom to do mostly as she wished?

She cast a glance at Mother, who met her gaze with a meaningful look.

A business deal, then. Despite her distaste for such arrangements, she had to admit the notion held some merit. Especially given the troubles she faced at Emberwild.

Would she be able to make any negotiations in this deal? Like keeping Arrow?

"You're of a reasonable age, as well," Mr. Dale continued when Nora still couldn't formulate a response. "Something I find quite favorable. Most women your age are widows."

Nora gaped at him and had to snap her mouth shut when Mother pinched her under the table.

Had the man really just stated he wanted an old maid?

"Young women tend to be a bit too flighty for my tastes. I'd prefer the companionship of someone more mature. The age difference will be beneficial for my son as well."

So much for getting to know one another first. Heat drained from her, replaced by a cold logic. Well, the man had said he was blunt. After so many secrets and clandestine glances, she had to admit she found Mr. Dale's manner refreshing.

If Mr. Dale could be trusted, she could set herself up for a life that didn't include scrubbing floors, fighting to be out in the barns, or being a drain on her mother.

Nora swallowed a lump in her throat. She'd also enter a life without her beloved Emberwild, possibly her favorite horse, and she'd never see Silas—

She cut the thought short. No. She'd never have any kind of future with a horse trainer merely passing through. Their shared glances and the things he did to her heart were fleeting moments of emotion that were impractical and could never last.

Though how could she be sure Mr. Dale would actually do as he said? Once wed, a woman lost all control—what little she had—to a husband.

"I see we've given Miss Fenton much to think about." Mr. Dale offered a charming smile and then turned to Amos. "What do you think about the Pennsylvania Railroad's claim that their train can run from New York to Chicago in eighteen hours?"

Nora missed Amos's response. Blood pounded in her ears.

"Remember what I told you," Mother whispered. "A woman with the ear of a man in power has power herself. Mr. Dale offers you far more freedom than I fear you will ever find here." She squeezed Nora's hand under the table. "For both our sakes, I pray you agree." She squeezed harder, nearly crushing Nora's hand. "Before it's too late."

chapter TWENTY

Neshoba County Fair
July 24, 1905

Where had all these people come from? Silas hefted Mrs. Fenton's trunk on his shoulder and worked his way through the river of humanity like a salmon trying to swim upstream. Men in straw hats and ladies in shirtwaists and skirts pressed together in a rather undignified way, all headed to find seats at the pavilion where Mississippi political candidates would give their speeches.

Asa had told Silas that the *Oxford Eagle* reported that more than twenty thousand people attended the 1904 fair, creating a temporary town in the fields eight miles outside of Philadelphia, Mississippi. Silas had doubted the man at the time.

Turned out he'd been wrong.

Families piled into the two hotels constructed solely for the event or stayed in tents or wagons of their own. A few families had built private cabins situated around the square.

Never in his years had he seen something like this.

He'd expected a day of picnicking families and the showing of a few prize livestock. Not a weeklong event with thousands in attendance. No wonder Nora had been so intent on Arrow making a good showing here.

The metal clasps of the trunk dug into his shoulder as he had to sidestep a boy of about eight begging his mother to forgo the political speech and buy him popcorn on the midway. Silas grunted and repositioned the heavy trunk. Why couldn't they have parked the carriage closer to the hotel?

Ahead of him, Silas caught a glimpse of Nora's straw hat with bright blue ribbons and quickened his pace. At nearly five months after her father's passing, Mrs. Fenton had declared Nora was no longer in mourning. Something he suspected had more to do with the new suitor and less to do with Nora's state of grief. Mrs. Fenton remained in shades of gray, but had discarded the heavy blacks he'd glimpsed her wearing on the few occasions she'd ventured out onto the porch.

The fact that the family had decided to travel out for such an event had surprised him. Not that he was one to speak on how affluent families were supposed to adhere to social norms of mourning periods. Perhaps a return to something festive would do them all good.

For Nora's sake, he hoped that would be true. Poor woman always toted an invisible burden.

"Hey, now." Amos suddenly appeared at his side, ducking out of the way of the trunk. "Careful you don't take my head off."

Silas shifted the weight. "Apologies, sir. This crowd."

The man chuckled. "Good turnout this year. Watch your step there." He gestured to the wooden steps at the front of the two-story hotel.

Inside, more people crowded the lobby. Silas lowered the trunk so as not to bump anyone and rested it on the floor next to his boot while he waited. Across the room, Amos secured the family's rooms from a harried-looking fellow at a long desk situated at the back wall.

For all the heat and press of the crowd, anticipation permeated the air.

Nora spotted Silas and slipped from her mother's side while the woman spoke with Amos. The brothers must have been very close, with as much care as Amos took with his brother's widow and her daughter.

"Exciting, isn't it?" Nora's eyes sparkled.

"I suppose."

She fanned her face, cheeks a warm pink. "Once Arrow qualifies, we'll want to run him in the daily races as well. As many as we can. There's a premium for best trotter or pacer, and that will gain Emberwild recognition."

"Yes, ma'am."

Nora glanced around the busy room and then eased closer, her arm brushing against his. "There's something I've been wanting to speak to you about. I'll meet you in the barn this afternoon so we can talk."

Her voice held a grave note Silas found disconcerting. "About what?"

Nora stepped away from him as Amos turned their direction. Had she not heard him, or was she pretending they hadn't been speaking? When she moved away without answering, he decided the latter.

Amos gestured for Silas to follow, appearing to be in a finer mood than Silas had ever seen him. Silas hefted the trunk once more—the women must have packed for a month—and made apologies as he picked his way through the crowd and up a flight of stairs to the second floor.

"Drop the trunk." Amos pointed to the third door down the hall. "I'll get it from here."

He deposited his load onto the wooden floor and then stretched his back. Though the place must contain dozens of rooms, the hotel was plain in nature with wooden walls, floors, and ceilings. No carpets or decorations. But then, why put such lavishness into a hotel that was only used during one week out of the year?

Amos unlocked two rooms—one for him and one for the women to share. Feeling out of place, Silas waited with his hands in his pockets until Amos dismissed him with a wave. He made his way back downstairs and out into the busy square. The heat of the late-July sun beat down on him, and he removed his hat to swipe the sweat from his brow.

The pavilion had filled with fairgoers awaiting a politician to spout promises of a better future. Children darted through the adults' legs, many of them begging to go to the midway and see the exhibits.

He turned east and headed toward the barns erected for the horses and livestock. The smell of pies and roasted meats hung on the sultry air, but by the time he pressed his way through the throng and neared the livestock area, the familiar musky notes of horseflesh and red clay greeted his senses.

Silas spotted Roger among the men making camp in the open field behind the barn. He'd pulled their wagon around and begun erecting the tents where they would camp for the next four days. A tent to himself in the open air was something he'd once been quite accustomed to on the ranch. Nights he'd spent with his father under the stars ranked among his fondest memories.

"Already stable the horses?" Silas asked as he approached.

Roger thumbed over his shoulder. "Carriage horses are in barn two. The colt's in the race barn." He bent to hammer a stake into the ground.

Silas set to work erecting his own tent, his mind more on Nora than his task. What had she been talking about? More instructions on how to handle the horse, no doubt. The way she'd spoken added mystery to her words. Why not just come out and tell him directly? Women. Always edging around a topic rather than speaking outright. Maybe they enjoyed making men guess their thoughts.

Tent completed, he tossed his small travel bag inside and tied the flaps. He should probably head to the barn to check on Arrow anyway. No telling how worked up the creature had become in the new surroundings. He could wait for Nora before checking in with the breed registry representative.

Apparently Amos had decided to let Nora come to the track after all. Would that change the agreement they'd made? Or did Nora once again plan to defy her uncle?

He hoped that fancy new suitor knew what he was getting into with Nora Fenton.

Silas pushed the thought from his mind. None of his business.

He entered the long barn filled with trotters, pacers, and saddle horses that had come to test their speed. Horses whinnied to one another from behind their chest-high doors. At least they hadn't merely used rope gates. He wouldn't trust Arrow with such a flimsy enclosure.

Hopefully, they'd stalled him away from any other stallions. He should have been here for that, not hauling a trunk for the women.

At the far end of the barn, he spotted a feminine silhouette near one of the stalls. Dressed in a deep blue skirt and white shirtwaist with a matching bow at her throat, Nora leaned over the stall door. Silas slowed his steps, watching her.

". . . and you'll be great."

Silas grinned. If anyone could calm the colt, it would be Nora and her sweet assurances. Who wouldn't want to do his best with a lady like that cheering him on?

Nora turned, spotting him. She stepped back from the gate and clasped her hands together. Had he made her uncomfortable by not announcing his presence?

Light filtered through the slats on the barn, creating lines across her face. She didn't offer a smile.

More evidence that whatever she wanted to say caused her distress. When she didn't speak he eased closer. "Everything all right?"

Nora nodded, though she twisted her fingers together in a fashion that said otherwise.

"Arrow will be fine. He's already looking more settled than I expected." He smiled. "Thanks to you, I'm sure."

She adjusted her hat and looked at the feisty colt trying to snag one of her ribbons with his lips. "He means so much to me. After his dam died, I would sneak out at night and stay with him so he wouldn't be lonely." She blew out a breath. "Father refused to put him with another mare, saying he was well enough weaned, but I couldn't bear the thought of the poor creature being so alone."

Something in her tone made him wonder if she'd been there to gain comfort as much as offer it. He glanced at Arrow as he nudged Nora's shoulder, seeking her attention.

"You certainly have a bond with him." Silas regarded her solemnly. "I promise to do my very best." He shifted his stance. "For you."

Her gaze slammed into his, and uncertainty crinkled the corners of her eyes. He shouldn't have been so forward. How had he allowed himself to let down his guard every time he was around this woman? He was her employee. A temporary one at that.

Despite her steady gaze, he couldn't bring himself to apologize. He *would* do his best by her, no matter her feelings toward him. She and Arrow both deserved as much. More, though he had nothing better to give.

"I know you will." She sighed and stepped closer. "There's something I've been meaning to discuss with you." Her chin dropped and she looked at the floor. "You must know I have a care for you, but I . . ."

His pulse ratcheted as she hesitated. This wasn't the direction he'd expected the conversation to go.

Her gaze met his once more. The muscles in her jaw firmed, tightening against her words.

Of course. He should have seen this coming. After the moment they'd shared in the carriage shed, he'd suspected she might have let herself be attracted to him. Attraction that could never bloom into anything more. Especially given her station and the suitor who'd come to call.

He should save her the embarrassment of having to tell him. "I understand." He offered the best reassuring smile he could muster, hoping she could see he held nothing against her. "I have a care for you as well, but I recognize that our relationship must remain professional in nature. There's no need to worry I'll cause issues for your suitors."

The color drained from her cheeks. She opened her mouth and then closed it again, flustered.

Had he spoken too directly?

"I didn't . . . I'm not . . ." She huffed. "What I mean to say is—"

"There you are!" Amos's voice boomed down the corridor. "Is it time for his run already?"

Nora stepped back, her rattled countenance instantly hardening into aloof calm. "If you'll excuse me, now that I've seen Arrow for myself, I'll be on my way."

Amos gave his niece a nod as she passed, then his features dipped into a frown. Once she was out of earshot, Amos leveled a flat stare at Silas. "Didn't I tell you to keep her away from the barns?"

Frustration boiled in his stomach. Amos had been the one to bring the women along with him in the first place. "As her kin, shouldn't you be the one to tell her where she can and can't go? Especially seeing as how you're the one who brought her here?"

Surprise drew Amos's head back. "Our relationship is in a delicate balance."

That didn't give the man the right to try to pin unreasonable responsibilities on him. "And our relationship is one of an employer and a hireling. Miss Fenton is determined to make sure her horse is well, and there's nothing I can do about that."

Amos regarded him for a moment. "I suppose you're right. I shouldn't have tried to put you in a position to engage with her more than necessary." He snapped open his timepiece and checked the hour. "The ladies will be entering the baking contest this afternoon, and I have an engagement. I trust you can handle the registration trials on your own? Mr. Sutherland will be marking the official paperwork."

Without waiting for a response, Amos turned on his heel and strode from the barn.

Silas groaned. The Fentons, without a doubt, were the most capricious family he'd ever met.

⁓

In the large exhibition tent erected to showcase all manner of baked goods and crafts, Nora impatiently waited with her barely passable entry for the "best six biscuits baked with Big Star Flour" contest clutched tightly in her hands. She didn't need to see any of the other contestants' trays to know she'd never win. Why Mother insisted she enter, she'd never know. If she'd actually wanted Nora to have a shot at winning, she should have baked them herself.

At least they'd come to the fair. For that, Nora would bake two dozen biscuits with burned bottoms and doughy centers.

She and Mother stood next to the quilting display where Mother soaked up the praise of a small handful of younger women fawning over her cathedral quilt pattern. The outing was doing Mother good, Nora reminded herself. She shouldn't feel so anxious to cut Mother's time short in favor of hurrying to her own desires.

They hadn't come to the fair in the past three years, and Nora hadn't expected they would this year either. Mother's abrupt announcement yesterday that they would accompany Amos had put everyone at Emberwild into a flurry of activity to prepare.

She'd do her best not to complain or upset Mother's surprisingly good nature. Even if she did have to stand around in the exhibition tent instead of staying at the barn. What time was it, anyway? It had to be getting late into the afternoon by now. She didn't want to miss the trial.

What had to be a quarter hour later, Nora could no longer contain her fidgeting.

How long would Mother carry on about quilting? If they didn't leave very soon, they would miss Arrow's run entirely. Mother, however, seemed in no hurry to leave the company of the gaggle of women. Disturbing her wouldn't go over well. She would consider the interruption rude, and besides—why ruin her fun?

Deciding it best to take the opportunity presented, Nora slipped away to place her tray on the biscuit table and then bustled out of the tent before she could be noticed and drawn into the conversation. Mother would forgive her.

Outside, she adjusted her hat to better shield her face from the glaring sun and ducked through the crowd to the racetrack. By the time she arrived, men already had horses attached to sulkies and the gleaming animals bobbed their heads in the heat, ready to begin.

For the life of her, she didn't understand why they didn't conduct the qualifiers and races in the mornings when it was cooler. She scanned the unfamiliar faces but didn't see Roger or Silas anywhere.

Where was Arrow?

Silas must be taking extra care harnessing him. The man was always fastidious with everything he did. The thought of the way he'd looked at her while giving her permission to toss him aside in favor of another man twisted her heart.

Heat flooded through her. She'd botched that conversation in more ways than one.

"I have a care for you . . . no need to worry I'll cause issues for your suitors."

He had a care for her. Had he merely echoed the words she'd foolishly spoken first? She'd meant to say that she cared about what had happened to his father and that he was a good man who deserved to know the truth. Starting with the truth that she suspected her father had been involved in some way. Instead she'd announced that she had feelings for him. What else could he have said without embarrassing her?

Regardless, he had made a logical point. Silas would be leaving soon. And even if he planned to stay, Mother—and Amos—would never allow the match.

Nora stepped out of the way of a youth leading a pretty bay filly that seemed completely comfortable in her harness.

She needed to think about her future, starting with Arrow. If he ran well today, he could impress buyers. Harness racing had continued to gain popularity and could well save Emberwild.

Of course, if she increased the property's prosperity, then Amos would be all the less likely to want to relinquish his hold.

And all the sooner marry her off.

She thought back to her encounter with Mr. Dale. Any woman would want the kind of security and easy life he offered, wouldn't they?

So why couldn't she find any excitement for the opportunity?

More thoughts to contemplate later. She must focus on the problems of today. After the trial she'd speak with Silas, and then she would leave him to his duties while she tended to her own.

A commotion in the field to the side of the barn drew her attention. A familiar voice shouted, and her heart plummeted.

Silas.

Arrow.

She gathered her skirt and raced around the side of the barn to find Silas hanging on to the reins as Arrow reared. Men around them shouted, further agitating the horse. Didn't they know they were only making things worse?

Pushing through the gathering crowd, Nora gained Silas's side just as he finally got Arrow's front hooves on the ground. The horse snorted, his eyes wild.

"What happened?"

Silas cut her a wary glance. "Spooked."

As she could clearly see. Nora eased closer, talking to Arrow in calming tones until he placed his muzzle into her palm and released a deep snort. His wild eyes rolled toward the men. "Easy, boy. Easy."

"I don't think he's ready to run today." Silas looped the reins around his hands, his face pinched. "He's too worked up, and I don't want another accident."

"Let me take him."

Silas's fist clenched, but before he could refute her, Nora gripped his arm.

"Please. I know all the reasons not to. I do." She clenched tighter, willing him to see the importance. "I'll wear trousers and a cap. No one will know I'm not one of the boys. I won't race him. Just the trials. If we could wait a few days, I would. But you know I have to have an official record, and that can only happen today."

He hesitated, uncertainty in his gaze.

"You know he will only trust me or you, and while he runs well with you, I'm much lighter."

Silas pressed his lips together.

"Please, Silas. I can do this. I was riding Arrow long before you showed up. If I'm to have any hope of saving Emberwild and a chance at a future of my own making, I *must* get Arrow to run today."

He glanced at the horse, then back to her, a war blazing behind his deep brown eyes. Her breath snagged in her throat. How she hated that every decision she wanted to make had to be ruled by a man.

Silas heaved a sigh, then gave her an almost imperceptible nod.

Relief swept through her and before she could think better of it, she lifted onto her toes and placed a kiss on his cheek, surprising them both. Then she dashed away in the most unladylike fashion to grab the trousers she'd stashed inside one of her petticoats for just such an occasion.

TWENTY-ONE

Nora would be fine, Silas told himself for at least the fifteenth time as he walked Arrow toward the track. Red dust hung on the air, clinging to men and horses alike. Arrow bobbed his head, pulling against the bridle in Silas's hand as he led the horse away from the barn and closer to what was probably a terrible decision.

Please, Lord. Let her be fine.

He didn't see another choice if they wanted Arrow to run today. Nora was the only person who could calm him. If she would ever get here. Where was she?

He glanced back to the barn again, walking as slowly as possible. He'd managed to convince Mr. Sutherland—the man who would officially record Arrow's time trial—to give the horse another half hour before they started the run. Thankfully, the man had been the agreeable sort. But how long could it possibly take for Nora to run back to the hotel and change?

Had she been caught?

Pounding footsteps sounded behind them and Arrow pranced sideways. A figure appeared dressed in an oversized brown hat, a baggy shirt, and trousers. Silas tensed. The last thing he needed was another fellow making Arrow spook.

The horse snorted.

"Hey, boy. Don't—"

Arrow leaned forward, nostrils quivering. Silas reached to grab the boy. Arrow nickered, knocking the boy's hat up, his ears pricked forward in greeting.

The kid giggled.

Nora.

Silas blew out a breath. He should have known. The getup had fooled even him. Maybe they'd get away with this after all.

She cast him a coy look from under the brim of her cap, bright eyes sparkling and a mischievous grin tugging at her rosy lips.

Silas's mouth dried, his throat refusing to form words.

The woman was mad. Totally mad and brave and beautiful—even dressed as she was with her hair stuffed under her cap.

He grabbed her fingers, giving them a squeeze. If something happened to her . . .

"Please," he whispered. "Be careful."

She nodded solemnly, chin ducked so that he couldn't read her features under the cap. "I will. Promise."

He released her, the tightness in his chest refusing to recede. She would try, but anything could happen. Part of him wanted to refuse. Insist she forget about the run and stay safe. But to try to cage Nora wouldn't be protecting her. He'd only be smothering her instead.

He tried his best not to watch too closely as she scrambled into the sulky. Once she was settled, Silas guided the colt to the starting point on the track and gave him a final pat before releasing him into Nora's care.

Please keep her safe. My heart can't withstand losing her.

The truth of the prayer pressed upon him. Somewhere along the way, he'd handed his heart over to a feisty woman who defied expectations and fought against the constraints of every restriction yoked upon her. A realization hit him. He'd come to Mississippi to find the truth about his father and ended up finding what his mother had wanted instead—a woman to love and devote his life to.

Determination stiffened his spine. He might not be able to offer her anything more than his heart, but if they made it through this run, he wouldn't give up without trying. If nothing else, she would know that she'd captivated his affections. Wealthy suitor or not.

Mr. Sutherland stood by the rail, attempting to hold his paperwork still in the breeze. His straw hat sat on hair nearly the same color, and a wide smile lit his brown eyes as Silas approached.

"Fine-looking colt you got there."

"Thank you, sir. The Fenton family is quite proud of him."

Mr. Sutherland looked around behind Silas. "Ah, there's Mr. Fenton now."

Silas kept his eyes trained on the track where Nora waited, both to make sure she remained safe and to lessen the chances that Amos would read any deception in his eyes. So much for leaving the run to him to handle.

Amos joined them at the fence and slapped Mr. Sutherland on the shoulder. "Good day for a run, isn't it, John?"

Mr. Sutherland returned the greeting with a sound agreement and then produced a watch from his jacket pocket. He gave a wave to let the jockey know he was ready.

"Who's that boy driving?" Amos asked, squinting toward the sulky.

Silas kept his voice level. "The only other person Arrow would allow near him. We had a time getting that horse settled."

Amos opened his mouth to say something, a scowl drawing his thick eyebrows together. At that moment Arrow lurched forward, drawing the attention of every bystander and silencing whatever Amos might have spouted.

For better or worse, there was no stopping Nora now.

Silas leaned into the rail, his pulse pounding.

The horse and sulky blew past them, dust boiling into the humid air. Silas gripped the wooden rail, splinters digging into his palms.

Nora ducked low in her seat, face hidden beneath a cap he had no idea how she was keeping on her head.

"Nice gait." Mr. Sutherland gave a whistle. "That colt can move."

Arrow careened around the first turn, the sulky's tire lifting slightly off the ground. Silas clenched his teeth.

Hold on, Nora. Hold on. Don't let him get too close to the rail.

She leveled out and Arrow lowered his head in the back straightaway, gaining speed.

There, now. Good.

He'd never seen a horse move that fast. What would he be like without the harness and sulky? Had Nora really ridden him at a full gallop as she claimed? If he moved like that at a trot, how dangerous would Arrow be at a dead run?

Dirt churned as Arrow made a smooth turn around the third and fourth bend, gathering several more onlookers. Men pointed, all fixated on Arrow.

Good, Nora. Good. You're almost done.

Arrow blasted past them, and Nora pulled up on the reins, trying to slow him. He fought against the bit, tossing his mane and refusing to yield.

Silas leapt the rail. Could he get to her in time before the colt got out of hand and caused a wreck?

Nora pulled again more firmly, and the two fought down the front straightaway until Arrow finally came to a heaving stop near the first turn. Nora leapt from the sulky before Silas could reach her and patted Arrow's neck.

He jogged to her side, his breath coming heavily.

Nora's bright eyes sparkled with excitement as though she hadn't been in any danger at all. "Well? What was his time?"

"I don't know." He reached for Arrow's bridle and took the horse firmly in hand.

Her mouth fell open, indignant. "What do you mean you don't know?"

"I didn't stand around to find out." He drew a breath and held it a moment before releasing it slowly. She was fine. He didn't need to cause a scene. He lowered his voice. "I was more concerned for your safety."

Her mouth puckered. "Oh."

Silas positioned himself between her and the track rail. "Your uncle is with Mr. Sutherland. Best you hightail it out of here before he realizes what you've done."

Nora frowned, hand coming to her hip.

Would she really be that stubborn right now? "Nora." She stilled at the firm use of her name. "I'll let you know Arrow's time as soon as you change and get back."

She hesitated but finally dipped her chin in reluctant agreement.

Obstinate woman. Brave, beautiful, obstinate woman.

Silas couldn't pull his gaze from her as she hurried away, her stride far too feminine. Anyone paying close attention might recognize her at any moment. Once she was out of sight, he took Arrow's bridle and gave the big colt a scratch behind the ear.

"Good run, boy."

He made a wide turn and led horse and sulky back to the waiting men. They stood with their heads together, looking over the paperwork.

"And you're sure?" Amos stroked his chin, his countenance serious.

Dread threaded through Silas's chest as he came to a stop. Had something gone wrong? Would they have to try to get Arrow to run again?

"Quite. One minute fifty-eight." Mr. Sutherland whistled. "Two seconds slower than Dan Patch himself." He shook his head, looking thoroughly impressed. "On his first run, you say?"

Amos grinned. "Excepting a few practice trials at home."

Mr. Sutherland scrawled a signature on two pieces of paper and handed one to Amos. "Expect to receive the registry paperwork in a couple of weeks." He tipped his hat. "Good day to you." He bobbed a nod to Silas, then hurried off, more papers tucked under his arm.

Spotting Silas, Amos grinned. "Good work, boy. Rebecca will be quite pleased." Amos slapped the papers against his thigh. "That horse is going to bring a fine price."

Amos sauntered off, a lightness in his step.

A good price? Silas's fingers curled into a fist. Amos was planning to sell Nora's horse right out from under her. She would be devastated, and the man didn't even care.

Silas gripped Arrow's mane, anger searing through him as hot as a branding iron. Sensing Silas's mood, Arrow pawed the ground.

"Don't worry, boy." His low tone caused Arrow to snort. "We won't let him get away with it."

Somehow.

Nora nearly tripped over her own feet in her haste. Dressed as a lady once more, she hurried down the stairs and to the lobby of the fair's hotel where people still lingered in droves. She just needed to slip out the door and get back to the barn before—

Oh no.

She slowed her reckless gait, taking the final stair more cautiously. Mother stood near the front door, her eyes scanning the room.

When Mother's gaze collided with Nora's, she hurried forward. "There you are. Where have you been?"

"In our room."

"Whatever for?"

What excuse could she give? "It's . . . terribly hot. I washed my face and neck to freshen up." Which was true. She'd had to wash the dirt off before changing back into her regular clothes.

Mother studied her. "Well, you do look fresher. Now let's go. We're going to miss the judging."

The judging? She withheld a groan. Why did she need to listen to the presentation of ribbons when she knew for certain her biscuits must have ranked last? She planted her feet against Mother's tugging. "I think Arrow has completed his time trial. Can we go to the barn and see how he fared instead?"

Mother slipped her hand through the crook of Nora's elbow, confusion etched across her forehead. "I'm sure we'll hear all about that later. If the run is finished, there's nothing else to see."

Nora's stomach sank. Mother was right. She could wait to find out what time the registry's man had clocked. She simply didn't want to.

They'd made a good run. She was sure of it. But had they beat the requirement of two and a half minutes? The suspense soured her stomach. Who cared about premiums for biscuits when the future of Emberwild was at stake?

Nora allowed Mother to draw her out of the hotel and down the front steps into the square. Men stacked wood for fires that would be lit around the square later this evening, and children scrambled around chattering about the midway and the oddities display. She and Mother threaded through the crowd and back to the exhibition tent where women gathered to hear the announcement for the winners of today's entries. Then these goods would be cleared away, and more would be put out for display tomorrow. At least she hadn't been forced to bake for multiple contests.

For the next hour, Nora suffered through the presentation of an array of baked goods proudly shown by women of all ages, though her mind kept spiraling away to entertain a dozen different questions.

Had Amos recognized her? Did Arrow qualify? Would Silas think something had happened to her when she didn't return to the barn?

"I'm sorry, dear. Perhaps next year." Mother squeezed her arm.

What? Oh. She hadn't won the biscuit contest.

"There's a premium for best horse and buggy driven by a young lady." Mother's tone was sweetly sincere. "Perhaps that would garner your interest?"

Mother would let her participate in a driving competition? What had come over her? "That's kind of you, Mother, but I don't think Arrow—"

"Of course not that wild colt." She waved a hand. "Don't be ridiculous." A shadow crossed Mother's face. "You are quite attached to that creature."

The statement required no response, and Nora didn't see the point in arguing. After a moment, Mother shook her head and returned her focus to the judging.

The man on the raised platform called for everyone's attention. "And this year's blue ribbon for best quilt goes to . . . Mrs. Rebecca Fenton."

Polite claps filled the tent as people looked around for the winner. Mother raised her hand and made her way to the platform to accept her prize of a woman's shirtwaist valued at three and a half dollars. The smile that graced her face sent a prickle of guilt through Nora's chest. How selfish of her not to want to share this moment. Mother had found so little to be happy about these days.

Nora clapped enthusiastically as Mother stepped down from the platform and walked back to her side. She pulled her into an embrace. "Congratulations."

Mother stiffened at the display of affection. "Thank you." She stepped back and straightened the collar on her charcoal-gray shirtwaist. A small smile tugged the corners of her mouth. "Seems I may not be entirely useless after all."

She spoke with pride, but the words made Nora cringe. Mother considered herself useless? Why?

"I suppose that's all for us. Would you like to go to the midway and try some of the popcorn?" Mother turned toward the open tent flap without waiting for Nora's response.

"May we go to the track now, please?" She took two quick strides to reach Mother's side.

Mother's smile faded.

"You know, if he does well, he could fetch us even better buyers for his colts than Ember." She took Mother's arm, leaning close

191

to her ear. "Think of how well we could do, you and I. We could make a good life for ourselves. Arrow is special. Others are going to know that now too."

Mother allowed Nora to draw her outside the tent, but as soon as they reached the shade of a young oak, she paused.

"Nora, there's something I should tell you." She drew her lip through her teeth, seeming uncertain. The expression was fleeting, however, and before Nora could form a response, Mother straightened herself into the stern posture she so frequently assumed. "Amos and I are considering selling all the horses."

What?

Blood thrummed in Nora's ears. She couldn't have heard correctly. The foals. Of course she meant the foals. "This summer's weanlings look good, but I don't think we should sell them until they are yearlings. We'll get a better price for them then."

Mother shook her head. "I mean *all* of them. No more trotters."

Nora tried to run her tongue over her lips, but both felt as dry as sand. "You can't be serious. How will we sustain a living without the horses? The crops hardly bring anything at all and—"

"Amos has other ventures."

She stiffened. *Other ventures?* What did that have to do with Emberwild? Nora struggled to keep the panic out of her voice. "That's his affair. Not ours. We can care for ourselves, Mother. I know we can. And Arrow is the key."

Mother shook her head. "There's so much you don't understand."

Resentment at the flippant way Mother planned to dismiss all of Nora's aspirations made her voice caustic. "Then tell me."

Mother drew back and glanced around the crowded square. "This isn't the place."

"Then why did you bring it up?" The words fired out of her mouth before she could catch them.

Rather than the indignation Nora expected, Mother only sighed. "Come, we'll take a walk."

They passed through the square and out to a large shade tree between the presenters' pavilion and the midway, finding a quiet space that, though far from secluded, kept most people out of earshot.

"Hopefully," Mother began as they stopped beneath the sweeping branches, "Mr. Dale will purchase Arrow for you, since Amos has been hesitant about my suggestion to include the colt in your dowry." She gave Nora a reassuring smile as though telling a child not to worry, her favorite doll had gone to the wash rather than being lost for good.

"My dowry?" She flung her hands out in exasperation. "I've only just met the man, so I don't see why Uncle is negotiating a dowry. And no one is selling Arrow. He's mine."

Sadness filled Mother's eyes. "You may care for him like he is, but none of the stock belong to you, no matter how much you may wish it so."

The truth of the words fell on her like a sack of rocks. "But . . . they belong to you."

Except they didn't. Her father's will had left everything to Amos, leaving his wife and daughter to his brother's mercy. Heat swelled in Nora's center as Mother offered no reply. "So that's it, then? You'll marry me off to the first man you find so you can get rid of me?"

"Nora, lower your voice." Mother glanced around, but no one paid them any attention.

Nora fumed. All Mother cared about was her reputation. Why had she ever let herself hope they could forge a happy life as independent women? Let herself think that Mother had changed? Mother had always had her own plans, and they had never involved Nora's wishes.

She glared at Mother. "Oh, I see. It makes perfect sense. I must be the ninny Father always said after all. Nothing like giving me the grand choice of marrying an old man or being left with nothing." She clenched her fists. "But of course you'd both want me gone so you can start your new life together without your spinster daughter messing up your newlywed bliss."

Mother paled, her expression stricken. "What are you talking about?"

The fire drained out of Nora, leaving her cold. She pressed her fingers to her lips. She'd meant what she'd said, though she wished she had been more kind. Regardless, there was no going back now.

Nora straightened. "Uncle Amos plans to marry you."

"Well, yes, but—"

"You knew?" The fire rekindled, scorching through Nora's limbs. How had she been so naive? All the covert glances between Mother and Amos. The games of toying with things left unsaid. Of course he'd already decided Mother was ready despite still being in mourning. She should have known. Mother had only entertained talk of an independent future to keep Nora complacent while they searched for a suitor to take her off their hands. Nora hardened herself against the pain threatening to lance her heart.

Mother's gaze sought the branches above. "I've always known he'd want to marry me if something happened to your father. Amos wanted everything that was meant for Hiram." Her eyes met Nora's. "Especially me."

"And you would let him take everything that should be yours by right?"

Mother pressed her lips together, refusing to answer.

"Have you even seen the will? Are you certain that's what it says?"

Doubt clouded Mother's eyes. "Why wouldn't it?" She dabbed at sudden tears.

Nora clutched the bow at her throat. They'd never even had a chance. All this time, she'd allowed herself the hope that she would be able to stay at Emberwild. To run the farm in her father's place. Tears burned her eyes. Foolish, childish hopes.

"I tried to tell you." Mother sighed. "All these years I tried to prepare you to leave home. To find something better. Mr. Dale can offer you all the things you want."

"I *wanted* Emberwild. I wanted to manage the horses and run the farm. I'm not meant to sit idly as some old man's—"

"That's enough." Mother's fierce gaze bore into Nora. "There's only one good outcome for the mess your father left us. You will marry Mr. Dale before he finds some other young woman with better sense than you. I will marry Amos. And then neither of us will find ourselves destitute." Her nails dug into Nora's arm. "Do you understand?"

Nora nodded, her throat clogged with anger and fear.

She understood. But that didn't mean she had to agree.

TWENTY-TWO

Something had to be wrong. Silas paced the aisle down the center of the race barn, nerves on edge. Nora had not returned after yesterday's trial. Nor had he seen her anywhere this morning. Had Amos found out what she'd done and forbidden her to come back?

Silas propped his arms on the stall gate and watched Arrow lazily swish flies from his back. Somehow, in a matter of a few weeks, Nora Fenton had wormed her way under his skin. Into his heart. Somewhere he suspected she'd hold permanent residency.

Why else would she continually occupy his thoughts this way? If he wasn't sliding down a slick slope toward deep affection—perhaps love—then why this unexplainable need to protect her?

He pushed off the gate. He had to go find her. Nora had been too fired up about Arrow's run time to have stayed away this long on her own. He marched out of the barn. Amos could send him off without any compensation. He didn't care.

He would find Nora and—

Silas's steps faltered. A striking figure headed toward the barn, causing his thoughts to stumble.

Nora.

She caught him watching her and a smile spread over her face, lighting her features. Had he ever seen a woman more beautiful? She was a splendor in a sunny yellow dress with matching ribbons in her hat and a basket looped over her arm.

If Amos had reprimanded her, she clearly didn't care. Chin lifted high, Nora strode toward him, giving a strange little wave that seemed almost . . . shy.

What had gotten into her?

"Silas. I've brought a picnic. Would you join me?"

The question caught him off guard. As did her demeanor. What had happened to the thorny woman who dressed in trousers and molded unsuspecting horsemen to her will?

Nora shifted from foot to foot, appearing nervous. He'd best find something better to do than stare at her before she realized what she was doing to him and hightailed it out of there.

He lifted his eyebrows in exaggerated surprise. "You'd like to picnic at the barn?"

Nora gave him a flat look, her feistiness returning. "If you're not interested, I'm sure I can find something else to occupy my time." She slowly started to turn away.

Silas laughed. "I can think of nothing better than sharing a picnic with you on this blistering day." He offered his arm, pleased when she looped her fingers through the crook of his elbow. "Do you have a place in mind?"

"Of course. Do you think me an impulsive woman?" She cut him a sharp look. "Don't answer that."

"I wouldn't dare call you impulsive." He chuckled. "Except perhaps when it comes to horses. Or racing. Or jumping in to save Arrow. Or—" Her playful elbow in his side cut off his teasing.

"There's a large oak to the east of the midway." Nora forged ahead. "Unless someone else has claimed the place, it will make a perfect spot."

Silas allowed her to guide him through the fairgrounds, the feel of her on his arm stirring a heat that rivaled the sweltering sun. He cleared his throat. "I take it you already know Arrow's run time? Seeing as you didn't return yesterday."

Nora's fingers tightened on his sleeve. "Yes."

She offered no further explanation and he didn't press, though he wondered what had siphoned her enthusiasm. They walked in companionable silence, skirting around the busy area at the pavilion where yet another political candidate enthralled the crowds. Nora had chosen a good time for her picnic—when the rest of this temporary town was otherwise occupied.

When they reached a large oak that spread stately limbs into a wide canopy, she released his arm and placed the basket on the grass. He should have offered to carry that for her. He shook his head at his own carelessness. Nora Fenton had a way of keeping him addled.

She lifted a thin blanket from inside the basket, and Silas took one side so they could spread the blue fabric out on the ground. Nora gestured for him to sit, then she took a place across from him and arranged her skirt around her ankles. "I've brought fried chicken, peaches, biscuits—don't worry, I didn't bake them—and a jug of sweet tea."

Taking that as his cue, Silas removed each item from the basket and placed the food between them. "Looks delicious."

She waved a dismissive hand in acknowledgment. "Thankfully other women have skills in the kitchen."

He took a bite from a chicken leg and chewed thoughtfully, the crunch of the batter igniting his hunger. "You don't enjoy cooking?"

Nora unscrewed the lid from the tea jar and poured a small amount into a pewter cup, but then set it on the ground next to her without taking a sip. "I'm not sure if I despise cooking because I'm no good at it, or if I'm no good at it because I despise it." Her lips twisted to the side, clearly annoyed.

Silas couldn't help but chuckle. "You can't be good at everything."

Nora didn't share in his laughter. She laced her fingers in her lap, leaving the food she'd brought untouched. "I have to tell you something."

Her tone sent a sour feeling snaking through his gut. He placed his chicken on a napkin and waited.

Nora looked out over the swaying grass toward where children played at the midway, avoiding his gaze. After a moment, her chest heaved with a gathered breath. "My father told me a secret before he died." She darted a worried glance at him. "One I fear may involve you."

Him? What was she talking about?

Fingers twisting together, Nora kept her gaze averted. "He said everything we had was built on a lie. After he'd told me we only had a floundering stallion and four half-starved mares." Her eyes sought his, imploring. "I didn't know. I promise."

Unease swelled through his chest. "Know what?"

"I've been thinking." She toyed with her lip between her teeth. "About what you told me about your father . . . and his horse."

The unease coiled into dread. "What do you know about my father?"

"Nothing." She sighed. "At least, not for sure."

"Then what do you know?"

"Amos told me that my father came home one day with a fine stallion and that where he got it always seemed . . ." Her gaze slammed into his. "Mysterious."

His pulse quickened. "Why didn't you tell me?"

"You have to understand. I don't know anything for sure."

He clenched his fists. "Yet when I asked you about it, you said you didn't know anything at all." Had she deceived him this entire time? Why? What reason could she possibly have for keeping any information that could help him discover the truth?

Nora's voice lowered. "Ember will be home when we return to Emberwild. You can look for yourself."

So that was it. She feared he would recognize his father's horse and thought she no longer had any choice but to come clean. He struggled for calm. Would she have kept silent if there hadn't been a chance he'd see Ember? "So you suspect your father stole my father's horse?"

"No." The word shot out of her like a volley. "I mean, I don't think so. But the coincidence does seem a bit odd." She stared at her hands. "At least, I think it's worth investigating." Searching eyes met his. "Don't you?"

"Of course I do." Silas shot to his feet. "It's the whole reason I came to this miserable town."

Hurt clouded in her eyes and she looked away again.

Silas rubbed the back of his neck. "I'm sorry." Regardless of her actions, she didn't deserve his harsh tone. How quickly he'd forgotten his desire to protect her.

Her throat bobbed rapidly, as though she kept swallowing.

Silas sighed and sat down again. "Nora. Look at me." Her eyes shimmered when they met his, and his heart sank. "I shouldn't have shouted at you." When she didn't respond, he continued. "I'm sure you had your reasons for keeping quiet."

"If my father lied, then our reputation will be ruined." She spoke with leaded words, each one falling heavy between them.

Silas took her hand in his, rubbing his thumb over the back of her knuckles. Odd how he wanted to be angry with her for hiding information from him, yet found himself trying to soothe her instead.

Nora scrubbed her other hand down her reddened face. "If the buyers have any doubt about Ember's bloodlines, we would lose all hope selling this year's foals. Worse, it calls into question every horse we've ever sold before." Nora pulled her hand from his grasp. "Emberwild would be ruined."

Consumed with finding answers, he hadn't considered the consequences for Nora. Consequences her father certainly deserved. But Nora?

She sighed. "But I suppose none of that will matter once Amos sells all the horses. Unless of course people start demanding recompense and . . ." She shook her head.

Wait. *All* of the horses? Silas frowned. "I thought he only wanted to profit from Arrow's speed. Why sell the mares?"

She barked a bitter laugh. "Because he can." Nora blinked, her eyes shimmering with moisture. She turned away from him, and he gave her a moment to collect herself.

Nora mumbled something about disposing of all their problems at once.

"What problems?"

She cleared her throat. "Never mind. That's none of your concern." She waved her hand again as though shooing uncomfortable emotions could truly make them go away.

Suddenly businesslike, Nora folded her hands in her lap. "Tell me everything you remember about the day your father died, and I'll do the same."

Silas repeated what he'd already told her about their stay in Philadelphia, the sheriff's assessment of a spooked horse, and the open barn doors. Nora nodded along, her features tight with concentration.

"Anything else? Any other detail you can think of?"

"I've thought about that night for years. There's nothing else."

Nora thought a moment and then suddenly gestured toward the food. "Aren't you going to eat?"

Was she stalling? Rushing her wouldn't help, so he snagged a biscuit.

Tense, Nora took one of her own but merely picked at the crumbling edges. Finally, she spoke. "My father said something about being desperate to make things better, so he didn't question him. But I don't know who *him* was. Then he said he should have known better, but he kept building on the lie anyway."

Suspicious, yes, but it didn't prove anything. "He didn't say anything about finding a horse, or . . ." Silas hesitated. "Or stealing one?"

Nora shook her head. "Only that everything we have was built on a lie. But then when you said that Arrow looked like your father's horse, I started to wonder. It's been gnawing at me ever since."

At least she'd finally spoken up. Not that her information gave him much. "Thank you for telling me."

Relief washed over her face, and she offered him a tentative smile.

After several moments of awkward silence, Silas lifted his hat and ran his fingers through his hair. "Yesterday Amos said Arrow would bring a good price, but I never thought he'd want to sell off the mares."

Anger flashed in her eyes. "Yes. Well. I'm still working on that."

Working on what? If her uncle wanted to sell horses he legally owned, Silas didn't see where Nora could do anything about it. He wanted to offer encouragement, but what could he say?

"I want to thank you for yesterday." Nora lifted a peach and picked at the fuzzy skin. "For letting me race him." A wistful look entered her eyes. "At least I got to see what it felt like. Just once."

The words had a note of finality to them that pinched his heart. "You should be free to race whenever you want."

"Yet women never have such freedoms, do they?"

As Silas struggled for an answer, Nora gained her feet and brushed her hands down her skirt. "When we get home, I'll find my father's paperwork on Ember."

"You have paperwork?" Hope that he'd moved one step closer to the truth sank. He stood, watching her carefully. If Nora really did have paperwork on Ember like Walter had said, then the chances the horse was the same one Papa had brought from Tennessee seemed slim.

"He kept all the registries in his office." Nora turned to look out over the fairgrounds, resignation filling her voice.

Silas reached for her hand again, wishing the caress of his fingers could erase the worry clouding her eyes. "I appreciate your help."

Nora looked at his fingers encasing hers, but she didn't pull away. "And if it's true? If my father stole your father's horse? Then what?"

Silas's stomach clenched.

Then he very well could have fallen in love with a murderer's daughter.

chapter
TWENTY-THREE

Emberwild
July 30, 1905

Anticipation and dread swirled in Nora's stomach as she slowly opened the door to her father's study. Hopefully, she would find what she needed here. She had no desire to have to check Roger's office in the carriage shed. To do so would likely rouse the man's suspicions.

Besides, she didn't want to have to explain herself to Roger. The man was as prickly as a porcupine with all the grace and manners of a red wasp.

Checking the hall for any sign of Mother, Nora slipped inside and gently closed the door behind her. Her father's study smelled of leather and dust, another unused place in the house Mother ignored.

Father's desk stood at the back of the room, flanked by two windows that would overlook the south pasture if the room ever came into use again. For now, the curtains hung limp, letting in only slivers of light to disperse the shadows.

Nora eased past two armchairs positioned by the cold hearth and ran a finger along the edge of the desk. She wiped her hand down her navy skirt and drew a breath.

Opening the first drawer, she found neatly stacked stationery, sealing wax, and writing utensils. She closed that drawer and opened the one beneath it. Her pulse quickened. These documents appeared official. Nora plopped into the leather chair, creating a puff of dust that tickled her nose.

Perhaps she would find the horses' documents here after all. She would find Ember's paperwork and clear her conscience that her father had found, or worse, stolen, the Cavalleros' horse.

Hopefully.

She hesitated. Did she really want to open doors better left closed? Without paperwork, no one could prove where Ember had come from. Just because both horses were the same age, the same color, and both had once had a small white spot didn't mean they were the same horse.

She thought of Mr. Dale as she riffled through banknotes and letters from businessmen she didn't recognize. Would he buy the horses from Amos if she asked? As his wife, would she be able to start a stable of her own?

Could she convince him they were good horses, even if her father had lied? Would he care about Emberwild's ruined reputation?

Nora closed her eyes and drew a long breath. Mother was right. Mr. Dale could very well be the solution to all of her problems. She would be a fool not to accept his offer.

As soon as the thought began to take root, Silas's face pushed out Mr. Dale's features in her mind's eye. Could she marry one man while her heart kept tugging her toward another?

She put her head in her hand, thoughts reeling. Too many questions, none with any answers or solutions.

She could marry Mr. Dale on the stipulations that he bought the horses and allowed her to start her own breeding program. In return she would manage his household and see to his son. A good arrangement. One that offered comfort and the realizations of her dreams.

Yet her heart squeezed at the thought.

Somehow, the dusty cowboy had taken up residence not only in her thoughts but in her heart. Gentle, understanding Silas had been the one person who never made her feel like a burden.

But there could be no future for them. Even if her father wasn't responsible for what happened with the Cavalleros' horse, Silas was only here temporarily. And even if he decided to stay, they would both be nothing more than poor horse trainers.

Would that be so bad?

That life, at least, offered some freedoms—and different confines.

Pushing aside all thoughts of men and the troubles they presented, Nora lifted a ledger containing the expenses of Emberwild. Flipping open the cover, she ran her finger down the lines of tallies accounting for each expense and asset. The final page ended months ago. No wonder they were struggling.

She should have come in here earlier and taken over running the account for the farm. How had Roger been paying the hands, ordering the supplies, and managing the inventory without keeping accounts? What had Amos been doing these past weeks running the farm? Did he have new accounts written somewhere else?

Why hadn't she thought to ask?

Perhaps she wouldn't have made a good manager after all. If she couldn't consider something so simple, she had no business taking her father's place.

Heart heavy, Nora pulled out more papers, scanning the contents for anything useful before placing them on the desk in turn.

Her gaze caught on a thick paper embossed with a seal at the bottom of the stack. She ran her fingers over the heading. The deed to Emberwild, listing out all four hundred acres, the house and buildings, and signed by both her father and someone named Mr. Davidson.

She carefully set the document aside. One item remained in the drawer. A bundle of pages folded in thirds. Nora unfolded the papers, her pulse quickening as she recognized the contents.

Father's will.

Nerves tingling, Nora read the first page. Then the next and the one after, her eyes flying over the words. With each line, sickness grew in her stomach, tangling with anticipation and anger.

It couldn't be.

He'd lied to them.

Nora gripped the papers in her fist, crinkling the edges. Blood pounded in her ears as she strode through the office. She flung open the door and marched into the hall.

"Mother!"

❧

Silas leaned against the fence, watching Ember. The stallion—easily over fifteen hands—tossed his head, ears flicking forward and back as though unsure if Silas posed a threat. Coat so light a gray it bordered on white, this horse didn't resemble the fiery red colt they'd gotten in Tennessee.

He shifted to look at the horse's right shoulder. No small white spot.

Though he couldn't really be sure. Not with the way the roan had grayed out. From what he understood of horse registration, every marking and coat pattern was documented to ensure ownership. Ember would look nothing now like he had when he'd been documented.

How would they possibly match the markings on the registry to a horse that underwent that much change?

"Silas!"

He turned at the sound of his name, spotting Amos walking purposefully toward him. With a sigh, Silas exited the stallion pen and headed toward the training corral. His shirt stuck to his shoulders, the midmorning sun bright.

What time was it? Well past when she should have been here.

He cast a look toward the house. Nora had promised to meet him this morning so they could look for Ember's papers.

Had she changed her mind?

He met Amos near the corral, the other man dressed in a linen suit and straw hat with a matching band. Silas ran his palms over his trousers in hopes of cleaning them before extending his hand to his boss.

Amos took his outstretched hand briefly, giving only one pump. "What are your plans now that you'll be leaving Mississippi?"

The thought of leaving Nora brought a pang he couldn't ignore. "I'm not sure." Best turn the subject and give himself time to come up with a plan. "What do you know about Ember? Was he always that color?"

Surprise lifted Amos's brows. "Why do you ask?"

Silas shrugged. "He's a fine animal. Not many Standardbreds have that coloring, I believe. I wondered if Arrow might do the same."

Amos looked in the horse's direction. "If I remember correctly, he wasn't quite as red as Arrow, and for years he remained a mix of red and gray. Wasn't until after his first decade he turned as white as he is."

If only that information could help in identifying where he came from. "How old is he now?"

Amos sucked his teeth. "Don't remember, exactly."

"Mind if I look at his teeth?"

A frown creased the center of Amos's brow. "Why?"

Silas forced a laugh. "A horseman's curiosity, I suppose."

"You'll more likely lose a finger than sate your curiosity." Amos removed the gold timepiece from his pocket and checked the hour. "I'm making a trip to town to withdraw your payment from the bank. Care to join me? You can be on your way from there."

"Today?" He cast another glance at the house. Where was Nora?

"As we agreed." Amos tipped his hat back, studying Silas. "Now that we're finished with Arrow's time trial."

Silas scrambled for a reason to delay. "If it's all the same to you, sir, I'd like to say farewell to the men. We've grown to be friends these last weeks, and I'd hate to disappear without the courtesy of wishing them well." A stretch. But he would at least like to have the opportunity to say his goodbyes to Asa and Walter.

His stomach twisted. And Nora. He couldn't leave without a word to her. She deserved far better.

After a long moment, Amos gave a nod. "Very well. In the morning, then."

"Thank you." Silas released a breath. One final day to seek the truth at Emberwild. A few remaining moments in Nora's presence.

Amos sauntered to the house, leaving Silas to make a decision. He had one afternoon remaining to figure out if Ember could be his father's horse. If so, then he had to prove it.

Then he'd have to decide what to do about Nora.

Mother burst from her room, eyes wide. "What? What's happened?"

Nora waved the papers. "This is Father's will. Have you seen it?"

She hurried closer, features tight. "Where did you find that?"

"In his desk." Nora folded her arms, keeping the papers from Mother. "Where any logical person would think to look. Why didn't you?"

"I had no need."

"You didn't?" Nora barked a bitter laugh. "Why? Because you already know what it says?"

Mother's shoulders stiffened. "It states everything is left to Amos."

"Except it doesn't."

The color drained from Mother's face. "What are you talking about?"

A satisfied smirk worked its way onto Nora's lips, and she didn't bother to squelch it. "Emberwild is yours."

Mother stared at her. "It can't be."

"Unless you remarry, then the property goes to your new husband." Nora sneered. "As of course the law always says. However, there's something more."

Lacing her fingers together in front of her black skirt, Mother's usual demeanor returned as she waited for Nora to continue.

"If I were to marry, then Emberwild is mine with the stipulation that you will be cared for here for the rest of your life." She scarcely believed Father had inserted a clause that would actually leave anything to her specifically. That he would insist on her marriage, however, did not surprise. "Unless I marry a man of ample means, then I am free to leave all of Emberwild to you and pursue my own life elsewhere."

Mother's mouth worked, but no words formed.

"Don't you see what's happened here?" Nora flung her arms wide, the papers fluttering. "If Amos marries you, he gets Emberwild."

"And if you marry Mr. Dale," Mother said slowly, "who is a man of ample means, then Emberwild reverts to me."

Nora clutched the papers. "Unless of course you've already married Amos."

Red splotches covered Mother's neck. "So he thought to see us both quickly married, thereby solidifying his claim on both accounts."

"Precisely." Nora shook her head, another thought dawning. "But then why sell off all the horses if he thinks he will inherit them?"

Mother pressed her fingers to her lips. "I don't know."

Hope pooled in her chest. Regardless of the plans Amos worked, they now had the leverage to devise a plan of their own. "Mother. Don't you see? Emberwild is yours. You don't have to marry anyone. Nor do I. We aren't going to be destitute."

Mother held out her hand and Nora relinquished the papers. She scanned the contents. "This was dated just after your father fell ill."

"Do you think it's different from the one the solicitor has?"

"Possibly." Mother rubbed the bridge of her nose. "I suppose we need to take this to his office and find out." She blew out a breath. "Something I should have already done instead of trusting your uncle."

"We mustn't let on that we know."

Mother opened her mouth, but a knock at the front door gave her pause. The women exchanged a look.

"Put this back. We'll deal with it later." Mother thrust the papers back at Nora.

Nora replaced the pages while Mother hurried toward the stairs. After stashing the papers, Nora made her way downstairs.

". . . would like for you to join me," Amos was saying, his voice coming from the parlor.

Nora slowed at the bottom of the stairs, listening.

"Not today, Amos. Thank you for the offer."

Where had he wanted her to go?

"You never wish to accompany me, Rebecca. I understand you're still supposed to be in mourning, but at least in private, can we not set such pretenses aside? Have we not finally reached *our* time?"

What in the world was he talking about?

"I don't think—" Mother's words suddenly cut off.

Nora frowned. What happened? She eased across the foyer and pressed herself up against the wall by the parlor. Slowly, she shifted until she could peek one eye around the doorframe.

Amos held Mother in an embrace, his lips pressed firmly against hers. Anger swelled in Nora's center. How dare he! She nearly burst into the room when Mother shoved herself out of Amos's arms.

"I'm not ready."

"I am," Amos replied, his voice tight. "I've waited years. Held my tongue. I honored my promise to you, but now that he's gone, it's time you honored your promise to me."

Promise? What promise?

Mother stared up into Amos's face as he cupped her cheek. Then after Nora thought her heart would burst from anticipation, Mother gave a slow nod.

chapter

TWENTY-FOUR

Where was she? Leaning against the barn, Silas scuffed his boot against the dirt and stared at Nora's house. If she didn't come soon, what would he do? Knock on the door? Leave without ever knowing the truth?

Or telling her goodbye?

Finally, the door cracked and a flash of brown fabric flew out of the house like a tumbleweed caught in a fit of wind. Nora's gait nearly pounded each step she took, her skirt whipping around the tops of her booted feet.

If coals could be blue, they couldn't have been any hotter than the eyes smoldering into him. Had something happened? She looked as though she meant to scorch him.

Tightness coiled around his stomach. She'd found something. Something that she didn't like. Had Nora discovered paperwork that proved Ember was stolen?

Silas stepped forward to meet her under the shade of Emberwild's ancient oak. The leaves shimmied in the breeze, creating a gentle whisper that did nothing to calm his nerves.

Nora stalked up to him and grabbed him by both of his arms.

"Nora? Are you all ri—"

Her lips landed on his. Hard. Silas froze. What in the world? Nora pushed up on her toes, still laying claim to his lips. Forgetting his shock and better judgment, Silas surrendered to the moment and wrapped an arm around her waist. He pulled her close, allowing himself to sink into the intoxicating sensation of her velvety lips beneath his.

Just as suddenly as she'd pounced on him, she thrust her hands up between them and shoved him away. "There." Nora's chin dipped decisively. "I had to know."

"Know what?" Lips tingling, Silas watched her flushed features for any indication she regretted her actions. He saw something akin to begrudging satisfaction.

Confounding woman. What did she think to accomplish, sending his senses through the wringer?

She smirked. Had she been toying with him?

"We're going to Roger's office to find Ember's papers."

His mouth worked, but words refused to escape. Nora turned on her heel, heading toward the carriage shed. Silas watched her skirt sway for several paces before he regained enough of his wits to jog after her.

"Care telling me what that was about?" What in the heavens was he supposed to think about a woman marching up to him, planting an unsuspected kiss, and then running off without an explanation?

"Roger will probably ask questions, but I'm in no mood to deal with his vinegar today." As though that statement made any sense, Nora thrust open the door at the side of the carriage house that revealed a narrow staircase to the quarters above.

She paused and sucked in a quick breath. "If Father had kept the horse papers with everything else, this wouldn't be necessary. Men. Fools, the lot of them."

Silas nearly reminded her that she had just rather unconventionally kissed one of those men, but since he *was* feeling rather foolish at the moment it didn't seem prudent. He trudged up the stairs behind her, refusing to repeat himself yet still at a complete loss as to the nature of her behavior.

He rubbed his chin. Women were a confusing lot to start, but this one in particular could make a fellow doubt he had any wits at all.

Muttering something about why couldn't they have electric lights like those fancy places in the big cities, she flung open the first door at the top of the landing. Inside, a small no-nonsense office housed a serviceable desk, one sitting chair, a side table containing one dusty ledger, and a wooden chest that had the looks of a lockbox.

Nora thrust open the curtains on the single window, sending up a cloud of dust. "Really. Does the man not even care enough to maintain his own working space?" She plopped down into the chair behind the desk, clearly not expecting Silas to answer.

Not sure where to best situate himself, Silas took a post by the door and watched the woman before him snatch open drawers like she meant to rip them from the desk.

"Look at this mess." Nora dropped a heap of papers on the desk. Her eyes—an unnerving mixture of blue flame and ice—pinned him. "Don't just stand there woolgathering. Are you going to help me or not?"

"As soon as you tell me what happened outside."

She stilled, but the tremble of papers in her hand gave her away. Was all of this an act to cover up her true feelings?

Silas closed the door lest Roger discover them in here snooping and took slow steps forward until he came to stand in front of the desk, forcing her to look up at him.

"I'm not accustomed to women kissing me out in the open." His lips quirked. "Especially with such . . . passion."

The color drained from her face. Almost immediately, however, pink rushed back in force. She tilted her nose higher and sniffed. "I should hope not."

Silas placed both hands on the desk and leaned closer. "What I'd like to know, my dear Miss Fenton, is *why.*"

The rogue. Why must he look at her like that? Worse, how could he stand there, clearly pleased with himself, asking her to speak about things better left unsaid?

She had no idea why she'd done something so brash. So forward. She'd been angry, confused, and plain livid with her mother. All she remembered was storming out of the house, unable to face the betrayal in the parlor.

If Mother could throw away their future for a man, perhaps she could too.

A stupid and ridiculous notion, she knew. Yet, when she'd found Silas standing outside waiting on her, she'd suddenly wanted nothing more than to throw out sensibility like last week's moldy bread.

There were simply no words that could justify why she'd kissed him in plain view of anyone watching. None.

Except that she'd wanted to know if doing so would send bolts of lightning through her.

It had. That and more. Not that she could tell him, of course. To do so would be completely indecent, and she couldn't go about making a mockery of herself any more than she already had.

Nora cleared her throat. "This is hardly a proper conversation."

Silas lifted his eyebrows, causing them to nearly disappear beneath his hat. The expression seemed to say that an improper conversation fit seamlessly with her improper behavior.

"You are quite an interesting woman."

She glowered at him. "So I've been told."

"You have?"

"Ever since I was a girl who dared to speak my opinion on which candidate would be the best choice for governor. Yes, I've many times been regarded as that *interesting* girl who couldn't find sense if it was the only onion left in the basket. Of course, that opinion probably had more to do with me embarrassing Mr. Cromwell in front of my parents' friends. I foolishly pointed out his grievous mistake in supporting the candidate who, ironically, had actually been the reason his daughter had to spend a year sequestered at her aunt's house in Atlanta."

Silas's eyes widened in surprise. She couldn't bring herself to clarify the girl had been in the family way, and the Cromwells' attempts to hide the matter were entirely conspicuous.

"I'm guessing that didn't turn out well."

Nora regarded him across the desk. "Father said I lacked even the wits God gave to a sow and vowed that such a loose-lipped twit could never be his offspring. He lost all his accounts with Mr. Cromwell's bank. Because of that, he didn't treat me with anything resembling affection for the remainder of his days." The memory brought the sting of tears to her eyes and she struggled to blink them away.

Silas leaned closer and captured her gaze. "I find you charming, fascinating, and quite alluring. That's my definition of interesting."

"You find me alluring?" The words left of their own accord.

"Even more so, I daresay, in light of recent events."

Nora huffed and reached for another stack of papers. Of course he would find a wanton display alluring. What man wouldn't? She dropped the documents on the desk and started unfolding one after another, her mind too stuffed with straw to be of any use. She had no idea what she was looking at. Silas—the scoundrel—continued to wait, his patient insistence on her answer as to why she'd kissed him eating away at what little composure she had remaining.

Finally, she threw down the paper she hadn't been able to focus on anyway. "I had to know, all right?" She shot up from the chair, sending it teetering behind her. "I had to know if what I feel for you could be real. If it could be worth . . . worth changing everything."

Deep brown eyes smoldered, hinting at fires that stirred beneath. Did he think her a loose woman? Or merely a fool?

"Is it?"

She crossed her arms over her chest to hide her trembling fingers, trying to glare at him. How dare he stand there so calmly? Nora narrowed her eyes. "What business is that of yours?"

Hardly fair, she knew. Yet somehow she could no more stop herself from acting like a termagant than she could command Arrow to fly.

Silas, however, remained infuriatingly amused.

"Quite a bit, I should think." He shrugged broad shoulders. "Seeing as how I'm the object of this little experiment. To which, I might add, I'm quite eager to hear the results."

Nora gaped at him. How could a man be so annoying and completely endearing at the same time? She tore her gaze from his disconcerting one and looked at the papers on the desk.

No. She would not get swept away by the electrifying way he looked at her or the appealing way his lips curved each time she got flustered. Obviously, Mother had gotten herself into some type of pickle with Amos. One she couldn't even begin to try to unravel in her current mental state. She wouldn't let herself get tangled up in the charms of a man and let such mercurial whims steal her future as well.

Never mind that she'd probably already hitched herself to that horse. Kissing him certainly hadn't helped. Especially if she'd wanted to keep such disastrous notions to herself.

Silas leaned even closer, stealing her already wavering breath. "Are your feelings real, Nora?"

Her tongue stuck to the roof of her mouth, and it took every ounce of her willpower to lie to him. "Perhaps."

Silas chuckled. "I'll take it."

Scoundrel.

"Of course, if you'd like to take another sample for evidence, I'd be happy to oblige."

Heat roared up her neck. Of all the—

Mischievous eyes danced with laughter as Silas tipped his hat back. What had happened to the stoic fellow she'd met a couple of months ago?

Had she really let a man carve out a place of affection in her heart in so little time? Her breath hitched.

His face suddenly grew serious again. "I shouldn't have made light." He shook his head. "I've never done this sort of thing." He rocked back on his heels, putting distance between them. "My mother always said I'd have a hard time finding a wife because I never could talk to a woman properly."

A wife?

Had he . . . ? No. His mother's saying, that was all. It had nothing to do with her.

"Think nothing of it." She gestured to the papers and did her best to turn this unseemly situation to the business at hand. Anything to douse the fires lighting in her and burning up all notions of reason. She straightened her shoulders and—with great effort—schooled her features into a sensible expression. "Look for papers with the breed registry at the top. We'll need one dated in 1890, if I'm correct. Ember was a sorrel then, so we'll have to—"

"Nora."

The sound of her name—and the way his voice embraced each syllable—stopped all thoughts in her head. She refused to look at him.

"Forgive my jesting. Any man would be honored to have a woman as wondrous as you turn her affection his way."

Wondrous? Men always found her overbearing, uncouth, or unfeminine. Never wondrous. She couldn't stop her gaze from returning to his. No man had ever looked at her as Silas looked at her now, either. As though she wasn't a surly old maid with a sharp tongue and a head full of air.

"You do know that, don't you?" A gentle look softened the planes of his tanned features. "Fearless beauty. As wondrous as the star-filled sky and as perfect as pure rain after the drought."

For all the emotions bubbling inside her, Nora couldn't think of a single reply.

chapter

TWENTY-FIVE

Best not push Nora any further. Silas had likely taken her as far down the revelation trail as she'd go for today. He picked up a stack of the papers on the desk between them and pretended to focus on the words. He avoided looking at Nora, giving her time to collect herself after his declaration. Where he'd found words nearing on poetic, he'd never know. He'd never once considered himself a romantic man. Until he met Nora Fenton.

"I . . . um . . . thank you." Nora tucked her chin as though the motion could hide anything from him. Her breath came quickly, and her hands trembled. Hope swelled.

She'd tell him the truth about her feelings when she was ready. He'd enjoy hearing the words when they came from those expressive lips, but her eyes had already given her away. Nora had soaked up his words like the cracked ground welcomed the rain's reprieve, and he'd seen his affection reflected back through sapphire blues.

She gestured toward the papers. "We should get back to the search."

Maybe he shouldn't have spoken so directly, but she needed to know her value, and he couldn't leave Emberwild without having told her the truth.

"Yes, ma'am." He withheld the urge to wink at her and shatter the professional mask she continued to struggle to set into place.

She needed time. A lady of her means would have considerations. Ones he must let her determine on her own. The rich suitor offered more than Silas ever could by way of a comfortable life. Would Nora consider throwing her hat in with a poor man?

Love made people do strange things. His mother had left a life of luxury for his father. The thought was bittersweet. Knowing he could be entrusted with the treasure of her heart—and what all she would have to give up to hand her love into his care—brought a well of emotions surging through him. But the vision of Mama's worn face after a lifetime of scraping a living from the ground chilled the warmth rising in him. How could he ask such a sacrifice of Nora?

"Did you find anything?"

At the sound of Nora's question, Silas snapped his attention back to the papers in his hand and forced himself to focus on the headings. Too new. Wrong color. Mare. Another mare.

He held one up. "Here. 1890. Sorrel colt." He frowned, scanning the lines. "This lists Ember's breed, age, markings, and run trial." Arrow ran the track fourteen seconds faster than his sire. Impressive. Silas read the page again. "Says here the sorrel colt was purchased from Clearwater Farm in Indiana. Officially stamped by the registry." Exactly as Walter had said. No mention of a small white spot on his side or a black mark inside his lower lip.

His shoulders deflated. He hadn't wanted to hope the Fentons had taken Papa's colt, but proof that they hadn't only left him with a stomach full of the same soured questions he'd lived with for the past fifteen years.

Nora leaned back in her chair. "I suppose that answers your question."

Perhaps. At least now he could be free to love Nora without suspicions hanging over them. "I don't think I'll ever have the answers I want."

Sympathy etched along the edges of her delicate eyebrows. She laced her fingers together on the desk and regarded him thoughtfully. "Unfortunately, I fear there are some answers we may never receive this side of heaven."

Silas tilted his head back and studied the ceiling. She was right. He could keep chasing the past, or he could put his energy into forging a future. He lowered his gaze to hers. "Amos wants to send me on my way in the morning."

Her eyes flickered with uncertainty, disappointment, and all too quickly, understanding. Wasn't she even going to—

"Do you smell that?" Nora lurched from her seat, features tight.

Acrid air stung his nostrils, sending off warning bells in his mind. Silas rushed toward the door and grabbed the knob. Warm to the touch. Concern kicked into fear as he wrenched the knob. "It's locked."

Nora pushed past him and took hold of the door, though her twisting yielded the same results. "Is that smoke?"

The pitch of panic in her voice had him futilely yanking on the door again. "Did you lock it?"

"You're the one who closed it."

Silas pounded on the door. The solid oak held unyielding against his efforts. The smoke curled under the door now, filling the office with caustic black tendrils that climbed into his nose and burned his throat.

Nora coughed and he wrapped an arm around her in a futile effort to shield her from the coming terror. "Find something to cover your nose."

Watery eyes latched on to his and held a moment. Determination mingled with fear, but she blinked hard and reached for her hem. Silas turned away as a ripping sound indicated she'd found a good use for the frilly fabric women kept hidden beneath their skirts.

While she busied herself with her underskirts, Silas moved for the window behind the desk. He flipped the latch and tugged.

Stuck.

Flaking paint clung to the edges of the seal. Someone had painted the frame without opening the window. He strained against the latch, but the dried paint held firm.

He might have to bust the window to get them enough fresh air. Possibly have to figure out a way to lower Nora down. But not before he tried to put his boot through the door. Silas reared back and kicked with all of his might. The satisfying sound of cracking wood encouraged him to try two more blows. His leg ached from the force, but the door still held firm.

Coughing, he leaned over and put his hands on his thighs.

"Here. Use this." Nora held out a length of soft fabric.

Her petticoat? Or worse, chemise. He started to shake his head.

"Don't be a fool. It's this or choke."

Silas took the band of cloth and tied it around his nose and mouth, pushing the ends of delicate lace up under his hat. The faint scent of something floral tickled his senses briefly before being swallowed under the burn of smoke.

Nora gripped his arm, her eyes asking questions he couldn't answer. Even if he succeeded in breaking down the door, Lord only knew what awaited them in the hall. He'd have to try the window. "Stand back and shield your eyes."

Silas grabbed the chair from behind the desk and flung it into the window. Glass shattered. An immediate rush of fresh air flooded the room, bringing momentary relief to his lungs.

"Nora!" He held his hand out to her, beckoning her to find a breath of relief.

She sucked in a lungful of clear air and leaned out the window. Her shouts for help carried on the breeze. Silas added his voice to hers, hoping the hands would be near enough to the barn to help. If they didn't contain the blaze soon, there wouldn't be anything left to save. This building was ready fuel for the flames already licking the walls.

Silas judged the distance to the ground below. "Take off whatever you have under that skirt."

"What?" Nora leaned back from the window, confusion clouding her features. "Why?"

"Just do it." Silas tossed his hat aside and pulled his shirt over his head. That should give him a few more feet of length.

He wrapped the fabric around his hand and brushed out as much of the broken glass from the frame as he could.

Nora scrambled out of a wispy white thing and left it in a pool at her feet. Silas couldn't tell if the red in her cheeks came from the heat or from the sight of him standing in nothing but his trousers and undershirt. He unhooked his bracers and tied them to the sleeve of his cotton shirt.

Wordlessly, Nora lifted the white lacy fabric toward him. He knotted the waist of the petticoat to the other sleeve of his shirt and then examined the length. It would have to do. He gestured to Nora.

"Hurry. Lift your arms."

She lifted her hands high, her gaze questioning in the hazy air. Her coughs caught on the fabric wrapped around her face, watery eyes leaking onto the silk. Silas wrapped the bracers behind her shoulders and under her arms, then knotted the material back on itself.

"I want you to hold tight here." He gestured to where the bracers were tied to one sleeve of the shirt. "I'm going to lower you out of the window and—"

"You'll do no such thing!" Nora wiggled in his grasp.

His fingers tightened around her wrists. "I can't open the door." The words pained him, and whatever pleading showed in his eyes forestalled her next protest.

"I won't drop you. I promise." Praying with all his might he could keep true to the words, Silas positioned Nora on the window frame. "Careful. Some of the glass might still cut."

He cast another look toward the barn. Where were the men? Shouldn't someone have come by now? The smoke billowed from below. At any moment the floor could drop out from under them. He had to get Nora to safety.

She clung to his arm as he swung her legs over the windowsill.

He brushed a sweaty lock from her forehead. "Hold on to the frame and let yourself dangle. Then I'll lower you as much as I can."

Fear widened her eyes, but she gave a determined nod. In one fluid motion, Nora twisted and dropped from the window, her fingers clinging to the frame.

"Good. Feel the pressure under your arms?" At her nod he gave a gentle tug. "I've got you. Let go."

Nora stared at him, her fingers digging into the window frame. Was he signing her over to injury with his foolish plan?

"But how will you get down?"

Silas's heart constricted. Nora held on not for fear of her own safety, but for his. "I need you to get help."

Her eyes widened in understanding, and without another hesitation she released her weight into his grasp. Silas grunted against the sudden tug and braced his feet against the wall. Inch by painful inch, he allowed the fabric to slip through his fingers until only the very end of Nora's petticoat remained wrapped around his white-knuckled fist.

"Can you reach the ground?" He flung the shout out the window, afraid to lose his grip by changing position.

"No. But I can—"

He suddenly fell backward, all of Nora's weight gone. Panic surged in a white-hot fire up his throat. He scrambled to his knees and lurched toward the window. In the grass below, Nora climbed to her feet.

"Are you hurt?"

She looked up at his shout and shook her head, coughs racking her body. Without another glance back, she bolted.

Silas coughed against the smoke filling his lungs, the air outside now not much better than what boiled into the office. He'd have to jump. If the men hadn't come by now, they'd never get him out in time. At least Nora was safe.

He pulled the knotted fabric back up over the window. If he secured the other end to the desk, he might be able to decrease the distance he'd need to fall to the ground. Hopefully enough to keep him from breaking an ankle. He knotted the bracer around the leg of the desk and gave it a firm pull. The weight of the desk held. With any luck, the desk would pull against the wall and then act as an anchor for his descent. Or the leg would break and he would tumble out of a second-story window.

He had to try.

Breathing through the silk around his face, Silas ducked out of the window and lowered himself to a hanging position. Wrapping the petticoat as best he could around one wrist, he breathed a short prayer.

He let go.

chapter

TWENTY-SIX

"Silas!" Nora raced across the yard, her skirt fighting against the stretch of her legs.

Silas lay on the ground, face up to the sky.

Unmoving.

Men's voices shouted behind her, but their words didn't register. She surged forward, something ripping and allowing her legs to swing more freely. The ground stretched on forever, grass quivering in the oppressive heat. By the time she reached him, he'd still not risen. She dropped to the ground at his side hard enough to jar her teeth.

"Silas?" She ran her hands along his arms and legs, looking for anything broken. Nothing felt out of place. Her hands returned to his face. Had he hit his head?

Was he breathing?

Nora leaned close. His chest wasn't moving. Panic wrapped cold fingers around her throat and squeezed.

No.

She placed her forehead on his. "Please. Breathe." Eyes closed, Nora held the sides of Silas's face, silent prayers forming on her lips in wisps of desperation.

Fingers suddenly slipped up the side of her neck and she yelped. She jerked back.

Deep brown eyes gazed into hers.

The breath went out of her in a rush. "You're alive."

Silas chuckled, the sound quickly dissolving into a groan. "Seems so."

Nora rocked back on her heels, relief flooding through her core and leaving her a bit dizzy. "What happened?"

"Came out of the window." He sat up, holding his head. "Fell farther than I would have liked. Took the . . . breath out of me."

She guessed he'd sustained more injury than he let on, given the way he rubbed the back of his head.

Heat blazed from the carriage shed in sudden force as though to remind her of the destruction at hand. She looped her hands under his arms. "Get up. We have to move. Does anything hurt?"

Silas grunted and rolled to his knees. "Ribs hurt. Head's sore."

The fire behind him blazed, the heat rolling off in waves from the inferno.

"Get up, boy!" Walter appeared at Nora's side, his wrinkled face covered in soot. "You looking for the Good Lord to take you today?"

With strength Nora didn't know the old man possessed, he grabbed Silas and hauled him to his feet. Nora slipped under Silas's opposite arm and the three of them scrambled away from the blaze.

Once they'd gained a safe distance, Walter let go of Silas and turned to Nora. "We got a bucket line started, but I don't think we're gonna be able to save it. Best we can do is keep them embers from taking hold anywhere else."

Nora stared into the flames. Yellow tongues licked at the carriage house, creeping higher toward the roof. Her father's papers. Roger's private quarters. All of their carriages and wagons. Gone in a matter of minutes.

Silas grabbed her hand, his fingers infusing a sense of strength. She straightened underneath the weight of responsibility. "Get the men to wet the ground around the building. Keeping the grass damp will help."

"Yes'm." Walter jogged off to do her bidding as the hands who had been working in the fields arrived to help the stable boys throw one bucket of water after another onto the flames.

Silas lurched forward, joining the efforts. She thought to call after him, but he wasn't the kind of man to leave an emergency to others, injured or not.

She could only pray they could keep the flames from reaching the barn or the house. Nora turned toward her home. Where were Amos and Mother? Hadn't they heard the shouts?

Nora ran toward the house only to find Mother standing with Amos on the porch, watching the flames. When she caught sight of Nora, she pulled free of Amos's grip.

"Nora!" Mother ran down the porch steps. "What in the heavens are you doing out here?"

Nora cast a glance at the porch where Amos stood, his solemn expression tight. "I called for help. Didn't you hear me?"

"I was in the parlor with your uncle." She shook her head fiercely, dislodging a lock of deep brown hair to swing against her cheek. "The men. They were yelling. We came out . . ." She swallowed hard.

She tugged on Mother's arm. "Come on. We need to help."

"There's nothing for women to do." Mother pulled her hands free and dabbed the corner of her eye. "The men will handle it."

Why had she expected anything different? Nora turned on her heel. Mother might be content to linger on the porch in a helpless show of femininity, but Nora wouldn't stand by and watch her property burn when she could do something about it.

"Where are you going?"

She ignored Mother's shout behind her. Heat rippled on the air in shimmering distortion, and the crackling fire popped in Nora's ears. Smoke caused each breath to burn in her lungs. Around the side of the barn, Pete worked furiously on the handle of the pump, water splashing over his scrawny arms. She grabbed his shoulder.

"Get more buckets. Every one we use in the stalls. Go!"

Pete raced off, and Nora grabbed a bucket from the pile at her feet. She pumped and filled, then passed it into the waiting hands of one of the men. Pete dumped more pails at her feet before rushing to join the men dashing back and forth between the water and the blaze.

Nora pumped until her arms lost feeling and her fingers trembled. She couldn't slow. Didn't dare stop. Fear kept her eyes on the task at hand, lest she look into the flickering orange glow and become overwhelmed.

The horses' panicked whinnies echoed on the air, adding another melody to the orchestra of terror sounding around her.

If the fire reached the barn . . .

She worked faster. She wouldn't let it. Hades' breath would not consume her home. Would not steal from them any more than she could help. *Up and down. Up and down.* The repeated cadence fired in her thoughts.

Bucket after bucket filled and passed. Filled and passed. When no fingers stretched out to take the next, she placed the pail on the grass by the hem of her tattered skirt and pumped again. Another. Filled and set on the ground. Three more ready. They must be ready.

"Nora." A firm hand landed on her shoulder. Tugged at her. "Nora."

Silas's warm voice washed over her, but she couldn't stop. "Another bucket's . . . over . . . there." Too consumed with her duty to produce more than heaving words, Nora thrust her chin toward the collection of filled pails at her feet.

"It's over." Silas pulled her from the pump. "We've done all we can."

Over?

Nora allowed her numb fingers to slip from the pump handle, her knees quaking. Silas tucked her up against his side, his own breath coming hard against the top of her head.

"The barn . . . is it . . . ?" She sucked a lungful of caustic air. "The house?"

"We kept it contained."

Relief eased through her, clearing the fog that had kept her moving through her exhaustion. *Contained.* Nora finally allowed her eyes to lift. The carriage shed lay in a smoldering heap, little more than a charred pile of lumber with the skeletal fingers of wagon wheels and bent metal poking through their grave. Her breath trembled. If Silas hadn't gotten them free, they would have been trapped among the charred ruins.

One moment they'd been going through the registry papers and the next . . . Nora shook her head. "How did it start?"

Silas leaned his chin against her temple. "Don't know."

They stared into the glowing heap, small flames still dancing at the center. So little remained.

"There he is!" Roger's voice slammed into Nora's ears, dislodging the stupor that hung over her like a shroud.

Silas released her, causing Nora to have to gather herself to stand upright. She hadn't realized how much of her weight she'd allowed to sag against Silas's strength. Roger and Amos approached from the house, both with faces as red as coals, though Nora didn't remember Amos having helped with any of the work.

The late-afternoon sun gleamed off the top of his uncovered hair, sweat glistening down the sides of his face. Nora's stomach tightened.

"Do you have an explanation for this, Mr. Cavallero?"

Lines formed on Silas's already tired features. "We smelled smoke. Called for help."

"He means an explanation for why you were snooping about." Roger crossed his arms over his thin chest, beady eyes glaring at Silas as though he were to blame.

Nora held out a hand. "No one was snooping. Silas was assisting me."

Close-set eyes roamed over her, disgust flickering underneath his brows. He opened his mouth, but Amos spoke before Roger had the chance.

"Collect your things. I want you off this property immediately."

Off the property? They acted as though Silas had done something wrong.

"Uncle!" Nora grabbed Amos's arm, her dirty fingers leaving a smear on his sleeve. "Silas didn't have anything to do with the fire."

Amos ignored her as though she were nothing more than a pesky fly. "Now. Before I send for the law."

Silas's features hardened and he narrowed his eyes. The air shifted between the men, crackling with an energy she feared would spark into a different kind of inferno.

If she didn't do something to defuse them, they would let their frustrations kindle into violence.

Silas clenched his fists at his side, soot and sweat darkening his features. Her stomach boiled up into her throat. After his fall and the strain of maintaining the bucket line, Silas was in no condition to defend himself. She'd have to be the one to keep the peace.

"Perhaps that's best?" Nora infused pleading into the look she turned on Silas, but the gesture only seemed to cause his nostrils to flare. "Please," she mouthed. His eye twitched and she thought he would refuse, but he suddenly turned on his heel and strode away.

Roger gave a satisfied grunt. "Didn't I say—"

Nora rounded on him. "How *dare* you!" She pulled her shoulders back, all earlier exhaustion forgotten. "You sour, ignorant . . ." she sputtered, insults and accusations curdling on her tongue.

Amos gripped her elbow. "My niece is clearly suffering from the shock." He turned her away, the pressure on her arm stealing the rest of her words.

"You've gone too far this time, Nora." Amos's fingers clamped down on her elbow as he nearly dragged her toward the house.

She craned her neck over her shoulder, searching for Silas.

He was already gone.

They blamed him? *Him?* Silas shoved his clothing into his saddle-bag and flung the worn leather over his shoulder. Of all the stupid things. Why would Roger accuse him of setting fire to the carriage shed?

And Nora. She'd turned on him. Disregarded him. How quickly her feelings fled with her uncle nearby. How had he ever thought she would side with him? Choose him over the will of her uncle? She'd sent him away like a mangy hound with a simple flick of her dismissive eyes, and then she'd had the audacity to plead his understanding while asking him to tuck his tail and scurry away.

Walter's boots slapped on the wooden floor and came to rest in the doorway. "Ain't right." He scratched the back of his head.

"Lots of things in this world ain't right." Like his father's death, his family's misfortunes, and his love for a woman he couldn't have. Sniveling wouldn't change anything.

"He's just riled over losing his stuff." Walter followed Silas through the kitchen. "He'll come around."

A man could be riled without accusing another of wrongdoing. It didn't make any sense. Silas stopped and Walter nearly ran into him.

"Do you think someone here wants me gone?"

Walter's eyebrows flicked upward. "None of the fellas care much for you, I reckon. Oscar sure had his hackles up with the way Miss Fenton responded to you. But what's that got to do with Roger?"

Silas headed toward the door. "First the cut strap, then the plow. Now this." He paused again. "Someone is set on causing trouble." Or causing him harm.

The old man's features scrunched, eyes pulling tight at the corners. "Well, now, I don't know about—" Walter scratched his chin. "Don't make no sense."

Nothing around here did. "Take care, Walter." Silas let the screen door slam behind him, leaving the old man inside. Guilt tugged at him. Walter deserved better. Of all the people on this backwater farm, the cook had been the one person who shot straight and dealt in kindness.

Outside, Pete held Starlight. Mama's old mare pawed nervously at the ground, her ears flicking forward and back.

Pete shifted his feet, the black soot smudged along his pale cheeks making him look like a waif. "They said I should saddle her and wait for you here." He rubbed the heel of his hand on one eye. "You leavin'?"

Silas tugged on the cinch, checking the youth's work. Satisfied, he swung into the saddle and draped his bag over his thighs. He accepted the reins held out to him.

"Will you come back?"

Silas looked over the top of Pete's head to the grand house on the hill. Nora was nowhere in sight. Clearly, she'd made her decision. He supposed it was better to know now, before he let himself care too much. The lie barely formed before crumbling to dust. He already loved her. The circumstances of her rejection made little difference, and knowing now rather than later did nothing to ease the feelings ripping through his chest.

"No, Pete. I don't reckon I will."

He turned Starlight's muzzle and pressed his heels into her sides. She launched forward, kicking up dust behind her.

At a full gallop, they left Emberwild behind.

chapter

TWENTY-SEVEN

Never had this house felt more like a cage. Nora paced from one wall to the next. Despite Amos's desire to marry her mother and regardless of the fact that he was her only remaining male relative, he did *not* have the right to treat her like a wayward girl.

She rubbed absently at the bruises he'd left on her arm when he'd dragged her inside the house. She'd been a coward. She should have stood up to him instead of hiding in her room. But Amos had looked so much like her father that fear had overtaken her.

Why hadn't she defended Silas and insisted he stay while they cleared everything up? She'd been too distraught to think clearly. Now he was gone, and it was her fault.

The murky predawn light peeked through the window of Nora's room, brushing the edges of her riding dress and poking tentative fingers into the sleeping shadows. Outside, the glow from the fire still smoldered, an unnatural companion to the sun's first rays.

Hand on the glass, she watched the world awaken, her nerves jittery. Despite her exhaustion, she'd hardly slept. Today she would have answers. Speak her own decisions.

And get Silas back.

Nora made her way down to the kitchen and flung open the

curtains. Mother would need a bracing cup of coffee this morning. Her trembling fingers indicated she might as well. She put the water on to boil, then added the fragrant grounds.

Soon the warm scent drifted through the kitchen and brightened her senses. By the time she set the tray with the coffee pot, two mugs, cooled cream, and sugar, her determination to find Silas and let him know he'd pried open the walls around her heart hardened into resolve. That resolve brought a sense of peace.

Peace that frayed around the edges, but peace nonetheless.

Nora carried the tray upstairs and tapped on Mother's door. A few moments later Mother appeared wrapped in her dressing gown, hair already brushed and shimmering down her back.

"I've been expecting you." Her tired eyes held little warmth, two cold amber stones set in a face unencumbered by emotion.

The mosquito netting had already been pulled back and tied away from Mother's bed, the serene blue quilts smoothed and draped over the mattress. Nora crossed the thick rug, catching a glimpse of herself in the floor-length mirror. The woman walking into her mother's domain strode with confidence and an unwavering calm that nearly surprised her.

On the other side of the dressing screen and washbasin, a cozy seating area snuggled against the two French-style doors leading to a private upper balcony. Nora placed the tray on the small table and then opened the doors to let in a sultry breeze still tainted with smoke. Without awaiting invitation, Nora settled into one of the two delicate chairs and poured the steaming liquid into the waiting cups.

Mother joined her at the table and wrapped long fingers around her mug. She lifted the rich brown liquid and drew a long breath. Nora looked out over the lawn toward the stables, the ruined carriage shed thankfully hidden from view.

After a few sips, she turned to Mother, meeting the gaze that lingered on her. "The truth, Mother, if you will."

She hadn't planned to start there, but she was tired of conversations that took the long route rather than stating the point. No more implications and vague answers. Something had happened between Mother and Amos. Something that she suspected led to Amos running Silas off the farm.

Even in her dressing gown with her hair tumbled around her shoulders, Mother sat as regally as a queen. "It started that night at the Cromwell house."

Nora paused with the coffee partway to her lips. The Cromwell house? What in the heavens did that have to do with Amos, the fire, or Silas? Perhaps she should have been more specific. Her childhood missteps had nothing to do with whatever had transpired between her mother and uncle in the parlor yesterday. She parted her lips, hot words on her tongue, but the ones leaving Mother's mouth stole them before they could fully form.

"Your father found out my secret that night. He became enraged. He wasn't thinking clearly, and he latched on to suspicions he refused to release. No matter what I tried to tell him."

Cold fingers wrapped around Nora's throat and squeezed as the words filled the space between them.

Mother put her coffee back on the table. Sadness entered her eyes, causing a spark of humanity that cracked her façade. "He looked for every excuse to prove his suspicions true. He insisted your wayward behavior and turning aside reasonable suitors was a punishment for my sins."

What sins?

And what did any of that have to do with the Cromwells and the ruinations she'd caused between Father and his banker? "You're speaking in riddles."

Mother sighed. "I loved Amos first."

The words fell between them as though someone had dropped a horseshoe on the table. Nora blinked, her mind refusing to grasp the meaning.

"I'd met him at a friend's picnic and . . ." She fiddled with the collar of her dressing gown. "You must understand how charming he was. I was young and foolish. The secret messages. The meetings when no one was looking. I found the entire thing wildly romantic."

Mother shook her head as if willing the painful memories away. She seemed to age a score of years in a matter of moments.

"Times were difficult then, during Reconstruction," she continued, her face becoming a mask of determination. "My father said he found a good match for me. A man who would be able to salvage our land and provide me with a good life. I had no idea at the time the suitor was Amos's older brother." She drew a deep breath and straightened already rigid shoulders. "I had a duty to my family. I needed to put aside girlish fantasies and yield to my father's wisdom."

Nora stared at her. She'd courted Amos, then ended up marrying Father? She blinked, trying to put the pieces together. "Is that the promise Uncle spoke of?"

Mother cocked an eyebrow. "Were you spying on us?"

This was hardly the time to feel scolded like a girl caught playing with her mother's perfumes. She kept her gaze level. "I heard you as I was heading outside. It's a wonder you didn't hear me shut the front door."

Red crept up the sides of Mother's neck but her gaze never wavered. "I tried to get Amos to understand that I had to make the match with the brother who had inherited. He promised to keep our affections for one another a secret so as not to poison the marriage." She swallowed and focused on her cup. "And I promised Amos that if anything ever happened to Hiram, we would be together."

Nora slumped against her chair, stunned. All these years. Did she love Amos the entire time?

"I wanted to be a good wife"—Mother's eyes appeared nearly pleading—"so I put the past behind me and focused on the life I would create with your father. Love has a way of blooming between the intimacies of husband and wife, and soon I realized that the fleeting infatuation I'd had with Amos was nothing more than a fondness for flirtations and romance. It held no comparison to the depth of shared lives and the bond of marriage. That kind of love was real."

Mother swiped at a tear, but her voice remained steady.

"As the years passed, I thought Amos's affections for me would wane, but he stayed true to his word. He never married." Mother's voice pinched. "Now that your father is gone, he believes I should keep my end of a foolish young girl's whispered assurances."

That explained the scene in the parlor. Perhaps many of the other conversations as well. It certainly played a part in his desire to so quickly wed his brother's widow. Perhaps she could even understand how Father could have grown bitter against his brother or his wife if he found out they'd had a hidden relationship. But what did any of that have to do with her?

Something Mother said earlier jabbed through the questions swarming in her mind.

"He insisted your wayward behavior and turning aside reasonable suitors was a punishment for my sins."

As though reading the question on Nora's face, Mother leaned forward and regarded her with an icy glare.

"A few kisses were all I ever shared with Amos." She tilted her chin higher. "Your birth so soon after our wedding and the lack of siblings in the years to come, however, put suspicions in your father's mind that no amount of assurances could dispel."

Nora slumped back in her chair. Her father had treated her as unwanted because he thought his wife had been with his brother? Had she suffered years of undue enmity because her mother had first loved another?

"All those years." The leaden words dropped from Nora's lips. She pulled humid air into her lungs, the mixture of summer blooms and lingering soot bitter on her senses. "All those years my father despised me because of you. Why didn't you tell me?"

Mother scoffed. "There was never a doubt you were your father's daughter."

Nora eyed the woman across from her, intimately familiar and yet somehow now completely foreign. How did one shift so suddenly from seeing only the mother who'd raised her to having her eyes opened to a woman who harbored an entire life filled with secrets and hurts?

The subtle game between Mother and Amos—the unspoken words and shared glances—all made sense now. Nora swallowed against the dryness in her mouth. "Are . . . are you going to marry him?"

Mother trailed a finger along the top edge of her coffee cup, refusing to meet Nora's eyes. It was all the answer she needed.

Nora rose. "I'm going to find Silas."

Mother's gaze shot to Nora, questions storming in their depths. "Why?"

"First, because he deserves the pay Uncle promised him." Her fingers clamped the back of the chair. "Secondly, the way he was dismissed yesterday was unfair." Third, because she loved him.

The smooth planes of Mother's face crinkled in dismay. "You care for him."

It was a statement, not a question. Nora adjusted her riding habit. "I'll not marry Mr. Dale."

Mother shook her head. "Fleeting affections come and go. A woman needs stability."

"Yet you will give up ours."

"That's hardly the same." The side of Mother's mouth twitched.

"Isn't it? You keep Emberwild if you remain unmarried. Marry Amos and everything becomes his."

Emberwild would be lost to her. Amos would surely see to that. Sorrow welled within her, but she pushed it aside.

Something simmered in Mother's eyes, but Nora couldn't decode the meaning. One thing she knew for certain. She didn't want to end up like Mother. Making all her choices about love and marriage based on fear.

She would not shackle herself to a man—or him to her—simply to seek security. If she ever married, it would be only to a man whom she could trust with her heart. A man who would never seek to destroy her freedom, but rather one who would stand by her side as they sought adventures together.

238

Nora held Mother's gaze. "You've made your choice. I'm making mine."

The woman before her no longer seemed the regal queen ruling over everything in her reach, but rather a tired woman who feared facing the world alone. Nora rounded the table and placed a hand on Mother's shoulder. As though her touch released something long held, Mother's tight posture drooped and her head lowered.

"He won't be able to provide you the comforts you deserve." The whispered words held a note of desperation.

"At least you'll be rid of me." The bitter words cracked from her heart, spilling into the light.

"Rid of you?" Mother's voice broke. "Is that truly what you think? I've only ever wanted for you to find security. A good life."

"There's more to life than property and comforts, Mother. With Silas, I can be free from expectations to be someone other than myself. He doesn't frown at my love for a wild gallop through the meadow or my wearing trousers to do so." Choosing Silas might not give her a life of means, but the call for an adventure of the heart pulled on her in ways she couldn't understand.

Yet wanted to embrace.

She squeezed Mother's shoulder. "Thank you for wanting to make sure I'm cared for. Please understand that your idea of how that is accomplished is different from mine."

A single tear streaked down Mother's cheek. Her fingers encased Nora's hand, then gave a small pat.

Nora leaned close and draped her arm over Mother's shoulders. "Take Father's will to the solicitor. Silas can help us run Emberwild, Mother. You don't have to marry Amos."

For several moments, Mother remained silent. Nora leaned down and placed a feathery kiss on Mother's temple. "You always have my love, no matter what you choose."

With one final squeeze, Nora released her mother and headed toward the barn.

chapter

TWENTY-EIGHT

Maybe she wasn't too late. Nora leaned down in the saddle, the ends of Arrow's mane fluttering in her face. The big colt's hooves pounded against the dry earth and sent clouds of red dust boiling up behind them. The sun hovered above the treetops, well on its way to the zenith.

Arrow ate up the ground between Emberwild and Philadelphia with exuberance. Gripping the reins in her gloved hands, she encouraged him to move faster. He tucked his hindquarters and shot forward, finding even more speed than she thought possible. The trees whipped by at an alarming rate, causing a tendril of fear to worm underneath the sense of exhilaration. Better ease up before their breakneck pace put one or both of them in danger. Nora tugged back on the bit and Arrow fought the bridle.

"Why must you be so stubborn?"

The horse twitched his ears at the shout above his head and to Nora's surprise slowed a fraction. They settled into a manageable gallop, fields and farms flowing by in streams of color. Finally, a cluster of buildings took shape in the distance. The moderate-size town of Philadelphia, Mississippi, where she hoped she'd find Silas.

By the time they neared the white tower of the county courthouse and the start of the paved streets, Nora and Arrow had entered into another battle of wills.

"Arrow!" Nora fought against the reins, but the horse refused to yield to her directions.

Townspeople dove out of her way as Arrow sped past the bank, the livery, and the blacksmith's shop. Nora barely managed to keep her saddle as Arrow careened around a corner. Fool horse had no problem obeying commands to turn. Only ones that forced him to slow.

The town's only inn came into view. Silas had to be there. "Arrow! Whoa."

They were barreling toward the building too fast. Nora planted her weight into her stirrup and pulled hard on the left rein. Arrow's powerful neck muscles fought against her and he kept his nose pointed forward. Would he plow right into the wall?

As though suddenly figuring out the detriment he was galloping toward, Arrow let out a high pitch squeal and ducked his hindquarters, rear hooves catching and sliding against the brick pavers. Nora's weight shifted forward, her momentum carrying her up over the saddle horn. Pain radiated in her middle as the air left her lungs. Fingers digging into Arrow's neck to keep her seat, Nora thrust herself back down toward the saddle.

Arrow flung his head and reared.

Nora rocked her weight, positioning her feet to come nearly to standing. With a snort, Arrow landed, jarring her teeth. As soon as all four hooves connected with the ground, Nora leapt from the saddle.

Her hands trembled as she gripped the reins. "Fool horse! You'll get us both killed."

"I was thinking the same."

Nora whirled at the sound of the masculine voice behind her.

Disappointment curdled in her stomach. Tall and lean, the man regarding her with interest in his deep brown eyes wasn't the cowboy she sought.

"Need help?" He eyed Arrow warily.

Nora shot a glare at her headstrong colt. "I'm looking for a man."

His eyebrows shot up and a smirk pulled his thin lips back from his teeth. "You're looking at one right—"

"I'm looking for Silas Cavallero." She pulled herself to her full height and forced her fluttering breathing to slow. "Dark hair and eyes, always wears a cowboy hat. Have you seen him?"

Disappointment flickered in the man's eyes. He shrugged. "Coulda been a fellow looked like that in the common room." He nodded toward the inn behind her. "But I didn't get his name."

Nora thanked him and tied Arrow to the hitching post. With any luck the horse wouldn't tear the thing down in the few moments she'd be inside and run amok through town.

"Please don't be stupid." She patted his sweaty neck.

Inside the inn she found a clean but rustic eating area with a long bar on one end and a set of stairs that led to an upper floor on the other. The half dozen tables stood empty this time of day, the only soul a large fellow wiping away at an already gleaming bar top.

A door swung open behind the bar area, and a middle-aged woman with a pile of curls perched on the crown of her head bustled out. Her gaze snagged on Nora and she scuttled across the wooden floor.

"Mornin', miss. Looking for a room?"

The man at the bar stopped his work, eyes fixed on Nora.

"No, thank you. I'm looking for Mr. Cavallero. Have you seen him?"

The woman shifted to share a meaningful look with the man. She smoothed her hands down the apron wrapped around her waist. "Your pardon, but aren't you the lady from Emberwild?"

Trepidation writhed through her center as she inclined her head in acknowledgment.

"Thought so. Boy was powerful upset when he came in here yesterday." She turned with a hand on her hip. "Weren't he, Joe?"

The man Nora assumed to be the innkeeper—possibly this woman's husband—nodded. "Probably would have left in the dark if I hadn't convinced him otherwise."

"Where is he now?" Had she already missed him?

They exchanged another look. "Don't know, Miss Fenton." The big man shrugged. "He was gone before Myrtle started the fire this morning."

Gone.

The weight of the single word draped around her shoulders. "Do you know where he was headed?"

Sympathy clouded the other woman's eyes. "Didn't say."

"Mentioned something about headin' back west." The innkeeper tossed the cleaning rag over his shoulder.

He wouldn't leave Mississippi for good without telling her. Would he? Nora clasped her hands in front of her and tried to maintain a cool composure. "If he comes back, would you mind telling him I was looking for him?"

"Certainly." Myrtle's smile touched her eyes.

Nora thanked them and stepped back outside. Arrow pawed the ground, his patience wearing thin. She shielded her eyes and gauged the sun.

West.

Not much to go on. But he couldn't have gone far, could he? She'd just start down the road. Arrow was fast. Much faster than old Starlight. She'd catch him. Tell him to come back.

Ask him to stay at Emberwild.

With her.

She untied the reins and swung into the saddle. Arrow pranced sideways, already eager to be on their way.

"Nora Fenton, you come down this instant."

Her knees instinctively tightened at the sound of her uncle's stern voice, and Arrow sidestepped. She held firm as Arrow pranced and chewed the bit. Of course he would be in town this morning. Had likely witnessed her crazed run through the streets.

"What are you doing?" Red crept up the sides of Amos's face, though from heat or anger, she couldn't tell. He eased closer, causing Arrow to snort.

Did he think her a child he could command? Nora lifted her chin. "I came to find Silas."

His posture stiffened. "Come down off that horse so we can talk."

Nora shook her head. "I need to go." What was he doing here, anyway? Had he come to the inn looking for Silas as well?

Before she could react, his hand shot out and seized the reins. Arrow tossed his head. Amos's arm wrenched forward, but he held firm. Arrow pawed and bobbed his head, then yielded.

Amos gestured toward the ground. "I won't ask again."

Ire scorched through her veins. She wasn't his ward or his daughter and she didn't have to—

"I've reported Mr. Cavallero to the sheriff."

The words hung in the air between them. She drew back, thoughts sputtering to a halt. "You did what?" What possible cause could he have for that?

Onlookers had paused to watch, and Amos gestured again toward the ground.

Nora leaned down closer and drew out the single word with as much authority as she could muster. "Why?"

The muscle in the side of his cheek twitched. "For destruction of property, of course."

"Destruction of . . ." Nora shook her head. "Silas didn't start that fire. Couldn't have. He was with me the entire time."

A noise rumbled low in Amos's throat. "How long do you think it takes for a fire to catch below and spread to the upper floor? He probably thought to burn up the evidence and you with it."

What in the world was he talking about? Nora tugged back on the reins, trying to free Arrow from Amos's grasp. She didn't have time for this. She'd never known her uncle to be the suspicious sort, but his accusation of a clearly innocent man bordered on paranoia. "You best look to Roger's carelessness if you're seeking a culprit for—"

Amos suddenly snatched Arrow's bridle with one hand and simultaneously used the other to seize Nora's arm and wrench her weight sideways.

She toppled from the saddle and barely kept her balance enough to land with both feet on the ground. Heaving, she stared up into Amos's stern face. She hardly recognized the man before her. Save the harshness in his gaze that rivaled what she'd often seen from her father. In that, the resemblance became strikingly clear.

Nora refused to let her fear show. Amos wasn't her father. She buried any outward reflection of her inner disquiet underneath an icy calm. "If you'll please excuse me. I need to be going."

"Don't be a fool, Nora."

Her hackles rose. "A fool? You are the one playing the fool, Uncle. Looking for ill intent where there is none. Accusing a man of wrongdoing without a single scrap of evidence. One would think you were simply looking to be rid of—"

"Then why was he snooping through the office?" Amos snapped.

Arrow snorted, tugging the reins in Amos's hand, but he hardly seemed to notice. He clamped his fingers around the tender flesh on Nora's arm, causing her to yelp.

"What was he doing?" Amos shook her arm, a wildness in his eyes. "Snooping through your father's things where he had no right." He shook her again. "Well? Speak, child."

"He was helping me." She gasped as he released his hold.

Amos's eyes narrowed. "Helping you? With what?"

Nora took a step back. "I . . . I asked him to help me look through Father's paperwork."

He stared at her a moment, something churning behind his eyes. Had he realized his mistake in going to the sheriff when Nora had been the one to go through Father's papers? Why did he care?

The will.

He must have known about Father's change in the will and didn't want anyone finding out the truth before he could wed Mother.

Amos closed his eyes, chin drooping toward his chest. Quiet

words slipped free, barely audible. "Why couldn't you leave well enough alone?"

Leave what alone? Did Amos know something about Ember's paperwork? Or Silas's father? "What do you mean?"

Amos's eyes snapped to hers and he shook his head. Nora tucked her hands behind her so he wouldn't see her fingers clench into fists.

"I should have known that boy would stir up trouble." Amos suddenly spat. "I should have gotten rid of him weeks ago."

Nora leaned back in surprise.

Amos rubbed the bridge of his nose, his tone defeated. "Instead, I'd wanted to keep you and your mother from the truth. It seems that's no longer an option."

Nora's pulse thrummed. "What truth?"

"I figured it out once Silas started asking questions, finally putting together the name and the incident from all those years ago." Amos shook his head. "Hiram is responsible for the death of Juan Cavallero."

Nora's breath caught.

Amos released a long sigh. "Indirectly, at least. My brother kept the secret to the grave, save what little he told you."

"But, I don't . . ." Words refused to form. She'd thought when they'd found Ember's papers that there'd been a mistake. All of Silas's worries had been cleared. Ember couldn't have been stolen. They had paperwork proving his legitimacy. So how would Father have been involved in another man's death?

"Hiram was failing. Losing the farm and everything he'd promised Rebecca. If only that fool had agreed to sell his colt, none of it would have happened." Amos stepped closer to her again, his voice barely above a whisper.

Her fingers clenched. More vague references. She needed him to state the truth. "*What* wouldn't have happened?"

"They had an argument. Apparently spooked the horse. There was an accident. Hiram left, not waiting to see what happened to the man." Amos's eyes were pools of remorse. "Silas must have found out that Hiram got into an argument with Juan Cavallero. Probably blamed the accident on him. I realized too late that he actually came to Emberwild to seek revenge."

Nora shook her head, thoughts spiraling. "No, that can't be right."

"Did he tell you a story about wanting to find out what happened to his father?"

"Yes, but—"

"And then did he tell you something to make you think that Ember might be the horse that ran off that night?"

Nora pressed her lips together. He had. But that didn't mean that Silas came seeking retribution. Did it? Silas didn't seem the type.

"I thought so." Amos blew a breath out long and slow. "You've been deceived, Nora. That man came to Emberwild planning to pin his father's accidental death on our family and claim that our legitimate foundation stallion belongs to him. All so he could destroy us in an act of revenge." He pinched the bridge of his nose. "Probably wanted to steal Arrow as well."

"None of that makes any sense." The pain in Silas's eyes had been too real. She regarded her uncle thoughtfully. Something didn't sit right.

"He used you and your affections to find the rightful papers." Sympathy dripped from Amos's lips. "Then he set the fire to destroy all the evidence. Probably even had you feeling sorry for him, didn't he?"

Yes, she'd felt sorry for him. Her heart had moved with his plight. But he wouldn't have used her affections to try to take advantage of her family. He wasn't that type of man.

A voice nagged in the back of her mind that every man she'd ever known had sought to use her in one way or another.

Nora tried to shove the doubts away. Silas wouldn't do that, would he?

Amos captured her gaze and spoke gently. "If there had been a stolen horse and a murder, don't you think the sheriff would have looked for the culprit fifteen years ago? Think about it, Nora. Why would

Silas come to Emberwild? Why now?" His eyebrows lifted with a new thought. "If fact, we don't even know that he's not just some drifter who heard the story and cooked up a tale to try to steal from us."

Despite her best efforts, doubt and hurt clouded her words. "But why would he do that?"

"Maybe he's a confidence man, child." He reached and took her hand. "Either way, he played on your emotions. I'm sorry I didn't get rid of him sooner. I fear I could have saved you a lot of heartache."

No. Silas hadn't done anything to prove himself anything but honorable. Nora pulled her hand from her uncle's grasp. "You're wrong. Silas didn't set that fire. And he wouldn't have lied to me."

Amos sighed. "What if I could prove it to you?"

"How?"

"He ran, didn't he? Probably as soon as he figured out the law would be coming for him."

Nora crossed her arms. "Because you dismissed him from the farm."

Amos lifted an eyebrow in challenge. "So he left without any of his pay?"

Doubt niggled through her again. She understood why he'd left Emberwild yesterday after what happened. But why had he left Philadelphia already?

Her heart pinched. Silas wouldn't have lied to her, would he? She thought back on their times together. His intensity about wanting to find out what happened to his father. To find answers. If he blamed Father, would he have thought to sabotage Emberwild?

"I think you're wrong." Nora drew herself tall, refusing to let the doubts sour her convictions about a good man. "Silas was looking for answers, yes. But I don't think he ever wanted to cause us any harm."

Amos appeared thoughtful for a moment. "Shall we put it to the test, then?" At Nora's hesitant nod, he continued. "A type of wager, if you will. If Silas is innocent, and his affections for you are real, then naturally he will return." He spread his hands. "At the least, he'll make contact with you once matters settle. Correct?"

He would, wouldn't he? He wouldn't have left her for good. Not after all the things he'd said to her. Not after the way his tender embrace had stirred her heart. "He'll come back."

"Then we are agreed. If Silas returns, we'll give him the opportunity to clear up what really happened with the fire."

What game was Amos playing? He couldn't have so easily gone from reporting Silas to the sheriff to welcoming the man back. "So if he comes back, you'll listen to all he has to say?"

"You have my word." Amos held up the palm of his hand. "But if he doesn't, then we'll put this behind us as a lesson learned and move forward with our lives. Agreed?"

Ah. There it was. The caveat. Nora crossed her arms. "And of course by *forward* you mean you'll marry my mother, take over Emberwild, and sell off all my horses?" She didn't mean for her voice to rise in pitch, but the words had the desired effect.

Surprise widened his eyes for an instant before his features settled back into patient composure. "I know you find this difficult to understand, but I care for your mother and want to make sure she is well taken care of. Emberwild is losing money. It will take selling the horses and most of the land to settle the debts."

Were they really doing so poorly that they were in danger of losing everything? Regardless of what happened with Silas, she couldn't stand idly by while Amos disassembled every portion of her life. She donned the mask of the doting niece, forcing her tone to lower into a respectful calm. "We only need a little more time, Uncle. You saw how Arrow runs. His stud fees alone will be enough to right the accounts."

Amos tapped the reins against his palm as he eyed Arrow thoughtfully.

She'd found an opening. Nora pressed the moment. "Let him run. Prove his worth. Why sell him for less as an unproven racer? He could be worth far more."

Calculation entered her uncle's gaze. "Perhaps you have a point."

Victory swelled and a sense of recklessness caused her to push harder. If she didn't try her luck now, she might never get a better opportunity. "Then you agree that if he wins, you step aside. I get to keep Arrow and run Emberwild, freeing us from the debts and allowing the farm to prosper once more."

Amos narrowed his eyes. "A woman isn't capable of running that place on her own."

Nora bit back the scathing retort about how it had been his and Roger's lack of management that landed them in this predicament in the first place.

Amos sucked his teeth. "But I will give you Arrow as a dowry when you marry Mr. Dale. Any worth he proves will only increase your asset."

Her stomach wriggled itself down to her toes. Would Amos keep his word on whatever deal they struck? She had to try. "No good. I don't want to marry Mr. Dale."

Amos studied her. "Very well. If Silas returns, then you two have my blessing."

He'd concede? Just like that? Why?

"I'll give you the chance to see if Arrow can reconcile the damages your father's sickness caused. If you can, then I'll allow you and Silas to manage Emberwild for me."

Her heart caught in her throat. He'd not only agree to the union, but he'd also give them Emberwild? Then it would no longer matter if Mother married him or not.

"But you must promise that if Mr. Cavallero doesn't return, then you accept Mr. Dale's proposition."

Nora swallowed, trying to work moisture back into her mouth. "How long do I have to decide?" Her mind scrambled. Silas would come back for her. Give her a chance to clear everything up. Of that she had no doubt. But they'd never keep Emberwild safe if she couldn't sell Arrow's stud rights for a hefty sum. "Arrow will need to race in order to prove his worth." He needed a year. Perhaps more. "Time to run the circuits and build his value."

Amos nodded along. "I'd like a fall wedding. Before then, I'd like to have matters settled with you."

This fall? It was almost August.

Amos removed his pocket watch from his vest and twirled the gold chain around his finger, causing Arrow to grunt and bob his head. "I'll let you enter Arrow in the harness races at the Mississippi and West Alabama Fair in October." The watch stopped spinning. "After that, you marry Mr. Dale and do with Arrow as you see fit."

"And if Silas returns?"

Amos spread his hands. "Then I'll sell the land and the mares to cover the debts, and you can keep the house, the barn, and Arrow."

He made the concession without ever thinking he would lose. Whatever he was up to, her only hope was to prove him wrong.

"Are we agreed?" He lifted the reins to Nora.

She accepted them, studying the leather in her hands. She wasn't as simple as her uncle likely thought. She knew the scales of this wager were uneven. If Silas returned, he had two people willing to run a failing farm and make it profitable for him. If he didn't return, Amos married Nora off with a dowry that she herself increased in value with Arrow, thus saving him the trouble of procuring more. A prize that cost him nothing.

For her part, if Silas never returned, she'd have one ornery stallion and a loveless marriage. Her beloved Emberwild would be gone, as would her freedom.

But she still had to try.

Please, Silas. Don't prove my faith in you misplaced.

Amos held out his hand, offering her a man's shake on a deal. Slowly, she slipped her gloved palm against his. Amos gave her hand a firm pump and smiled.

"It's settled, then." He patted her shoulder. "Let's head home, shall we?"

Nora cast one final look at the western sky before mounting Arrow once more.

She'd just bet her entire future on a man.

chapter
TWENTY-NINE

Emberwild
August 29, 1905

Twenty-nine days. Nora stared out over the southern pastures and watched the ripe seed heads sway in the grass. Arrow snatched at the stalks contentedly, his red coat in harmony with the colors painting the morning sky.

Another sunrise. Another morning that would slip into a day filled with directing the stable hands to finish the work of cleaning up the ruins of the carriage shed, helping Mother, and avoiding her uncle.

One more day to try, but fail, to keep her hands and her mind occupied, desperately hoping to distract herself from the one thought that continued to pluck away at the fibers of her soul until she felt as raw and exposed as a turtle pulled from its shell.

Silas hadn't come back.

The ache in her center had dulled a little more with each passing day, settling from a churning, maddening thing—a tempest of hope, expectation, and anxiety—into the residual floodwaters that now threatened to drown her in their mire.

Tears stung the back of her throat, but she wouldn't let them form. To do so might release the dam struggling to hold her emotions in check. It was cracked and crumbling already, and the smallest leak would cause a greater fissure she feared she couldn't contain.

Where is he?

She'd given him the first two weeks in hopeful impatience, knowing he would need a little time for emotions to cool and for his wounded pride to step out of his way. Men could be like that. Stubbornly refusing to yield if they saw the move as a sign of weakness. Had he considered coming for her a weakness?

Arrow snorted, his patience with Nora's lingering growing thin. She plucked another seed head and let the pieces crumble between her fingers.

"There's no reason he didn't come back for us."

The horse tossed his head as though agreeing with her statement. Nora tangled her fingers into the comfort of Arrow's mane.

Amos had lied.

The weathered sheriff's face hovered in her mind. His confused expression branded into memory. *"Don't know what you're talking about, Miss Fenton. There's no report filed for that fire."*

The revelation had left her cold.

Why had Amos lied about going to the law? To frighten her? How did the deception play into whatever he planned?

How had she let herself bet everything on Silas? She didn't know him. Not really. Never mind that something about him coiled her insides into knots, drawing her to his steady presence with a pull she couldn't define. Betting her entire life on a feeling had been reckless. Stupid.

The morning air hung heavy with moisture and the smells she'd loved her entire life. Fresh grass, dew-laden air, horses. The reins grew slick in her hand and she had to squeeze her eyes shut a moment.

Amos's promises were a rusty bucket. Not holding anything for long. Yet somehow he'd weighted everything in his favor, and the scales tipped all the way to his side. Arrow could save the farm, she felt that deep in her marrow. She really could bet her future on him.

Silas, on the other hand . . . Nora huffed. What had she been thinking?

The dull ache residing in her chest intensified, bringing barbs that cut into her heart. She'd been thinking he cared for her. Perhaps loved her, as she did him.

Nora thrust her foot back into the stirrup and swung her leg over the saddle.

Maybe Mother had been right all along. Emotions were fickle things. A woman couldn't base a future on them.

Nora let Arrow have his head. The big horse tensed beneath her. Was her affection for Silas nothing more than a firefly's flickering light? Beautifully pulsing one day, yet gone the next?

If she chose to marry Mr. Dale, would they be able to grow something more powerful out of the union? Her heart stubbornly disagreed, but what did she know?

She'd finally found the courage to make her choice. Fine lot of good it had done her. The decision still landed her in the same predicament she'd been in months ago.

Lose Emberwild. Marry a man she didn't know. Leave everything behind.

Perhaps not everything. "At least I still have you." The whispered words fell on ears that flicked back toward her for only an instant.

Arrow tossed his head, waves of energy waiting to be released.

This was why she'd always preferred horses. They were simple. Easy to understand. Care for them, respect them, and they offered you the same in return.

She leaned forward in the saddle and drew a deep breath. "Ready?"

An idea half formed in the shadowed recesses of her mind.

What if she took Arrow and ran?

She tightened her knees and squeezed.

Arrow lurched forward, his power erupting beneath her. Wind

rushed over her. Nora threw her head back and let the wind have its way.

They could make the race circuit together. Travel the country. Arrow would win.

It would be a chance. An opportunity to make her own decisions and her own mistakes.

Arrow galloped across the field. Nora loosed the reins and let him fly, surrendering them both to the desperate need for freedom.

Hurt cloaked her heart. She embraced it. Used the pain to fuel her courage. She squeezed her eyes tight and let Arrow take her wherever the wind blew them.

Leave Emberwild.

Her eyes flew open and she lowered herself in the saddle. "Run, Arrow. Run as fast as you can."

Charged by her words, the horse gained speed until the world around them became nothing but a blur.

Arrow would run.

Could she?

chapter
THIRTY

Emberwild
October 12, 1905

Nora flung the light covers from her sweaty legs and left the bed she'd hardly slept in. Dawn would be here soon, bringing with it another day to chip away at her heart.

Arduous days had melted into weeks, and still nothing had changed. Mother hadn't voiced a firm decision. Amos's patience with her wore thin. Twice Nora had brought up the will, only to have Mother shake her head and infuriatingly insist on avoiding the discussion. What in the heavens was the woman up to?

Silas still hadn't returned.

Hope steadily drained away, until she felt little other than the sharp pain of rejection.

Silas had chosen to leave her. That, or he was dead.

The second thought threatened to open a hole so deep within her that she almost welcomed the first. He'd chosen to leave. Fine. She could live with that. She'd always known men to be a fickle species, following pride or whims wherever the notion took them. Hadn't she always expected that surrendering her heart and making herself vulnerable would only leave her trampled? She hardly had the right to be angry with herself now when she'd let such foolishness consume her.

But she could be angry with him.

Holding on to that anger would give her the fuel she needed to take the next steps. To follow through with the plan she'd spent weeks formulating.

Now it was nearly time.

After dressing in a plain day dress, Nora decided to leave the length of her hair down around her shoulders with two simple braids to hold it back from her face. Then she tidied her bed and moved to the door. Coffee on the porch as the birds greeted the day and then a visit with Arrow would provide her with enough fortitude to endure another day.

Predawn light warmed the wallpaper in the hallway. She closed her door quietly, not wanting to disturb Mother. She'd been withdrawn again, and the purple shadowing her eyes indicated she could do without Nora waking her too early.

She stepped quietly across the carpet and then paused, a sensation creeping over her and causing her skin to pimple into gooseflesh. What was that?

Whispers?

Nora paused and strained her ears. Perhaps she'd imagined it. Her overcrowded mind had started playing tricks on her.

The voices came again, louder this time. One male, one female. Coming from the first floor. Nora frowned. Who would be here this early in the morning? She tiptoed closer, listening. At the top of the stairs, she dropped down into a crouch. From this vantage, she could make out two figures in the foyer below.

Amos. She should have known. She shouldn't be eavesdropping, and true, she felt a bit childish hiding from her family, but her uncle had hardly been transparent, and sneaking would likely be the best way to learn anything of use.

"Don't worry, Rebecca." Amos smoothed a hand down Mother's hair.

Bile rose in Nora's throat. How long had he been here? Surely he hadn't stayed the night.

Mother stepped away from him. "You always say that, yet the more times you do, the more I worry."

"The drifter isn't coming back. I promise."

Nora's stomach clenched. Had he done something to Silas? The idea sucked all the moisture from her mouth. He'd been sure that day in town. Confident. She'd dismissed his assurance that Silas would never return as another facet of her uncle's overconfidence in his own schemes. Or simply because Amos saw the odds as too stacked in his favor.

But had Amos actually harmed him? Nora wrapped an arm around her middle. Would her uncle do such a thing? Would he hurt Silas simply to have his way with the Fenton women?

"And *how* do you know that?" Mother's voice rose with a sharp whisper, clearly wondering the same terrible thing as Nora.

"Because I've taken care of it," he scoffed. "When will you ever learn to trust me, woman?"

Fire rose up in Nora's center. How dare he speak to Mother that way? What right did he have to think he could—

"I'll not suffer that tone, Amos." Mother drew herself into her familiar regal bearing, her dressing gown and haphazardly pinned hair unable to diminish her. "When will *you* learn that I will not be maneuvered?"

Maneuvered? Had she been so submerged in her own problems that she'd missed the ones simmering between them? Nora angled herself to get a better look at the two figures squaring off against one another.

They looked nothing like a couple who might soon marry. Or had she simply refused to look past Mother's forced smiles?

"I've done everything in my power to give you what you want." Voice raw, words weighted with meaning, Amos stepped closer to Mother, every line and angle of his form screaming barely contained desperation.

Would she reject him?

"I never wanted this." Mother's words were so soft that Nora nearly missed them.

"Everything will be fine, Rebecca. You'll see. And if it's Nora's suitor that has given you qualms, then I'll find her another match." He stroked Mother's arm. "I'll take care of everything for you."

Nora inched closer and lost her balance, sliding down another step. She caught herself on the rail, heart lurching into her throat. Had they heard her? She held her breath, trying to listen past her own frantic breathing.

"It isn't only Nora's future I'm considering."

Nora let out her breath in a rush and pushed herself higher up the stairs and deeper into the shadows.

"You're ready to put this place behind you, remember?" Amos crooned as though Mother hadn't even spoken. "We are ready to start our life together, the way we should have all those years ago."

Nora eased down again, trying to see their features. Was *that* what this was all about? Amos wanted to be rid of Emberwild, his niece, and everything that reminded him of his brother? Was he trying to erase the past three decades and pretend that he'd been the one to marry Mother all along?

Was he that delusional?

"Amos." Mother shook her head, the movement carrying a tangible sadness. "I've considered. At great length. As you asked me to do." She took another step back toward the stairs. "I'm sorry. I truly am. But I never meant for the promise to extend so far."

"Of course you did, my love. The years have just made you forget." The words slipped like silk through the air, carrying a sweet tenderness. "But I've never forgotten. I've waited. Patiently. And now I finally have everything worked out for you. Everything's in place." He took Mother's hands in his, his face now close enough for Nora to read affection and command warring in his gaze. "I've only ever wanted your happiness. Surely I've proven that."

Mother's shoulders sagged. Nora clutched at her skirt, heart pounding furiously. Surely Mother didn't love Amos. Not anymore. Fear kept Mother grounded to the ways of the past. Kept her from thinking she could do anything on her own.

Mother shook her head and pulled her hands from Amos's grasp. "I know about the will. Nora found the revised copy, and I've already submitted it to the solicitor. He informed me yesterday the judge is letting it stand."

Silence settled on the room, thick and palpable.

Nora leaned forward, her nerves tingling. Mother had taken the will to the solicitor? Had garnered the judge's approval? Hope fluttered. Was that why she'd been putting off giving Amos an answer? Why she hadn't wanted to say anything to Nora, lest the new will would not hold up?

Appreciation for Mother warmed her heart. The woman was more clever and brave than Nora had given her credit for.

Amos's voice came out low and controlled. "That changes nothing. A married couple shares everything. Regardless if Hiram left this place to me or to you, it's still ours. Together."

"I don't want to marry you."

Mother's words came clear and strong, and Nora's heart somersaulted. She couldn't help dropping down another step, hoping for a better look at Amos's face. Red boiled in his cheeks, but his voice remained calm.

"You don't mean that, my love."

"I do." Mother pulled her dressing gown tighter. "You say you want to give me what my heart desires? I want to keep my home, my daughter, and my husband's memories close. He was a good man, once. Despite the bitterness he let overtake him and the pain my secrets burned into him, Hiram wanted to care for me, even in his death." Her words gained force as she tilted her chin higher. "I'll not force our daughter into a marriage and sell the home he built for me, all so you can pretend I'm the foolish girl you once courted."

A cheer rose up in Nora's throat and she had to clamp her hand over her mouth to stifle it.

Amos growled. "I've done everything for you. Everything!"

His shout brought Nora to her feet and she scrambled down the stairs. Both pairs of eyes swung to her. She rushed forward and grabbed Mother's hand, a sense of empowerment bringing boldness.

"She doesn't need you."

Rage flickered on Amos's face. "Stay out of this, girl."

Nora refused to be cowed by the bite in his tone. "Mother doesn't want to marry you. Perhaps you should take this opportunity to bow out gracefully."

Pain flared in his expression, and she almost regretted the words. His dark eyes sought Mother, and Mother's hand trembled in hers.

Mother hesitated only a breath. "I'm sorry. I know how this must pain you."

Nora squeezed Mother's hand.

"This isn't what you want, Rebecca." Amos clenched and relaxed his hands. "You're letting the girl cloud your judgment."

"No, Amos." Mother sighed. "It's you who I've let cloud my judgment."

"You won't make it without me, you know that." His tone held an odd mixture of annoyance and pleading.

"Perhaps."

Not exactly the determined retort Nora had hoped for, but Mother had given far more than she'd ever expected.

Amos shoved his hat down on his head. "This isn't over."

Before either of them could reply, he stormed out and slammed the door behind him.

They stood in silence as pounding boots sounded across the porch. After a moment, Mother sucked in a breath as though coming out of a stupor.

"Shall I make coffee?"

Nora grabbed her. "You don't want to marry him? Emberwild is ours?"

"Yes." The single word seemed to pain her, and Mother turned toward the kitchen.

Following behind her, Nora sought resolution to another question. "Why was he here so early?"

"Because today was the day I promised an answer. Apparently, he couldn't wait an hour longer. Of course, I'm sure he was expecting something much different."

Nora was almost afraid to ask, but the question had to be spoken. "Is this really what you want?"

Mother remained silent as she filled the kettle and lit the fire in their iron stove. Impatience filled Nora, but she gave Mother the time she needed.

Finally, the words came out slow and even. "I want to stay at Emberwild. Not start my life anew as though every moment I shared with you and your father never existed."

The admission brought a flood of relief to Nora's veins. "We can do it, you know. We can forge a life for ourselves here. Just the two of us."

Mother quirked an eyebrow. "Don't you want a husband? Children?"

Her throat thickened. "Not without Silas."

Tears glistened in Mother's eyes and she pulled Nora into a tight embrace. "Then perhaps we should try to find him." She rubbed Nora's back in soothing circles. "But only if you want to. Otherwise, we'll throw all reason to the wind and figure out how to run this floundering horse farm on our own."

Nora breathed in the lavender scent of Mother's hand cream before pulling away. "Never underestimate Fenton women."

Mother smirked.

Living here with Mother as two independent women. Running Emberwild as she saw fit. Training her own horses. Running Arrow in the races. It was everything she wanted.

Wasn't it?

"Did . . . do you think . . . ?" She couldn't even form the words.

Mother read her thoughts anyway. Conviction filled her voice. "Amos may have sent Silas away, but I don't think he'd ever harm the young man."

Nora wasn't so sure. "Then why hasn't he come back? It's been weeks."

Mother pulled two mugs from the shelf and scooped a generous amount of coffee grounds into the heated water to brew. "Perhaps he thought he had nothing to return to."

Nothing to return to? Not his job or his earnings, or . . . her? She knew what Mother meant. She stilled her restless pacing. "I made my feelings clear."

"Did you? Or did you tell him it would be best if he left after the fire?"

Ice formed in Nora's stomach. She'd meant that for the moment, to avoid more conflict. Not for good.

"He thought I dismissed him." Her throat burned with the realization of how Silas must have taken her actions. "He thinks I don't want him here."

Mother squeezed her arm, compassion lining the timeless beauty of her face. "How about we put an ad out for him? Let him know he has something waiting for him."

"In the paper?" The idea brought a tingle of excitement. "Do you think he'd respond?"

An impish smile turned Mother's lips, transforming her features. "I don't know. But there's nothing wrong with a lady taking a little initiative, wouldn't you say?"

What would Amos do if he saw the notice? Did she care? A surge of determination pulsed through her. She wouldn't leave everything up to Silas, nor would she quake in fear of Amos's wrath over his ruined plans. She'd let Silas know disaster didn't await him at Emberwild.

Hope bubbled through her core, breaking through her despondency. She returned Mother's mischievous grin. "Why, no. I don't think there's anything wrong with that at all."

chapter

THIRTY-ONE

If she didn't hold on tight, she might just fly away in this whirlwind of activity. Nora checked the account registry again and double-checked the inventory in the feed room. They'd lost a lot of the previous records in the fire, but in some ways she was glad to have a fresh start. Do things her own way.

Roger grumbled as he handed her the accounting sheet for the sales of last month's hay bales. He still chafed at her authority, but given the choice between staying and working for Nora or finding another place of employment, he'd found it in his heart to decide taking orders from a woman might not be so bad.

As long as he continued to share knowledge with her and offer counsel rather than commands, Roger would keep his place here. Especially now that she knew the majority of his earnings went to help his widowed sister-in-law and her two sons. For that, she could put up with a little vinegar.

"And the receipt for the grain?" Nora wiggled her fingers.

Roger grumbled something and produced another sheet of paper from his jacket pocket. They'd need to work on taking better care of paperwork, but for now, having a dirty accounting record was better than none at all.

Nora smiled sweetly. "Thank you." She goaded him, she knew. She'd need to work on that. Still, the temptation to kill him with kindness had led her to stretching out her smiles and sugaring her words.

He turned to go.

"Oh, and Roger?"

"Yes, ma'am?"

Nora shifted, confidence wavering. "Did you go by the post?"

What appeared to be genuine sympathy softened the hard lines of his face. "Sorry, Miss Fenton. Ain't been no reply to your advertisement." He shifted his feet, then drew a breath. "I know he didn't cause that fire." He shook his head. "He didn't deserve the way we treated him, and I'm sorry for my part in it."

Nora swallowed the thickness in her throat. "Thank you." What else could she say?

She turned her attention back to the preparations to keep her mind from sticking on Silas too long. She and Mother had gone to the bank and discovered that while Emberwild was in desperate need of better management, they weren't in a dire condition. With a little leanness in their personal spending, careful accounting, and Arrow's winnings, they shouldn't have to sell any of the horses.

Amos had left on a business venture, and no one had seen him in town since. At least he'd had the decency to find a place to lick his wounds in private. The space would give them all time to heal. Surely now that he knew Mother's true feelings, he'd be able to move on with his life.

As they were moving on with theirs. She and Mother had finally come to enjoy a friendship. They could talk to one another, dream together. A life as independent women was within their reach. The relationship had been a balm to past wounds, edging out hurts and fostering a deeper love between them.

Nora leaned over Arrow's stall gate. "We're all counting on you."

Arrow snorted as though to say any worries she might have were totally unfounded. He would run well. He would win. She checked her timepiece. Only a few more hours until supper, and she still had a lot to do to get ready to travel the eighty miles to Columbus, Mississippi, for the fair. There'd been a lot of advertisements in all of the papers for the harness races—she knew because she'd run notices for Silas in all of them. The premiums would not only bring them in a fine profit, but Arrow would also start building a name for himself.

A welling sense of accomplishment filled her, momentarily pushing out the constant worry that nagged in the back of her mind. The sensation lasted only a moment, however, before everything came rushing back.

Where was Silas? Surely any living man would have read a paper by now. Unless he'd already traveled so far away that he was beyond the circulations. Nora filled her lungs with hay and horse-scented air and breathed out a small prayer.

"Please, Lord. If it be your will, bring him back to me."

She didn't need him to help her with the farm, train the horses, or provide for her. In all the ways that she'd been taught a woman needed a man, Nora didn't need Silas.

The way that she did need him, however, made her heart quiver. She wanted to love him. Care for him. Kiss away his worries and concerns. Explore the feelings of electricity that shot between them. She wanted to lean on his friendship and quiet strength.

No, she didn't need a man. But she did need Silas Cavallero.

She completed her duties for the day, paid Asa for overdue farrier work, and made sure Walter had all the supplies he needed, then left the barn feeling both satisfied and exhausted.

After an in-depth look at their expenses and a long talk with both Walter and Roger, Nora had determined that the men her father had employed were hardly more than useless gamblers. She'd sent them on their way with little hesitation. Walter and the Reed boys could tend the horses, and Roger could maintain the land. He'd somehow seemed pleased with the idea of spending more time with the tractor and less time with the horses.

She and Mother passed the evening with a supper of biscuits and preserved strawberries on the porch at sunset, making their plans and laughing over the antics of the foals. They talked until dark about their goals for the future and the prices they'd ask for the horses in the yearling herd. By the time Nora retired for the evening, her heart felt full.

Contentment with her new life. Longing for Silas. Worry for Arrow. Concern Amos would suddenly pop up one day and Mother would change her mind. Every thought and emotion toyed with her, dragging her from one scenario to another until she thought she might be ripped in two.

With effort, she forced the tempest within her to settle. There were so many things she couldn't control, but she wouldn't let worry rob her of the contentment she'd found. She'd pray for peace and let God work out the details.

Tomorrow they would ride for Columbus in a wagon loaded with jams and jellies Mother had prepared for the fair. Her new sulky had been delivered last week, and her big beautiful boy was ready to race. The fair held possibilities for a new beginning. A new future.

They could do this.

chapter

THIRTY-TWO

He'd almost made it. Silas stared across the Arkansas River, the moment of decision upon him. For a time he stood there, emotions warring within him. A choice that he sensed would change the course of his life. Finally, he gave the river a parting nod and turned away.

He kicked out his campfire and searched his saddlebag for something to quiet his hunger.

This mission would never bring him peace. Finding the truth and finally confronting his father's killer wouldn't soothe this emptiness.

He'd chased the scent of the man who'd killed his father and stolen his horse as far as this river. Another day's ride, maybe two, and he'd find his quarry. But try as he did, he couldn't dislodge a nagging sense that pulsed in his spirit, warning him this path would only lead to destruction.

Gentle words whispered to his soul to let the past die. Perhaps he could. In time. But then what did he do with his future? That also held little appeal.

Not without Nora Fenton. And she had made her feelings clear.

Silas pulled the girth on Starlight's saddle and tied off the cinch.

Leaving justice to God alone grated against his every instinct. As did returning to Mississippi and humbling himself before a woman who didn't want him. He gave the leather another yank and Starlight snorted.

He patted her neck. "Sorry, old girl."

His mother's sweet mare bobbed her head, forgiving him as easily as Mama would have.

Find a better life. Love a good woman. Rest once in a while.

Mama's final words echoed in his soul. She'd wanted him to find a love like she and his father had shared. Nora was a good woman. One worth fighting for.

He gave one final look in the direction his retribution would take him, then mounted his horse. His stomach rumbled, reminding him he'd spent too long in the saddle nibbling on stale bread and dried meat.

So far he hadn't spent a single cent of the money Nora had left sitting outside his door at the inn. He'd awoken the morning after the fire to find an envelope stuffed with bills and a letter that had been seared into his memory.

Please accept this payment for all you've done at Emberwild with my deepest thanks. Know that you will forever hold a place of fond memory here. However, now I need to make the choice that's best for me and my family. What started between us can never be. As my parting farewell, I believe you should know the truth. I discovered my father and a man named Bernard Grant approached your father to purchase his horse. There was an argument and a fight, and Bernard pushed your father into the stall. When they realized the man had been killed, my father ran, and Bernard took the horse. The man you are looking for is in Pine Bluff, Arkansas.

I hope you find peace and a good life.

Nora

She didn't want him. How could he blame her? He had nothing to offer.

His stomach growled again, and he rubbed his fist against his middle to quiet the ache. If only the pain in his chest was as easy to relieve. He'd accepted her decision. Or at least, he'd told himself so. But if acceptance meant living with this regret, then he was done accepting her choice.

Mile after mile he rode, closer and closer to the town that represented both his past and his hopes for a new future. His thoughts made continuous loops until finally he turned them to prayers.

By the time Philadelphia came into view, he felt lighter. Wagons lumbered down the main street, the horses' hooves clicking on the brick pavers.

Silas entered the Philadelphia inn to find Joe Elroy wiping counters, men gathered around the tables playing cards, and a fellow pounding away at an out-of-tune piano. Nothing had changed. Joe's wife, Myrtle, spotted him as soon as he stepped through the doorway. He offered her a tired smile. Her kindness had sent him running from his problems with two saddlebags of vittles. He owed her more, but a friendly greeting was all he could muster.

"You came back!" The creases in her face deepened with a wide smile. "See here, Joe!"

The innkeeper lifted a hand from behind the bar where he served a customer.

"Which one did you see? We had a wager going on it."

Silas studied the woman, her words not making any sense. "See what?"

"The notices. Surely you saw one of them at least. She put them in every paper from here to Jackson."

She? His pulse tripped over the word. "Care to explain?"

Myrtle put her hand on her hip and pointed a finger at him. "Good thing you came back. Folks was saying you wouldn't and that you'd leave that poor gal to a heap of heartache. Me, though, I knew you'd come to your senses. Men usually do, once they've had time to stew." She wagged her finger. "Took you so long I almost gave up on you."

Silas stepped closer, causing her to tilt her head back to keep her pointed gaze on him. "I have no idea what you're talking about."

Myrtle dropped her hand. "You don't? Huh."

Before he could stop her, she turned and bustled out of the common room, leaving him to stare after her. He tried to make sense of anything the innkeeper's wife had said, but he felt as useless trying to solve the puzzle as he would trying to wield one of Asa's blacksmith hammers.

Might as well get a table and ask after a room. He needed a real meal and a night's sleep under something more substantial than the stars if he was going to face Nora tomorrow.

He chose a seat at a back table and ignored the looks sent his way. Her ire at his unannounced return he could handle. He didn't dread her thorny tongue. Truth be told, he feared indifference far more. At least if she was angry, he knew she still cared.

A stack of newspapers landed on the table in front of him.

Myrtle stood over him with her hands on her hips. "You see there? One every week. In every paper."

Silas eyed the tall stack in front of him and thumbed through the folded edges. "One *what*?"

For an answer, the woman huffed, flopped open one of the papers in front of him, and jabbed her finger at a small square of print.

Silas. I'm sorry. Things aren't what you think. Please send word. Nora.

He read the words three more times. Nora had put a notice in the paper, looking for him?

"Well?" Myrtle crossed her arms over her ample bosom. "You mean to tell me you ain't seen a one of these?"

"Haven't been buying newspapers."

"Then what brought you back?"

Heat scorched up his middle and culminated in a smile he couldn't hold back. "Nora."

Her grin could have rivaled his. "Good. Then what are you doing here, boy?"

Suddenly no longer tired or hungry, Silas tipped his hat to the matronly woman and dashed out the door.

chapter

THIRTY-THREE

Columbus, Mississippi
October 24, 1905

He'd kill them all at this rate. Nora held fast to the reins as Arrow reared, his hooves flying dangerously close to her face. Men shouted all around her, their voices only causing Arrow further distress.

She pulled hard, trying to get the creature to plant all four of his hooves on the ground. He was in no condition to race.

Thanks to Amos.

The man stood at her side barking orders as though he hadn't been thoroughly ousted from their lives. She cut him a scathing glance. "I said step back!"

The fury in his eyes two smoldering coals, Amos nonetheless complied. Finally, Arrow settled again, his nostrils quivering. She ran her gloved hand along his neck, whispering assurances everything would be all right.

"Should have sold him," Amos mumbled. "That thing is a menace."

The crowd that had gathered around the race barn began to dissipate. Nora collected her composure and turned to face her uncle. "Why are you here?"

"I've told you already. I was in Columbus on business. Came to watch the races."

She narrowed her eyes. Surely he didn't expect her to buy such a tale of serendipity, did he? Amos was here for a purpose. One she suspected had something to do with Arrow.

"We haven't changed our minds. None of the horses are being sold." Never mind the state of the finances at Emberwild wouldn't require such drastic measures. Amos didn't need to know what she'd discovered or how she planned to right their debts.

He grunted and checked his timepiece. "Shouldn't your jockey be here by now?"

Was he planning to pay the man off and get Arrow to lose? Could he really be that petty? For the sake of family, Nora tried extending a splinter of the olive branch. "I'm sorry about Mother. I know you wanted something different, but I thank you for conceding to her wishes."

Amos's nostrils flared, but his words came out serene. "I've only ever wanted her happiness." He flicked a hard glance at Arrow. "When this little adventure you're dragging her on crumbles, I'll be there once again to help her pick up the pieces. I've always put her first." He shoved the watch back in his pocket. "Pity you don't care for her enough to do the same."

He strode away, his back stiff. So he blamed Mother's decision on her. She couldn't say she was surprised. She sighed and ran her hand down Arrow's slick coat. Whatever he planned, she didn't have the slightest intention of playing into his hand.

Still, her nerves tingled. Would he find Mother in the exhibition tent and manipulate her into conceding to a wedding? To selling Arrow or the other horses? Arrow tossed his head, sensing the tension swirling in her. She could hardly follow Amos and see what he was up to. She had to think of Arrow and pray that Mother's newfound independence would stick.

There were no official rules stating a woman couldn't race. It just wasn't done. Well, just because something wasn't done didn't mean she couldn't do it. She would simply have to race Arrow herself. Let the men scoff. What did she care?

She led Arrow around the side of the barn to where the sulkies were stored and headed toward their shiny new bicycle tire model. Now all she needed to do was figure out how to get Arrow to stand still while she hitched him to it without needing to tie him. Sweat slithered down the back of her neck despite the pleasant drop from the summer's intense heat to fall's more temperate touch.

"I saw your notice."

The sound of the masculine voice behind her sent an electric current through her heart. She whirled.

"Silas."

He stood a few paces away, his stance wary and his unshaven face unable to hide the weariness underneath. She stared at him, yearning to throw herself in his arms, yet kept at bay by the callous expression shadowed beneath his hat. Behind her, Arrow nickered.

Even the horse was happy to see him. But he certainly didn't look happy to see her. Had he only come for the payment? Had he found out what Amos said about Father being responsible for Juan Cavallero's death?

The hope that he truly cared vanished. Whatever he'd come for, it wasn't her.

❧

How could one woman cause so many conflicting emotions to crash through him? Trying to hold them back was like trying to lasso an entire herd of wild stallions. It took every ounce of his willpower to keep his feet rooted to the ground and his face passive.

She'd sent him away. Then put the notice out for him. Let her be the one to say why.

"Why are you here?" She wound Arrow's reins time and again around the palm of her hand. Her clipped words reminded him of the woman he'd first met. Covered in thorns. But he knew the rose underneath.

"When I got to Emberwild, Walter said you'd left for the fair." And he'd ridden poor Starlight hard all night to get here. He took a step forward, hoping she would give him any indication that she'd sent for him because she missed him. Cared for him. Loved him.

Her expression remained unreadable.

"Why did you post the notice?"

Nora straightened to that annoyingly haughty stature he despised. The one that indicated she was trying to hide vulnerability underneath a hard shell. "Amos didn't report you to the sheriff. I thought you should know."

The words threw him off guard. "I didn't start that fire."

"I know." A lock of honeyed hair caught on the breeze and flitted across her nose, but she remained statuesque. "You should also know Mother and I have taken control of the farm."

"Is that why you sent out the notice?" Would her independence change things between them?

"No, not exactly."

Annoyance surged. Heaven help him, but he couldn't bring himself to beg her. "Then *why*?" He didn't mean to bark the word, but this woman had scoured his nerves too thoroughly for his senses not to be raw.

Nora didn't flinch. "I only sent you away because you were in no condition to suffer a fight."

Silas ground his teeth. What did that have to do with her letter? Or the notice in the paper?

"That day. At the fire when I said it would be best for you to go. You'd been injured. I didn't want foolish men to let their pride spark into a brawl that might put you in need of a surgeon." She stared at him, daring him to tell her she was wrong.

Did she think him such a weakling that he couldn't handle Roger? Even with sore ribs, a pounding headache, and arms tired from the strain of the bucket line, Silas could hold his own.

Uncertainty entered pools of liquid blue that stared up at him, but her voice remained firm. "Roger was acting the madman and my uncle . . ." She shook her head and absently rubbed her elbow. "Well, Amos wasn't acting himself either."

Had the man hurt her? Protectiveness stirred inside him, adding to the tempest he still struggled to keep under control.

Nora released a long breath. "I was simply trying to protect you."

Pride swelled. He didn't need a woman to protect him. He was—

He cut the thought. She sought to protect him as he did her. This fierce woman who never fit any mold thrust upon her had tried in her way to save him.

"Your letter said you wanted me to leave. Do you still want that?"

"What letter?"

"The one you left with payment and the name of the man who killed my father."

Nora's eyes widened. "I never wrote you a letter. I came to the inn and you were gone. Then Amos . . ." She trailed off, shaking her head. "So that was his plan. Why he was so sure you'd never come back." Her eyes softened. "Silas. I didn't pay you or write you a letter. Amos must have done that. I came to find you, but you'd already left."

She stepped closer, enough so that the floral scent of her meddled with what little sense he had remaining. "Will you come back to Emberwild?"

His thoughts reeled. She hadn't written the letter. Emotions threatened to break through his crumbling control. He wanted nothing more than to tell her the depth of his feelings. His mouth wouldn't form the words. He couldn't do anything but continue to drink in the sight of her. She hadn't sent him away.

Nora clenched her skirts and huffed. "I didn't really want you to go, all right? I wanted you to stay."

Warmth spread through his core and out through arms that longed to sweep her into an embrace and kiss her until neither of them harbored a lingering doubt. He opened his mouth to tell her so, but she marched forward, chin thrust out.

"I wanted you to stay with me." Nora flung out her arms. "There. Are you satisfied now?"

Silas tipped his head back and laughed.

"I hardly find that funny. How dare you stand there and—"

Silas pulled her against his chest in an entirely improper public embrace. Arrow snorted, displeased with the sudden tension on his reins. Nora gasped, long lashes flying wide. "Yes, Miss Fenton. I do believe I'm quite satisfied."

She stared up at him, questions written on her features. He'd answer them all. But for now, he needed to be sure she understood the truth. "I should have never left you, Nora. My love for you was what brought me back to Mississippi. Not an advertisement in the paper." He rubbed his thumb down her smooth cheek. "Will you accept the suit of one poor, dusty cowboy with nothing to offer you but his undying devotion?"

He looked down into her face and fought off the urge to press his own smile onto the one blooming on her perfect lips.

"I do believe I'd like nothing more." She lifted onto her toes and kissed him. Soundly. Before he could melt into the passion welling inside him, she pulled back, leaving him thirsting like a man stranded in the desert. She lifted her eyebrows, teasing in her eyes. "Now that that's settled, if you'll excuse me, I have a race to win."

She handed him Arrow's reins, a pleased smile toying with her lips.

THIRTY-FOUR

She could do this. Nora transferred the reins to one hand while she tried to rub away the itch that sweat caused inside her glove. Trepidation sloshed in her stomach, threatening to make her heave its contents. Silas had helped her into the sulky, his reassuring eyes giving her the courage she needed. She wouldn't let him down.

Three jockeys had protested. The fair commissioner had frowned at the rules, but finally stated there was nothing that said she couldn't race. This was her chance. She'd prove not only Arrow, but herself. If only she could get her erratic pulse to slow.

They made their way to the starting line, Arrow pinning his ears at the horses on either side of him as they bunched together at the gate. Crowds filled the raised stands along both straightaways, children waving colored ribbons in the air. The atmosphere tensed with thrilling anticipation and mounting pressure.

They were in the middle of the pack. She'd hoped for the outside edge. The inner gave an advantage of tighter turns and quicker speed, but the outside would keep her from getting bunched up with the other racers. Arrow was fast enough to get around the turns without the advantage.

He pawed the soft ground, though she couldn't tell if the movement came from impatience to run or annoyance at the closeness of the other horses. Three other horses spread out on each side of Arrow, their nearness making his ears flick back and forth.

"Hold together, boy. You'll be fine."

The jockey to her left, a small man with a mustache far too large for his narrow face scoffed. Nora ignored him. One trip around the track. One trip to prove themselves. Careful on the turns.

Don't let him swing too narrow.

Silas's words echoed in her head. Worry had been written all over him, but he'd never once tried to dissuade her from mounting the sulky.

Arrow was quick on the start. He could get out in front. Once the other racers were behind him, he'd settle into what he did best. They would be fine.

Everything was coming together. Silas was back. He would stay with her at Emberwild. Her Emberwild. Arrow would win and—

A shot rang out and the other horses bolted forward. Arrow squealed and sidestepped, nearly crashing into the bay horse driven by the sneering mustache man. Nora snapped the reins to get Arrow's attention. She'd been too busy worrying and hadn't been prepared for the starting signal.

She hunched over the reins, every muscle tensing in anticipation. "Go, boy!"

Arrow lunged forward, hooves driving into the dirt. The six other racers on the track pulled ahead, leaving them in a cloud of choking dust. She could hardly see. She tapped the reins across his back, trusting him to see where she couldn't. They had to get out in front.

Arrow gained ground quickly. Nora blinked moisture through her eyes, clearing her vision. The roar of the crowd intensified, mingling with the pounding of the horses' hooves and the drumming of her heart. They passed by the mustached jockey and a thrill reverberated through her.

Ahead, the racers clustered together in what appeared to be an impenetrable knot. She tugged on the outer rein, nudging Arrow to the right. They'd have to go for the outside. It was longer, but he was fast enough.

They cut across the track and headed for the outer rail. The ground flew by beneath her, but she refused to let her focus drift from the steady bob of Arrow's head as he fought to gain more ground.

Arrow picked up speed, swerving to pass another horse. The driver shouted an obscenity at her. Nora lowered her head, willing her galloping pulse to keep calm.

Watch the turns.

They hugged the outside rail and passed another jockey, then dove for a position. As though sensing her plan, Arrow barreled toward the first bend and cut hard, ears pinned. He was too much of an alpha to let another horse take the lead. The sulky tipped dangerously. Nora thrust her weight in the opposite direction and held tight. The bicycle tire reconnected with the ground, jarring her teeth. Two more sulkies fell behind her.

They were in the straightaway. Arrow's powerful muscles churned. The two lead sulkies bounced together in the middle of the track, vying for position. Nora guided Arrow to the inner rail. They could take them on the inside. Arrow lowered his head and cut to the left, snatching the conveyance behind him. Terror rose in Nora's throat but she fought it back, focus tunneling into the narrow strip of dirt between her competitor and the edge of the track.

They would never fit.

Arrow surged forward. Nora tugged the reins. The inside wouldn't work. They'd need to go to the outside again. Skirt around them and then make up the distance with his speed. Arrow clamped the bit and thrust his nose in the gap between the other sulky and the rail. He wouldn't slow enough to let the other horse pull forward so they could move behind him and then take the outside. Nora pulled back harder, but Arrow ignored her.

They slid farther into the hole. Nora clenched her teeth.

The other driver turned to glance at her, a shout rising in the air only an instant before her sulky wheels caught on his.

The world lurched beneath her.

Arrow squealed, a high-pitched sound that sent waves of icy terror through her and nearly stopped her heart. The sulky tipped. She thrust her weight again.

The sulky rocked dangerously. Nora fought with the reins to no avail. Arrow wouldn't give up the fight for the inside rail. For a place at the front.

He was going to get them killed.

She screamed and pulled back on the reins. The win wasn't worth his life or hers.

The horses collided. Vibrations lurched through her as the sulkies tangled. Panic fled, leaving only a brief sensation of floating in a void.

Her body lifted from the seat, and suddenly she was flying through the air.

∽

A roar ripped through his throat as Silas leapt over the rail and landed on the track. Nora had collided with another driver. Horses tangled. Sulkies overturned.

Nora lay in a heap on the ground.

He pushed his legs faster, dodging out of the way of a loose horse trotting back toward the barn. The crowds that had gathered to watch shouted, adding to the cacophony of noise. Blood throbbed in his ears, pushing out the sounds.

Silas skidded to a halt, dropping to his knees and sliding across the dirt to Nora's side.

She groaned. "Arrow. Is he hurt?"

Relief surged through him. "Are *you* hurt?"

Nora shook her head and struggled to a sitting position. "A little tender, but mostly unharmed."

It was a wonder she hadn't been trampled. Silas scooped her into his arms and gathered her close. "Let's get you out of here." For once, Nora didn't protest, though her eyes continued to scan the track. "I'll find Arrow as soon as I get you to safety."

"Don't let Amos take him."

Amos? He was here? He'd thought she'd said she had control of the farm. He pushed the questions away. An issue for another time. For now, he had to get her to safety. Crowds pressed close and he had to shout for people to get out of his way. Finally, he made it through the press and to the barn, where he gently set Nora on her feet.

"Find him, please." Her pleading gaze made him waver. He didn't want to leave her, but she didn't seem badly injured. Merely shaken.

A figure burst through the crowd, stalking their way. Silas's jaw hardened, and he stepped in front of Nora as Amos approached.

"Do you see now? This is why women don't race." Amos's face reddened, making him look like a man who'd spent all day over a blacksmith's forge. He looked through Silas, his rage pinned on Nora. "What will your mother think?"

"Perhaps now isn't the time?" Silas forced his voice to remain even.

His gaze slammed into Silas, as though just now noticing exactly who stood between him and his niece. "What are you doing here?" Amos snarled, baring teeth like a cornered wolf.

He owed the man nothing. He took Nora's hand. "Come on. Let's get you inside."

Nora cast her uncle a glance and followed Silas to the cool of the barn. A jockeys' room near the double sliding doors offered a dusty seating area. Without complaint, Nora settled gingerly onto a wooden bench.

"Arrow?"

He gave a nod and strode for the door, hoping Nora would have enough sense to stay put while he stalled the horse and checked him for injuries. When he stepped back into the hallway, Amos had disappeared.

Good. At least the man had enough sense not to try to lecture Nora at a time like this.

As he crossed the short yard to the track, a young groom approached with Arrow, the horse trailing placidly behind him.

Silas thanked the young man and gathered the long reins, another wave of relief crashing through him. A miracle neither of them had been harmed. Arrow seemed to be walking fine, his usual fire subdued. The horse nickered at Silas as though thankful for a familiar face after the ordeal. Silas ran a hand down the horse's muzzle. "You sure gave us a scare."

Arrow would be getting a lot more training before he raced again. He'd be just as fast next year. And maybe then he wouldn't risk getting anyone killed.

Silas entered the barn, and Nora immediately came to her feet.

"Arrow! Is he hurt?" She ran her fingers over his legs, checking for herself.

"Once I have him stalled I'll give him a thorough check." Her face scrunched with hesitation, but he continued before she could protest. "Let me handle him for you. Take a few moments in the jockeys' room to recover. We'll still be here when you're ready."

She gave Arrow one last pat and then nodded before turning toward the door across the hall.

Her ready agreement made him hope she wasn't more injured than she let on. Once she disappeared inside the room, he took the colt on to the stall.

No sooner had he pulled Arrow's bridle free than Amos appeared at the gate. Had the man been stalking him? The muscles in his shoulders tensed.

"What do you want, Amos?"

"What do I *want*?" The man nearly growled. "I thought I was rid of you, boy. Why are you here and not in Arkansas?"

Rid of him? Silas gripped the edge of the stall, nerves tingling as he positioned himself in the stall opening between Arrow and Amos. "You wrote the letter. Pointed me to Pine Bluff. Why? You could have dismissed my employment at any point."

Amos fumed. "You were supposed to go to Arkansas."

Realization swept over him. What fate had been waiting for him if he'd gone across the river? "Does Bernard Grant even exist?"

"You'd have found out. Then I'd finally have had this mess settled."

Silas tightened his grip on the doorframe, pieces of the puzzle falling into place. "All those accidents at the barn. That was you?"

Amos snorted. "Fool. Tossing cats and cutting leather like he really thought that would get you to leave. Roger was easy to prod but useless in execution."

Roger had sabotaged him? "Then why not simply dismiss me?"

"You'd ask too many questions." Amos glared at him like he was a fool. Had the man gone mad?

Silas tried for another answer to a question that had plagued him. "But how'd he get that plow to fall?"

Amos snorted. "That was God's own hand. Telling you to mind your own business. You should have listened."

The words chipped at him, further unraveling the mystery. "The fire. That was you."

Rage contorted Amos's face, making him nearly unrecognizable. He stepped closer to Silas, the vein in his neck throbbing. "I knew Roger wouldn't have the guts." He sneered. "Almost knocked out two problems at once."

Silas's fingers twitched at his sides, energy tingling through him. "Me and Nora?"

"Think you're smart, don't you, boy? What'd you find, huh? The papers that proved Ember belonged to my brother all along? You were looking to dig up ghosts. Looking for anything to try to prove a story you wanted to be true."

His blood cooled. "What story?"

"The one where you think my brother had anything to do with your father's accidental death. Where you want to pin a crime on us and steal everything we've built."

There'd never been another man. Bernard Grant had been nothing more than a trap. Silas studied the man in front of him. Why go to such lengths to cover up the sins of his dead brother?

Unless Hiram had never been there at all.

Amos pulled the watch from his coat pocket, his fingers stroking the pattern on the front. "You should have gone." His breath came in gasps now, as though something that had been festering inside him boiled out of its confines. He stroked the face of the watch he always carried.

Silas stared at the watch. He'd seen it before. Without Amos constantly spinning it in circles, he could clearly see the pattern on the front. Two horses running, the clouds behind them a tangle of swirls mingling with their manes.

A memory burst forth, stealing his breath. His father's pleased expression. His mother's smile. A treasure for better days.

"My father's watch." The words scraped past his throat. "You . . . you have my father's watch."

Amos suddenly lurched forward, shoving Silas with both hands. He fell backward into the stall. Arrow reared.

Silas rolled, narrowly missing the pounding hooves. He jumped to his feet and slammed the stall door behind him, trapping Arrow inside.

Where was Amos?

Turning and catching a glimpse of Amos's retreating back, Silas leapt forward and slammed all of his weight onto the man, bringing them both tumbling to the ground.

Amos roared and struggled beneath him, but Silas used every skill he'd ever learned tying calves to keep the furious man pinned to the floor. Knee in his back, he pulled both of Amos's arms upward until the man howled.

"I yield! Let me up."

"And give you the opportunity to escape?" Silas pushed his knee harder. "I'll hear the truth." Keeping the man pinned, he searched around in Amos's pocket until he found the watch and snatched it free.

Releasing the clasp, he opened the watch to reveal an inscription inside.

To Juan with all my love, Mary.

His father's watch. This man had kept his father's watch. Stroking it with murderous hands and—

Amos thrust upward, knocking Silas off-balance. In an instant, he was on his feet. The two men squared off.

"Why did you do it?" Silas clenched the watch in his sweaty palm. "You killed my father. Stole his horse."

Ember. He'd felt it all along.

Amos sneered. "Hiram was a fool. Always was. But he got everything. Everything that should have been *mine*." He clenched his fists, wild eyes looking everywhere but at Silas. The words tumbled from him, faster and faster as he went. "She loved me. But she was faithful to her vows. I couldn't stand to see the mess he'd landed her in."

Mrs. Fenton? What was the man talking about?

"He gave me the money. Charged me with finding them a horse that would save them. I did it. For her. Doubled that money in a wager. Should have doubled it again if that cheating pox-faced Harvey hadn't stolen it from me."

Amos started pacing, hands flexing. He laughed, and the eerie sound echoed along the walls. Silas glanced behind him at the closed door of the jockeys' room where Nora stayed safely hidden inside.

Where was everyone else? Cheers arose from outside. Another race. They were in here alone. He took a small step toward Amos.

"Fate shined on me then. A horse even better than the one I'd been sent to buy turned up right under my nose. I offered a good price. All he had to do was take it." Amos turned glassy eyes on Silas. "Why wouldn't he just take it?"

"So you killed him?"

"He should have taken it. The horse spooked. Wasn't my fault."

"Yet you stole his watch and his horse and left him for dead?" Fury burned inside him. He'd lost his father because of another man's greed? His pride?

A gasp sounded behind him.

Nora. She'd heard everything.

Amos's eyes swung to where she stood in the open doorway, eyes wide. "You killed Silas's father? Stole his horse?" She clutched at the fabric around her throat.

"Nora! Get back in—"

Pain erupted in his jaw. His vision blurred. Amos flexed his fist and turned toward Nora. Silas felt himself sway.

Then everything went black.

THIRTY-FIVE

Nora screamed. Silas crashed to the floor, his body landing in a heap. She rushed to him, panic rising in her throat. Amos snagged her arm.

"Couldn't leave well enough alone." He hauled her up against him.

She fought, another scream erupting in her throat. Amos pressed his hand over her face, smothering her. She struggled, but he was too strong.

"Now I'll have to create another accident." He bit off the words like the necessity was Nora's fault. "Rebecca will have another to grieve, but I'll be there for her. I'm always there for her." He hauled Nora away from Silas's crumpled form toward the back of the barn.

"You wanted to go for a ride. The horse spooked. A pity your stubbornness is what ended up breaking your pretty neck."

Nora's feet scuffed the floor as he dragged her along. What was he going to do with her? They neared a stall, and he shifted her to one side to free a hand. Nora brought her knee up hard into his groin while thrusting her elbow into his gut with all of her might.

With a grunt, he released her. Nora ran.

Footsteps pounded behind her. She'd never escape him. She grabbed for the latch on Arrow's stall. Her fingers slipped.

"Nora!"

She threw the door wide. Arrow pawed the ground. She grabbed his mane and flung herself up onto his back. Arrow bolted through the gate and galloped through the barn toward the open doorway.

In the hallway, Silas scrambled to his feet. He shouted for her, but she couldn't stop.

Please, God. Let him be safe.

It was the only thought that she had time for as she buried her face in Arrow's mane and tried to hold on for her life.

Hooves thundered behind him and Silas barely dove out of the way as a gray horse streaked by him, a man pinned to his back.

Ember?

Amos.

The thoughts barely had time to register. Amos was going after Nora. A boy leading a racehorse into the barn shouted and scrambled out of the way just as Amos thundered by. Ignoring the pain pounding in his skull, Silas ran after them.

"Hey!" The boy protested when Silas snatched the horse's reins from his hand. In one fluid motion, he was on the filly's back and turning her around. The boy yelled about a stolen horse, but Silas couldn't stop to explain.

Shouts followed him as he dug his heels into the horse's sides, chasing Ember through the fairgrounds.

People screeched and dove out of their way. Silas did his best to steer the filly with the long racing reins flying out behind him.

"The law!" Silas shouted as he plunged through the crowd. "Get the law!"

Ember took a sharp left and galloped between two towering canvas tents. Silas squeezed the filly's sides harder, urging the creature to do his bidding. She turned between the structures, leaning hard enough to one side that Silas nearly came unseated.

They burst through the midway and out into an open field.

Nora.

She held fast as Arrow shot across the ground. Ember thundered behind her, but Arrow was too fast. They would escape. But for how long?

Suddenly Arrow's body lurched forward, his front leg stumbling. Nora screamed. Silas urged the horse beneath him to run faster, every moment feeling as though he swam through mud. Sticking and pulling. Keeping him from reaching her in time.

Ember gained ground.

Amos lunged.

He hit Nora, toppling them both to the ground. The filly galloped closer. Silas dove from the horse's bare back and hit the ground hard. He rolled to his side, barely catching his breath as the horse he'd ridden fled.

He stumbled to his feet. Amos had Nora pinned to the ground. A feral rage boiled through him and he sprung for the man's back.

Nora's screams assaulted his ears as he and Amos rolled on the ground, grappling for a better position. His fist connected with a satisfying crunch against the side of Amos's face, just as a blow cracked one of his ribs.

Amos shoved Silas back and leapt to his feet, reaching for Nora. Silas scrambled after him.

Shouts accompanied the sound of pounding hooves. The law. Silas grabbed Nora, taking advantage of the second Amos flicked his attention to the approaching horses. He thrust her behind him, body tensing for the fight.

Amos shouted a string of obscenities and snatched Ember's reins. The horse snorted and sidestepped as Amos tried to mount.

Nora grabbed at the back of Silas's shirt.

Cursing, Amos got his foot in the stirrup and mounted Ember as the posse neared. He kicked his boots into Ember's sides.

The old stallion reared.

Amos flew through the air, landing on the ground with a sickening thud.

He lay still.

chapter

THIRTY-SIX

This couldn't be happening. Nora buried her face in Silas's shirt, finding a strange sense of comfort in letting him handle everything brewing outside of the protective encasement of his arms.

She clung to him, the voice rumbling from the chest beneath her little more than a pleasant thunder. There were questions, curt answers. A command to have Amos taken away.

Her uncle. Dead.

Had to be. Wasn't he? Nora pressed her eyes into the hollow place beneath Silas's throat. What would Mother say?

Someone groaned, and she lifted her head. A stout lawman helped Amos to his feet. His body shook as his feral eyes raked over her.

"You did this." Amos's voice rasped like metal on bone. "You ruined everything for her."

Silas shook his head. "You did this to yourself. Tried to kill me the way you killed my father. Instead, you nearly shared his fate."

The lawman pulled Amos's arms behind him. Nora stepped out of Silas's embrace. "At least you get to live. Live with knowing how much hurt you caused." She took another step closer. "Poor Mother will be devastated."

Amos lunged at her with a howl, but the stout man pulled him away.

It took three men to bind him, kicking and cursing, to a placid mare. As the horse turned to take her uncle to his fate, Nora's knees trembled.

In an instant, she was encased in a warm embrace once more. Silas's arms gave a gentle squeeze and then eased her back so that he could look at her. His somber expression carried a weight that settled on her.

"He tried to . . . to . . ." Her voice hiccupped and she clenched her fists. Her uncle had tried to kill her. As he'd killed Silas's father.

Silas ran a hand down her arm. "I know."

Nora suddenly became aware of the crowd surrounding them, their faces stern and eyes holding countless questions.

"Are you harmed?" A short man in an oversized hat with a badge indicating his authority approached and regarded her with a keen expression.

Of course she was. The lies and deception tainting her life would open painful wounds for all of them. But she wasn't harmed in the way the man meant. Nora shook her head. "A bit sore. But I'm otherwise unhurt."

The gentle squeeze on her arm said Silas understood the bruises she carried couldn't be seen. Those would need time to heal. Her gaze drifted to where a young deputy held the reins for their two stallions. Ember held his head high, his stately form not diminished by his increase in years. The horse Juan Cavallero had died for. The horse Amos had coveted and killed for.

The foundation stallion her father had staked their livelihood upon. Had likely lied to the breed registry and forged purchase papers to keep. Amos had apparently stolen him from Emberwild and, for reasons she might not ever understand, had brought him here.

"Everything we have is built on a lie."

Her father had known. All this time she'd suspected Father had been the one who had cheated or stolen, but he'd only covered up his brother's sins. Had held up the lie. Knowing his life was constructed on top of the tainted gift his brother provided for the woman he'd always coveted had likely festered the bitterness already growing in his soul.

Silas watched her, shoulders taut as though the weight of the truth fell as heavily upon him as it did her. There was only one way to set things to rights. Only one thing she could think of to mend what her father and uncle had broken, though she knew her gesture wouldn't begin to replace all that had been lost.

"He's yours." The whispered words brought a freedom, a release from the burden her father had draped on her shoulders. "Arrow, too, as a fraction of recompense."

The muscles in Silas's jaw flexed, then relaxed. He didn't answer. He took the reins from the waiting deputy and stood in stony silence. He didn't need to say anything. She understood.

Nora took her place at his side, her heart stinging in anticipation of the conversations that would soon come. For her mother's heartache. For what the truth of Amos's deceptions would mean for all of them.

What would happen to Amos now? Would they have to endure a trial?

"If you'll come with us, please?" The man in the hat nodded in the direction they'd taken Amos. "We have questions."

Silas nodded. "We'll be right along behind you."

The man hesitated a moment, then gave a curt nod and mounted a dun horse. He and the other two lawmen retreated toward the fairgrounds.

Silas slipped his hand into hers, his rough fingers infusing her with hope that not all had been lost.

"I'm sorry." Did he realize how much she meant by those simple words?

He ran a finger down the side of her face. "You've nothing to apologize for. The actions of your relatives are not yours to bear." He tilted her head back. "And I won't take your horse. You love him."

"Not as much as I love you."

The side of his mouth twitched and he swept the hat from his sweaty locks. His gaze slammed into hers, carrying with it all the promises of forever that she'd never dreamed of. Whatever became of Emberwild, her heart would be safe in the steadfast hands of Silas Cavallero.

He pulled her against him, the heat of his body radiating through her. Slowly, tenderly, he kissed her. Until their problems melted. Until the aches faded.

Until the old wounds confining her ripped open and somewhere deep inside, she finally felt free.

Emberwild
October 25, 1905

After all these years, Silas finally knew the truth. They'd spent several hours with the deputies from the Lowndes County sheriff's department and had finally been released to travel home.

Home.

The word held new meaning to him. Another truth he'd found.

Silas rubbed his thumb over his father's watch as he mounted the front steps to the house Nora shared with her mother, lingering a moment. In some ways, he'd always known the truth. His father had died under Ember's hooves. An accident. In other ways, he'd always been right. The accident wasn't entirely unintentional. Amos had shoved Papa and startled the horse, all because Papa refused to sell. Then he'd taken Ember and gifted him to Hiram. All in an attempt to provide for the woman he loved but could never have.

The knowledge brought a sense of closure, but also a weight of its own. His father had died because Amos had lost Hiram's money in a card game. How differently would things have turned out if Amos had won that night, or if Papa had sold him Ember?

He stared at Nora's door. Then he wouldn't be here. Wouldn't know her. How like God to weave a pattern where men's evil and tragedy could somehow be twisted into something beautiful at the end.

The front door opened and Nora startled. "Oh! I was just coming to look for you." She stepped outside and pulled the door closed behind her, studying his face.

"How's your mother?"

"She's cooking up a meal much too large for the three of us." Nora offered him a gentle smile. "The truth pained her, but in a way I think it also finally let her find peace." Nora bumped her shoulder into his. "She said you had better take off those boots before you track mud across her clean floors."

They took seats on the porch and for several moments allowed companionable silence to settle over them. That was one of the many things he appreciated about Nora. She didn't feel the need to stuff every moment with conversation. Simply being together was enough. She brought comfort to him, soothed the places in him that had felt raw and untended. Mama had been right all along. He needed a good woman to love.

"What do we do now?" Nora's words were filled with meaning.

He didn't take the question lightly, giving himself a moment to give due consideration to her query. But he didn't need to think long. The past couldn't be changed. Their fathers' actions and Amos's sins didn't have to rule the life he wanted.

"I'd never try to take your horses, Nora." He shifted to face her. "Arrow is yours."

"Then at least take Ember. It won't bring your father back, but I—" She turned watery eyes away, and he dropped to a knee in front of her.

He grasped her hand, placing a gentle kiss to the smooth skin on the back of her knuckles. "I want nothing in this world that I can't share with you."

A laugh hiccupped out of her. "Mother said you'd say something like that."

He lifted his brows.

"And I told her you were more than I deserve."

He stood and pulled her to him. "You deserve more than I could ever give you." He placed a kiss on the top of her hair and pulled her close. "Where would I be if not for this fierce beauty who makes every day an adventure?"

She shifted to look up at him, a hint of mischief in her sapphire gaze. "I'm guessing Pine Bluff, Arkansas."

"Thankfully, I had enough sense to not leave my greatest blessing behind."

She drifted her fingers lazily along the edge of his jaw, stirring desires that went far deeper than attraction. He wrapped her in his arms, and for the first time he could remember, peace seeped deep into his heart.

THIRTY-EIGHT

November 6, 1905

Nora's beloved Emberwild spread out before her, painted in the beautiful rays of morning's early light. Underneath her, Arrow munched grass, his sides expanding with a contented breath.

She cut a glance at Silas where he sat atop Ember. He stared out over the field. What occupied his mind? Nora settled into her saddle, leaving the moment to develop as it would. If Silas had something on his mind, he'd share when he was ready. She wouldn't break the serenity of their morning ride or disturb the taste of new mercies they found under the sky at the break of each new day.

Everyone at Emberwild had settled into a routine. Roger had confessed his part in Amos's schemes, and they'd chosen to let him stay. For the time being, Silas lived in the bunkhouse with Roger and Walter, though she had distinct plans for him to move into the main house.

Of course, if he didn't hurry up and officially ask her to marry him, then she'd have to broach the matter herself. Life was too precious to waste. Love was too rare to not embrace every elation, trial, and challenge with abandon. Even if she had to break another social convention along the way.

In addition to the racing, they needed to make better use of their land and find buyers for the new foals. Silas had thought he had nothing to offer her, but every horse that had come from Ember was already half his by right. At least as she saw it.

Her mind wandered to operations and new plans for the farm, excitement mounting as she considered each new idea.

"What thoughts consume you so early in the morning?" Silas's teasing tone pulled her attention from calculating the expenses of hiring a housekeeper and purchasing a small herd of cattle.

When she turned to face him, her breath caught. Had a man ever looked so handsome in a wide-brimmed hat? "Just going over our expenses."

"Our?" He played with the word, drawing it out as though tasting it.

His stallion had founded their herd. Her mares had produced the foals that would sustain them. Both had given them Arrow—a certain legend in the making. She gave Silas a coy smile. "You know my mind on the matter. You just like for me to say it."

Silas swung down from the saddle and offered her his hand. He chuckled. "You've found me out."

She easily swung down from her perch, pleased to finally be able to wear trousers without someone telling her she shouldn't. Her shoulder-length hair blew freely in the breeze.

They walked hand in hand, leading the two stallions along behind them. Ember rolled a big eye at Arrow and snorted, but with one look from Silas he settled down. No doubt who had become the alpha of the herd.

"Under the circumstances, I wanted to give you some time. But I'm tired of waiting."

Nora tilted her head to study his profile. "Waiting for what?"

"Us."

Her pulse quickened as he turned to face her. This man. He was everything her father and her uncle had lacked. Resolute. Faithful. Honorable. He was somehow both gentle and strong. A man of consideration and thought, but also one of action. She'd learned that while she didn't need a man to be complete—only God could touch and heal the places deep within her to make her whole—having him at her side made life more abundant.

She waited for him to continue, giving him a moment to gather and speak his thoughts without her jumping in.

He caressed the back of her gloved hand. "Nora Fenton, I've been smitten with you since the moment I realized you weren't a brave boy on a wild horse."

Nora snorted a laugh. "That is the worst compliment I've ever heard."

His eyes remained serious. "Since that moment, I've discovered a headstrong, spirited woman who makes my life feel adventurous. You're everything a man could hope for."

She pulled closer to him, savoring the feel of his arms around her waist. "And you, Mr. Cavallero, are honorable, kind, and more than a little headstrong yourself." She tipped his hat back to better see his eyes. "A woman could be no prouder to have such a man willing to stand at her side."

Silas tangled his fingers in her hair. "Marry me?"

She locked her hands around the back of his neck, her words coming out more breathless than the teasing sound she'd intended. "I've been waiting forever for you to ask."

His lips hovered above hers, sending sparks through her veins. "Is that a yes?"

No sooner had her agreement formed on her lips than it drifted away beneath the expression of his love.

Eager for more from

Stephenia H. McGee?

Turn the page for a sneak peek at her next enchanting historical romance.

chapter
ONE

Atlanta, Georgia
May 1912

Her entire life was a sham.

Somewhere deep inside, Lillian Doyle had always suspected there had been more to the story she'd been fed since girlhood. Yet in that moment, as Mother lifted her chin in defiance of the truth, Lillian longed to be wrong. Without the veneer of the shiny lie that kept their lives polished, what would become of her?

The solicitor's stuffy office smelled of stale tobacco and pomade, neither of which helped Lillian's roiling stomach. She and Mother sat in matching leather chairs across from Mr. Riley, who regarded her from behind round-rimmed spectacles.

"As you can see here." He jabbed a bony finger at the paper on the gleaming desk between them as though doing so would make the words any easier to comprehend.

Mother maintained her poise. "Yes, of course." Her honeyed tone dripped from lips used to forming deceptions. "And she is to inherit everything, you say?"

"As he had no wife or legitimate children, yes."

The words landed with a crushing weight, shattering the last bits of the veneer Mother had maintained for so long.

No wife.

No legitimate children.

Just Lillian.

Mother's glance warned her not to breathe a word. She couldn't speak if she'd wanted to. What did one say to finding out a dead man had died?

If that were not scandal enough, however, it would seem Mr. Floyd Jackson had bequeathed the sum of his earthly possessions to the sole care of his estranged daughter. One he'd never met.

A strange whooshing noise filled her ears. He'd been alive all this time.

"Did you hear me, Miss Doyle?"

Lillian's attention snapped back to the solicitor's pinched face. "Sorry, sir."

He tapped his finger on the desk. "You have claim to Mr. Jackson's portion of the business as well as his house and furnishings. The solicitor in Dawson County will assist you further."

Mother sniffed as she rose from the small chair. "Thank you, Mr. Riley." She ushered Lillian from her seat and gestured to the door.

"Do you understand what I've told you, Miss Doyle?" Concern pulled his bushy brows together.

"She understands." Mother grabbed Lillian's elbow and tugged her from the office. "Thank you for your time."

The paperwork. Did she take that? Lillian turned to ask, but Mother closed the door firmly behind them and stalked past the reception desk. Lillian lingered in the hall. Should she knock, or . . . ?

The door opened, and Mr. Riley nearly ran into her as he stepped out. "Oh." He straightened his glasses. "You'll need this." He glanced behind her, clearly looking for her mother. He lowered his voice, though Mother had already headed for the front door. "Are you all right, Miss Doyle?"

"Um, yes, sir. It's a bit of a shock, is all." Lillian accepted the paper that announced her father's death.

In prison.

A knowing look entered his blue eyes, followed swiftly by pity. "If you have any questions, please feel free to stop by again."

He scurried back into his office and shut the door before she could reply. Lillian stood there a moment longer before tucking the page inside her skirt pocket and hurrying to catch Mother. She stepped outside onto a street teeming with people, horses, and the occasional automobile with a purring engine. Lillian situated her hat on her upswept hair and practiced the conversation she'd have with Mother.

"Why didn't you tell me my father was still alive?" she would ask.

Mother would tilt her chin in her defiant way. "You didn't need to know. As far as you were concerned, the man was dead."

She would set her shoulders and keep Mother's gaze. "That's hardly true. It seems I have much to be concerned with, as he has left me a sum of money. Me, his illegitimate daughter."

Faced with the unveiling of the truth, Mother would apologize and explain that she had been protecting Lillian all this time.

Then Lillian would say . . .

She blinked, unable to think through where the conversation would go next. So much depended on how Mother responded. What else had she lied about?

"How did he know where to find us?" The question slipped between her lips instead of staying properly confined to her head. At least until she'd had the time to iron out any wrinkles in her delivery.

"Not on the street." Mother had the uncanny ability to bark words under her breath while still maintaining a pleasant smile to passersby.

Not on the street. As though any of these strangers would know what they were talking about. Lillian pressed her lips together and let the matter drop. For now. But the moment they stepped inside the privacy of their townhouse, Mother would have to answer her questions.

Her father had been alive all these years. Meaning Mother was *not* the bereaved widow as she'd claimed. Nor had she been Mr. Jackson's wife.

Were you ever planning to tell me I was born out of wedlock?

Lillian watched her mother retreat down the busy walk. If she wasn't a widow, had they survived all this time because she was a kept mistress?

If not for Mr. Jackson's will, would Mother have kept the truth of Lillian's birth a secret forever? Probably.

If Mother had been able to go to Mr. Riley's office and collect the inheritance without her, would she have? Apparently. Lillian's presence had been required or Mother wouldn't have taken her to the solicitor's office with nary a word as to what the call was for.

Lillian stepped to the side to let a lady with a baby carriage pass on the sidewalk. Too many questions. Her head swam with how she'd ask Mother each one. How she would insist on an answer.

Then there were the technical issues to consider. They would need to travel to a rural town and find the solicitor there. Had Mr. Riley given her the solicitor's name? She couldn't remember. Then there would be paperwork, followed by some legal procedures. Then she would need to sell the assets, leaving her with a tidy sum.

Then what?

For the next four blocks, Lillian's mind created and discarded several possibilities. Such a sum changed much. Would the money truly be hers alone? If so, what would that mean for her future? For Mother?

The cool May breeze lifted the edge of her wide-brimmed hat, causing her to take notice of the surroundings she'd not paid much heed to. Where was Mother? Lillian turned, finding the woman now trailing behind her. She must have been more lost in her thoughts than she'd realized.

When Lillian paused, Mother breezed past her, the heels of her fashionable shoes clicking as she mounted the steps to their modest townhome. Lillian didn't waste a moment. As soon as the door closed behind them, she launched into the conversation she'd practiced.

"Why didn't you tell me my father was still alive?"

Mother lifted her chin in exactly the way Lillian had anticipated. "To save us from scandal, of course."

Lillian gaped. That hadn't been what she'd expected.

"Good riddance to the man."

Good riddance? How terrible of a relationship had the two of them shared? "But he knew where to find us." Didn't that mean they had stayed in contact?

Mother unpinned her hat and tossed it on the rack by the door. "Sally!" She tugged the gloves from her fingers. "Of course he did. This is where he sent the money."

The young serving girl they couldn't truly afford scurried down the steps and stumbled to a stop in the entryway. "Yes, ma'am?"

"Tea in the parlor. I am expecting Mrs. Montgomery any moment."

Mrs. Montgomery? Now? Today was hardly the day to deal with that pretentious woman and her—

"I'm not up to answering a bucketful of questions," Mother said as soon as Sally rushed off to prepare tea and refreshments. She pulled back her shoulders, stretching the too-tight fabric against a figure that had rounded considerably in the past year. "Mr. Jackson did not accept responsibility as a father, though his guilt saw to it that we were cared for." She gave a derisive sniff. "Until whatever schemes he was involved in failed, and then my monthly allowance disappeared. Now it seems he died in prison, leaving you whatever property remains. A good thing too, as we are on the verge of becoming destitute."

Lillian blinked, all her practiced poise flying away before she could grasp it. Mother took her silence as acceptance and bustled into the parlor.

"Sally!" Mother poked her head back through the doorway. "Didn't I tell you to have the parlor spotless?"

Lillian followed her mother into the room, finding nothing out of place or lacking shine. The end tables gleamed, and the curtains had been opened to allow sunlight to splay over the furniture upholstery and create stripes across the rug.

"But, Mother, why didn't you ever tell me that . . ." The words "I was born out of wedlock" lodged in her throat at Mother's pointed glance.

"We'll discuss the specifics of collecting what's ours later." She fluffed a pillow that didn't need fluffing and replaced it on the settee.

A knock sounded in the entry. When the hem of Mother's gauzy gown disappeared through the parlor door, Lillian's breath left her in a rush.

That hadn't gone at all like she'd imagined. Though she shouldn't have expected anything different. Mother had always been tightly guarded, even with her own daughter. Lillian shouldn't have anticipated a little thing like her father's death to spark any heartfelt moments of connection.

Cheery voices twittered in the hall as though this morning's events hadn't entirely altered Lillian's world. How dare Mother pretend at a time like this?

But then, was not that the whole of life? Pretending?

"Smile, Lillian. You could at least appear to be glad to be here."

"Tell the grocer his payment was sent last Tuesday."

"Wear the gown for the station of life you want, and that is what people will see."

Lies, all of them. And those only from this week. Lillian pinched the bridge of her nose to ward off a headache. She was in no mood for Mrs. Montgomery, and given the change in circumstances, she didn't see why she had to entertain the woman at all.

Mother would expect her to feign a smile and pretend to be the lady worthy of a gentleman out of her reach. What would Mrs. Montgomery think if she knew the truth? Mother would likely no longer be invited to any gatherings. Neither would she, for that matter.

Reginald Montgomery would most definitely be out of her social circle.

So much the better. She was an heiress now, after all. She didn't have to keep up any pretenses if she didn't want to. In fact, she would tell Mrs. Montgomery that she no longer found herself interested in further discussions about—

"Why, Miss Doyle, are you quite all right?" Mrs. Montgomery's airy voice snapped Lillian out of her thoughts and made her drop her hand from her face. The woman's slim frame graced the doorway, concern etched on her delicate features.

Before Lillian could formulate any type of proper response, Mother patted Mrs. Montgomery's arm and leaned close, whispering something about "indisposed" and falling victim to "women's troubles."

Another lie. And an entirely unnecessary one. Mother bent the truth whenever the need suited her, but today the very notion of playing along with another of her falsehoods made searing heat climb up Lillian's neck.

Mother pinned her with a warning glare as though suspecting that today might actually be the day Lillian learned to loose her tongue. "Perhaps my dear daughter should lie down for a bit, hmm?" Her honeyed tone warred with the hard glint in her eyes.

Lillian stared at her.

"Oh my, yes." Mrs. Montgomery patted her perfectly coifed hair. Assessing eyes slid over Lillian as though the woman wondered why Lillian didn't possess the fortitude to maintain herself even while experiencing a woman's discomforts. Such a girl wouldn't be worthy of her Reginald, certainly.

The woman had no idea. Reginald would never marry her if he found out about Mother's situation. The temptation to let the sordid truth take wing made her heart hammer. Instead, pitiful words she'd not meant to speak squeaked through her tight throat. "I do hope you will forgive me."

Mrs. Montgomery slowly tugged kid gloves from her fingertips. "Of course, my dear. You are such a delicate thing. Mrs. Doyle and I can handle these matters."

Mrs. Doyle.

The name stabbed at Lillian. Mother had never been *Mrs.* anything. What did that mean about her family? Had Mother lied about Lillian's grandparents as well? And what about her father's family? How would they accept finding out he'd had a daughter?

"Certainly." Mother took Lillian's arm when she'd still not managed to move from the center of the room. "Mothers are supposed to help with such important decisions for the children."

Children. She spoke as though Lillian and Reginald were both mere toddlers who needed every decision made for them. At the moment, however, she had an escape, and she wouldn't let wounded pride steal it from her. They could plan whatever they liked. That didn't mean Lillian had to abide by any of it.

Mother may intend for Lillian to marry Mr. Montgomery, but she would soon discover that Lillian would no longer consider such a drastic option.

AUTHOR NOTE

Dear Reader,

Thank you for going on this ride with me! I have always loved horses, so I particularly enjoyed writing this story where I finally got to put my equine science degree to use! There were a lot of things to research for this book, including horse training methods and tack of the time as well as how harness racing would have been in the early 1900s. While I did my best to stay true to the era, I apologize if I overlooked any details.

The Neshoba County Fair is a tradition that continues in Philadelphia, Mississippi, to this day. Every July, an entire population moves into a small city of fair cabins for a full week of horse races, contests, the midway, and time spent with family and friends. Cabins have been passed down for several generations, and it's a place where you almost feel as though you've stepped back in time. Neighbors fellowship on the front porch with their sweet tea while kids play in the square and forget about their electronics for a little while.

For this story, I got to go back to the early days of the fair when two hotels stood around the square with the original founders' cabins. I dug through the Mississippi historical archives and studied maps laid out from the early 1900s fair. I was also able to find several newspapers from around the state advertising both the Neshoba County Fair and the Mississippi and West Alabama Fair, which heavily publicized their harness races. Most information prior to the 1940s was difficult to locate, however, so I took what information I was able to verify and combined it with the atmosphere of the later years of the fair to create the scenes in the book. I apologize for any elements that I may not have gotten quite right.

Thank you for stepping into Nora's world with me. I hope you had fun on our gallops with Arrow!

ACKNOWLEDGMENTS

This book marks a new chapter on the author journey for me, and it has been quite the adventure! I'm still amazed at how far the Lord has brought me, from those first days jotting down story ideas in a gas station notebook to seeing the work of my imagination on bookstore shelves. There were moments I almost gave up and more than a few tears, but God in his faithfulness kept nudging me along, encouraging me to walk in the purpose he had for me. His kindness and mercy are without end.

He also blessed me with a whole bunch of completely awesome humans who walked with me along the way. First, to my amazing husband. You bought me that gas station notebook and kept encouraging me to put words on the page. Every step of the way, you have been by my side and helped me reach my dreams. You are my greatest blessing.

Not only do I have a mama who is my dearest friend, but she's also my very first reader and biggest fan. Thank you for reading my stories, discussing plot ideas over coffee, and always being excited when a new book comes in.

Thanks, Janet, for being an awesome critique partner and helping me make these chapters somewhat decent before the editors see them! I'm also very grateful to all my beta readers who helped make this book better. Becky, you are the best assistant an author could ask for. Thanks for keeping all those details straight when my writer brain is off in story land.

Jim Hart, thank you for believing in me and for your enthusiasm for my work. It's been a pleasure working with you as my agent.

Kelsey, the size of the thanks I owe you probably weighs more than Arrow. Without you, this book wouldn't have been possible. You've been with me through the entire process, and working with you has been incredible. Thank you for starting me on this journey and for all the moments in between. You are the best.

Brianne and the marketing team, Laura and the design team, and Jessica and the editors at Revell, as well as all the other amazing people who make the wheels turn, thank you for each touch you put on this book!

Finally, to my wonderful readers. My amazing team of Faithful Readers is dear to my heart. Thank you for your encouragement, enthusiasm, and willingness to review and share about my books. You help more than you know.

And to every reader who picked up this novel, thank you! We are a team, you and I. For a story is never truly complete without you to bring it to life. You have my forever thanks.

Stephenia H. McGee is the award-winning author of many stories of faith, hope, and healing set in the Deep South. When she's not reading or sipping sweet tea on the front porch, she's a writer, dreamer, husband spoiler, and busy mom of two rambunctious boys. Learn more at www.stepheniamcgee.com.